POWER IS T

MARIANNA CUI
superstar is swept
the role of Empress to a captivating Mid-Eastern
Shah. Her marriage begins on the highest crest of
love and ends on the strongest note of revenge.

SELMA SHAPIRO—a driven woman, unattractive
and sexless, she rises from file clerk to executive producer of Hanover Studios. Her handsome and ungrateful husband can't possibly stay faithful to her
and Selma's only success and happiness—her career
—is about to be sabotaged by Marianna.

DOUG BRADEN—his career as actor and ladies'
man is on a downhill slide. Now, only the Empress—
whose heart, and body, he once possessed—can put
his name back in lights . . . and he's willing to do anything to persuade her.

CALVIN GROPPER—as advisor to the President,
he has wielded extraordinary power by providing
playmates for international heads of state. He was
the one who introduced Marianna to the Shah of
Bahrait and now the unhappy Empress is going to
make him pay for his mistake with something worth
more than money.

EMPRESS

BY SYLVIA WALLACE

GOLDEN APPLE PUBLISHERS

EMPRESS

A Golden Apple Publication / December 1984

*Grateful acknowledgment is made for use of lines from
"I Wonder What the King Is Doing Tonight" from
Camelot. Copyright © 1960 & 1961 by Alan Jay Lerner &
Frederick Loewe Chappell & Co., Inc., owner of publication
and allied rights throughout the world*

Golden Apple is a trademark of Golden Apple Publishers

ISBN 0-553-19817-3

PRINTED IN CANADA

COVER PRINTED IN U.S.A.

0 9 8 7 6 5 4 3 2

For Irving,
with love

A king's wife is a widow for life.
—WELSH PROVERB

EMPRESS

The two dark-suited men were weary.

Stepping aboard the commercial jetliner that would take them from Paris to Washington, D.C., they ignored the young stewardess's cheerful welcome and, unaided, found their seats side by side in the first-class section of the plane. Glumly they surrendered their black raincoats to a second stewardess, but each clung tightly to the locked briefcase under his arm.

The long journey from the Mideast city of Ryal to the frenetic Charles de Gaulle Airport in Paris had tired them. The immediate connecting flight to Washington had deepened their exhaustion and the stifling boredom they felt for each other.

As diplomatic couriers their weekly round-trip flights between Ryal and Washington had been the most demanding part of their lives for the past two years. In the manner of couriers everywhere, they were obliged to travel as a pair. They had long ago said whatever they had to say to each other and they resented the fate that bound them in wordless passage halfway around the world. Yet they fulfilled their assignment without complaint. In Bahrait, their native land, whispered discontent could be as dangerous as treason.

At Dulles International Airport, still clutching their briefcases, they passed through customs without inspection and headed for the exit and the familiar car that awaited them. The nondescript station wagon, distinguished only by the DPL license plate provided by the District of Columbia to all members of the diplomatic corps, was in its usual parking place. The driver who left the wheel to open the rear door for the two couriers ventured a greeting and was rewarded with thin smiles.

In moments the station wagon was on the highway. Cutting through the shadowed greenery of Virginia, it crossed into Maryland on the Cabin John Bridge, then headed down River Road onto Massachusetts Avenue and the splendor of Embassy Row.

The day had been overcast and misty. Now it slipped imperceptibly into evening. The passengers in the station wagon, oblivious to the view, gazed dully ahead as the car sped up Massachusetts Avenue. Passing the magnificent embassies, chanceries, and diplomatic residences that lined the stately street, the two men were blind to the uniqueness of the individual mansions that housed the British, the Japanese, the South Africans, the Bolivians, and representatives of most of the countries recognized by the United States of America.

At last in the fading light the couriers could make out the glossy red marble facade and columns of their own embassy —its windows protected by graceful blue and white grillwork, its double doors by a gilded lion clasping a sword between his paws. At the rear of the embassy the blue-tiled dome of a Bahraitian mosque caught the last light of the day.

Within the building the two couriers hastened toward the chancery, the section of the embassy set aside for business affairs. A secretary admitted them at once to the inner office of the head of the chancery.

Arriving at a heavy desk, they placed their briefcases before the official who lounged behind it. The official scowled as he reached into a drawer for a ring of keys. Selecting the key he wanted, the official unlocked the briefcases, withdrew a cluster of documents from the first, glanced at them fleetingly, then turned to the second briefcase. A small packet of parchment envelopes bound with a ribbon fell to his desk. Undoing the ribbon, he spread the envelopes before him. He studied the name and address on each, then looked up questioningly.

One of the couriers spoke. "Get them into the mail immediately," he said. "They're from *her*."

Selma Shapiro planted her chunky body before the picture window in the Executive Office Building of Hanover Studios and parted the gauzy curtains an inch. Just an inch, no more. Greedily her lashless rabbit eyes devoured the scene below. It was lunchtime and the streets inside Hanover Studios brimmed under the California sun. Actors, directors, writers, laborers passing beneath Selma's window singly, in pairs, and in groups, joked, growled, confided—all grateful for the break that released them from the morning's tension at their desks or on the vast studio soundstages.

Selma savored this moment in the day. They were hers, all hers, these talented, envied people: the cocky and the frightened, the newcomers, the old-timers, and all those in between, the grips who brown-bagged in the sun and the upper echelon favored with Green Room dining privileges. She relished the fact that she controlled their present and, for many, their future as well.

As production head of Hanover Studios, the first woman ever to hold the office, she could hire and fire at will and often did, but never out of feminine pique. Although she was only thirty-seven years old, to the community of Hanover Studios Selma Shapiro was totally sexless. Her decisions were cool and implemented without pity, for Selma too was an employee, answerable to a coterie of eastern bankers and international stockholders who judged her as ruthlessly as she judged the people below.

Performance was all that counted. In five years as studio head Selma had performed outstandingly. Under her shrewd supervision various Hanover productions had scooped up twenty-four major Academy Awards, spelling stunning revenue for the studio. Unexpectedly, three of her critical clunkers had been transformed by public quirkiness into worldwide box-office bonanzas. Jealous peers described her as "hot," that begrudging Hollywood endearment meaning ragingly successful—for now.

The envy of her colleagues delighted Selma. So did their underlying wish that she would soon trip and fall from grace.

She did not intend to gratify the ill-wishers. She had paid her dues—she deserved her success. Hanover was her own hard-won turf. She would allow nothing to threaten her position within its magic circle.

Still, she missed the camaraderie she had enjoyed as an underling. Selma rarely mingled with her employees. Occasionally, if a dignitary visited the studio lot or if an actor vital to a production needed soothing, Selma would appear at her reserved table in the Green Room, her presence there a benediction. Most of the time Selma lunched in the private dining room that was part of the suite she had inherited when her predecessor, J. J. Courtney, was discharged for squandering outrageous sums of studio money in a doomed attempt to make his nitwit Peruvian mistress a star.

Today Selma would eat alone. Earlier in the morning, while she was surrounded by the production staff of a troubled film, her conference room door had been thrown open by her secretary, Miss Thornton, who nervously handed her an impressive envelope.

It would have astonished Abigail Thornton to learn that to Selma she was as precious a symbol of power as the private dining room and J. J. Courtney's French chef. Abigail, a rawboned virgin pushing thirty, was the daughter of an old-money Philadelphia attorney and his socialite wife. Educated at snob-appeal boarding schools and polished at Wellesley, Abigail spoke unaccented French and German, dressed with conservative starchiness, and never split an infinitive.

Abigail's advantages, secretly envied by Selma, had proved valueless in the marketplaces of romance and commerce. To repay a debt owed the elderly Thornton, J. J. Courtney had invited Abigail to Hollywood. In Courtney's office Abigail's presence had lent a touch of class which Courtney himself lacked. He had settled her at the telephone in his reception room where her crisp manner and chilling eastern accent suggested to callers that the man she served was at least as important as she was herself. Abigail worried about losing her job when J. J. Courtney was booted out, but Selma had never intended to let her go. To Selma, Abigail was an ornament, the finishing-school diploma she had never achieved.

As the production staff looked on, Selma had thanked Abigail and glanced at the envelope. It was from Bahrait, from Marianna. She had received many like it in the past. What was unusual about this one was that it bore, in Marianna's own hand, the words *"Strictly Personal."* Casually she tossed it aside and continued the meeting.

At the conclusion of the meeting Selma once again took the envelope in hand, studied it briefly, and reached for her Gucci letter opener. Careful to preserve the turquoise wax that sealed the envelope, she applied the opener to the top fold, slit the fold slowly, and withdrew the enclosure. It was, as she had expected, an invitation to Bahrait. Not a routine invitation. Those came on the telephone when she and Marianna talked between Ryal and Hollywood. This one, with its black and red calligraphy and elaborate flourishes, resembled a page stolen from a fourteenth-century illuminated manuscript. Like the envelope, the invitation was addressed to Miss Selma Shapiro and Guest. (How Gino would hate that!) She fingered the parchment paper, then read:

H.I.M. RAMIR, SHAH OF BAHRAIT

AND

H.I.M. EMPRESS MARIANNA

REQUEST THE HONOR OF YOUR PRESENCE IN CELEBRATION

OF

FIVE HUNDRED YEARS OF THE ZAHEDI DYNASTY

AND

THE FIFTEENTH ANNIVERSARY OF THEIR MARRIAGE

Selma's avid eyes swept down the parchment page, past the date, past the place—she knew it all. The event, still months away, had been huckstered throughout the global media for the past year by press agents in the employ of the Shah. It was to be a week-long affair held in a lavish tent city, presently under construction on the desert sands adjoining Ryal. Wildly coveted invitations could be anticipated by all recognized heads of government and the most glittering members of royalty, both incumbent and deposed.

Selma had never doubted she would receive her invitation. In recent telephone conversations Marianna had urged her to filch the time from her hectic studio schedule. Frankly thrilled, Selma had attributed the tension in Marianna's voice to temporary pressures and had promised to be there, with or without Gino.

What did surprise Selma was the personal note enclosed by Marianna.

"Please, darling Selma, come here to me. I need you. Try

to be in Ryal one week before the royal circus begins. I've
invited a couple of our old studio colleagues but it's you I
must see. Please don't let me down. Ever, Marianna."

Selma had read the note a second time, frowned, then
canceled her luncheon date with a powerful Hollywood agent.
She was aware the agent would be furious. It amused her that
he was in no position to protest.

Selma needed time to think.

Now, seated alone in her oval dining room, surrounded by
coral silk walls backgrounding antique French prints, Selma
permitted Josef, her chef-waiter, to set a seafood salad and a
few soda crackers at her place. Before the luncheon was
ended Selma would ring for a basket of bread and a bar of
butter, which she would consume with zest. It was a game she
and Josef understood. Miss Shapiro dieted with the fervor of
a zealot, but she did require a tiny snack to keep her energy
up.

Five years ago when she had risen from the rank of
producer to studio chief, Selma had placed herself in the
hands of Margaret Delaney, head costume designer at Hanover, and Casper Rittenhouse, the studio's leading set decora-
tor, and ordered them to give her a new image.

Selma knew they had done their professional best, and she
recognized the incongruity of the results. The carefully
planned wardrobe, updated frequently, did nothing to soften
the blunt body. The exquisite suite of offices, created for a
woman of impeccable taste, had accomplished the coordina-
tion of every detail except its occupant. Only the pink
fluorescent sidelights at the makeup-table mirror, cleverly
placed to flatter the heavy face and the squinty eyes, pleased
Selma. When no one was in sight she would sit at the table
and gaze wistfully into the mirror, wishing Gino could see her
as the mirror did.

Gino. Her husband of three years. She hardly needed an
adding machine to count the number of nights they had slept
together. What was he doing this very minute, she wondered.

It was nine hours later in Italy. In Venice, where Gino was
directing his third picture for Hanover, the lights would be on
in the Piazza San Marco and the cocktail crowd at Harry's
Bar would be breaking for dinner. And Gino, he of the
butterscotch skin, the carefully tousled hair, and the whippet
hips that had made him the leading male fashion model in
Rome—where would the son-of-a-bitch be tonight? In some

tiny projection room reviewing the day's rushes? In his Hotel Danieli suite blocking out the next day's shooting? Like hell he would. She was a fool to have handed him a third directorial assignment after the mess he'd made of the first two. And she was a masochist to dwell on him now.

Absently she raised her dinner bell and rang for Josef. When the white-jacketed man had removed the demolished salad and placed the bread and butter before her, she reread Marianna's note with increasing curiosity and an undeniable tinge of satisfaction. She, Selma Shapiro, late of Brooklyn, New York, was not only invited, she was *needed* by Marianna, the Empress of Bahrait.

Momma and Papa, she thought, they would go shouting through the streets waving the invitation if they could get their hands on it. This evening she would show it to them. Not Marianna's note, of course, but the fancy invitation and the envelope with the turquoise wax seal. She and Ma and Pa would sit around the table in the nice two-bedroom house she had bought for them in Tarzana, in the San Fernando Valley. Over dinner, as she did every Friday night, Selma would bring them juicy gossip from the remote world she inhabited on the other side of the hill.

Tonight, she knew, her news would be almost as breathtaking as it was the time she had phoned them in Brooklyn from her Century City apartment to tell them she had been made head of the studio.

"Ma," she'd hollered, "it's me, Selma!"

"So?" her father had said on the extension. "Every Friday night it's you, Selma. What's so special?" Then, his voice gentler, "How are you, sweetheart? How's Daddy's little girl?"

"Daddy's little girl is Hanover's chief executive," she'd shrilled. "Today—are you listening too, Ma?—today those big shots in New York made the big decision! Ten men they passed over for the job and they picked me—Selma! I'm gonna be boss of the whole goddam studio!"

"Selma," her mother said in a choked voice. "Such language—I always taught you you shouldn't . . ." Then she had broken down completely, saying only, "Yes, yes, we'll come, we'll stay," as Selma described the dream home she would find for them in the San Fernando Valley, reminding them how close they would be all the time, how Papa could raise chickens in the backyard and join a new *shul* and wouldn't feel lost anymore because years ago, when she had advanced from publicist to production assistant and begun to earn decent money, she had persuaded him to retire from his dry-cleaning shop and accept financial help from her.

The shop still haunted Selma. She shuddered, recalling the dim cubbyhole, wincing at the memory of her father, blunt-bodied as she, hoisting soiled clothes over the wooden counter that separated him from his patrons, forced to examine each garment as customers pointed out stained armpits and snickered over spotted crotches. Poor demeaned Papa, promising everything would soon be as good as new. And in the rear of the shop her crunched little mother, graying hair bobby-pinned behind her ears, patiently sewing buttons back on dresses and repairing zippers on pants which had once held those revolting spots.

Selma had never been a conscious rebel determined to rise above the sordidness of the shop, the dreary flat, the run-down neighborhood. Without forethought she had sought her own landscape, losing herself in the local movie houses and in the fan magazines which told her how beautiful the world could be.

In her bedroom behind the shop Selma devoured the fan magazines, reading of Lana Turner, Katharine Hepburn, Bette Davis, and others, daydreaming herself into their lives. On the bus riding to the typing jobs she held after school hours and during high school vacations, Selma read her magazines. Later, in the subway she rode to Hunter College —where, to fulfill her parents' dream, she studied to be a teacher—she continued to read her movie magazines, concealing them behind the covers of *Collier's* and *The Saturday Evening Post*.

After two years at Hunter it dawned on Selma that she did not have to be a teacher. The fill-in jobs had made her a skilled typist and an efficient file clerk. She had something to offer and she knew where she wanted to offer it.

In New York City were the home offices of the great motion picture studios of Hollywood, the real power bases from which a half-dozen studios on the West Coast were governed like far-flung possessions of empire. She would find a job in one of these, accept anything thrown her way, pay them if only they would let her work.

Selma began her campaign. For months she knocked on

doors, impervious to rudeness, encouraged by a smile even when words offered no promise. She was armored now, insensitive to rebuff because, at last, she knew what she wanted—a chance to touch the hem of movie glamour. She recognized she did not have what newspaper ads called "front-office appearance" but she was confident she had *something*.

Then one day it happened. Selma slipped past the switchboard gnomes and once again presented herself to the personnel head of Hanover Studios. Mrs. Perugia, a sour-faced woman with tightly bunned hair, looked over her glasses and groaned.

"I've told you a dozen times we have nothing," she said. "We never have anything. Someday maybe we will. I'll call you, I promise. Please go away."

The chunky, eager girl, narrow eyes bright, gasped with pleasure. "You mean that? You'll call me? You'll really call me?"

Mrs. Perugia put down her pencil and studied this oddity. "Selma, that's your name, isn't it? Selma, sit down—but just for a minute, understand—sit down and tell me what this is all about. There are thousands of offices in New York. Why this one? So it's Hanover Studios. So what? You think Rock Hudson is going to walk in and invite you to lunch? This is an office like any other office. In twenty years, sometimes they give me free tickets to a premiere. If I'm lucky I see a movie star walk down the aisle. That's it."

Selma's eyes never stopped shining. "It sounds wonderful," and said in a hushed voice.

Migod, Mrs. Perugia thought, this one is a *fan*, a real fan. Not one of those crazies who stands outside of hotels and theaters waving autograph books.

This one has an obsession. And an obsessive fan just might be an obsessive worker.

"Selma," said Mrs. Perugia, "you start on Monday, back in the file room. The stars get some mail here that needs answering. Let's see how you handle the job."

Selma breezed through it all. A joyous fiend, she plunged into the most tedious work and begged for more. In time a secretarial opening occurred in the publicity department and Mrs. Perugia, out of revenge for an old hurt, foisted her onto a reluctant senior publicist, Al Collins. Although he found her unappetizing, Collins soon learned to appreciate the longer martini lunches and golfing sprees made possible by Selma's fervid devotion to the most obnoxious and demanding tasks he threw her way. When it became apparent to Al and to other jaded members of the publicity department that Selma was an actual threat, they conspired to have her kicked upstairs. Upstairs was the West Coast offices of Hanover Studios. Upstairs was Hollywood itself.

Her mother and father, shedding tears of pride, shaken by fear of loneliness, borrowed Uncle Abe's car and drove her and her suitcase to the airport. Selma cried, too, but not for long. By the time the plane was over Newark she was dry-eyed and ready for the future.

A former school friend, Ada Fischer, now married, took her in temporarily and drove her around town until she found a one-room bed-in-the-wall apartment just off Hollywood Boulevard. Selma bought her own used Chevy and visited Grauman's Chinese Theatre, Forest Lawn, and the corner of Hollywood and Vine. The few dates Ada lined up were brushed off quickly. Selma wanted no life beyond Hanover Studios.

It was the Hollywood of iron-handed moguls that Selma came to. Monarchs like Samuel Goldwyn, Darryl Zanuck, and Watson Wagg still ruled the land. To Selma they were names to be considered briefly, then forgotten. For it was also the Hollywood of Sophia Loren and Gregory Peck, of Natalie Wood and Cary Grant, of Shirley MacLaine and Jack Lemmon—the people who *mattered*.

As in her New York years, wars, famines, elections came and went while Selma remained blissfully unaware of them and of anything that did not concern Hollywood. She haunted the vast Hanover soundstages, always careful not to trip over cables, sawhorses, and floodlights. She hovered outside the stars' commissary and sneaked onto working sets when the warning light switched from red to green. There she gawked openly at stars like Gene Kelly, Elizabeth Taylor, and the great Astaire until studio guards chased her outside.

Inches away from Frank Sinatra she felt faint. Snubbed when she delivered a publicity department request to Marlon Brando, she blessed her lucky stars. Turning a corner and coming face to face with a bigger-than-life portrait of Grace Kelly, she wondered what she had done to deserve all this.

At first her assignments were modest. She wrote press releases, scurried from the publicity department to the photo gallery and back again, and captioned pictures to be distributed to the media. Her day-to-day reading was limited to *The Hollywood Reporter, Daily Variety,* Hedda Hopper, and Louella Parsons. Weekends she drove to the public beach at Santa Monica, flopped on a straw mat she'd purchased at The Akron, and devoured her beloved fan magazines. On their shiny, richly illustrated pages she discovered tidbits about the newer players, the movie stars-to-be: Joanne Woodward, Jane Fonda, Ann-Margret, Paul Newman, and Elvis Presley. But none among them awed her as much as Hanover's own Marianna Curtis.

Marianna Curtis.

A New York theater critic, witnessing the young actress's stage debut, had dubbed her the Porcelain Madonna and the name had stuck. Selma knew that, and everything else there was to know about Marianna Curtis. The movie magazines, claiming "intimate," "revealing," "confidential" interviews with Marianna Curtis, rhapsodized over her patrician Boston parents, the splendid New England boarding school that had educated her, the run of Broadway triumphs that had paved her entry to Hollywood. And always they spoke of her abiding dream of becoming a great actress.

No one resented Marianna Curtis's smooth road to her present eminence. Her private self remained shy, faintly remote, and undeniably aristocratic. Shed of her natural inhibitions, she became an actress of excitement and sexuality because, as she explained in her smoky voice, "then I'm not really me." Interviewers, marveling at the long cornsilk hair and delicate uptilted nose, gazed into thickly lashed, innocent blue eyes and were mesmerized.

No one, including Selma, read meaning into the full, sensual lips and the firm set of her jaw.

Marianna Curtis's life since arriving in Hollywood was an open book suitable for children. *Photoplay* and *Modern Screen,* along with Hedda and Louella, attested to that. The star lived quietly in a tree-shaded colonial house in a cul-de-sac behind the Beverly Hills Hotel. The town's most notorious rakes were her escorts, yet it was said they advanced no farther geographically than her front door, and no further physically than a hasty kiss on her cool cheek. It was

rumored that many a frustrated man returned to his own
shower or another woman's bed to relieve the sexual tension
she aroused. Undiscouraged, they continued their hopeless
pursuit of the Porcelain Madonna.

Marianna appeared content and no longer talked of returning to Broadway. This piece of intelligence, revealed in an
exclusive chat with Hedda, was a source of considerable
comfort to Selma, who had seen movies about backstage life
and thought the New York theater too wicked for Marianna
Curtis. Moreover, Marianna was one of the few stars on the
Hanover lot who responded to Selma's timid smiles with a
slight nod of her blond head and an occasional wave of her
white-gloved hand.

Although Selma attempted to imitate her idol by posturing
before the mirrored doors that concealed her in-the-wall bed,
her merciless reflection confirmed she was a lost cause. No
miracle would transform her squat frame into the graceful
reed that was Marianna Curtis's body. In her bathroom Selma
color-treated her healthy brown hair from a bottle labeled
Glorious Glints. The result, a sickly yellow, was a disastrous
contrast to her sallow skin. She was a million light-years away
from the pink and white glow that enveloped Marianna
Curtis.

Still musing in her executive dining room, Selma plucked
the last bread crumbs from her plate, ran her fingers through
her cap of frosted curls, and allowed herself a slight chuckle.
Christ, what a *klutz* she had been in those days. What a
goddamn jerk. But that was long ago. Since that foolish time
she had had fifteen years of maturing, of toughening, of
learning about respect—how to earn it, how to demand it,
how to retain it.

And she had Marianna Curtis to thank for that.

Brusquely Selma rang the dinner bell, which brought her
waiter trotting. Signaling for him to clear the table, she
thanked him for the fine lunch and returned to her office
desk. For the rest of the day she functioned crisply. She
talked to London, Paris, and Tokyo. She bested a cunning
agent in a battle over a new director's contract. In a screening
room she viewed the daily rushes of a 30-million-dollar
musical and, with Abigail Thornton beside her jotting notes,
she ordered film cuts of what displeased her and authorized
an additional budget for retakes. Not until she slipped behind

the wheel of her black Porsche and sped along the San Diego Freeway for the traditional Friday night dinner with her parents in Tarzana did she allow her thoughts to return to the invitation from Bahrait and Marianna's note.

Fifteen years . . .

"Hey, dopey." She could still hear Jerry Crane, head of Hanover's publicity department, calling out to her. "Got a job for you, better than a Christmas bonus."

Stupid bastard, wherever you are, she thought, pressing harder on the Porsche's accelerator. But that day she had looked up hopefully. "How'd you like to get off your butt and hustle these new portraits over to Curtis's dressing room? See that she puts her okay on every damn one of them. They gotta go into the mail this afternoon."

Selma, clutching the folder of 11 × 14 glossies, had torn across the lot to Stage 18. Clusters of workmen, lunching in the sun, looked up and snickered as Selma flashed past them, pleated skirt flying. She stumbled onto the huge stage and found it deserted for the noontime break. Ducking between lighting setups, avoiding heavy cables coiled like menacing black snakes, she ran to the portable dressing room emblazoned with a silver star and the name of Marianna Curtis.

Without bothering to knock she flung open the dressing-room door, stepped inside, then stopped, frozen. From a dim corner of the lamplit room a male voice, thick with heat, muttered, "Shut the door, you goddam idiot."

Selma did as she was told.

Rooted in terror, she could make out Douglas Braden, world-renowned leading man, sprawled naked in a chair, his heavily muscled thighs spread wide, his eyes glazed, his face twisted in impending orgasm.

And between his legs, her nude back damp with sweat, knelt Marianna Curtis, the Porcelain Madonna.

Oblivious to Selma, Marianna filled her mouth with Braden's erection, her gleaming ivory rump quivering with excitement. The golden hair swung wildly as she tongued his testicles. Her lips made sucking sounds as she rode them up and down the engorged prick, pausing to kiss, to tease, its velvet tip. Suddenly Braden grabbed her head, lurched over it and plunged his penis deeper, deeper into her throat until Marianna gagged. When his prolonged groan filled the dressing room, Selma clámped her eyes shut. Opening them again, she saw Marianna rubbing her mouth tenderly against the deflating organ. Lost in loving him, she raised her face to Doug's. But Doug was not looking at her.

"You stupid bitch," he roared across the room. "Get the hell out of here!"

Selma had spent the rest of the day in a daze. Returning to the publicity office, she informed Jerry Crane that Miss Curtis was busy and had refused to look at the pictures. Crane bawled her out, grabbed the pictures, and started for the door.

"No, Mr. Crane, please, Mr. Crane, don't go! She's in a mood. Believe me, I tried. She and Mr. Braden, they have a tough scene coming up. They're ... they're rehearsing. They don't want to be disturbed!"

Jerry Crane put down the pictures. He studied the distraught girl and his eyes narrowed with comprehension. "Jeezus," he said at last, "you are gauche. Didn't anyone teach you to knock before opening a door?"

Selma spent a sleepless night. The next morning, when Jerry Crane told her Marianna Curtis wanted to see her, she crossed to Stage 18, rapped on Marianna's dressing-room door, and waited.

"Selma?" The voice that called out was friendly. "Come in. I've been expecting you."

Selma opened and closed the door and leaned against it, shaking.

"Sit down, Selma," Marianna said from her makeup table. "There's nothing to be afraid of."

"Miss Curtis, I'm so sorry! I want to die. I'll never tell a soul. I swear on the heads of my mother and father. I swear it! See, I forgot the whole thing already. Please, Miss Curtis, please don't get me fired!"

Marianna placed her makeup sponge in its container and fixed her eyes speculatively on Selma. "That's not going to happen, I promise. Neither Mr. Braden nor I will ever mention the incident to anyone. We're not angry with you."

"You mean that?"

"I do."

"Oh, God bless you, Miss Curtis." Selma wheezed with relief. She dug into her pocket for a ragged piece of Kleenex. Before she could get it to her nose, Marianna was speaking again.

"Your job is safe, but I have another plan for you."

Selma kneaded the Kleenex in her hands fearfully. "What do you mean?"

"I've been watching you. I like what I see. I'm going to instruct Mr. Crane to assign you to me exclusively. Would you like that?"

"Would I like that?" Selma said. "You'd make me the happiest girl in the world!"

"Then it's settled. I'll inform Jerry today."

"Miss Curtis, you're a great lady. I always knew it. Yesterday, that was nothing. Just give me a chance, I'll be your slave."

Marianna's lips twisted into a mirthless smile. "Pull your chair closer, Selma. Let's talk . . ."

As Selma swung her Porsche off the freeway at the Tarzana ramp, her mind replayed that long-ago morning. Marianna had bulleted questions at her, about her family, her schooling, her financial situation.

And then more intimate questions. "What about your personal life? Men friends, a special one, perhaps? Your new job will mean traveling from time to time."

"Miss Curtis, look at me, fat and funny-looking. No, I don't have a man."

"And your future plans?"

"All I want is to stay with Hanover. It's like a dream, being at Hanover. And now a chance to serve you . . ." Selma stopped, overwhelmed.

Marianna nodded. "It's new, glamorous. What about ten years from now? Won't Hanover begin to pall? Suppose I'm not here. There'll be other Jerry Cranes. And stars who are monsters. Is that what you want, a lifetime of humiliation?"

Selma's full face crumpled. "I never admitted it, not even to myself. It's been humiliating right from the start. Jerry Crane makes fun of me, and the rest of the department—they do what he does. And last week . . ."

"What happened last week?"

"Jerry sent me out to Edna Salters' house, up in Mandeville Canyon, with a writer and photographer. Her being such a big swimming star and all that, they took lots of pictures near the pool. Then they wanted her faking the domestic type. She got dressed like a Sears, Roebuck housewife with new shoes and an apron. After some kitchen shots the shoes began to pinch. Instead of finding another pair she kicked off the shoes and told me to walk up and down and break them in."

"And . . . ?"

"And I did. My feet are wide. I hobbled around till I had them stretched enough to satisfy her. Everyone laughed. Me, too, but I felt ashamed."

"How old are you, Selma?"

"Twenty-two."

"I'm twenty-three. I feel a hundred."

"Miss Curtis . . . !"

"Marianna, please."

"You can't feel that way—Marianna."

"Think so? Let me tell you about myself."

And Marianna had begun, the whole story, from the beginning in Boston to this moment in the dressing room. Selma, her head muddled by fan magazine interviews and studio publicity puffs, sat disoriented, unable to sort it out.

"Are we friends?" Marianna asked when she was finished.

"Yes, Miss Curtis . . . Marianna," Selma breathed. "Forever."

That evening she unfolded the parchment invitation for her parents. Her father looked pleased, then troubled. "Gino?" he asked. "What about him?"

"He'll be in Italy. He can't leave the picture. I'm going alone."

"Good."

"Now, Pa."

Her mother, hypnotized by the royal seal, murmured, "Marianna, the Empress of Bahrait. What a lady."

"Yeh, Ma, a real lady."

3

The mail was soggy when Carrie Malone brought it to him. Soggy like his mind and his body, soggy like Charlestown, the Boston slum he could see through the curtained window of his parish house. Father Rory Flynn brooded over the rain, falling steadily for the second day on sloping Bunker Hill Street.

"Put it here, Carrie." The priest swiveled in his chair and cleared a space on his desk for the letters and periodicals the young woman with the brick-red hair was bringing toward him.

"Not yet, Father. It's a drippy mess."

"Right, Carrie." Father Flynn spread the morning edition of the Boston *Globe* over the desk's mottled surface. "Wouldn't want to ruin the splendid finish, would we? Thirty years, it's picked up a scar or two. No need to make it worse."

"The *Globe* won't mind. We won't tell them, will we?"

"No, Carrie, we'll save that for confession."

Bending toward him, the young woman laid the mail on the newspaper. "Anything else, Father?"

"Nothing I can think of. Soon as I get through this, I'll be going to call on Mrs. Dwyer and the children."

"Polly Dwyer." Carrie jutted her chin in anger. "Just between you and me and the Lord, I shouldn't think she'd mourn that brute husband. It's good riddance, I say, after the way he beat up on her and the kids, regular as a clock striking the hour."

"Ed Dwyer had his devils like the rest of God's children."

Carrie lowered her green eyes. "I know what you mean, Father."

Father Flynn observed the girl as she pattered from the study, the late Kate Moynahan's oversized carpet slippers flapping on her feet. He took unabashed enjoyment in watching Carrie perform her household duties. She was clear-faced and pretty and hopeful. Since coming to live with him, she had done more for his spirits than he had done for hers.

Father Flynn ran his fingers through his brush of gray hair, remembering. There had been considerable whispering, and vulgarity straight to his face when he, nearing sixty, had taken Carrie Malone under his wing. It was soon after Kate had had her stroke and he had needed a new housekeeper. Carrie, a teenager orphaned by the strife in Belfast, had been shipped to Boston to live with a maiden aunt on upper Bunker Hill Street. Shortly after her arrival, her affair with a married man had been a juicy morsel for the neighborhood. It was not until her pregnancy became obvious, causing general shock and titillation, that her aunt had thrown her out. Homeless, she had turned to the Church and to Father Flynn. Disregarding sly insinuations and open attacks on his good name, Father Flynn had guided her through the ordeal. Gently he convinced her that abortion was wrong. He taught her to hold her head high when with swelling body she strode the neighborhood, and to shut out the crude street taunts intended for her hearing. The following spring when the baby was born she named him Rory and gave him up for adoption to a fine Roman Catholic family in Salem.

Father Flynn took paternal pride in what Carrie had accomplished. Pride and satisfaction. Satisfaction with the peace on Carrie's face and with the tentative steps she was taking into her future. Young men were coming to call—unmarried this time. The suitors were courageous, too, for they came in defiance of self-righteous parents, offering what their elders would not—forgiveness.

Satisfaction was what Father Flynn felt. But absolution was what he sought and would seek for the rest of his life on this earth. And all because of Mary Anna Callahan.

When Carrie's footsteps had receded into a far corner of the parish house, Father Flynn shook himself from his reverie. Riffling through the hill of mail on his desk, he was not surprised to find the oblong parchment envelope bearing the turquoise wax seal of Bahrait. For months the *Globe*'s stringer in Ryal had been filing stories about preparations for the dazzling celebration to be hosted by the Shah of Bahrait and his Empress, Marianna.

Father Flynn had anticipated this invitation. Not that he and the Empress were in regular communication. Hardly that. Her short, scribbled letters came at Christmastime and Easter, and there had been invitations to Ryal when each of her three babies was born. Always he had acknowledged the letters and declined the invitations. He would do so again. He was not ready to face her. Not yet.

Despite the infrequent reachings out, the Empress was seldom far from Father Flynn's thoughts. Nightly at prayer he begged for forgiveness for himself and for what he had done to the soul of the trusting woman first known to him at her christening as Mary Anna Callahan.

The delicately boned child with the cornsilk hair huddled small on the concrete stoop of the apartment building. It was almost dark and beginning to grow cold. She had had a fine day. The sweet glow, inspired by rare praise from the severe sisters at the convent school, was still with her. On the stroll home she and her best friends, Rose and Sally Jo, had stopped at Rose's house for a glass of milk, then hurried back outside to play their favorite sidewalk games—jacks and hopscotch. With the coming of twilight and the early evening chill the other girls had returned to their homes. Mary Anna had gone to hers, too, on shabby Pleasant Street where narrow two-family row houses, built of clapboard and shingles and painted brown, gray, and green, abutted each other like a defeated regiment standing at listless attention.

Mary Anna had buzzed her doorbell, waiting patiently for her mother to appear at a second-story window to summon her indoors. When no answer came, Mary Anna's narrow shoulders sagged and she decided to wait on the stoop until her father returned from work. She hugged her slender body to keep away the cold, adding new creases to the lightweight white cotton blouse and red plaid jumper that were her parochial school uniform. Mom would have a fit and complain bitterly about thoughtless eleven-year-olds who bedeviled their mothers by adding unnecessary washing and ironing to an already overburdened woman's day. Mary Anna was familiar with the rambling words. She had suffered the scolding many times.

"Isn't it enough that I have to keep your father looking like a bridegroom for that stupid job of his? Do I have to look after a sloppy baby, too? Good thing the boys are grown and gone their way. Let their wives learn what it's like to watch the years go by knowing you'll never be anything but a cook and a cleaning lady and a damned *laundress*."

Mom wasn't always that way. Sometimes she covered Mary Anna's face with kisses and, if she was feeling well, used her best hairbrush to coax curls into the long yellow hair so like her own. They had good times, too, when Mom, laughing and teasing, taught her to bake and sew. Other times, Mary Anna would let herself into the apartment and find Mom asleep on the sofa or bed with that terrible smell around her. When she was like that, not even a good shaking could rouse her.

Today was another of those troubling days when Mom had not come to the window. Despite the chill, Mary Anna was glad she was outside. Pop had said he'd be home early tonight.

"Hey, there's my beautiful angel!" Pete Callahan, his athletic body tall and straight, rounded the corner and raced down the hill toward his daughter. "How's my little lovely?" he asked, lofting her overhead until she squealed with delight. Holding her close, he warmed her against his stiff black chauffeur's uniform. Then he set her down and, in a familiar ritual, raised the visored cap from his glossy black hair and swooped before her in an elaborate bow.

"Madam, I am your servant."

She clapped her hands joyfully. It was always like that when Daddy came home and found her on the stoop. But soon the game would end. As he laced her slender fingers between his own powerful ones, his smile would vanish and, his head indicating the front door, he would ask, "How is it today? How's your Mom?"

"I didn't go up. She didn't answer the bell. Guess she's sleeping real hard."

"All right, my darling, we'll just tiptoe in and rustle ourselves a bit of supper. A picnic for you and me."

That night Mary Anna lay in her bed, tense beneath the covers. Through paper-thin walls she heard them quarreling.

"Madge, it's got to stop. Never mind about me and Mary Anna and the boys. It's you I'm worried about. You're killing yourself with the booze. Why? That's what I don't understand. Why?"

"You know why! It's because I'm stuck. That's the truth of it. Stuck! Nothing to look back on, nothing to look forward to. You, you're out all day and most nights, driving that fat limo you don't even own, meeting exciting people who have exciting lives and exciting places to go to!"

"Look, honey. Don't take it out on me. That's their lives, not mine. I'm just hauling them around, a guy for hire. My life is here with you and Mary Anna. What did you expect when you married me—a royal carriage to pull you up the avenue?"

"I don't know what I expected. You were chauffeuring then, you're chauffeuring now." Her voice through the wall was contemptuous.

"I had other chances," she went on. "I was prettier than Agnes. I could be living up there on Beacon Hill if I hadn't been so hasty and stupid."

"Madge, dear God, what more can I do?" He sounded tortured. "I'm doing the best I can."

"And that's nothing, do you hear me—nothing! You'll always be a dumb chauffeur and I'll rot here, waiting."

"Waiting? Waiting for what?"

"For my life to begin, for something to happen."

"The booze will get you first."

"Let it. It would be a mercy. I won't have to think about you—how much I hate you. Do you hear me? I hate you!"

Then, from her bed, Mary Anna could hear an exchange of terrible words, the kind of words decent people never used. And suddenly the sound of a stinging slap and her mother's whimpering: "Pete, what's to become of us?"

The neighbors downstairs knocked on their ceiling with broom handles, demanding silence. There had been no silence, only muffled sobs.

Mary Anna slept a few hours. The next morning she had a quiet breakfast with her father at the kitchen table. Her mother did not appear.

"We woke you, baby, didn't we?"

"Sort of—"

"Try to forget it. Married couples, they sometimes lose their tempers. It's not serious. When the boys were growing up, things were different. She had more fun." He heard his own words and stopped abruptly. "Not that we don't love you as much. After the boys went away, you were such a wonderful surprise, a blessing."

"Yes, Daddy."

The following afternoon she had invented an excuse for not playing with Rose and Sally Jo and crossed the street from the parochial school to the parish house to call on Father Flynn. Responding to Mary Anna's tapping on the glass-paned door, Kate Moynahan, flushed and breathing hard, came from the laundry room to welcome the little girl. "Well, you're a pretty surprise," Kate said warmly.

"I'd like to see Father Flynn, if I may."

"And I'm sure he'd like to see you," Kate replied.

Cushioning the solemn child's hand in hers, the housekeeper led Mary Anna to Father Flynn's wood-paneled study. The priest rose from the worn leather chair behind his desk and came forward to greet her. "Mary Anna," he exclaimed. "I've been thinking about you. Come join me near the fireplace. Kate, will you bring milk and cookies? Tell me, child, how are you today?"

"I'm wicked," Mary Anna whispered from her seat. "I make them fight."

"You make who fight?"

"Mom and Pop."

"How?"

"I'm not sure. They were happier without me. Mom said so. She doesn't like me."

"You misunderstand."

"No, Father, I upset her. She cries most of the time, or she sleeps so hard I can't wake her. I think she doesn't want to look at me. Then she gets upset at Daddy. Because of me. I drive her crazy."

"What did you do?"

"I got born."

The priest sighed. "You were right to come to me. Tell me about it."

In a halting monotone Mary Anna had described the scene of the night before, leaving out nothing, not even the frightening, forbidden names her parents had flung at each other. Recalling the absence of conviction in her father's voice, she passed quickly over his explanation at the breakfast table.

"So you see, Father, I had to come to you. Momma won't, and she told Daddy she'd kill him if he did. She didn't say I couldn't come though."

Father Flynn had been kind that afternoon, and in so many of the afternoons of the years that followed. "Listen to me carefully," he said, speaking very, very slowly. "You must understand what I am about to say. You are not responsible for your parents' problems. You never were. All the troubles began before you were born, before they met. You cannot solve them. Is that clear? You are guilty of nothing. Come to me whenever you wish. We will visit together here in my study—"

Relieved, she bade the priest good-bye. At last she had a friend, an ally to turn to whenever things got bad.

After that terrible night Pete tried harder to ease the friction at home. Throughout his years of chauffeuring, he had developed friendships with a number of clients who enjoyed his quick wit and willing sympathy when they poured out their own problems. Confident that certain clients would not report him to the company, he fell into the habit of stopping by for Mary Anna at the end of the school day and slipping her into the front seat beside him.

Soon Mary Anna Callahan became a familiar and welcome sight to many of the passengers Pete picked up at Logan Airport. Movie stars, stage stars, visiting authors, politicians up from New York and Washington, all looked forward to seeing her, often arriving with trinkets for the serious golden-haired child who sat alongside the handsome Irishman. Her mother never asked how she passed her time or how she acquired the gifts she brought back to the dreary linoleum-floored flat on Pleasant Street.

Riding with Pete from the airport to the stately Ritz-Carlton Hotel overlooking the Boston Common, to the brilliantly lit theaters, the bustling broadcasting stations, the parklike estates beyond the city, Mary Anna had glimpsed and begun to understand the world her mother yearned for.

The day Pete told her he had to chauffeur a producer to Quebec and would be gone for several days, he made her promise to be especially well-behaved around her mother.

"You're going on twelve, Mary Anna. You know how to take care of yourself. Come home from school promptly. You can cook and do the housework. Help Mom in every way you can, and be nice when she has her headaches."

Headaches. Mary Anna had asked herself why Pete couldn't be truthful. One afternoon, after a particularly bad night in the bedroom behind the flimsy wall, her dad had joined her on a visit to Father Flynn. Kate Moynahan had placed the usual cookies and milk before her, and the priest had poured a whiskey for himself and Pete. Together the two men had talked to her about Mom's drinking.

"Not social drinking like this," Father Flynn had apologized observing her widening eyes. "Your mother has a sickness. It's called alcoholism. We don't know why it reached out for her. Maybe for the reason she gives—life hasn't brought what she hoped for when she was a youngster like you. Sometimes people aren't strong enough to make adjustments to reality. Believe me, she despises the drinking as much as you do. It's an illness of the soul she has. Your Mom doesn't have the strength to fight it."

Every day since, Mary Anna had reminded herself of the priest's words. They eased her conscience but did nothing for the embarrassment that engulfed her when she read pity on the faces of the nuns. Nor was she relieved of outrage when neighbors, idling on the tenement stoops, clucked their sympathy as she passed.

At home she dealt with the illness stoically. After school her friends continued their outdoor games while she hurried home to Mom. As her mother slept stuporously or lay awake quietly staring at the ceiling, Mary Anna performed the household chores. She cooked for herself and Mom, mopped the floors, scrubbed clothes in the big tin tub, and ironed them until her arms ached. Sometimes Mom asked her to sit on the side of the bed. They held hands, silent except for an exchange of "I love you." After dark, in her own bed, she drew her body into a tight ball and wept softly, heartbroken for tragic, lost Madge, for Pete, so burdened, and for herself. She had counted the hours till Pete's return from Quebec.

The apartment was quiet the evening he telephoned. "Baby, I'm staying over a few extra days. Nothing I can do about it. Mr. Snyder changed his plans."

"I understand."

"How's Mom? How're you managing?"

"Everything's fine, Daddy."

"Can she come to the phone?"

"Not just now, Daddy."

"I see." Then cheerfully, "I have a present for you."

"Thank you, Daddy."

She hadn't told Mom about the call. And she hadn't told Pete how much she needed him.

Determinedly she kept up her school work, anticipating the only brightness in her day, the carefree moments when she and Sally Jo and Rose walked home from school together. Occasionally she stole a few minutes for a street game or for a glass of milk at Rose's house before hurrying back to Mom.

On the day she would never forget, she did both. She played a game of jacks and she succumbed to Mrs. Gargan's urging to come inside. With the other girls she sat around the plastic-covered table, giggling, telling stories, pouring extra glasses of milk.

A glance at the kicthen wall clock had brought her to her feet. "Look at the time. Mom will be worried sick." She lunged for her school books and lunch pail and hurried to the door.

Sally Jo put down her glass. "Wait, I'll go with you."

"Me, too," Rose said.

Mary Anna hesitated. "You can't come in, you know."

"Don't want to. It's just for the walk," Sally Jo said and Rose agreed.

It was Sally Jo who saw it first. Arriving at the top of Pleasant Street, she had spotted the gathering, unnaturally subdued, around Mary Anna's stoop. An ambulance, its siren stilled, stood at the curb. From the far side of the stoop Father Flynn stared fixedly ahead as he gestured for them to stay back. Sally Jo looked at Mary Anna. The dancing blue eyes, so alive with fun a moment earlier, were dulled with horror.

"Momma," she screamed. "Something's happened to Momma!"

Breaking free of Sally Jo's restraining hand, she ran crazily down the hill. "Please, dear God, don't let it be! Don't let anything hurt my Momma!"

Shrieking, elbowing her way through the enlarging crowd, she saw Father Flynn struggling to get to her. Someone standing behind tugged him back. Helpless, he stood with the others who formed a clearing between the stoop and the rear door of the ambulance. The crowd hushed as a stretcher borne by two white-clad attendants came through the gaping doorway.

Mary Anna had reached out to the stretcher but Mrs. Egan, the downstairs neighbor, caught her and held her fast. "It's not a sight for your young eyes, poor sweetie."

It was too late anyway. She knew it was her Mom. The face and the still-shapely figure were draped with white sheeting, but someone had been careless. As the stretcher bumped down the stoop, a hand slipped loose. Madge Callahan's ashen fingers were lifeless, the plain gold wedding band visible.

Once more Mary Anna screamed and tried to break away.

Mrs. Egan, strong arms around the child's waist, would not let her go. "Baby, baby," she crooned, "you can't reach her. No one ever could."

The attendants slid the body into the ambulance, slammed and locked the doors, and scrambled for the front seat. Sirens wailing, the ambulance tore down the street. To the morgue, the hospital, the police station? It didn't matter anymore. Madge Callahan was dead. The doctor had said so earlier. Everyone knew she wanted to be, and now she was.

In the mumblings of the crowd Mary Anna heard, for the first time, the dread word "suicide." The drinking, and the hoarded pills prescribed by a doctor to help Momma sleep. Suicide. The sin the Lord could not forgive a good Catholic. Suicide, the crime that would forever doom her mother to unconsecrated ground.

Dazed, she watched the neighbors drift away. A few stopped to pat her head, to murmur condolences. The pale child had stopped screaming. She stood stone-still, biting her lips, not touching the tears that spilled down her cheeks. Mrs. Egan, protective instincts depleted, gratefully relinquished her to Father Flynn.

"We're going to the parish house," the priest had told her. "Mrs. Moynahan will watch out for you. We'll find Pete and locate the boys. Meanwhile you'll be safe with us."

Her hand in his, she finally had dared to ask. "Is it true, Father, did my Mom kill herself?" Father Flynn looked over her head to Mrs. Moynahan who stood near the parish house steps, waiting. "Nonsense, absolute nonsense," he responded with assurance. "Madge Callahan died of natural causes. Dr. Shaw will tell you so himself. That's what the death certificate will say."

After the funeral, her three brothers and their wives had gone away, disappeared to distant cities where they had their real lives. Mary Anna and Pete stayed on in the apartment. Without discussion, Mary Anna assumed her role as sole caretaker of the tiny flat. Ended were the cookie-and-milk visits with Father Flynn, the street games and leisurely strolls from St. Francis de Sales with Sally Jo and Rose. No more the stolen interludes of gossipy phone calls to schoolmates made possible by Momma's drugged sleep. She was twelve years old now, the woman of the house. She marketed with care, using the scant household allowance Pete left on the kitchen table once a week. She cleaned and cooked without complaint and never failed to have a hot meal ready for Pete when, beaten and unsmiling, he returned from work.

What did upset her were the occasions, which grew more frequent, when he told her to have an early supper ready, then rolled in late, filling the small apartment with the same whiskey smell she thought had departed with her mother. Other times he'd come home punctually and eat in silence before dropping into his chair in front of the TV set. There he would sit, downing cans of beer, staring vacantly at the screen.

Once, while driving the limo, Pete jumped a red light and had a minor accident, shaking up a new passenger. Mr. Ryan, who owned the limo service, reprimanded him mildly, then forgave him. Everyone knew of the terrible tragedy that had befallen Pete Callahan.

Each Sunday, like a dutiful South Boston father, Pete tried to make it up to his daughter. He put aside his black chauffeur's uniform and, handsome in his pin-striped brown suit, he would enter the church with Mary Anna walking proudly by his side. After services and lunch in a nearby sandwich shop, he left the choice of their afternoon activity to her. An amusement park, a museum, the zoo, a drive to the country or seaside, a movie. Usually she chose the movie.

Summer, fall, and winter came and went. Their routine never changed. One evening Pete was later than usual. Mary Anna, about to reheat his supper for the third time, heard a rapping on the door followed by the voice of Father Flynn calling her name.

Carefully she replaced the pot on the stove and hurried to let the priest in.

With foreboding she scanned his face.

"Mary Anna." He had difficulty getting the words out. "They telephoned me—"

"Who telephoned you—?"

"The limo company. Mr. Ryan himself."

"Another accident?"

"Yes. He'd been drinking again."

"Are they angry?"

"They're not angry."

"They should be angry—they *must* be angry. Unless— Oh, God, no!"

"He was alone," the priest said helplessly. "Driving fast.

Like he wanted to get somewhere in a hurry. There was a tree—"

The priest knelt, bringing his face close to hers, and held her to him. Mary Anna wept soundlessly against his shoulder. Soon she began to emit dry gulps, signaling the end of her outburst.

Father Flynn straightened. "Get some things together. I'm taking you out of this doomed place. We're going to the parish house. Mrs. Moynahan will look after you." He raised her chin. "You'll be all right. You're stronger than Madge and Pete. You've had to be. You and I, with the help of the good Lord, we'll figure out what's next."

The cubicle that was the guest room at the parish house was furnished with a single brass bed, a varnished chest of drawers, a wickerwork chair, a crucifix on the wall, and a hand-painted picture of Mary holding the infant Jesus. In this peaceful room her emotions exploded. She had screamed throughout the night, refusing to be comforted by Mrs. Moynahan who came to sit beside her. Exhausted, she slept away the day.

The brothers and their wives turned up once again, for the second funeral. After the burial Father Flynn met with them in couples, then gathered the group together. The decision was unanimous. They had little money, young children, growing responsibilities. Good-bye, Mary Anna. Good luck. They had heard that the nuns in the parish orphanage were strict but kind. Father Flynn would know better than they how to accomplish the placement of Mary Anna. They would leave all arrangements to him. They had kissed her and promised to write from time to time.

The elaborate invitation from Bahrait lay before Father Flynn, a symbol of the grandeur that was now Mary Anna's. Turning his chair from his desk, he gazed once more at the mournful day outside his window and thought about the everlasting poverty of the parish he sought to serve and solace. The contrast with the heralded splendor of Ryal troubled him. Yet he knew that he, of all persons, had no right to indulge in comparisons. He had allowed himself to do so once, only to succumb to the cleverness of a stranger—and to barter away the faith of Mary Anna Callahan. He wondered if God would forgive her. He knew there could be no forgiveness for his own sin.

Father Flynn heard a light tap on his study door. Carrie stuck her head in to remind him of the obligatory visit to the bereaved Mrs. Dwyer and her children.

Father Flynn sighed heavily. Later he would write to Mary Anna, remind her of the pressures of his parish work, beg her to understand that the trip to Ryal was impossible. Mary Anna would, as she had in the past, respond with a letter expressing her own regret. The matter would end there.

And then he saw the single folded sheet that had slipped from the invitation. He picked it up and read:

"Dear, dear Father Flynn,

"This time you *must* come. Before the festivities begin. It is vital that I talk to you. I need your guidance. You alone can help me. I would come to you if I could, but circumstances make it impossible. *Help me*. I know one cannot go backwards in time but I must try. Love, Mary Anna."

His hands shook. To steady them he flattened the letter on his desk, pressing hard to keep it in place.

Perhaps there was a way out. Not only for Mary Anna, but for a hapless priest as well.

4

It was their fourth round of margaritas and Joe Curtis was smashed. His florid face and bald pate glistened in the sunshine that illuminated the playroom of his suburban Boston house. The invitation from Marianna, dropped off with the morning mail, demanded a rousing celebration. Only a pair of clods would allow such an occasion to pass unmarked, he told Aggie. And Aggie, needing no encouragement, had snatched up the parchment pages—one, the formal invitation from Bahrait, the other a dashed-off note from Marianna saying, "Do come a week earlier. In a way it's a family affair."—and gracefully waltzed her way to the bar.

Pouring—almost squeezing—the last drops from the blender, Joe vocalized along with the show tunes blasting from the hi-fi. Moving from behind the bar, brimming cocktail glasses held tight in his beefy hands, he stopped to admire his wife. You had to hand it to Agnes—she was quite a gal. Forty-one years married and there she was, gyrating to the music, orange hair flying, her undulating body in the green satin jumpsuit still satisfying to his undiminished appetite.

"Sit down, horny bitch," he called. "It's juice time."

She stuck out her tongue without breaking her rhythm. "You go ahead. That's one thing you can start without me."

"Cunt," he said good-naturedly. Setting the glasses on the coffee table, he flopped his bulk into the rattan sofa, tossed aside a flowered cushion acquired during a vacation in Honolulu, and continued to admire his wife.

None of his onetime buddies had a wife like Agnes. Not that he saw the old gang much anymore. Some people changed and grew; others stayed glued to the pot so long there wasn't much left to talk about.

From the beginning Agnes was different. He owed her plenty. The day they took their vows in St. Francis de Sales Church, she let Joe know they were more than husband and wife—they were a team. They were moving on—up, up, and away from the drabness of their slum backgrounds.

Joe had been a hod carrier then. As an eighteen-year-old

bride, Agnes packed his lunch pail with bulging sandwiches and steaming coffee in a thermos. When he came home she had the apartment spick-and-span and dinner ready. That wasn't all she had ready. She had schemes, plans, strategies. "You'll get a hot poker up your ass, Joey, if you don't go in tomorrow and do this—ask for that—tell the son-of-a-bitch —" He went along because he knew she was right and it was what he wanted, too. He had risen rapidly, becoming foreman of his crew within a year. Later on he had launched his own general contracting firm and prospered. In time the newspapers referred to him as a construction tycoon. One careless reporter actually called him "the engineer, Joseph Curtis."

While Joe advanced, Aggie hadn't let any grass grow under her feet. Joe admired her spunk. In the lean years she joined the Y, where she did bone-breaking exercises and swam until she was exhausted to improve the terrific shape God had given her. When they could afford to buy into a country club she hired pros to teach her tennis and golf. She studied skin care and gourmet cooking, and read books beyond her comprehension. Joe could still remember their first TV set. Agnes would pull a chair up to the console and carefully mouth the words of news announcers and British movie stars.

"What the hell you think you're doing?" he had wanted to know.

"Learning to speak proper English. Wouldn't hurt you any," she'd snapped, and returned to the set.

A damn good wife, and he had been a damn good husband. Straight as a die for years. Still was, not counting the infrequent hanky-panky on the side. A man grew successful and the cooz was out there begging for it. Nothing serious. Merely a touch of variety for a guy who'd married young. Not that he could prove anything, but, the truth be known, he wasn't altogether sure about Aggie, either. There had been times he'd come back from a business trip and the smell of sex was around her. He'd grab for her in bed and she would slide away, pretending to be asleep, smiling with her eyes closed. He never questioned her—he didn't want to know. The money was rolling in. Their friends were getting classier— lawyers, corporation presidents, real engineers, a college professor. Why stir the waters? They were an unbeatable pair.

Even the good Lord had been on their side. In his wisdom he had rendered them childless. They had sought medical advice and lit candles at the altar but their fate was unalterable. Their sorrow was known to everyone. Alone with each other, they rejoiced.

Children had no place in their grand design. Agnes's sister Madge and her husband Pete had been blessed with three boys and a girl, enough for all of them. Watching the Callahan kids growing up had reinforced the Curtises' gratitude for their sterility. The boys, dependable and dull in childhood, had fulfilled their promise of mediocrity as adults: a used-car salesman in Pittsburgh, a mechanic in Trenton, a liquor store clerk in Chicago. They never sent money home, though God knows Madge and Pete could have used a remembrance from time to time. Nor did the boys bother to keep in touch. Their wives were wary of Madge, who was either sodden with drink or sober and melancholy. They liked Pete well enough but they had seen Madge drag him down too many times.

And the youngest, Mary Anna, wispy and quiet as a ghost, with the moody sides of Madge and Pete overwhelming the radiance of her yellow hair and the frightening clarity of her blue eyes. On appropriate occasions—birthdays, Easter, and Christmas—Agnes and Joe mailed clothes and toys to Mary Anna. Days later, a scared little voice would come on the telephone to thank them hastily and hang up before they could respond. Once, too busy to shop, they had sent a check, only to have an ungrateful Madge return it without comment.

When Madge died they had been properly solicitous. Agnes had volunteered her maid's occasional services to keep things orderly in the small flat, a gesture Pete had rejected. "We'll manage, Mary Anna and I, won't we, sweetheart?" The dry-eyed child had nodded assent.

Soon after Pete's fatal accident Agnes and Joe departed for the Caribbean. "A business conference," Joe complained to the knot of neighbors gathered at the graveside behind the church. "Not as terrific as it sounds. That's how things get done in my line of work." At his side, Agnes dabbed her tears with a lace-edged handkerchief and declared she too would die if she didn't get away after this second tragedy.

Now, sipping his margarita, Joe grimaced, recalling how the boom had fallen on him and Agnes, shaking up their perfect lives. Upon returning from the Caribbean they had found a note from Father Flynn. "It is imperative that I see the two of you. At once." Reluctantly they put away their resort clothes, donned something somber, and invited the priest to call.

Father Flynn wasted no time. Seated in this very den, whiskey in hand, he came directly to the point.

"The parish can't keep Mary Anna forever. The boys are hopeless. It's up to the two of you."

Agnes and Joe exchanged uneasy glances. It was Joe who spoke. "If it's money you're talking about, Father, no problem." He smiled expansively. "Anything, Father. You name it."

Agnes agreed. "Mention any amount—you got it."

Father Flynn looked from one to the other. "Cut the crap, you two," he said. "It's a home that child needs."

The Curtises were silent.

"A home," Father Flynn repeated. "A mother, a father, a family to belong to."

The Curtises continued their silence.

"I'm hearing you plainly," Father Flynn said rising. "Obviously other plans are called for."

"You don't see our side of it." Agnes was plaintive. "The good Lord never meant for us to have kids. If He had, He'd have bestowed them on us."

It was Father Flynn's turn to be silent.

"Joe and I, we've been married nearly fifteen years," Agnes floundered. "We don't know anything about kids. We move around a lot. How can we be parents to Mary Anna?"

"You can't," Father Flynn responded flatly. "Too bad. After the boys, you're next of kin. There's only one solution, then. She goes into the orphanage."

Relief washed the Curtises' faces. "It would be best," Joe said. "They understand about kids there."

Agnes picked up. "And there'll be lots of playmates. It'll be real nice—"

"Then it's settled." Father Flynn found his hat. "Of course it won't look so good, will it now? I mean, when word gets out that Joe Curtis, noted philanthropist and bigmouth, and Agnes Curtis, admired social leader and head of the Boston Children's Fund, let their only niece go into an orphanage run by charities. But so be it. I'll make the arrangements."

The following day, Mary Anna Callahan went to live with the Curtises.

Agnes and Joe moved her into a guest room. They enrolled

her in a private school, bought her party dresses and pumps at Filene's, and engaged an attorney to secure her adoption. The adoption papers passed through the courts without challenge. When they emerged from the courthouse, Mary Anna Callahan had a new mother, a new father—and a new name.

She was Marianna Curtis.

Unexpectedly, the child proved a social asset to Joe and Agnes. The adoption won the approval of friends and business associates, who lauded the Curtises for their compassion. Marianna was the prettiest youngster at the country club, well-mannered, reserved, graceful, and obedient.

Within the Curtis household the situation remained awkward. It was an uneasy alliance at best. Marianna noiselessly trailed Joe and Agnes about the house, carrying her homework to the den where her new parents sat downing their predinner drinks. Sometimes she crept into a corner chair to read while the Curtises whooped with laughter or talked back to the stars of their favorite television shows. Dinner hour became the most difficult time of all. Gathered at the oblong mahogany table, Joe and Agnes at either end, Marianna between them on one side, they struggled to find small talk. Politenesses were exchanged over soup and salad and then conversation died. Joe and Agnes, accustomed to a raucous flow of gossip and profanities with their evening meal, had ruled out both in the presence of the child. "I don't trust her," Agnes said. "She'll go quoting us all over town." The Curtises' lovemaking, too, became inhibited. Joe's bellowed orgasms, Agnes's drawn-out squeals were stifled by their awareness that Marianna's bedroom was down the hall.

"The kid's turning the place into a tomb," Joe grumbled when they were alone.

"We're screwed, chum. Face it."

"Yeah, but for how long?"

"A year. Two, maybe."

"Then what?"

"I've got an idea. Listen."

Joe heard her through. When she was finished, he playfully pinched her bottom. "You're a genius, Aggie," he exclaimed. "I should have thought of it myself."

Meanwhile, Marianna solved the dinner problem for them. She asked permission to take her evening meal earlier, in the kitchen with Florrie, the cook. She also learned to go directly to Florrie for an after-school snack, and to climb the stairs to her room to do her homework and watch TV.

Joe and Agnes dealt with their sex life in their own way. They said, "To hell with the kid—we've got rights in our own house," and resumed their noisy routes to gratification.

Joe and Agnes stuck it out for two years. When Marianna turned fourteen they grabbed at the only face-saving way to be rid of her. With relief they enrolled her in a boarding school in Vermont. The Windsor School, a wooded paradise in the eastern part of the state, was idyllically rustic, co-ed, and far enough removed from Boston to enable the Curtises to put their youthful charge out of their minds.

As a final parental gesture they personally delivered her to the school for the start of the autumn semester. There they introduced themselves to Harold Ruskin, the headmaster, and to the assembled instructors. They looked in on the sparse quarters, approved the bunk bed and bare wooden floors and, as an afterthought, informed the headmaster that he was to telephone if ever there was a problem. "She's a fine girl," Agnes said. "We don't expect to hear from you."

Nor did Marianna expect to hear from them. At school that year she found two or three confidantes—shy loners like herself. She picked up fair grades and she never overspent her allowance. To everyone she was a model of diligence and decorum. During school breaks, if the Curtises were in Boston she returned to them and was exhibited among their friends like a recently unpacked objet d'art. More often Joe and Agnes were out of the city. On those occasions a sympathetic schoolmate would invite her to spend her holiday on Cape Cod or on Nantucket. It was an ideal arrangement.

The Curtises experienced their first jolt when a telephone call from Mr. Ruskin stopped them at the front door. Agnes was headed for her Mercedes and her tennis game. Joe had a chauffeured car waiting to deliver him to the airport.

"We caught her." Mr. Ruskin in faraway Vermont sounded hysterical. "We suspected it was going on but we couldn't prove it."

"Dammit, Mister, get to the point. I got a plane to catch."

"One of our teachers walked in after bed check and caught her—in bed with the Carstairs boy."

"Fucking!" Joe's face reddened with fury. "You gotta be mistaken. That girl was raised to be a lady! You telling me she disgraced us?"

"Cool it, Joe," Agnes said on an extension. "It's only a disgrace if it gets out. That's not going to happen, is it, Mr. Ruskin?"

"Mrs. Curtis, we have the school's reputation to consider also. No, it won't get out. Not through us, not through Marianna. I've talked to her myself. So has her counselor, Mrs. Edwards."

"Then what the hell you bothering us for?" Joe demanded.

"As her parents, we thought you'd want to know. It's your problem, too."

"*Our* problem!" Joe's booming voice rattled the phone. "We're hundreds of miles away. She's *your* problem!"

"She's your daughter," Mr. Ruskin said.

"Oh, yeah! Who's paying the bills?"

"You are, sir."

"Keep that in mind," Joe said, and hung up.

By the time Marianna returned for Easter vacation there had been three more reluctant calls from Mr. Ruskin: the Jaxon boy, the Havermyer boy, the Dempster boy.

In the car, driving Marianna from the airport to the house, Joe and Agnes snarled between tight lips that they did not wish to discuss the matter except to say they were shocked by her ingratitude and disgusted by what a tramp she had become. Marianna, alone in the rear of the car, said nothing.

The next morning she told Agnes and Joe she would like to see Father Flynn. They agreed she sure as hell had a lot to confess.

At the parish house Mrs. Moynahan squeezed Marianna to her fat, spongy breasts. "Father told me to bring you to him. He's waiting in the study."

Father Flynn came from his desk to embrace her. Observing how she had grown and developed, remembering why she was there, he placed his hands on her shoulders instead.

"Smile for me, Mary Anna," he coaxed. "It can't be that bad."

"It is, Father."

He scanned her troubled face, then led her to an armchair before the cold fireplace. Tea and cookies were on the low table between them. He poured the tea and offered her the cookie tray, meanwhile chatting easily, hoping to make her eyes meet his.

She took a cookie, decided she didn't want it, replaced it on the tray. "I can't eat, Father. My mouth is dry. I wanted so desperately to see you. Now I can't talk."

"You could always talk to me."

"I let you down, Father. Badly. They tell me I'm the worst sinner they've known."

"Who tells you that?"

"Aunt Agnes and Uncle Joe. That's all they'll say. They won't let me explain. The school calls me a problem. It's not *what* I do, going to bed with boys and all that. Nobody really cares. They just don't want it spread around." She giggled nervously. "They can't stop me, either. Oh, I'm not the only one. I'm just the unlucky one—the one who gets caught."

"Why do you suppose that happens?"

"I want to get caught," she said. "I want them to know—I mean Aunt Agnes and Uncle Joe, maybe all of Boston—I want them to know that someone touches me and needs me even if it's for a half hour." She shrugged. "The boys brag—they tell each other I'm easy. Word gets around fast. What's the difference?"

"Mary Anna, what will we do with you?"

"Don't lecture me and don't assign me one hundred Hail Marys. I *need* to be touched. Don't you understand?" Blushing, she rushed to apologize. "Forgive me, Father, of course you don't. You've taken your vows. You're peaceful with the Lord. Me, I've had no calling from Him." Suddenly her mood changed. Her eyes shone with satisfaction. "And there's something else," she said defiantly. "When I get those boys excited, they're crazy for relief. I can walk away or I can give them what they want. They're at *my* mercy. *I* make the decision. *I* have the power. It's a great feeling."

The priest shifted uncomfortably in his chair. "This is a sad, lonely time for you. Soon you'll be grown. You'll find people to give you the loving affection you deserve. You won't have to play games. Until then—what can I say?" His voice began to fade. "It will all work out—one day."

In the end he recommended to Joe and Agnes that they consult the school about programming Mary Anna for physical activities of a more acceptable nature. On her return to Windsor, Mr. Ruskin scheduled her for extracurricular lessons in tennis, ballet, horseback riding and, conditions permitting, Alpine skiing. To distract her further, she was assigned classes in modern dance and drama.

In her remaining years at Windsor she was never again found in bed with a boy. Her drama coach, Eddie Kalber, kept an apartment in nearby Hanover, New Hampshire. He became her lover and, because it was convenient to do so, she remained faithful to him until she graduated.

For Agnes and Joe her misbehavior was reduced to a teenage aberration to be erased from memory as soon as possible. Thereafter, whenever she visited Boston, Marianna avoided Father Flynn and his pieties. Moving on to New York, she met other men and was accountable to no one.

Now, so many years later, Joe and Agnes sat in their den sipping their margaritas and rereading the invitation they had found in the mail.

Agnes's head rattled with wonder. "Who would have believed it, Madge and Pete's daughter an Empress," she said for the hundredth time.

"Our daughter," Joe reminded her. "We had her for the years that counted. We brought her up to be a queen. All that fancy schooling, the special lessons—they cost a mint."

Agnes sobered. "Wish we had some of that money today."

Joe placed an arm around her, slipping thick fingers over the heavy breasts spilling from her green satin jumpsuit. "Don't worry, pet. Business is gonna improve. We'll be back on easy street. Marianna, she remembers it was my professional contacts got her on the stage without all that sleeping around other girls go through. Agnes, baby, we did the right thing and she knows who to thank." He paused, fondling fingers stilled. "Married to a *Shah.*" The title, the man himself still awed him. "That little unpleasantness we had in the beginning—it's all forgotten."

"Sure, so much has happened since. . . . Move your ass, Joey, and mix me another drink."

5

In this early hour of the morning, the exclusive Malibu beachfront was deserted except for a skittering flock of sanderlings chasing the foamy shoreline.

Douglas Braden, his broad chest inflating, stood on the upper deck of his wildly expensive home and breathed in the tangy Pacific air. Hands on hips, he exhaled with gusto. This was a splendid day. He had already completed an hour of exercise in the fully equipped gym adjoining his bedroom. Now he was ready for a brisk jog on the sand and a quick swim beyond the breakers.

The athletic regime devised for him by Ricky Hubbard, the most sought-after "physical instructor to the stars," was as rigorous as it was successful. At fifty-five Doug could proudly exhibit a body that was tough and firm and limber, hardly changed from the old days when he had been hailed as "the new Gable." Admittedly, Ryan O'Neal, his neighbor on the beach, was tougher and firmer and more limber. That was to be expected. Ryan was considerably younger. On the other hand, matched against Paul Newman, who often visited Ryan, Doug felt he came out the winner. Paul was fifty-five also, but he did guzzle all that beer.

Doug allowed himself a moment of bitterness. Paul didn't know there was a contest between them, nor would he give a damn if he did. Paul was still a star while Doug Braden was well on his way to becoming a has-been.

How to explain such things? It was a question he put to himself and to his agent again and again. Gradually over the past years job offers had dwindled. Instead of being the pursued he had become the pursuer. In the grand days of his stardom he had never dreamed it could come to this. He had accepted the fact that everyone grew older. Still, Fonda had weathered well, as had Peck and Mitchum. And before them Tracy, Bogart, and Wayne. He would bet a bundle Newman would go on forever.

On his next inhale-exhale, he resolved to shake the bad thoughts from his head. Ricky Hubbard, to whom he had confided his discontent, vehemently disapproved of any negativism. It brought wrinkles and a loss of skin tone, according to Ricky, and frequently induced overeating. Ricky was right. Besides, he wasn't to be counted out yet.

A day earlier the postman, a young snot from Oregon who unfailingly and messily shoved letters and magazines into Doug's box, had actually rung the doorbell and personally— carefully, in fact—delivered the mail into his hands. It was the invitation from Bahrait, of course. The heavy parchment envelope with the turquoise wax seal had knocked the kid out. Movie stars, especially those older than his father, no longer impressed the kid from Oregon. Regal seals were another can of beans.

Doug had no intention of opening this particular can in front of the postman. He accepted the delivery and reminded himself to take the little prick off his Christmas-tip list.

After shutting the door in the boy's face Doug had dropped the rest of the mail on his entry-hall table and carried the parchment envelope outside to his favorite deck chair. With on-camera casualness (at the beach you never knew which neighbor was training binoculars on you), he had opened the envelope from Bahrait. Reading the invitation made his pulse jump. The personal note from Marianna was intoxicating.

"Doug, dear," she had written. "It's been so many years. Over fifteen, as you can see from the invitation. Much has happened to each of us, yet I have never forgotten our friendship. It is as a friend that I ask you to come to Bahrait. Not merely for the celebration—although that will out-Hollywood a hundred Hanover Studios premieres. No, it's the future I'm thinking of. Something that may concern us mutually. Do come a week before the formal festivities begin." She had signed the note "Sincerely, Marianna."

The indifferent "Sincerely" had troubled him. He had considered it, then shrugged it off, attributing it to protocol or discretion.

This morning the vitalizing charge induced by the invitation continued to build. Last night he had vigorously entertained a statuesque twenty-one-year-old brunette with high oval breasts (he suspected a silicone touch-up) and long California legs. She was a stranger to his bed, a cocktail party pickup. In a celebratory mood he had invited her to follow him home. He had offered her a peak performance and the girl had matched him stroke for stroke. The experience had been a delight and he planned to have her back if he could find her name and number. Sex with young women was a special high. It boosted his ego, reassured him he was the equal of men half his age.

Ah, Ryan, ah, Paul, he thought: You should have seen me at midnight.

He had seldom been better. Finished with the girl, he had patted the solid behind and told her it was time for her to leave. The girl had protested, her lower lip quivering with hurt. To appease her, he had dropped between the raised V of her knees and manually brought her to orgasm three times. Her responsiveness and the passage of time had revived him. Plunging into her wetness, he had jackhammered her until she collapsed beneath him like a rag mop.

Pleading to spend the night, the girl (her name was Doris, he suddenly recalled) had promised more exotic joy before breakfast. Mindful of Ricky Hubbard's strictly imposed regimen, he had rejected her offer. He had helped her to shower and dress—if you could call that side-slit disco slip a dress—and hustled her to her car parked on the Pacific Coast Highway.

Solitude was what he wanted—time alone to dwell on the past and that interlude in his life named Marianna Curtis. However, the present needed attention first, he reminded himself. After receiving the invitation he had tried at least a half-dozen times to reach his press agent. The bastard had not returned his calls, probably suspecting it would lead to one of Doug's periodic outbursts demanding to know what the lazy idiot was doing to earn his $250 a week. Well, Doug had a meaty story for him this time, a perfect item plant for *Daily Variety* and *The Hollywood Reporter*. Both could be counted on to run dignified, straightforward news about the invitation to Bahrait. The items would remind the New Hollywood that Douglas Braden was still a figure of international importance, the final round a long way off. He would take his own sweet time about responding to Marianna. A week at least. Then he would send a terse cable, accepting the invitation. No need to appear overeager.

With both pieces of business mentally disposed of, and with Doris dispatched, Doug lay awake till dawn. The rhythm of the surf, usually a hypnotic seduction to sleep, could not overcome his inner excitement. He lay quietly in bed, his memory traveling back, way back to the days and nights of his love affair with Marianna Curtis.

Golden Marianna. Divine Marianna. Marianna, the Porcelain Madonna. Remote, courteous, untemperamental even after she had won her Academy Award. A studio makeup man who had survived the pyrotechnics of Joan Crawford and her ilk swore he had seen her halo.

From the start she had had the mark of royalty on her. What did not emanate from her person was written into her contract. To lure her from the theater, Watson Wagg, the head of Hanover Studios, had acceded to every demand made by her agent. Yes, she could return to the stage whenever she wished. Yes, on her arrival in Beverly Hills there would be an authentically furnished colonial house, reminiscent of her native New England, placed at her disposal and paid for by Hanover. Yes, she could have script approval, and director approval, and approval of her leading men. Yes, yes, yes.

Her steel was in her agent's glove. The fair-haired young woman who was led from the plane to the studio limousine by Watson Wagg himself gave off a white marble serenity and never raised her voice except in a role that demanded it.

Doug Braden knew that one day he would have her as he had had every leading lady throughout his career. It was a bonus he gave himself, one that alleviated the tedium of moviemaking, transporting it to a loftier realm.

Doug's own contract, one of the most rewarding in the history of the movie business, paid for his five-acre wooded estate in Bel-Air. It also sent his two sons to a high-tuition military school in the San Fernando Valley and his two daughters—to preserve their virtue—to an all-girls' school in Bel-Air. It provided his ex-dancer wife, Rita, with foreign-label cars and clothes, luxuries which kept her off his back each time he bedded down a new leading lady.

Doug never asked Watson Wagg to cast him opposite Marianna Curtis. He waited for Marianna Curtis to come to him. He wanted her seasoned first, at ease with the relaxed morality of Hollywood, devirginized in attitude if not in fact. He watched from a distance as she made pictures, one after the other, with handsome, ballsy leading men. No rumor ever surrounded her, not even when she worked with Frank Sinatra—and Doug was sure nothing happened there because Frank was still in love with Mia.

The day Watson Wagg sent over a crimson-bound script of *The Shadow Darkens*, a remake of *Wuthering Heights*, with Doug himself to play Heathcliff opposite Marianna's Cathy, he tossed the script aside without reading it. Days later, when a call from Watson Wagg brought him from his tennis court, he told the anxious studio head that he'd given it some thought. It wasn't much of a part, he'd said, but what-the-hell, if Watson wanted him to do it, okay, he'd go along.

Before shooting began, Ellen Wagg, Watson's wife, arranged an *intime* dinner party, as she called it, for the principals involved in the making of *The Shadow Darkens*, Watson's sole personal production of the year. An experienced hostess, Ellen—at the foot of the table—had placed Doug at her right and Marianna next to him. Facing the stars, to Watson's right, were Doug's olive-skinned, steamy-eyed wife, Rita, and Marianna's escort, the director Justin Wright—a fag and a creep in Doug's book. To emphasize his lack of interest in Marianna, Doug attempted to devote himself to Rita. Refusing to be drawn into his game, Rita devoted herself to her food.

Frustrated, Doug reluctantly turned his attention to Marianna Curtis. He was suitably polite about her past work, cautiously avoiding overt flattery. In turn, she praised his performances and was modest about her own. Her coolness disturbed him, as did the pulsating in his groin. In a rare attack of self-doubt he wondered whether he would ever succeed in penetrating the iciness and the cunt of Marianna Curtis. The evening was not improved when Rita, reading his thoughts as only the damn bitch could, raised her wine glass in salute and muttered, "Strike out this time, ol' buddy."

On the first shooting day of *The Shadow Darkens*, Doug knew Rita had picked up the wrong signals. Justin Wright had chosen to open the production out of sequence with a scene depicting the star-crossed lovers in impassioned embrace on a windswept English moor. While the wind machine whirred off camera, Doug, wearing a billowing shirt, drew the breathless Cathy to his bared chest. Under Justin's direction and in clear view of cast and crew, Doug pressed his hand into the small of Marianna's back and forced her body against his. His action was intended to be no more than a hint of possible pleasures whenever she wished to play. To his mortification, his penis responded independently and stiffened.

Thankful that Heathcliff's loose-fitting breeches concealed his hardening, Doug moved in closer. Blurrily he looked into Marianna's eyes, found them expressionless, then closed his own as she unexpectedly rubbed with him, her feigned breath-lessness grown real. Choked, unable to speak his lines, Doug released his costar. He coughed theatrically, apologized, and asked for a glass of water.

The moment passed so quickly it went unnoticed by all but Justin Wright, peering at the pair through a camera lens. Smirking, the director called "Cut." Unwilling to waste valu-able production time, Justin shuffled the script and led his stars into a sequence that did not involve body contact.

From then on it was smooth sailing, with Doug at the helm. Marianna never reproached him for the incident on the set nor did she trouble to explain her response. She remained consistently courteous. She was never inviting.

Doug did not attempt to rush her into the inevitable liaison. Instinct and experience informed him this one was confused, although hungering for it. Tact was definitely called for.

When their on-screen work did demand physical contact, Doug painfully restrained his impish organ. Offscreen he assumed the role of protective uncle. The big guns could be brought up later when her defenses were weakened. Mean-while, at the end of each day's work he sat beside her in the blackness of the plush studio projection room watching the daily rushes. He lavished approval on the skilled fragility of her performance, offering no flirtatious comment on her beauty and scorching sensuality. Occasionally they spent lunch breaks in her star bungalow running through the lines of a difficult upcoming scene, his brazen masculinity incon-gruous in her fluffy feminine quarters.

Sometimes he drove her to the studio in his own sports car when her driver was ill and a substitute chauffeur could not be found to take her to an early morning call. Prudently, she always awaited him outside, on the road in front of her Angelo Drive house. He wanted to grab her then—she looked so desirable in the misty morning light—drag her back into the house, and shove it to her good. Doug relished early morning sex just a bit more than he enjoyed it at other hours of the day or night. It had a special erotic quality that his doctor had once linked to his boyhood enjoyment of mastur-bation. Doug had not pursued the subject. The mindless give-and-take of sexual exercise suited him perfectly. He had no curiosity about scientific theories of copulation.

In time, as he knew it would, her resistance cracked. He

made her fall in love with him, employing small attentions, silly gifts, and his own apparent romantic indifference. He could tell he'd scored by her growing shyness, her gulped speech during their dressing-room rehearsals, her unblinking eyes fixed on him as she sat set-side in the canvas chair stamped *Marianna Curtis,* watching him perform a scene without her.

One afternoon when the shooting had gone particularly well, Justin Wright called an early end to the day's filming. "You've been good children," he told the cast. "Why don't you skip off and play? We're finished with this set and we're striking it. The next one won't be ready till morning. Leave, have fun, come back refreshed."

"Doug?" Marianna was at his side. "Would you like to stop by for a drink? I won't keep you, I know you have other things to do—" Her voice trailed off weakly.

He followed her to Angelo Drive, waited for her driver to leave, then swung his own car up to her front door. He heard the electric gates, operated by someone inside, snap shut behind him.

Marianna opened the door herself. "No maid today," she apologized. "A sick husband. I sent her away. What would you like to drink?"

"Cream," he said. "Fresh rich cream." He tossed his jacket on a sofa.

"I don't think—" She pretended puzzlement. Wise from boarding school and the New York days, she understood.

Moving awkwardly, she went about darkening the living room, fastening wooden shutters, stopping once to switch on an insignificant green-shaded lamp. Over her shoulder she could see him twirling the lock and setting the chain on her front door. "Sealing out the world," he said.

Easy as a tomcat he crossed the room and helped her undress, meanwhile flicking open-mouthed kisses on her soft hair and taut throat. When his lips moved on to suckle her breasts, her nipples sprang up, twin pink erections. She welcomed his exposed penis, manipulating it adoringly.

Her aggressiveness, her unsuspected skill excited him. It also dispelled his reason. Roughly he swung her about, positioning himself behind her. While one strong arm encircled her, he pressed his heavy prick between her buttocks. She heard his clothes, loosened by his free hand, drop to the floor, then felt his palm on her neck forcing her to arch for-

ward. She did not protest until he rode the tip of his stiff
penis against her anus.

"Doug, no, please not that," she whimpered. "It hurts that
way. I know."

"I'll never hurt you," he promised. "I love you too much."

Breaking free, she lowered herself to the carpet and opened
her legs, touching the tiny nub where her need centered.
"Now," she said urgently. Dropping to his knees, he leaned
forward and lapped at her thirstily, teasingly, until her fingernails drew long scratches on his back and she cried out, "I'm
ready, goddammit. I'm ready!"

She accepted him then, out of her head, loving the way he
loved her, in the good old-fashioned missionary way. The
New England way.

Fifteen years later he had to admit he had never experienced anyone like Marianna Curtis. He couldn't count the
women who had followed her. Stars, starlets, secretaries,
script girls, daughters of his friends, and friends of his
daughters, none had been the equal of Marianna Curtis. Yet,
he reassured himself, he had done the right thing in ending it
when he did. How could he have guessed it would turn out
the way it had?

Today he was alone, breakfasting on some health-food
straw recommended by Ricky Hubbard. Only the sounds of
the sea filled his house. Back then he had had Rita and the
kids, and the anticipation of all the women still to be enjoyed.
How could he have behaved in any other way with Marianna
Curtis? He wasn't a fortune-teller, was he?

With hindsight he knew better. Marianna had been so
giving, so rare, he never should have let her go. That icy
facade—dissolving at his touch—had brought him new sensa-
tions, exquisite, mind-bending, never again equaled. After
that first time she was eager to learn his needs and to satisfy
them. Kinky sex, they called it these days. But with Marianna, as their affair progressed, nothing had been too outrageous to suggest.

She complied so willingly, a sweet child eager to please,
gratified if he was gratified.

He recalled the time they lay nude on her bed, relaxing in
the aftermath of what she, in her boarding-school French,
described as their *cinq à sept,* the hours between five and

seven in the evening when working Frenchmen traditionally
visited with their mistress of the moment before returning to
home and family. "If you're fishing, my darling," he said,
"put it out of your mind. You are not my mistress of the
moment."

"I believe you. I love you," she said. "I'll always love
you."

"My Porcelain Madonna." He touched her unbelievably
fair skin, still moist from their lovemaking. "If the press
could see you now—you're a pornographer's dream."

"Doug." She took his face between her hands and studied
him seriously. "Doug, we belong to each other. Stand up," she
commanded. She led him by the hand to the full-length
mirror in her dressing room. Together they marveled at
themselves, her white body luninous beside his sunlamp-
darkened skin. "Look, we're beautiful," she said. Freshly
aroused, she aroused him. Longing to give, she turned her
back, bent forward, inviting the entry she had once denied
him.

Afterward, she clutched him to her. "Forever, Doug?"

"Forever," he murmured, not meaning it. "I've never
known anyone like you." He had meant that.

Indeed, *The Shadow Darkens* had been a fantastic experience for everyone. It had had a three-months' schedule, was
shot entirely on the sets and back lot of Hanover Studios, and
became known in industry vernacular as a "happy picture."
Not because of its theme, certainly, but because of the
general high humor of the two stars. Their sexual needs met,
they were unfailingly cooperative and their mood pervaded
the production.

Justin Wright, Doug heard, had actually scurried home to
tell his roommate, Billy Clinton, that henceforth he would
dispense with screen tests and demand that his costars submit
to bed tests instead.

"Nothing smutty, of course, Billy. Just a bit of fooling
around to see how they mesh."

"And who's going to direct them?"

"Your li'l friend Justin, Billy, my boy. It'll be fun seeing
how the other half loves."

Memories were giving him a headache. They had no place
in his life today, not with the future suddenly so bright. Still,

swallowing his morning ration of vitamin pills with a papaya-juice chaser, Doug helplessly conjured up yet another scene out of his affair with Marianna Curtis.

He had been lounging on a sofa sipping wine when she came from her bedroom dressed uncharacteristically in faded jeans and a tailored silk shirt. He had looked at her questioningly.

"I don't want to play seductress tonight," she'd said. "It's hard to explain. I feel—I don't know—sort of cozy. At peace. Married. You've done that to me, Doug, given me emotional safety. Can you take a compliment? I trust you as much as I love you. I've never said that to a man. You know what I mean, don't you? Sex—it comes and goes—but trust, that's what it's all about. When my parents died, somehow it seemed they'd betrayed me. Since then I've been afraid to commit myself to anyone. When you trust someone you give him the power to hurt you. I don't want to be hurt, not ever again."

She stretched on the sofa, her head nestled in his lap. "I want you to belong to me." She looked so serious, so childishly appealing that he lowered his own head and kissed her brow.

A flicker of foreboding grazed him. "You have nothing to worry about. Not with me, my darling." He eased her face toward his groin. She sighed contentedly and found his zipper. Silently he congratulated himself. Tonight she would be mellow and yielding.

And he had succeeded in changing the subject.

It had been Marianna, eager to spend every waking moment with him, who suggested they add the studio lunch break to their *cinq à septs*. In the past Doug had conducted his affairs far from the studio lot. He had not forgotten the tale of the legendary Hungarian director who had laid—*stood* was a more accurate term—a willing minor behind the schoolhouse on the Hanover lot. The pair was discovered and word of the incident rapidly made the gossip rounds of Hollywood. It was the director's bad luck that a report on his misbehavior reached the bankers in New York. Dreading scandal and the possibility of a lawsuit filed by the youngster's parents, the bankers had issued an ultimatum. Resign at once, they told the chagrined Hungarian, or remain to face a morals charge. The director had wisely chosen resignation and overnight had been spirited back to Europe. There he pulled off a stunning tour de force—an all-female film about novices in a Roman convent—which won him an Academy Award. On his return to Hollywood to collect his Oscar, the bankers rallied to his side. The unfortunate child and her parents, still awaiting court action, were branded liars and threatened with libel suits. Frightened by a legal firm which listed fourteen attorneys on its letterhead, the plaintiffs disappeared into the Hollywood side street from which they had emerged, and were never heard from again.

Marianna had hardly been jailbait. Nor, given her reputation for purity, was it likely anyone would suspect what went on beyond her dressing-room door. There was no risk. Only added titillation. Doug relished the danger, the *sneakiness* of their lunchtime encounters, even more than the *cinq à septs* he had come to accept as normal. It was zestier, like making love behind a gauzy curtain in I. Magnin's window on Wilshire Boulevard.

Only one incident had marred, although not terminated, their daily dressing-room rendezvous. That was when Selma Shapiro had burst in upon them. Fat, homely Selma who had chosen the celestial moment of his orgasm to stand at the door, gaping like a dead fish.

Later, when he told Marianna what had happened literally behind her back, he had insisted the girl be fired.

"No," Marianna had replied. "Let me handle her my way."

He never learned what Marianna and Selma said to each other. Marianna refused to tell him. All he knew was that a friendship grew between them that baffled everyone on the lot.

Selma Shapiro, the present head of Hanover Studios. How could he have guessed that the gross, sloppy girl would one day be among the most powerful personages in the industry? He should have humped her then, given her his Sunday Afternoon Special with all the trimmings and placed her in his debt forever.

Maybe it wasn't too late. He brightened at the prospect. Surely Selma would be at Marianna's shindig. Just as surely she wasn't getting much action from that Italian model-turned-director she had married. Gino what's-his-name? The stud would never make it in the business. He had no talent.

Body and face weren't enough these days. The times demanded talent, real talent, like his own. And sometimes that
wasn't enough, or why would he be in this bind today? If
nothing came of the reunion with Marianna, he would definitely toss something Selma's way. An iron in one more fire,
so to speak.

He glanced at his bedside clock. Four A.M. Lately he had
begun to experience small bouts of loneliness. The kids had
been gone for years. He had always expected the kids to
leave. Kids did that. But Rita! No woman ever before had
walked out on Douglas Braden. Rita's defection had astounded him. He had stopped loving her ages ago, but she
had been *there,* a presence, a sensational body, an affirmation
that although he was incorrigible he was also irresistible. Yet
Rita, bawdy, overripe, not-so-young-anymore Rita, had
shipped the last kid off to school, then calmly mounted the
staircase and begun to pack her suitcases.

He remembered leaning against the doorjamb of her bedroom. "Off to camp?" he asked. It was a joke between them,
he thought. Whenever one of his affairs became too flagrant,
Rita, tough as she was, would work off her wrath by signing
on for a couple of weeks at a beauty spa or an expensive
tennis ranch in Arizona.

"Not this time, Doug."

He put the back of his hand to his brow in mock horror.
"Ah," he intoned, "you are leaving me."

"Fucking right I am."

His hand dropped and his face registered concern. Real
concern. "What kind of shit is this? You can't go." His large
frame filled the doorway, attempting to block her although
she was still packing placidly. "Why?" he demanded. "Nothing's changed."

"It changed long ago, Doug. You didn't notice."

"Those other women, they never mattered."

"They mattered to me, pal. Cheap thrills for you, maybe,
but they sure as hell chipped away at little Rita. Chipping is
painful, Doug, when it's happening to your pride."

"This is crazy—"

She looked up from the compartmented bag she was
stuffing with lingerie. "Don't get sloppy and talk about love
and the kids and the good times we had. I won't cry. I'll
vomit."

"Rita, we've been married—how long has it been?"

"You don't even know. No reason you should. It's not important. You're not in line for a service badge. You can keep the house or sell it—I don't give a damn. Just don't forget, California is a community property state. Half of everything is mine."

In the end she had made off with a bundle. He had sold the Bel-Air estate to a British rock star and bought himself this house on Carbon Beach in Malibu.

The beach house suited him fine. The kids dropped by often, bringing friends for a volleyball game on the sand. And he could always find a woman to share his bed. Times were different, thank God. The women, bless them, never talked of marriage.

The way Marianna Curtis had.

That had been the most difficult scene of his life, harder than the one when Rita walked out.

The Shadow Darkens was almost wrapped up. His next film, still unannounced, was scheduled to begin shooting in a month on the Côte d'Azur, near Antibes. The kids would be out of school and he had invited the whole family to join him. The studio was still dickering with Brigitte Bardot for the female lead. He was in sublime condition for the demanding athletic role. And for a new love affair.

"You still love me, Doug?" Marianna asked. A week earlier Rita had taken the kids to Chicago to visit her mother and he had begun to stay the night on Angelo Drive. They were breakfasting on the patio when she popped the question.

"Dumb bunny, I adore you." He tore a slice of toast in half and lathered it with marmalade.

"It's been beautiful, hasn't it—you and me alone in this house?"

"Beautiful, like you." He wiped his sticky fingers on his napkin and added sugar to his coffee.

"Well, what about it, Doug?"

"What about what?"

"Going on, the two of us, together."

He gulped the coffee. "We'll always be together. You know that."

"Do I?"

"Look, Marianna—I don't want to spoil this precious interlude. It's an idyll, a dream."

"But . . ."

"Well, you'll have to know sooner or later—next month I leave for France—a three-months' location."

"Am I going with you? I'll be free when *Shadow* finishes. The studio's giving me a vacation."

"Marianna, how can I say it?"

"Say what?" She looked perplexed.

"A year ago I promised this trip to Rita and the kids. They're looking forward to it."

"And then, Doug?"

"And then what? I'll be back. Everything will be the same—the way it is now."

"I don't like the way it is now."

"Marianna, it's great. It'll be great again. Nothing can spoil what we have between us."

"You're not reading me, Doug. I'm talking about marriage. I want to marry you. I want us to have our own children. What's Rita to you? Nothing. You said so yourself."

"Rita's not well," he stammered. "She's seeing a shrink. It would kill her if I asked for a divorce. And the kids, where would they be, with a sick mother and a father gone from the house?"

"I see," she said dully. "Get out."

"But I thought you understood—affairs, real love affairs, they go on all the time. You don't break up a family because of them. Look at Tracy and Hepburn. What they have is magnificent, better than any marriage. Who knows, maybe it's because they can't get married. Wife, kids, religion, whatever. They've made their peace with the situation and they're happy. I'll be back, Marianna, and we'll pick up as though no separation had happened."

"Get out," she repeated lifelessly. She came to her feet, her face bled of color. "Get out before I kill you!"

He had got out. With a sense of relief. In the past he had never encountered a sticky situation at the end of an affair. Other women had been *grateful* for what he had given them and had gone away quietly.

Sure, he knew about Marianna's soap-opera childhood, the death of her drunken parents, the narrow escape from an orphanage, the rejecting adoptive parents, the screwing around in boarding school and in New York. She had confided everything and he had listened sympathetically, offering tenderness and reassurance. How could he have guessed she was sopping it up, taking all his romantic bullshit seriously? He had given her credit for more sophistication.

Yes, he had got out. And he had never seen Marianna Curtis again. On location in Antibes—he had not scored with the leading lady, but her hairdresser, a farm girl from Normandy, had been sensational—he read in *Nice Matin* about what was happening in the life of Marianna Curtis. Watson Wagg had announced the engagement. Marianna Curtis was going to marry the Shah of Bahrait. Marianna Curtis would become an Empress.

Doug was pleased for her. And secretly smug because he had been in there first, luxuriating in those warm, dark, and mysterious places, paving the way for His High and Mighty Majesty.

And now, all these years later, Marianna Curtis wanted him to come to her. To talk about the future.

Dawn was nearing. Rosy streaks were appearing on the horizon. He'd hardly slept, yet he had never felt better. In skimpy white swim trunks he descended the wooden stairs leading from the deck to the sand.

He was still young, he told himself, breathing in the daybreak air. Yes, young and virile and free.

Easing into a gleeful jog, he started down the beach. Past Ryan's house, past the other dozing celebrities.

I'll show those bastards, he vowed. I'll show them yet.

6

The luncheon had been a disaster. The parting handshakes with his two German guests, movie financiers from Munich, had lacked enthusiasm, confirming his premonition of yet another failure. Following the initial hearty greetings and first drinks on the patio of Hollywood's chic Ma Maison, the entire meeting had gone downhill.

"We'll think it over, Mr. Wagg," one of the Germans had said over dessert.

"We'll get back to you," the other added.

Leaving him to settle the bill, the Germans had walked to the Melrose Avenue curb where the parking attendant waited with their rented Mercedes. Observing them go, Watson Wagg was certain of two things: (a) They had already thought it over, and (b) they would never get back to him.

Watson Wagg was a realist. In the half-dozen years since his forced resignation from Hanover Studios nothing had gone right. His extraordinary record as a movie money-maker, his dedication to the art of film, his decades of friendships with studio titans had added up to zero—no one had come to his rescue.

Not after he was found with his hand in the till.

It had been a matter of bad timing. Ellen knew when they met as seniors at Stanford that he had this flaw. He had gambled away his allowance from home and she had bailed him out then, as she would in all the years of their long marriage. Because it distressed her so much, he often tried to conceal the fact that he was in the hole again. The six-figure salary from Hanover, the luxuries paid for by the studio—a chauffeur-driven limo, charge accounts for lavish entertainment, unlimited travel expenses—did nothing to assuage his need for risk. Santa Anita, Las Vegas, high-stake poker games in Beverly Hills, all lured him. He heard the call and he was helpless, his numberless promises to Ellen and to himself forgotten. Large winnings, more exciting than any of the women he could have had, inflamed his habit. Losses were rationalized. The luck of the draw. Tomorrow was another day.

Many times before his disgrace, he had tampered with money that belonged to Hanover. But always, until that terrible day, he had managed a killing and restored the borrowed sum. He had never worried about that part of it. He was confident the funds would be there when he needed them.

It was just a rotten break that without his knowledge, and with no suspicion of his misconduct, eastern auditors for Hanover had unexpectedly descended upon the studio to review the ledgers. What they discovered astounded them. Watson Wagg, one of the most respected figures in the industry, had been borrowing—"stealing" they called it—from funds under his control. A few more days, a week, and no one would have known the difference.

Overnight, it was too late. He was permitted to resign with dignity. The press was told of "artistic differences" and that he was leaving to "embark upon independent production." Nonetheless, the story had got around—been magnified, actually—and since that nightmare period six years ago, no one would take a chance on Watson Wagg.

Ellen's death shortly after had broken his heart. To repay Hanover he sold his magnificent Holmby Hills estate, complete with obligatory swimming pool and tennis court and forty-seat theater built for him by the studio. Humiliated, he offered his resignation to the Los Angeles Country Club, which accepted it before he could change his mind. With a fair degree of grace he adjusted to the defection of nearly all of his friends and business associates. He was thankful he was not sent to prison. The studio, ever alert to repercussions in the stock market, refused to press charges.

Guilty over Ellen's death, shaken by his fall, he had found therapeutic help in a rehabilitation group for compulsive gamblers. The treatment was a success. Pleased with himself, he had spread the word that he had beaten his habit, only to learn that he was still looked upon as "chancy." Ruefully he recalled the many times he, as head of Hanover, had turned away talented people who had fought and won their battle with alcoholism. "How can we take the gamble?" he had asked their desperate agents. "Millions of dollars ride on a production. What if your client tumbles midstream?" Well, he hadn't tumbled, but he wasn't standing upright either. The fact that he lived handsomely in a spacious condominium off the Sunset Strip he owed to Ellen, to her prudent investments and

to her insurance policies. He had a live-out mistress who
managed the Better Dresses Department at Saks, and a new
circle of friends who were not judgmental of his past.

It was his exclusion from the movie business that tor-
mented him. Every day he read the Hollywood trade papers
with the passion of a starlet. It was on their pages that he
learned of the German businessmen who, seeking investments
abroad, were coming to town to scrutinize the film industry.

A loyal friend had put him in touch with the two gentlemen from Munich. The shrewd Germans had let him do most
of the talking. Quickly they sized him up for what he was,
one more Hollywood promoter with nothing concrete to
offer. Watson Wagg had no desirable story property, no
studio support, no bankable star. Little wonder they had
grown restless halfway through the meal.

Driving up the semicircular ramp of the Sierra Towers, he
blamed himself for the disappointing meeting. He had
suffered through too many similar lunches to have permitted
himself the optimism he had felt earlier in the day.

In the vast lobby a neatly clad receptionist handed him his
key and his mail. "Sorry, Mr. Wagg," she said regretfully, "no
messages, yet."

As the self-service elevator swooped to the fourteenth floor
he held fast to the packet of letters tucked within his
subscription copy of *Weekly Variety*. Inside his apartment he
deposited his mail on an end table and stepped to the window
wall. Hands in pockets, he stared at the sprawling town
below. His town. Once, long ago. Recrossing the room, he
moved behind his miniature wet bar and poured himself a
half-tumbler of scotch which he downed in a few hasty
swallows. The scotch was reaching his head when he returned
to the mail and saw the envelope from Ryal. He tore it open
and read the contents, first the formal invitation, then the
personal note.

It was marvelous, dizzy-making. He poured a second drink
and sat down, grinning like a fool.

Naturally the royal couple would think of him at a time
like this. Hell, without Watson Wagg there might never have
been a marriage. And three gorgeous children. They owed
him a lot, those two. Something told him the payoff, fifteen
years coming, was finally on its way. If not, why Marianna's
cryptic words, "talk about the future—"?

Watson Wagg had deliberately played down his role in the

conspiracy to bring together Marianna Curtis and Ramir, the Shah of Bahrait. He had confided the full details to no one but Ellen.

It all began after the wrap-up of *The Shadow Darkens,* the picture which was to become his greatest success. The cast and crew had scattered. In the cutting and dubbing rooms there was that special fever that rose when everyone smelled a hit.

Douglas Braden, before taking his sulky wife and four disagreeable children to France, had put his head into Watson's office to say good-bye. "Hear we've got a smasher," he proclaimed exuberantly. "Expect a call from my agent. He'll be dropping by to talk about doubling the ante on the next one. Wouldn't want the hero of Hanover to be unhappy, would you?"

Marianna Curtis, looking wan, had visited his office, too. "I'm leaving town," she said.

"Good, you deserve a rest." He had handed her a brandy from the bar concealed in a *bombé* chest. "Where are you going?"

"Away." She brought the glass to her lips, then put it down untouched.

"Alone?"

"Alone. Away."

"Marianna, something's wrong. Is there anything I can do? You can't be depressed about *Shadows.* It's better than *Chambers.* You'll win another award. Migod, your performance was inspired!"

"Inspired? I suppose it was. Well, I'm all out of inspiration. I'm tired. I'm leaving town today."

"Of course, my darling," he soothed. "Where can I reach you? I won't bother you with new scripts, not now. Relax, get the bloom back in your cheeks. But you must tell me where I can find you. Something may come up."

"Watson, don't push me," she said. "I have a problem to solve. I want to cut out completely. In a few weeks I'll be back."

He knew she was too important to be harassed, so he had not persisted.

He never did learn from Marianna Curtis where she had gone. When the long-distance call came from Calvin Gropper he had had to admit that the most valuable star on the Hanover Studios roster had dropped out of sight.

"No, no," he assured the man in Washington, "she hasn't *disappeared*. There's no cause for alarm. I simply don't know where she is."

"Then find her," Calvin Gropper had ordered in his familiar accented guttural, "and get back to me immediately. Is that clear?"

Watson Wagg's stomach curdled. Who did the son-of-a-bitch think he was? His impulse was to slam down the receiver. Then he reconsidered. This was no ordinary caller. This was Dr. Calvin Gropper, adviser to a succession of American presidents, crony to reigning heads of state, intimate of that exclusive web of sinister men who ruled the world through their control of far-flung consortiums and multinationals.

Watson Wagg was not intimidated by Calvin Gropper. He hoped the arrogant bastard would stew in hell one day. But not just yet. Watson Wagg could recognize the value of a friend like Calvin Gropper. Hanover's foreign productions frequently required the cooperation of men in high places. A careless word, an unneeded enemy, could jeopardize the chance of winning that cooperation, whereas a nod of the right head could save the studio millions of dollars.

Watson Wagg had chosen to be placating. "Certainly, Mr. Gropper," he said heartily. "I'll help in any way possible. Can the matter wait a few weeks? Miss Curtis is vacationing. She just wound up a strenuous production—a magnificent one I might add."

"This matter cannot wait," Gropper had replied. "I am surrogate for a man as powerful as our president. He does not willingly countenance delay."

Wagg was intrigued. "Who is he? I'll do everything possible to find Marianna, but what am I to tell her?"

"Tell her I represent Ramir, the Shah of Bahrait. His Majesty wishes to meet Miss Curtis. At once."

"My dear Mr. Gropper, I think I may speak for Miss Curtis. She has met kings and princes and presidents. She will not be impressed by your Shah."

Could a man sneer over the telephone? Watson Wagg sensed that Calvin Gropper was doing just that.

"Did I say meet Miss Curtis, Mr. Wagg? I understated the

situation. The Shah of Bahrait not only wishes to meet Miss Curtis—he has decided to marry her."

And marry her he did. Because of Watson Wagg's intervention. Because Watson Wagg had gone to the mat for her, fought with the New York board of directors when it waved her contract over her head, trying to squeeze one last picture out of her, hoping to cash in on the publicity generated by the announcement of her engagement. Watson had fought for her and he had won.

It hadn't been easy.

His initial discourse with Calvin Gropper still rankled. Gropper had clipped off instructions like a general commanding a subordinate, while Watson Wagg, leaning back in the burgundy leather chair from which *he* usually issued orders, suppressed his irritation. Calvin Gropper had been explicit. The Shah's ultimate intention was not to be disclosed to Marianna. Affairs of the heart, like affairs of state, required subtlety. The Shah's plans for Marianna were to unfold gradually. She was to be informed that he was her ardent admirer, having spent long lonely nights in the projection rooms of his palace in Ryal and in his villa on the Caspian Sea, running and rerunning her films. Since his divorce from his first wife and the death of his second, the Shah had acquired a well-deserved reputation as a playboy. Gropper conceded that much. But Marianna was to be told she was the only woman in years to have truly captivated him.

It was Watson Wagg's responsibility to deliver Marianna Curtis to Paris in ten days, Gropper said. Arrangements would be made for her stay at the Hotel Plaza-Athénée on the Avenue Montaigne. She could bring a maid or companion if she so desired. Wagg was to persuade her to accept the Shah's generous invitation. That accomplished—and Gropper did not allow for failure—Wagg was to arrange a meeting between Marianna Curtis and himself. At that point Wagg was to step aside and Gropper personally would carry on the romantic negotiation.

Thoroughly baffled, Wagg had rung up his wife to report on the call from Washington.

"Where is she?" Ellen said.

"I haven't the faintest idea. Calcutta for all I know. She wouldn't tell me where she was going."

"What about her agent, her housekeeper?"

"Blank walls. If they know, they aren't saying. If I don't find her, Gropper will have me before a firing squad." He tried to make it light. "Not literally, but he has his own ways of liquidating people—professionally, without bloodletting."

"Watson, you're scared!"

"Of what? I was a struggling lawyer once. You wouldn't mind starting over, would you?"

"Indeed I would," Ellen snapped. "Start thinking—fast. What about that publicity girl?"

"Selma? Selma Shapiro, Hanover's heaving hulk?"

"Don't be nasty. The girl is overweight and uncouth but she's Marianna's friend. Hang up this second and give her a try."

She clicked off and Wagg asked to be put through to the publicity departmnt. "Send Selma Shapiro to me," he ordered.

The fearful girl who stood before him minutes later, voice quavering, had surprised him with her stubbornness.

"I'm sorry, Mr. Wagg, I gave my word. Miss Curtis is up north somewhere. I can't tell you any more than that."

"Sit down, Selma. Do you think I would intrude on Marianna if I didn't think it was important?"

Selma sat. Her heavy lips caught between her teeth formed a tight slash in the fat face. When she spoke, her words were uncompromising. "You can fire me if you like, Mr. Wagg. I gave my word to Miss Curtis. If she wants to hide, that's her privilege."

"Come now, Selma, loyalty is admirable. But what you're doing can hurt Marianna."

"I'd never do that!"

"Pull up your chair," he said conspiratorially. "Let me tell you what's going on."

He had told her what he could. Not the marriage part. Gropper had warned him about that. But about Gropper himself, the Shah, his infatuation with Marianna. The trip to Paris.

Selma protested immediately. "She's not feeling well. I can't go into it—"

"Look here, miss," Watson began with irritation, "a studio is like a small principality. I don't employ spies—not in the usual sense. I don't have to. Here in the executive suite everything is reported to me. Do you think I'm in the dark about what's troubling Marianna? Doug Braden's behavior is ancient history to me. I know everything that went on between him and Marianna. I followed their affair from beginning to end. All of it. Your tactless entry at—shall we say—an inappropriate moment, I know about that, too. I could have predicted the outcome."

"Then, why didn't you—?"

"Warn Marianna? Try to talk sense to a woman in love? It would have been futile." He leaned closer. "I am the head of this studio. It is my responsibility to get every picture completed on schedule. Why cause heartbreak prematurely? It doesn't alter the outcome and it runs up the cost of production."

Selma's body struggled to shift within the narrow confines of the armchair. "You're sure this is good for Miss Curtis? I mean, this man, the Shah—I read the gossip columns. His reputation isn't so great."

"Marianna will be more cautious this time. She won't fall into the same trap that bastard Braden set for her."

He saw the young woman waver. "Look at it this way, Selma. It will be a diversion. A glamorous one. Isn't it better than holing up somewhere, brooding? Now will you tell me where she is?"

Selma came to her feet. "No, Mr. Wagg," she said, "I won't. I'll do this though. I'll call her and tell her everything you told me. Except about Mr. Braden, of course. As for the Shah, she can make her own decision."

"Good. Go back to your office and get her on the phone."

"Sorry, Mr. Wagg. Not from here. The studio operator would get hold of the number—"

He had concealed his exasperation, "All right, go home, go to a telephone booth, go anywhere. Just get back to me by evening." He scribbled something on a piece of paper and handed it to her. "My private number in Bel-Air. I'll be waiting."

It was a while before he learned how she did it. Early that evening Selma reported that Marianna needed more time to think it over. Embarrassed, he had been forced to report to Calvin Gropper that his plan was not proceeding smoothly. "Stay with it," Gropper said impatiently. "The Shah is standing by. So am I."

The following morning Selma reached him through the studio switchboard. His flabbergasted secretary had been instructed that any call from Selma Shapiro was to be put through at once, whether he was in a meeting or in the john.

"Is it okay with you, Mr. Wagg, if I come right over? I have good news."

"Splendid, my dear. I'll be free when you get here."

Hurrying to his private bathroom, he had to admit his stomach had been giving him trouble since the first call from Calvin Gropper. However, he was composed and at apparent ease behind his desk when Selma was shown in.

"I can tell you where she is—where she's been—because she left already," Selma began. "She went up the coast to Mendocino County, to a cottage at Heritage House. It's quiet there. Rocks and sand and rain, and meals private. That's what she wanted. Believe me, Mr. Wagg, it took some talking to get her out of that place. She was crying, I could tell. And between you and me, she doesn't give a damn—excuse me, Mr. Wagg—she doesn't care about any Shah. When I mentioned Paris she refused absolutely. I knew what she was thinking. Paris is in France and so is Mr. Braden. So I said, 'Look, hon, Paris isn't anywhere near Antibes. Give yourself a break. Have a little fun, a change of scenery.' And I said if she got your permission I'd go with her." Selma hesitated. "It's okay, isn't it, Mr. Wagg? I'll make up the work somehow."

Wagg had beamed at her with affection. His patrician face, so unexpectedly kind, incongruously recalled her devoted Uncle Abe in Brooklyn. "My child, that's no problem at all. Let's call it a vacation, richly earned. When will she be here?"

"She's driving. She wants a couple of days for traveling and then getting some rest. You can tell Mr. Gropper it suits her if he comes to her house on Thursday night. After dinner, she said, around nine. Nobody will be there except me. She wants it secret is what she said. No one-two punch for her, she said. She thinks the whole world is laughing because of what Mr. Braden did." Selma frowned. "Isn't it sad, Mr. Wagg? She's got an ego like the head of a pin. Jeez, suppose she looked like me."

"Nonsense." Wagg led her to the door. "You're both lovely women—in your different ways."

Alone again, he had put in a call to Washington. "Done, Mr. Gropper," he informed the man at the other end of the telephone. "Thursday at nine." Then vindictively: "I'll switch

you to my secretary. She will give you the address." He cut
off, not waiting for thanks, not sure there would be any from
that pompous pimp. Calvin Gropper.

As Watson Wagg brought himself back to the present the
Hollywood skyline was darkening. One thing you could say
for the condo. It was built higher, much higher than the
estate in Bel-Air. The view from his living room was fantastic. Dammit, who was he kidding? He longed for the mansion
he had shared with Ellen. He poured another scotch and
swallowed it raw, letting his imagination float free. Who
knows, he asked himself, rereading the invitation, maybe
Marianna Curtis held the key to his old front door.

7

Naming the estate The Farm had been absurd in the first place. A touch of whimsy on the part of Hilary Gropper's forebears. The mansion, set deep in the wooded acres of Beverly Farms, Massachusetts, had been modeled after Jefferson's Monticello more than one hundred and fifty years ago. In the years since, it had nurtured nothing more than splendid alleys of oak, maple, and hemlock trees, cutting beds for spring and summer flowers and, during World War II, a victory garden consisting mainly of carrots, potatoes, and peas. Nonetheless, it had continued to be known as The Farm. Since its creation it had never passed out of the hands of the Westfield family.

Its present owners, Hilary and Calvin Gropper, had received title to the estate on the occasion of their marriage five years earlier. To Helen Westfield, Hilary's mother, it seemed the only appropriate gift for her thirty-three-year-old daughter and the unlikely mate she had chosen. With no regret Mrs. Westfield had transferred ownership of The Farm to the newlyweds and moved off the premises to a comfortable apartment on Commonwealth Avenue in Boston.

Hilary accepted the estate as her due—the belated return of property wrongfully held by that usurper, her mother. In Hilary's view Helen, a former schoolteacher, was not a true Westfield but an interloper who had, in fact, diluted the aristocracy of Hilary's genes by blending her own with those of the late Austin Westfield.

The marriage of Helen and Austin Westfield had been an agreeable one. To their mutual sorrow it had produced only one child. All the indulgence and love intended for a half-dozen offspring had been poured into Hilary.

Seated in the morning room of The Farm observing the end product, Helen Westfield asked herself where she had gone wrong. Hilary was, had been, always would be a contemptible snob. Intimations of the adult she was to become had surfaced early when, in a childish treble, she had terrified nursemaids, cotillion masters, and riding instructors.

She had inherited her long bones, concave chest, and sharp profile from her wellborn father. Her mother's more plebeian genetic contributions—glistening chestnut hair and a clear olive complexion—failed to soften her horsey appearance. Today, as always, Helen repressed her inclination to check Hilary's pronouncements by calling "Whoa!"

A slim French maid wearing a round-collared bombazine uniform and a white scalloped apron had left a tray of cucumber sandwiches and tea on the sideboard. Nibbling a sandwich, Helen Westfield watched her daughter work her way through the morning mail stacked on the Adams desk.

An uncommon chuckle escaped Hilary's pinched lips. "Mother, have you ever seen one of these?" Hilary held out a parchment envelope sealed with shiny turquoise wax. She pulled it back as Helen reached to take it. "Huh-uh, we're not opening it."

"It's impressive."

"You impress too easily."

"Aren't you curious?"

"About this? Not in the least. I know what it is. It's from the Shah of Bahrait and his Hollywood Empress. The invitation to their anniversary splash. Calvin's been talking about it for months."

Hilary waved the envelope in her mother's face. "I'm putting it aside for Calvin. He's such a little boy about celebrities." Her smile was indulgent. "The entire world is in awe of Calvin. Can you believe he still tingles when someone famous calls him by his first name? Amusing, isn't it?"

"You amuse so easily."

Hilary's marriage to Calvin Gropper still fascinated Helen Westfield. Certainly Calvin was a personality to be reckoned with. In government he had outshone the presidents he served. Since his withdrawal from government, his activities, largely mysterious, fanned to every corner of the earth. Socially his presence bestowed unrivaled glitter on distinguished gatherings in the major capitals of the world. All these attributes, Helen surmised, had been run through Hilary's computer mind when Calvin proposed. Obviously they had triumphed over the unfortunate and conspicuous reality that Calvin was a Jew.

"Where is Calvin now?" Helen asked.

"Flying up from Washington. Tomorrow he's lecturing a

graduate seminar at Harvard. He's speaking on international
relations and the current power struggle." Hilary's face
softened. "Tonight I'll have him to myself."

Helen Westfield placed her empty teacup on the sideboard.
"I have my own seminar this afternoon. I'd better start back
to town."

"Mother, I can't believe it yet—you returning to teaching,
and at your age. And those pathetic Southies. It's so useless."

"It's tutoring I'm doing, Hilary. I'm sorry if it offends you."
She found her shoulder bag. "One day you and Calvin may
have children. Then you'll understand about them."

"Don't nag me, darling. Calvin and I aren't ready for
parenthood." Hilary accompanied her mother through the
front hall and out to the small coupe parked in the cobble-
stoned driveway. They touched cheeks in parting.

Starting up her car, Mrs. Westfield glanced back at her
daughter—her husband's daughter really—and called out,
"Give my love to Calvin." Turning onto the road leading to
Boston, she greedily inhaled the air of the common people.
She had never been happier than the day she moved away
from The Farm. In Boston she had promptly formed a
delightful alliance with a Puerto Rican professor from MIT
and, for the first time in her life, was blissfully in touch with
the physical side of her nature, a phenomenon which Austin
Westfield had barely ruffled. Her lover's face rose before her.
"Poor Hilary, poor Calvin," she thought. "You don't know
what you're missing."

Helen Westfield would have been more pleased with her
daughter had she seen Hilary that evening. Showering with
Calvin, lathering him front and back, running her long fingers
between his chunky thighs, fondling the circumcised penis,
Hilary was almost beautiful. Responding to her soapy
caresses, Calvin dipped his head and with pursed lips nipped
at the walnut-sized breasts. Using both hands, he toyed with
her clitoris until she came with a howl thankfully muffled by
the water spilling from the shower head. It was one of the
minor drawbacks of their sexual coupling that Calvin, a good
six inches shorter than Hilary and paunchy, could not enter
her comfortably while standing. Accommodating to this difference, they toweled hastily and concluded their lovemaking
in bed.

Later, as Hilary slept, Calvin nestled into his pillow,

clasped his hands behind his head, and sighed with contentment. He had it all. Power, success, financial rewards, each in
its way had appeased his many hungers. Marriage to Hilary
had been the crowning glory, elevating him to the discriminating domain of Old Money and Social Status. Hilary's
unabashed lust was a bonus.

It was Hilary's secret that she, too, believed she had
married above herself. The last Westfield of distinction, a
well-respected United States senator, had died in a fancy
Chicago bordello soon after World War I. Hilary had longed
to restore the Westfield line, if not the name, to its previous
eminence. In Calvin Gropper she had found not only a
husband she could love but a statesman worthy of fathering
her children. Pressed by her age rather than maternal longing,
she planned to get down to the nasty business of pregnancy
one day soon.

When Hilary's ladylike snore, an undulating hum, grew
deeper and regular, Calvin knew it was safe to leave their
bed. Slipping into a silk Charvet robe, a gift from a colleague
in Paris, he padded down the stairs to his study. From his
desk he retrieved the invitation from Ramir and Marianna,
which Hilary had tossed aside after teasing him about his
excitement.

"It's just another bash," she had said. "I'll go if you want
me to."

He'd smacked her bony bottom. "Of course you'll go, and
you'll adore it. After all, the Shah and his Empress. What has
Massachusetts got to match them?"

"Love him, loathe her. At least he represents tradition. But
Marianna—a parvenu."

"Hardly. Don't forget she comes from a good family. She's
also a superb actress who walked out on a brilliant career."

"Good family." Hilary pounced. "The Joe Curtises of
Boston? Her so-called father began as a hod carrier."

"Mine was a shopkeeper," he reminded her gently.

"Calvin, I'm sorry! You're different. You make no pre-
tenses. She thinks she's royalty."

"She is, Hilary. Look again at the invitation, read her
letter."

Hilary held the letter between her fingers like an oily rag
and read aloud in antic singsong.

"Dear Hilary and Calvin,

"This invitation comes as no surprise to you. Our Minister

of Propaganda (dreadful title) has had his public relations people drumbeating the event everywhere. We can't be accused of entertaining quietly, can we?

"Yet, as you both know, we do have our private life, and that we wish you to share with us. Ramir and I appreciate how busy your own lives are. However, we hope you will be free to spend a week here in Ryal before the hullabaloo begins. A quiet week. Some old friends from Hollywood, a priest from Boston, my aunt and uncle, and the two of you whom we think of as family.

"Please say you will come. It would make us so happy. Love, Marianna (and Ramir)."

The Farm was quiet at midnight. Without Hilary nearby to tease him, Calvin reread the letter and gave full rein to his satisfaction. Clutching the arms of his deep chair, he pulled his plump body erect. The occasion called for a drink. Passing an heirloom Chippendale mirror, he glimpsed the complacent smile on his round face. So be it. He had earned the right to be complacent.

At forty-eight (and at thirty-eight and twenty-eight) no one could have described Calvin Gropper as physically attractive. His body with its thickened midriff was egg-shaped. His lips, like his nose and the springy hair on his head, were too heavy. But his gray eyes, when they were not clouded with concentration, twinkled with humor. His witticisms and thoughtful utterances were noted and quoted by the media of the world.

The story of his tragic unpromising beginnings, the Nazi murder camp which had devoured his parents, the good-hearted bourgeois Dutch family which had sheltered and educated the bereft boy, were known to everyone and referred to as his "past." To Calvin Gropper nothing was in the past. His life was a continually rotating wheel to which all of his personal dramas clung.

By the time he was ten Calvin had recognized that power would be his vehicle of salvation. He had recognized, too, that he was equipped with the brilliance and the drive to achieve it. At the Swiss boarding school in Paudex-Lutry to which his Dutch patrons, the Van Zyls, sent him, he frequently sat on the dock, dangling his legs in the clear water of Lake Geneva, staring at the lordly Alps and plotting the route to his destiny. There, too, he grew proficient in six languages and came to know young people from diverse countries and cultures. Groundwork. Contacts. Foundations for the years to come. The school officials, like his foster parents, were astounded by his progress. They called him clever and dedicated. They avoided the one word that most accurately described Calvin Gropper—ambitious.

Summoning memories of the years in Switzerland, Calvin Gropper applauded himself. He poured a generous brandy and returned to the armchair, noting with satisfaction that the seat was hopelessly indented not by one of the spare-assed Westfields who had preceded him but by Calvin Gropper, a middle-aged German Jew who still spoke accented English.

Thomas Jefferson had visited here once, Hilary had told him. A great man, Jefferson. But history would decide whether he was any greater than Calvin Gropper—the Calvin Gropper to whom presidents, premiers, and kings turned before deciding to avoid or dare their wars; the Calvin Gropper whose advice was heeded by industrialists possessed of empires larger than many nations, the Calvin Gropper who influenced the political and financial fate of the world more than any man of his time. The same Calvin Gropper who once had splashed his feet in Lake Geneva and who now sat sipping his brandy in a Wasp home with a well-laid Wasp wife snoring in the room above.

Prince Ramir of Bahrait had fit perfectly into Calvin's plans. The two young men had appeared as undergraduates at Harvard in the same year. Calvin, confident, determined, accepted by the school on a scholarship. Ramir, heir to the potentate of a Mideast kingdom, shy, exotic in the Western world, accompanied by servitors and spiritual guides entrusted with keeping him close to his Moslem faith.

From the start Calvin believed he admired Ramir for himself alone and not as a potential stepping-stone to the future. The eighteen-year-old prince had been vulnerable yet winning, revealing no traits of the dictator he was to become. In the years after Harvard, as Calvin's stature grew and as Ramir made the transition from prince to Shah following the exile of his father, it gratified Calvin to meet Ramir as an equal.

In the matter of Marianna Curtis, Calvin had proved invaluable. It had been an inspiration, an incontestable coup. Calvin, the undisputed architect of the marriage, had pulled it off with the same diplomatic skill he brought to seemingly

impossible truces between opposing nations. Whether or not
the marriage of Marianna and Ramir would grow into a love
match had not been Calvin's concern. The union was conceived as a political arrangement and he had seen it through
deftly, from the initial meeting in Paris to the dazzling
wedding ceremony in Ryal fifteen years ago.

As in other matters of state, Calvin sometimes deemed it
necessary to conceal sensitive details from one or all of the
principals involved. Certainly Marianna Curtis had been denied any information that might have obstructed the plan
Calvin Gropper contrived to manipulate her life.

Calvin thought of Hilary upstairs. In the second stage of
sleep she would be wheezing lightly, her rest serene after their
frolic in the shower and on their bed. He loved Hilary
without reservation although he disapproved of her appetite
for international gossip and the bitchiness with which she
employed every crumb. To appease her he served up luscious
tidbits: the lesbian affair, flaunted on three continents, between the wife of an Asian leader and the ex-wife of an
American oilman; the tawdry romances of the bored consort
of a European queen; the married premier who brazenly
drove his sports car out of the forecourt of the Élysée Palace,
past the toy soldiers in their guardhouses, and onto the
Faubourg Saint-Honoré, to meet his movie-star mistress in
the boudoir of her apartment on the Avenue Marceau.

Hilary lapped up his insider's information and repeated it
to her closest friends with unwholesome relish. "I never
reveal a name," she swore to Calvin. "Just a few hints,
darling, spicy enough to tantalize but not inform. More,
Calvin."

He told her more. But he had never told her the truth
about Ramir and Marianna. Even now the facts were politically volatile. Prudently he limited his story to the myth he
himself had concocted: The lonely Shah, longing to find a
woman with whom he could spend the rest of his life, had
viewed the films of Marianna Curtis, been bewitched by her
sultry voice, the porcelain perfection of her proud face and
body, her extraordinary talent, and had fallen helplessly in
love with a woman he had never met. Like a doting father
repeating a favorite fairy tale, Calvin told Hilary again and
again how he had tapped the proper sources and brought
Ramir and Marianna together in what the world would
forever remember as "the love match of the century."

The inspiration for the royal marriage had come to Calvin on a gloomy winter afternoon in Ramir's town house on the Boulevard Maurice Barrès in Neuilly. Seated before a dwindling fire in the drawing room overlooking the Bois de Boulogne, the two bachelors had toasted their reunion with a rare aperitif brought from the cellar of the four-story mansion.

Despite their long friendship, Calvin deferred to his host and waited for Ramir to call the meeting to order. It *was* a meeting, a matter of business, Calvin sensed, that had brought him here this day.

In the past week, as special represetnative of the busy President, he had persuaded two opposing African nations to open a dialogue, and he had been granted his fourth private audience with the Pope in the Vatican. Reached in Rome by an emissary of the Shah, he had canceled a day of dalliance with a nymphomaniacal fashion model in Milan and hurried to Ramir's *pied-à-terre* on the outskirts of Paris.

The Shah, his intimidating black eyes recessed beneath bushy eyebrows, glowered at Calvin. Although his opening words were jovial, the nostrils of his long, beaked nose flared in a manner that to Gropper signified repressed rage.

"Calvin, you old lecher, do you know my staff keeps a special file on you?"

"I am not surprised. I would be dishonored if your capable agents overlooked me."

The Shah waved his hand. "Not *that* file," he said. "Monitoring your political activities is routine. My secret police are in charge of that. It is your personal life I refer to—your sex life, so charmingly documented by every lousy tabloid on two continents. Is it all true? When do you find time to serve your country?"

Calvin lowered his eyes modestly. "Let us say half true. Power is sexy, I am told. The ladies drop like plums at my feet. They come with the job, an undeclared bonus. I would be a fool not to harvest them while I can."

"And you are no fool, Calvin."

"Agreed."

"Do you know why I sent for you?"

"The proposed armaments purchase."

"Dependable Calvin. Your antennae pick up everything."

"I am overly conscientious. It blights my existence."

"Then you know I need new planes, new guns, new tanks,

and replacement parts for those I have. Also more instructors to train my armed forces."

"I know that. And I know our most powerful congressmen are opposed to letting you have them."

"Tell me why. I pay my bills. I am a friend of the United States."

"Blame the American free press. Every day it relates your imagined torture of dissidents and your most recent acts of repression. In America your own students riot and shout for your downfall. You're standard fare on television."

Ramir brought his fist down on the arm of his chair. "What do they know of my problems? Are your congressmen concerned with the threats I must deal with? Do they understand the dangers I face from neighboring states and hostile elements within my own country?"

"They understand you. You do not understand them. Remember this about our elected representatives—they are concerned first of all with their own re-election. They cannot go back to the people who sent them to Washington and explain why they voted to sell military hardware to a ruler the press calls a tyrant."

"A tyrant! I do what is necessary, no more. If I am deposed the entire area could fall to the Soviets. Can't your Congress grasp that much?"

"They can and they do. Secretly many support you. Unhappily, few are willing to risk their own political necks to save yours."

"You Americans are insane! Are we talking of political realities or public relations?"

For long minutes Calvin was thoughtful. Suddenly his face lit up and he pressed forward excitedly. "Ah," he exclaimed. "As usual you have put your finger on the problem!"

"I don't know what you are talking about."

"Can't you see? We are talking about public relations. It is your image, not your performance, which must be altered. You have a Ministry of Propaganda. What does it tell the world? That you are a misunderstood man who sometimes must resort to disagreeable practices to protect your subjects, but always with a heavy heart because you wish only to serve the people, and because you alone know what is best.

"Everyone recognizes your media is controlled. It doesn't dare criticize you. Foreign journalists tell another story. They are not afraid to expose the excesses of your secret police.

They dote on stories of corruption, jailings, beatings, executions."

"Every country has the same. They go by different names," Ramir responded angrily.

"True, but perhaps your agents are thought to be a little more—shall we say—creative? Good friend, so much was expected when you succeeded your father. You have disappointed the idealists. How can Americans accept selling you additional hardware when you are said to be using guns against your own people. Your image—which you and I know to be false—is that of an insatiable, high-handed dictator. *Image.* That is the key word—*image.* Other rulers are pitiless yet they preserve the illusion—the *image* of benevolence. There, Ramir, you have failed. That is what you must change."

"Idiot! What are you proposing? That I, the leader of a great country, buy myself a press agent—a Hollywood-type press agent?"

Calvin sat back and puffed his Cuban cigar calmly. "Hollywood—of course. But not a press agent—a wife."

"You're mad!"

"No, it's perfect. An American, an adored symbol. Someone who holds the public in the palm of her hand. A singer, an actress, perhaps. I know I'm on to something. There must be some woman, the right woman, a woman who is loved and respected." He came from his chair and stood over Ramir. "Think of it. Whoever she is, by marrying you she will make the world see you with her own adoring eyes."

Ramir rose, laughing, and forced Calvin back into his seat. "Off your rocker. That is one thing I learned at Harvard. To recognize a man who is off his rocker."

"Don't dismiss the idea," Calvin warned. "Marriages of convenience, for political advantage, have been made for centuries. Forgive me, but you have already made two yourself."

"But an American? Ridiculous." Ramir ran his fingers through his wiry black hair. "Yet, intriguing. Who do you have in mind?"

"Not so fast. I have contacts in the entertainment world. You said yourself—I get around a bit."

"Your affairs attract more attention than the government's."

Calvin shrugged. "Image, all image. Women worship me on

sight because of my image. Many of them will go to bed with any man who is famous because it titillates them and their friends. I seldom discourage them. I am strong as a bull. As for the gossip, I help spread it."

Ramir sat musing. "Remember our Harvard days—how I was a prisoner of the courtiers of Bahrait? God, I was horny. They meant me to be celibate then. Only you understood— and provided lovely ladies to end my torment."

"You have managed well enough since."

"Yes, but I cannot do what you suggest. I cannot leap into a bed you have made ready for me. I send for you to help me get armaments and you are trying to sell me an Empress."

"You will have both."

"It will work?"

"Leave it to me."

"And what of my own people? How will they feel about a foreign consort?"

"A detail. Give me time to think. It will be more difficult than Harvard. But I promise, you will have your Empress— and your hardware."

It was almost too easy. Subtle inquiries, a weeding through of possibilities. And all channels had led to one name: Marianna Curtis.

There had been roadblocks, of course. That was normal in diplomatic negotiations. The priest had been a sticky situation. So had the studio. Not the chief, Wagg, but the money- men in New York. And that doughy creature, Selma Shapiro, now risen so high in the picture industry. She had argued against the marriage, telling Marianna she was being reckless, falling in love on the rebound. And Marianna herself—chary, suspicious, determined to remain uninvolved.

In the end, as he usually did, Calvin Gropper won. Mari- anna Curtis surrendered. For fifteen years she had been an Empress.

And Ramir got his hardware.

8

Except for the illuminated bedside clock, the room was in total blackness. The jewel-studded timepiece, a gift from the Emir of Qatar, bore twenty-four numerals on its platinum face and informed the Empress it was precisely six o'clock.

Bringing her arms from between the ivory satin bedsheets, she stretched them high overhead, exposing her breasts with the motion. Her fingers clawed at the air. Angered by the infernal lyric that drummed through her head, she slid back between the sheets and shut her eyes.

"I wonder what the King is doing tonight.
I wonder what merriment the King is pursuing tonight."

Long ago, in the fervid days of their courtship, she and Ramir had seen the French version of *Camelot*. Listening to the lyrics from their theater box, they had moved closer to each other and giggled. They knew what the King would be doing *that* night.

"I wonder what the King is doing tonight.
I wonder what merriment the King is pursuing tonight."

The King is fucking, that's what he's doing tonight. In London, tonight. Far from Bahrait, tonight. Far from his Paradise Palace in Ryal, tonight.

And farther yet from the ornate bedroom he was no longer permitted to visit.

More than fifteen years had passed since that radiant evening, and she was furious with herself because he still invaded her morning thoughts. She was through with Ramir, done, finished. By mutual agreement they tried to conceal their estrangement from the public and, they hoped, from their children. As best they could they upheld the appearance of the magical couple they had been on their wedding day and for the cloudless decade that followed.

Their growing apart had begun five years after the birth of their third child, a daughter named Nariam. That was when

Marianna had first learned that the gossip about other women, casually dismissed as "nonsense" by Ramir, was not gossip at all but bitter truth. Before, overhearing disturbing stories, she had continued to love him, placated when he assured her she was the only woman in his life. That fantasy was behind her now, had been since the disastrous scene with Azar in Switzerland.

Her own involvement with Luke Tremayne, embarked upon when Nariam reached nursery school age, was not that spiteful Hollywood exercise known as a revenge fuck. It was a firmly rooted affair which had deepened steadily in the four years since they had become lovers.

Sometimes after Luke left her bed Marianna lay still, reveling in thoughts of her love for the sloe-eyed, rugged American with the shining rumpled hair and full black moustache who had come into her life as the children's tutor.

It had all started when Karim, the Crown Prince, was ten. Accompanying Ramir to Qatar, Marianna had left Karim and the younger children in the care of nannies and tutors. As a guest of the Emir, she had met the powerful leaders of the Gulf States as well as the then ruler of Iran, Shah Mohammed Reza Pahlavi, and his Empress, Farah Diba. While the men conferred in air-conditioned council halls, she and Farah had escaped the smothering heat, swimming lazily in the Emir's indoor climate-controlled pool. Later they had stretched out poolside on spongy mattresses and bewailed the problem of educating their children in volatile lands like Iran and Bahrait.

Farah, exquisite in a swimsuit the color of cranberries, had propped herself on an elbow and spoken with intensity. "My husband and I," Farah said, "we wanted our four children to go to the best schools in Teheran. We soon agreed it was impossible. The country bitter, so full of hatred. The risk, we saw, would be too great. Yet we did not want them tutored at home—lonely little captives confined to the palace. An English friend provided the answer—a real schoolhouse on the palace grounds and regular classes with other children."

"Whose children?"

"There are so many to choose from," Farah had said. "The children of shopkeepers, lawyers, businessmen, architects, members of the military. Foreigners, too. The students we select are bused in. After school they are bused home." She had smiled. "I know that sounds odd to you. For us, it works."

Marianna, her pale cheeks flushed with inspiration, had hugged the Empress of Iran and thanked her for sharing her experience.

On the flight back to Bahrait she had cautiously mentioned the Iranian solution to Ramir. He had grunted and picked up a magazine.

In the past when Marianna had cornered Ramir to discuss injustices suffered by the people of Bahrait, she had found him impatient and unsympathetic. Frustrated at being treated like a foolish child, she invariably withdrew defeated. In the matter of her children's education she would not be turned away.

"I object to tutors coming to the palace," she said that evening. "Our children are isolated from other children. They're being stunted by book learning alone. They need outside stimulation."

"It is unimportant now," he snapped. "When they are older they will go away to school as I did."

"You were miserable when you got there. You told me so yourself."

"I adjusted as they will."

"Must they be unhappy first? We can do better than that."

"How? Think of the mood of the country. It is unsafe for them to leave the palace grounds. Kidnappings, or worse, could occur. The best guards are no guarantee. How can you be so reckless with their lives?"

"You know I'm not reckless," she flared. "Why can't we have a schoolhouse right here—bring other children to them? And another thing—"

"Yes?" He waited peevishly.

"I'm an American. I love your country, but I want the children to know something of mine, too. I insist upon an American to supervise their education."

He was thoughtful, calculating the depth of her feeling. "You have my consent," he said finally. "I will talk to Calvin."

"Calvin!" She was outraged. "What the hell has he to do with this?"

"Can you think of anyone better? He knows American

educators. He knows us. He will find the most suitable person."

And Calvin had come through. He had explored the credentials of numberless candidates and settled, without reservation, on Luke Tremayne.

Marianna squirmed pleasurably between the satin sheets as she recalled the first time she had set eyes on Luke Tremayne. Seated alongside Ramir behind his massive desk in the cavernous Golden Lion Room, she had been immediately struck by Luke's easy, confident stride as he approached the royal couple. Mentally she reviewed Calvin Gropper's dry resumé, concentrated on unadorned facts: candidate Luke Daniel Tremayne, born in Oklahoma; English ancestry with Cherokee blood sneaked in somewhere; thirty-six years old; son of a surgeon; trained as an educator, Brown and Stanford; two years in Peace Corps, Philippines; headmaster at private schools in Maine and Vermont.

And the personal history, brief, to the point: divorced after ten years; unmarried at the time his ex-wife, Harriet, confessed—too late for abortion—that he'd made her pregnant; one child, a boy; numerous affairs before, after, perhaps during marriage; presently uninvolved. Unable to tolerate confrontations with ex-wife when exercising visitation rights; desired employment abroad, specifically with youngsters; annual trip to vacation with son in U.S. essential; otherwise prepared to devote foreseeable future to royal children.

Calvin had omitted one ragingly obvious detail. Filled with his own conceit, he had failed to recognize the disturbing aura of virility that surrounded Luke Tremayne.

As Luke had neared, Marianna could feel his magnetism across the room. Without rising, Ramir had performed a brusque introduction of his wife and waved toward the single chair facing the desk.

"Be seated, Mr. Tremayne," he said.

Luke sat.

Fingering the resumé, Ramir began the interview. "Born in Oklahoma."

Luke nodded.

"Educated at Brown and Stanford. Good schools."

Luke nodded again.

"Divorced, I see."

"Guilty," Luke replied.

"You have a son."

Luke fidgeted irritably. "That's what it says, doesn't it . . . *sir?*"

Ramir looked up surprised, then returned his attention to the page in his hands. "You're thirty-six years old," he said.

"Right again . . . *sir.*"

Now Marianna studied the American with increased curiosity. And admiration. No one, ever, had risked speaking to Ramir with such naked disrespect.

As Ramir began another query Luke interrupted. "Your Majesty, Mr. Gropper impressed me as an exceedingly thorough man. He asked me questions—I answered him. I had questions of my own—he answered me. I doubt anything was omitted on either side."

Ramir thrust aside the resumé. "The interview is concluded, Mr. Tremayne. The children will be told you have arrived. As soon as possible, school will begin. You will report to Her Majesty regularly."

"We're in business," Luke said, coming to his feet.

When Luke had gone from the room, a scowling Ramir turned to Marianna. "I don't trust that man," he said.

Marianna grinned wickedly. "Calvin does," she said.

Admittedly, she had been attracted to Luke with the same sudden surge she had experienced upon meeting Douglas Braden and Ramir. But this time she was determined to be more cautious. Observing Luke at work in the schoolhouse, she remained regal, testing him with her bad humor and seeming indifference. Disappointingly, Luke did nothing to reveal his own emotions. He swaggered about in jeans and open-necked shirts that bared his hairy chest, and talked fondly of women friends in Ryal's foreign colony. When reviewing the children's lessons with her, he kept at a respectful distance. As time went by she noticed that his words slurred and his once-insolent eyes softened when he was near her. Then she knew he cared and she was happy.

She seduced him early one morning. They'd fallen into the habit of meeting at the palace stables at dawn and riding their horses through the woods. "Luke," she said after they dismounted, "meet me in my apartment after breakfast. There's something I'd like to give you."

No pang of conscience troubled their love affair. The history of his marriage—the vindictive ex-wife and the disappointing finale to the custody battle for their son—was known to her. The publicized history of the romance between Marianna Curtis and the Shah of Bahrait was known to everyone.

To Luke, the man who loved the Empress, the stories he read in yellowing press releases were not enough.

"How did you get into all this?" he had wanted to know.

They were lying between the satin sheets after making love.

Her head rested on the tangle of damp black curls matting his chest. "Into what?" she yawned.

"This romance of the century. Ramir. You had it made in Hollywood. Why did you leave?"

"I'll tell you about it someday." She yawned again. "Now I'd like to doze."

"Whatever pleases Your Majesty," he said. He kissed her lips and held her close. But she did not doze. Instead, spurred by his questions, she closed her eyes and replayed in memory the beginning of her courtship, and of her marriage. . . .

After the break with Doug, she hadn't wanted to see anyone, not even her best friend, Selma Shapiro. She drove north of San Francisco to Mendocino County and rented a cottage overlooking the Pacific. She needed solitude and time to think through the mess her life had become. There was no escape. Her mind was like a hamster going round and round in its cage, getting nowhere. And then Selma telephoned.

"Hi, Marianna. How're you doing?"

"Lousy. In the pits."

"That stinking actor. Someday . . ."

"Please, Selma, don't start that. . . . What do you want?"

"I got news for you."

"I don't want to hear it."

"You gotta listen."

"You're the new president of the D.A.R."

"Not yet. No, it's about you."

"Then talk fast and hang up."

"So that's the way it is? The country air isn't doing it?"

"Selma, I'm so low I want to go over the nearest cliff."

"You won't when you hear what I have to say. Guess who

wants to see you? Don't guess, I'll tell you—ever hear of Calvin Gropper?"

"The playboy of the western world? Thanks loads. I don't want to see him or any other man."

"Waita minute. Gropper's not asking for a date. He's an emissary."

"A what . . . ?"

"An emissary. He's representing someone important."

"He's still adviser to the President, isn't he?"

"Yeah, but he's in the emissary business on the side. It's sort of wild."

"Get to the point. I'm about to hang up."

"I don't know too much. Gropper called Mr. Wagg from Washington. Mr. Wagg was all flustered—he didn't like admitting he couldn't find you. Mr. Wagg, he tried to squeeze the info out of me. I wouldn't even burp for him."

"Good girl."

"All he'd tell me is that Gropper represents some big shot—bigger than the President—who's in love with you long-distance. A bachelor. He wants to meet you real bad."

"That's ridiculous."

"Listen, you're ready to go over a cliff anyway. What's to lose? See Gropper. Find out who he's pitching. For my sake. I'm *plotzing* with suspense."

"Selma, you're pushing."

"Maybe. But it sure sounds better than breaking your neck in the Pacific Ocean."

In the end Selma had won. It was misty and bleak in Mendocino. The alternatives weren't promising. She knew she didn't want to get involved with another man but she wasn't ready for a nunnery either. She took the coast road and nearly did go over a cliff, thinking of Doug and crying.

At home, there were a half-dozen messages, all from Watson Wagg. When she telephoned him he said Calvin Gropper was standing by in Washington. Unless she objected Gropper would be at her door at nine sharp the following evening. She did not object.

It was all very cloak and dagger. She and Selma had had an early dinner. At nine o'clock someone punched the doorbell. It was Gropper. Two men, Secret Service, stood behind him. Gropper snapped his fingers without looking back and the men retreated to a limo. Selma pulled Marianna aside so that

Gropper could come in. Gropper glared at Selma but she would not budge until Marianna told her to wait in another room.

Gropper followed Marianna into the den. Curious, she asked him about the men outside. He said they were assigned to him by the State Department and had accompanied him to the Coast in a presidential plane. At the airport the trio had been picked up by the black limousine which had swept them off to Beverly Hills.

In her den, Gropper told Marianna he represented Ramir, the Shah of Bahrait. Of course she knew of Ramir. Who didn't?

Gropper was jovial that evening, exuberant about his assignment. "It is my privilege to invite you to be the guest of the Shah in Paris in two weeks time. He keeps a simple *pied-à-terre* in Neuilly. Naturally, you will stay at a hotel. The Shah would be honored to have you join him at dinner on the night following your arrival. There will be other guests. After that—who knows?—you may wish to stay on to enjoy more of Paris and of His Majesty."

Gropper talked rapidly without pausing for her reaction. "I will be waiting at Charles de Gaulle Airport. Your suite has been reserved at the Hotel Plaza-Athénée. A car and driver will be at your disposal. Plan to stay a week, two weeks, as long as you choose. Bring some gowns for evening, a few costumes for street wear. Dior will send around anything else you need."

She had felt herself going under. It was moving too fast. She hadn't accepted, yet she heard herself say, "I'd like to bring a companion."

"Why not?" His expression was a cockeyed blend of affability and pain. "I suppose you mean the young woman in the next room?"

She hadn't liked the way he'd said it. "Selma Shapiro is my dearest friend," she told him sharply.

"Do as you like. Suitable arrangements will be made for the two of you." He kissed her hand and left.

When the door closed, Selma tumbled into the room. She hadn't missed a word. She was squealing, "Baby, baby, baby, you got it made! You're gonna live happily ever after!"

Two weeks later Selma and Marianna had arrived in Paris. They were swept through the airport. No passport control, no

luggage delay, no dragging through customs. All the wheels
and palms had been greased.

Gropper was waiting at the curb with another of those
limousines. The standard everyday type, without crests or
flags. Att he hotel he saw them to their suite and helped them
find their way through the flowers, fruit, and champagne.
There was a solid gold compact for each of them with a card
that said simply, "Welcome. Ramir."

Selma had never been east of Brooklyn. She was ecstatic
and a bit paranoid recalling all the spy movies she'd seen. She
peeked behind drapes and under furniture, searching for
listening devices, and was disappointed when she could find
none. Thrilled about being in Paris, she did not feel snubbed
at being excluded from Ramir's dinner party.

When Gropper called for Marianna the next evening, he
was in formal dress. There was a blinding shine on his
patent leather shoes. She suspected he was wearing a corset.

Ramir's "simple" *pied-à-terre* was situated on a lamplit
residential street. It was concealed behind a wrought-iron
fence overgrown with shrubbery.

Inside, it was a miniature palace. Crystal chandeliers,
marble floors, Persian rugs, and porcelain *objets*. Marianna
had the eerie sensation of being transported backward in time
to a Hanover soundstage where she had once played Marie
Antoinette. There were voices and laughter coming from a
room off a landing on the floor above.

A butler took her white mink wrap. Gropper had dropped
enough hints to persuade her to dress to the nines for the
occasion. Another butler led them up the stairs, past niches
with Grecian statuary, to a wood-paneled study with shelves
of leather-bound books, and family snapshots on a grand
piano. There were fewer than a dozen people in the room.
Ramir stepped out of a small group and came toward them.
He was glorious to look at. Only thirty-five then, taller than
she'd expected, stunning in evening clothes. His face was
familiar, naturally, from television, magazines, newspapers.
But no picture had ever caught the beauty of his coloring, the
scorching black eyes—the bags came later—the smooth skin,
like coffee with a dash of cream, the glow about the high
cheekbones. And that graceful body. She thought, no, this
man can't be the monster the press says he is. She told herself

she must not find him attractive. Only weeks ago she'd sworn off men forever.

After Gropper introduced them Ramir took her hand. He bent from the waist and grazed her fingers with his lips. He thanked her for coming.

Marianna's attempt at being aloof did not deceive him. Women had always responded to him. He knew it and he accepted female attention as his divine right.

While Gropper made his way among the guests Ramir, still holding her hand, drew her into his group. He introduced her to his mother, a handsome matron who examined Marianna as though she were an haute couture gown the Dowager Empress was not sure she wanted to own. Azar, Ramir's older sister, was there too. A doll-size woman. Plastic surgery gave her the semblance, if not the reality, of youth. With her was Aldo, her young lover of the moment. Azar, Marianna knew from newspaper accounts, was the widow of a pauper prince chosen by her mother. She had not mourned the prince nor, as Marianna was to learn, did she expect to mourn the death of her mother. The two women doted on Ramir and competed for his attention. The others in the room were staff aides and their wives.

The women were breathtaking, dazzlingly bejeweled, exuding confidence. Marianna felt like a street waif. She reminded herself they'd probably known riches all their lives. They'd never heard of a depressed neighborhood called Charlestown. If they had, it would have affected them as little as the deprivation in their own country.

At dinner she was seated at Ramir's right, his mother at his left. Azar requested that the twin crystal chandeliers over the dining table be dimmed. Everything shimmered. The diamonds and emeralds of the women, the white teeth against the caramel skin of the men, the gold platters and serving pieces, the wines in fragile glasses. Everything sparkled— except the conversation. It was muted—because of her. Later, when she knew them better, they were animated. Sometimes it was the animation of fury, but at least it was human. That night she sensed she was on the auction block, merchandise under consideration. She couldn't understand the whole charade and it made her uneasy.

Whispering, Ramir confirmed what Gropper had told her in California—that he'd screened her films over and over again in his projection room in the palace in Ryal and in his villa on the Caspian Sea. He said he felt he knew her but not yet as well as he hoped to. His black eyes seemed to eat her. Across the table Gropper purred.

When Ramir rose and proposed a champagne toast to Marianna as guest of honor, she longed for a screenwriter to give her her lines. On her own, the best she could offer was an actressy nod and a choked "Thank you." She was overwhelmed, not only by the rich trappings but by Ramir himself.

In the limousine returning to the Plaza-Athénée, Gropper had patted her hand. "You exceeded his highest hopes," he said.

She found that patronizing and told him so. "What did he expect, Eliza Doolittle?"

"Don't be upset. Ramir is the world's most eligible bachelor and you pleased him."

She was incensed. "And I am not Cinderella. If we're counting brownie points let me remind you that I am one of the world's most desirable women."

"Indeed you are. But together—what a couple!"

"Look here, you bloated Cupid. I didn't send for you, *or* for him."

"A thousand apologies. My imagination is fired by the possibility of a meaningful relationship between you and my old schoolmate. We must plan our next move."

"We must *what . . . ?* You're being insulting! If there's to be a next move, your old schoolmate will have to make it himself."

Gropper sputtered, "He's the Shah. Things aren't done that way."

"Then I'll pick up my marbles and go home."

"You can't do that!"

"I can and I will."

"Now listen to me . . ."

"You listen to *me*. If there's to be a relationship, it doesn't need a middleman. Exactly when were you planning to step aside—at the bedroom door?"

Gropper had sputtered some more but he knew she was serious and quickly became his usual fawning self. "I see your point and so will the Shah. He will personally telephone you in the morning."

"I sleep until noon."

Gropper and Marianna did not exchange another word

until they reached the hotel. He saw her to her door and said goodnight.

Selma, bursting with questions, leaped from the sofa when Marianna let herself into the suite. Marianna made her wait until she had changed into a gown and robe. Then they sat on a bed like a pair of sorority sisters. Selma's mouth hung open as Marianna described Ramir and his guests.

Then the realistic Selma surfaced. "You really fell for each other?"

"Yes."

"He's an all-right guy? He won't give you trouble?"

"He's a kind man. He'd has more than his share of tragedy. Being forced by his ministers to divorce his first wife because she was barren. Losing his second wife in a plane crash. He hasn't had an easy time."

"Barren?" Selma snatched at the word. "You mean the first wife couldn't have a kid?"

"That's right. A Shah needs a male heir to inherit the throne."

"You mean if you get married to him you get thrown out if you don't produce? Do you give him a money-back guarantee? You've never had a baby."

Marianna gave her a sickly smile. "Look, Selma, I'm *too* fertile. I'm a good Catholic, but I've had four uncomplicated abortions. I've confessed them and I've done penance. Believe me, I felt awful each time, but my career was moving so fast, I couldn't stop for babies. Especially illegitimate ones. You know very well that I have three brothers and they all have sons. Sure, it's Russian roulette but the odds are with me. Anyway, I don't want to think about that. I'm too happy. Besides, he hasn't asked me to marry him."

The next day Ramir phoned at noon. It was a glorious blue-sky day. He suggested a drive into the country, lunch at Coq Hardi. A limousine would pick her up, he said, and bring her to him on the Boulevard Maurice Barrès. She forgot her spat with Gropper and her resolve to transform this into a normal man-woman relationship. She heard the snap of authority and folded like an accordion.

Ramir was in front of the town house at the wheel of his Jaguar. He told her Gropper and the family had gone their separate ways.

That afternoon Ramir and Marianna visited Versailles. In the days that followed they drove to Chantilly, through the forest of Fontainebleau, and to the wild animal reserve behind the Château de Thoiry. At restaurants, by prearrangement, they slipped through side doors to private rooms. If bodyguards were about, she never saw them.

Their favorite dining spot became the *cave* in L'Hôtel on the rue des Beaux Arts. In the years since Oscar Wilde had died in a cramped upstairs bed-sitting room, L'Hôtel had become a chic hostelry with the same *fin-de-siècle* decor it had had in poor Oscar's time. At L'Hôtel they had laughed and kissed and clung to each other for dear life, as they tried to reach the dark cellar without falling down the narrow curved stairway. They had their own hideaway in the *cave*—a round parlor, candlelit, with a round table set for two. There were red plush banquettes, a vitrine with Dresden figurines, a tiger-skin rug, and iron gates to close them into the dim seductive room. After dinner the waiter would place a screen in front of the gates, cutting them off like a pair of hibernating bears. But they did not hibernate. In the beginning Marianna was shy, awed like Selma, and a bit scared. The third evening they ate very little and allowed the champagne to do its work. Marianna grew woozy. Before she could shake herself sober they were on one of the banquettes and he was guiding her hand between his thighs. She murmured, "Yes." They left L'Hôtel and drove back to Neuilly.

It was the first time she'd been inside the town house since Gropper had escorted her to dinner. Ramir unlocked the door. No one was in sight. She was nervous and still a bit drunk mounting the marble staircase. In his bedroom they undressed each other slowly. He was so committed, so unselfish in lovemaking, she never doubted they were right for each other.

That night he asked her to marry him. She had consented before the words were out of his mouth. They made love again and slept.

When she opened her eyes it was morning. She saw a chiffon peignoir on a chaise longue near the bed. Ramir was seated across the room watching her awaken. Before she could get to the peignoir he had removed his dressing gown. They made love again as joyfully as they had in the night.

In a pink marble bathroom—she learned later that his bathroom was on the opposite side of the room—she found feminine toiletries and, unexpectedly, one of her own daytime outfits.

An impassive butler rolled in a breakfast table. They sat opposite each other near a window, drinking strong coffee and gobbling croissants and madeleines, hungry, happy, full of plans for their wedding.

"Calvin Gropper will make the arrangements," Ramir had begun. When he saw her stiffen, he pulled his chair alongside hers. "My darling," he said, "in our bedroom we will be as other couples. It is our public faces that will be scrutinized. For my country, for my people—and they will be yours, too—we must perform according to expectations, rules, formalities. In all of these Calvin is expert. He is my friend and he will be yours. You and I, beautiful Marianna, we cannot elope to a little Swiss village for a quiet civil ceremony. There is much to do when the head of an Islamic state marries. There is your conversion to the Moslem faith . . ."

"My *what?*"

"My bride must be a Moslem. I owe that to my people."

"But I'm not a Moslem. I'm Catholic!"

"No problem. You will study with a mullah. There is a simple rite for conversion. In Bahrait there is historical precedent for taking a foreign bride. You will be accepted."

She was indignant. "You haven't asked what *I* want."

"Forgive me, I assume too much."

"You do. I have hard thinking to do. So do you. What do you know about me? Publicity releases? Magazine profiles? You think that's Marianna Curtis?"

"Darling Marianna, I have been informed of everything. No one dares keep secrets from me. It is my business to know cold, even brutal, facts as it is yours to know how to please an audience."

"What are you telling me?"

"That I know it all. Your chauffeur father, your mother's covered-up suicide, those adoptive parents in Boston, your school and theater days—promiscuous, I believe. The abortions. I know everything."

"Everything?"

"The affair with Douglas Braden, yes, that too."

"That's disgusting!"

"Only if you view it that way," he said. "My life has been the public's business from the hour I was conceived, yet you accept me, both the good and the bad of what you've heard. I am not reproachful of you. What right have I to be? I am aware of certain truths that you might have wished concealed. What of it? I adore you the more for your sad little secrets. Isn't that a sounder basis for our marriage?"

She was frowning and he asked her why.

"I was thinking of Father Flynn."

"Ah, the Boston priest. I know about him, too. Perhaps you would like his opinion before you decide about the conversion."

"I would."

"Then Calvin will see that you have it."

"Calvin again?"

Ramir sighed. "If you wish, you may deal with Father Flynn yourself. However, recognize this: Once you have made your religious peace with Father Flynn—and I am confident you will—you will become my Empress. The nuisances, the intrusions you will endure as a royal figure are enormous. Greater than those you've endured as an actress. Think of it this way—movie studios are notorious for smoothing the way in delicate situations, yet you have accepted their services without question. Your conversion is also a delicate situation. It will be helpful to have a skilled intermediary. Calvin will prepare Father Flynn for your arrival. Certain emotional roadblocks will be down. You will find it easier to meet again with the good Catholic father."

She had agreed. She knew she wanted to spend the rest of her life with Ramir and she suspected she would convert regardless of what Father Flynn said. But she desperately needed his approval to ease her conscience. She wanted him to understand and to remain her friend.

Selma was shocked to the bottom of her Jewish soul when she heard that Marianna might change her religion. Selma believed there was a special hell reserved for anyone who rejected the faith he was born into. She was as amazed as Marianna when, a week later, the actress walked out of Father Flynn's parish house not only with his blessing but with his encouragement. He had appeared to be *urging* her to become a Moslem. Her relief was enormous, her eyes lit up Boston. And why not? Seated in that familiar study, searching the priest's beloved face, she could almost touch her heart thumping outside her skin. She had been afraid of calling down the wrath of the Lord and afraid of the pain she would cause her old friend.

Instead, Father Flynn was reassuring. He had said something about the Lord's moving in mysterious ways His wonders to perform. He told her the Lord *wanted* her to give up her faith.

"Don't look so confused, Mary Anna," he had said. "When the Lord tries us He has His reasons. If you love this man, you must marry him. It is a step with a high purpose. Before the eyes of the world you will prove that people born to different faiths can be united by love. Obviously the Shah cannot join you in celebrating Catholicism. Our Lord will forgive you for sacrificing your Church."

Then there was Watson Wagg to be told. Under her contract she owed Hanover Studios two more pictures. The legal wolves in New York pressed hard to hold her to the agreement. She would be a bigger money-maker, more bankable than ever with this new splash of publicity. Watson was marvelous. He convinced them it would be an ugly, losing situation, that they would come up against the formidable Calvin Gropper, an adversary no one wanted to provoke. The New Yorkers gave in. They labeled her release a gesture of international goodwill and called it her wedding present.

At her home in Beverly Hills there was a letter from Doug Braden, postmarked somewhere in France. She had handed it to Selma, who tore it in half unopened.

Winding up her life in California took several weeks. It seemed an eternity. Ramir phoned a dozen times a day from his palace in Bahrait. Secretly, they arranged for the wedding announcement to be released simultaneously by the Royal Court in Ryal and by Watson Wagg in Hollywood.

The media went wild when the story broke. She was trapped everywhere, from Le Bourget airfield in Paris where one of Ramir's planes brought her from Los Angeles, to Christian Dior's salon in Paris where Ramir helped her select more than one hundred costumes for her trousseau. She had sent him away when the time came to choose her wedding dress. Selma joined her at Dior's. It didn't matter that Selma's taste was nightmarish. Marianna was sentimental and wanted someone close to share the moment. Joe and Aggie Curtis came out of the woodwork, primed to be loving parents, but Marianna kept them away. She missed her own mother terribly.

In Ryal she studied with a mullah. The simple conversion was performed in the mosque on the palace grounds with only Ramir's family present.

The wedding was something between an Arabian Nights ball and a Hanover Studios spectacular. Heads of state, royal guests, many in native costumes, acres of food and drink, the newlyweds holding hands, smiling and waving for the cameras. Reuters took a poll of the most widely recognized figures of the twentieth century. Only Marilyn Monroe, Jackie Onassis, and Mao led the royal couple. What a joke, Marianna had thought. It wasn't more recognition she wanted —just peace and privacy with Ramir.

They had honeymooned on his yacht in the Caspian. When they returned to Ryal she was ecstatic—and pregnant. She believed nothing could disturb their future.

She had no premonition of what lay ahead.

The Empress contemplated the Emir's clock and rebuked herself for wasting time in useless reflection. She tapped the button that would bring Narit with her breakfast tray. Lying back, she allowed her fingers to glide fondly over the pillow on which Luke Tremayne had drowsed till midnight.

Narit would notice the pillow and the rumpled sheets. She always did. Her morning smile would be approving as she settled the tray across the Empress's lap. A withered woman whose face bore a cluster of spiky warts and a faint moustache, Narit had served two previous Empresses in this vast suite. She owed her tenure to her kind and accepting nature and innate sense of discretion. The ugly sounds of anger—as well as the happy noises of abandon—that she had heard spilling from this bedroom were never the subjects of her backstairs gossip. An emotional woman herself, she believed in all expressions of passion short of murder. Always, Narit's inquisitive kitchen colleagues were faced down with blank stares and a shrug of rounded shoulders if they dared pry into the intrigues of the succession of Ramir's wives that Narit had served.

From the start Narit had been Marianna's accomplice, barring entrance to would-be intruders who approached the Empress's quarters when Luke was with her. The affair, begun as an early morning rendezvous, was presently conducted with minimum caution at any convenient hour of day or night. In his role of schoolmaster, Luke strode the corridor to Marianna's suite, his arms laden with books and folders, a briefcase stuffed with reports of the children's progress tucked under his arm. Departing, his briefcase still unopened, he would tip his head and wink as Narit rushed past him to change the satin sheets.

"Why does he stand for it?" Luke had asked one night. "Whenever he's away, I'm with you. Everyone knows it."

"Not everyone, yet. So far we're mostly palace gossip, jet-set speculation. If he moved against either of us, the story would be trumpeted around the world. Imagine, the Shah of Bahrait, a common cuckold. The humiliation would be more than he could bear." Her brow furrowed. "There's something else restraining him. I don't understand . . ."

"But we can't live out our lives like this, Marianna. What's your future? What's mine? Karim is at Le Rosey. In a few years the other children will leave for Swiss schools. The palace school will close down. My work will be finished here. What will happen to us?"

She had smiled a cat smile. "One thing at a time, Luke. Be patient . . ."

When she had awakened he was gone, as she knew he would be—as usual remaining beside her until she slept, then reluctantly leaving for his own spartan quarters adjoining the schoolhouse. Never furtive, he would have openly greeted servants or guards he encountered as he exited through the great iron doors to the graveled driveway and turned onto the treelined path that led to his cottage.

Now Marianna poured herself a second cup of strong coffee still steaming in the high-gloss silver pot on her breakfast tray. Narit, tugging strenuously, pulled apart the heavy damask drapes. From her bed Marianna could see that the morning would be drizzly. It was her kind of morning. She cherished the touch of the cool damp air, softer than ermine as it wrapped itself around her, a pewter cloak on those infrequent dawns when she and Luke still met at the stable for an early canter.

There would be no canter today, nor a visit to the children in their schoolhouse. Not this day.

In one hour the American television crew would be ready for her.

Last summer Hamid Agil, the palace press secretary, had received a clever letter from the head of a major American television network. The executive had hinted at the Shah's dubious reputation in the United States as well as his tenuous hold on the Paradise Throne.

"A television tour of the palace, conducted by the Empress Marianna, would be incalculably useful to the monarchy when viewed by millions of Americans," the executive had written. "If you will think back to Jacqueline Kennedy's widely acclaimed tour of the White House and Princess Grace's effective interview in the palace of Monaco, you will grasp the advantages to all parties involved. It will also be a perfect curtain raiser to the televised anniversary celebration you have so generously invited us to cover."

Halfheartedly she had agreed to do it. Recent decisions had made her regret her commitment. Her professionalism told her it was deceitful to mislead the network chief, his hard-working crew, and the potential audience with an inaccurate portrait of palace life. She was going along with it today because she knew the film would still be valid when it was aired.

Yes, it would be all right. She was not yet ready to make her move.

Marianna descended the Grand Staircase grudgingly. Underslept, uninspired, she paused at a wall mirror for a final check of her costume.

"Please, Your Majesty, select something simple," Agil, the press secretary, had urged. "I think no jewelry would be best. The overall impression should be, as you say in America, 'homey.'"

"Homey." She repeated the word, wondering why the fool had bothered saying anything. Did he think she was going to send to the underground vault for her best diamond tiara? Except for state occasions she dressed simply. It was her style. The wraparound apple-green skirt and the dyed-to-match blouse she wore were not unlike most of her daytime outfits.

She glanced at her makeup and was grateful to the Hollywood wizards who had taught her to conceal the shadows under sleep-deprived eyes and to erase the fine lines, etched by tension, at the corners of her mouth.

The scene that awaited her as she turned into the salon was disorienting. The usually pristine room had been torn apart to make space for television equipment. Hot lights focused on the tall, gold brocade wing chair she was to occupy. A blond woman sat in the chair—a perspiring stand-in suffering the hot floodlights—as the setup was readied for the Empress.

Marianna had a sense of *déjà vu* discomfortingly reminiscent of her Hollywood past—the bustling grips, the frantic director, the insipid script served up to her days earlier by the press secretary, filled with bland responses to stupid questions expected to be asked by the network's star interviewer, the obsequious Chester Rudolph. She had run through it once and tossed it aside, considering it idiot food.

Seated in the wing chair vacated by the unintroduced stranger, Marianna smiled into the camera, embracing the anticipated audience with her warmth.

Scrutinizing her, Chester Rudolph vowed he would dispose of *that* piece of film. He was the star of his shows. No one upstaged him. Following a brief introductory statement to "our unseen friends out there," he faced Marianna.

"Fifteen years, Your Majesty. Does it seem that long?"

"It seems only yesterday. It has passed like a dream."

"A dream. A beautiful dream. One which you and the Shah so generously have let us share with you from your wedding day to the present. And the three lovely children who have blessed your union, how old are they now, Your Majesty?"

"Crown Prince Karim is fourteen. He is at school in Switzerland. We miss him very much. We are a close family. Prince Jannot is eleven. Our daughter, Princess Nariam, is eight."

"They grow so fast." Rudolph verged on tears. Pulling himself together, he continued. "We know something of your good works for the people of Bahrait. Can you tell us exactly what you do?"

"With pleasure. First let me remind you that Bahrait is still an emerging country. We have far to go to catch up with the West. Education, health care, improved housing—so much, so much. My husband and I consider those the areas that most demand our attention. Since he is occupied with immediate affairs of state, I am his eyes and ears. I travel about the country visiting with the people, observing their needs. I make recommendations and supervise remedies whenever possible."

"Does the Shah consult you on diplomatic matters?"

"Seldom." Marianna smoothed the green skirt. "He has more knowledgeable advisers."

"Is there something more you do—something you have not told us?"

"Let me repeat—Bahrait is constantly evolving, and not just economically and politically." Marianna looked away from the camera and into the limpid eyes of Chester Rudolph. "For centuries our women have remained in the background serving their men. New attitudes are appearing in that area, too. I present them to my husband and to his ministers. With considerable success."

"For example?"

"For the first time in its long history, Bahrait is educating women to be doctors, lawyers, professors, economists. Even TV interviewers, Mr. Rudolph."

"Indeed. I see Her Majesty has not lost her American sense of humor."

"Thank you."

"And now, Your Majesty, would you be kind enough to treat our television audience to a glimpse of this splendid palace?"

"I would be delighted. Please follow me."

While the camera crew shifted its equipment Chester Rudolph slid behind her. "Just like the good old days, isn't it, Miss Curtis? Remember me?"

Marianna looked around, startled.

"I didn't expect you would. I worked at Hanover myself. In the publicity department. Remember Jerry Crane? I was his assistant. Wrote press releases. Worked on your last picture. What was it called?" He tapped his head. "Got it, *The Shadow Darkens*. With Douglas Braden. Ever get lonesome for the old days?"

"Your question isn't in the script, Mr. Rudolph."

"Forgive me."

"For your information, the answer is no. If my attitude toward show business needed reinforcement, you've provided it today. Please excuse me, I must freshen my makeup. Send for me when you are prepared to continue the interview."

Somehow she got through the day. With Chester Rudolph and the camera crew tagging along she passed through the portrait gallery, a long corridor hung from ceiling molding to paneled dado with dynastic predecessors, terminating with an oil painting of Ramir in full military dress, looking formidable. Gazing into the camera lens, she was winning and sincere as she related the history of Bahrait through the portrait of each leader.

When the gallery sequence was concluded Rudolph caught up with her. "Smashing, just smashing. Our audiences will eat it up. Just one question. Off camera, of course."

"Again?"

"An innocuous one. Why are there no portraits of women?"

"Because no woman has ever ruled Bahrait."

"I understand that. I mean the consorts, the wives."

"Mr. Rudolph, you have not prepared for your assignment. In the past it was customary for a Shah to have several wives at the same time. In modern Bahrait that is no longer acceptable. My husband's father chose to remove all portraits of earlier Empresses to avoid questions like yours."

Rudolph chuckled. "They say old customs die hard."

"What does that mean?"

"Nothing, Your Majesty. I was just thinking, some men get all the breaks. At least they did in the good old days."

"You have a quaint sense of history, Mr. Rudolph. I'll rejoin you in ten minutes in the State Dining Room."

After roving the dining room they visited the kitchen, chatted with individual chefs in charge of meat, vegetables, fish, fowl, and pastries, took a lunch break and moved on to the Grande and Petite ballrooms, the gymnasium, indoor swimming pool, and the miniature hospital. Trailed by equipment, Marianna and Rudolph stepped outside to view the exotic creatures assembled in Ramir's private aviary and zoo. Hours later the tour wound up in the family sitting room.

"This is where we gather," Marianna said, "my husband, the children, and I. We play table games, watch television, or read quietly. Sometimes I bring my needlepoint. When the Shah is absorbed in paper work, I sit nearby and speak when I am spoken to." She smiled adorably into the camera. "Not so different from other families when you get right down to it."

"Come now, Your Majesty."

"Oh, that's the truth. Of course my husband travels more than most men. Affairs of state constantly demand his attention. He is in London now. I accompany him when he thinks I can be helpful. On other occasions he can accomplish more if he does not have to be concerned about me."

"They also serve who only stand and wait?"

"Mr. Rudolph, you do understand. Naturally we regret the

separations. However, when he is abroad we keep in touch by telephone several times a day."

"Thank you, Your Majesty. After this most agreeable visit, we appreciate how difficult the Shah must find it to be apart from you."

"Thank *you*, Mr. Rudolph. And good-bye."

9

"Perks" they were called, those extra dollops of luxury, the fringe benefits that came with the job when the job was sufficiently important. Like being a corporation executive or a president, or a premier. Or an Empress.

Those who rated perpuisites (their full and proper name) could tick off such hedonistic advantages as yachts, vacation retreats, country-club memberships, chauffeured limousines, voluptuous food and drink, and custom-fitted private planes like the one that now bore the Empress Marianna from Ryal to Paris.

"It's free, all free," Selma had exulted when the coveted perks began to come her way. Then, embarrassed, she had caught the amusement in Marianna's eyes. "*Someone* pays for them," she admitted.

"Sure." Marianna agreed. "Someone known as the Government or the Stockholders or the Taxpayers. Don't feel guilty, Selma. If you don't grab the perks, the person standing behind you will. It's all borrowed anyway. Once you're out of power the pretty toys vanish. You're back picking up your own dinner checks and chasing down taxis in the rain. Enjoy it while you can."

Today, giddy over a martini in the ornate Persian-motif fantasyland that was the interior of her personal jet, Marianna asked herself if the perks were the subtle devils that tied her to her job. She decided they were not. On too many occasions when she stepped aboard the plane it was to carry out official assignments passed on to her by Ramir. Most recently, as his representative, she had attended a British wedding that bored her and the funeral of a prime minister she had never met. Before that there had been an exhausting journey to a South American disaster area, undertaken to show the world that the Shah and his Empress cared.

Today's flight was different. She was on her way to Paris and, unlike the duty circuit she so often traveled, this trip belonged to her. Luckily, Ramir approved of her jaunts to Paris. Whether she came back buoyant from a shopping spree or remote after visits with French friends, her mood when she returned made no demands upon him. Further, he was thankful for the closeness that existed between Marianna and his daughter, Dahlia. Almost nineteen and a student at the Sorbonne, Dahlia led a life complicated by problems and romances her father seldom wished to share. Early on he had shifted the burden to Marianna, leaving her free to visit Paris as often as she pleased. And it very much pleased her to do so now.

Curled into one of the silk-covered chairs in the lounge area of the plane, Marianna watched Fred, the white-jacketed steward, place a fresh martini on the mosaic table beside her. Surprised, she glanced at the glass in her hand and saw that she had drained it.

"Freddie," she said, "how many does that make?"

"Only two, Your Majesty."

"Two down, two to go, and then we close the bar. Agreed?"

"Agreed."

"Wouldn't do to have the Empress of Bahrait miss a step and disembark on her face, would it?"

"No chance, Your Majesty. I made 'em like you said—easy on the vodka."

Marianna was fond of Fred, the sassy redheaded youth she had selected to be part of her crew. She had spotted his mischievous freckled face at an American engineers' club, one of many that had sprung up in Bahrait, and had got a kick out of the irreverent manner he adopted toward the pompous engineer types. She had also grown nostalgic listening to the ripe Boston accent that reminded her of the long-gone Pete Callahan.

Her decision to hire Fred had been a fortunate one. Aboard the plane they were not employer and servant but two expatriates who had become friends. It was to Fred, and Fred alone, that she had confided the secret of her frequent visits to Paris.

"Who's meeting the plane?" Fred asked.

"Princess Dahlia."

"Pleased to hear that. She'll cheer you up."

"Not this time. She has her own troubles."

"Lucky kid, having your shoulder to lean on."

"Think so? I try my best. And Fred—"

"Yes, ma'am?"

"Tomorrow Dahlia and I, we're going to spend the national

budget at the couturiers'. His Majesty's orders. He wants us to be the two most gorgeous women at the Jubilee. We'll use Claude to drive."

"And the next day?"

"Dr. Lasseaux. Usual time."

"I'll be waiting."

After Fred had served her third martini Marianna rested her head on the back of the chair and closed her eyes. Her thoughts still with Dahlia, she recalled her introduction to Ramir's only child. Dahlia had been four years old when Marianna first visited Bahrait. Although their marriage was still months away, Ramir had insisted she come. "You must see your new home. You may wish to call off the wedding if you find the palace too modest." Then, anxiously, "You must meet my daughter. She will be yours also."

Ramir had ordered the nursemaid to bring the child to his second-floor suite. The encounter was not a success. The forlorn little girl with the round black eyes and the large fleshy nose that dominated her oval face was presented to Miss Marianna Curtis from America. The child nodded solemnly and said nothing. Informed by Ramir that the fair-haired stranger who stood before her would soon be her new mother, Dahlia promptly burst into tears. Touched, Ramir had swept his daughter into his arms and tried to comfort her. When he attempted to pass her to Marianna's open arms, the child turned her back and buried her wet face in her father's shoulder.

"It's going to be all right," Ramir said. And it had been. Once the excitement of the wedding and the separation of the honeymoon were behind them, Marianna and Dahlia began to develop the precious intimacy they shared to this day. Satisfied that his daughter's emotional needs were met, Ramir had gradually receded from Dahlia's day-to-day life.

With the birth of Karim less than a year later, Ramir's paternal instincts had resurfaced, but only to focus on his son. Although enthralled by her firstborn, Marianna had doubled her attention to Dahlia and the lonely child had blossomed.

To the people of Bahrait, Karim's appearance was a thrilling national event, erasing all suspicion about their Shah's bride. At last the monarchy had an heir. The two children who followed, a second son called Jannot and an almond-eyed, dark-complexioned daughter named Nariam, were the icing on the cake. Ramir's mother, the Dowager Empress, openly hostile since meeting the foreigner who had captured her son, took a second look at Marianna and concluded he might have done worse.

Only Azar, Ramir's older sister, remained remote. Dwelling in France and Switzerland with a succession of young lovers, she was a shadowy figure who turned up unwillingly when summoned by Ramir. Usually it was to participate in photo studies of the royal family destined for distribution to the wire services and worldwide television, "to illustrate the unity of our dynasty at a time when there is so much discord around us." Pictures taken, Azar would erase her smile, repack her bags, and vanish into her own mysterious habitat.

Azar was of no importance to Marianna. Yet it was Azar who had taken the shimmering bubble that was Marianna's life and ruthlessly smashed it onto the hard earth of reality.

10

St. Moritz, that snowy playpen of the very rich, that unrivaled grande dame of Alpine winter attractions, is never more spectacular than in the merry months of December, January, and February. Like a selective magnet circling the globe, it lures the moneyed, the pampered, the glamorous to its glorious peaks and valleys. They come by plane and train from countries as distant as Mexico, Argentina, and Brazil, and as nearby as Germany, Austria, France, and Italy.

Discriminating prostitutes brighten the landscape on the arms of former patrons or in pursuit of new ones. No purse-swinging floozies, these. Graceful skiers by day, they appear superbly gowned and jeweled for evening, their scrubbed-faced youth all that distinguishes them from women of established means. That, and the fact that they move on to their next poaching preserve taking their elaborate attire with them, unlike the men and women of wealth who keep wardrobes in a half-dozen resorts, and who store their winter clothes and furs in St. Moritz until they return to pick them up the following holiday season.

In the lobby of the old Palace Hotel, famed jewelers like Cartier's, Harry Winston, and Van Cleef & Arpels fill their bolted vitrines with emeralds, diamonds, sapphires. Conservatively dressed salesmen preside discreetly over their wares, confident that there is no such thing as a priceless jewel. Sooner or later a buyer will appear and the most staggering cost will be met.

Everyone comes for the Season. Only the nouveaux riches arrive before December or linger into March. Most crowd into outrageously luxurious hotels. Others, with fabled names like Niarchos, Onassis, Agnelli, and von Karajan, dwell high above the town in secluded chalets ranging from ostentatiously simple to unabashedly lavish.

Members of the chalet set are cliquish. They lunch in the restricted Corviglia Club, cocktail and dine in private villas with small peer groups, and are fond of venturing into the King's Club, a disco in the Palace Hotel, to dance and drink till dawn.

Of all the chalets in St. Moritz, the one owned by the royal family of Bahrait is the most eye-catching—its single distinguishing feature being its remarkable ugliness. Set close to the road, it is constructed of depressing grayish stone blocks. Its heavy oak double doors and its narrow leaded windows are trimmed in dispirited brown. To passersby it is an architectural alien among its neighbors.

Standing in the driveway, confronted for the first time by the dour villa Ramir introduced as their "true vacation home," Marianna was aghast.

She waved a fur-gloved hand in the direction of the distant mountains and pine forests. "Magnificent," she said.

"But you don't like the villa. It resembles a fortress, admit it."

"It's—unexpected. You did say it was old." She pointed toward the peaked roof. "Why all the paraphernalia up there—the cables, the antennae?"

"Shortwave, for communication to Ryal. It is always possible to reach me here."

"But we're vacationing!"

"Of course we are. You and I, we will play all of the time—except for a few hours in the late afternoon."

"What happens then?"

"I go to work in my quarters at the Suvretta House."

"The Suvretta House—what's that?"

"We passed it on the road. It is a hotel, very grand and correct, a sedate old lady. It is not for St. Moritz high-lifers like us."

"Why can't you work here?" she had protested.

"On holiday, I do not work where I sleep. It would be unfair to you. Aides underfoot, telephones ringing, secretaries rushing about with documents—you would be unnerved. The Suvretta has always maintained accommodations for my staff. It also provides more sophisticated high-frequency equipment than we have here."

He cupped her face in his hands. "You are disappointed with me. My darling, you are not married to a tradesman. A Shah cannot close up shop for a month and hide the key. Only a few hours a day—what difference? You will find many ways to amuse yourself."

She had relented and smiled. "Take me inside."

Her city boots slid on the icy driveway. He had clutched

her around the waist as he led her to the house. Unsummoned, a male servant opened the doors. Ramir greeted the man who bowed and then scuttled away.

Marianna stood in the entry hall, her eyes aglow. She scanned the room that spread before her and gaped at the dazzling view beyond.

"What do you think now? Is it so terrible?"

"It's incredible," she breathed. "Who—?" She stopped abruptly. She did not want to know which of her predecessors had introduced so much beauty into her new home.

"Watch the steps," he cautioned, guiding her from the entry hall into the sunken living room.

The forbidding house she had seen from the driveway had prepared her for an austere baronial interior. Instead she encountered gay chintzes, furry rugs scattered on random-width oak floors, mellowed hand-painted antique Swiss furniture, and enticing bookshelves flanking a rustic fireplace.

"It's exquisite," she had finally whispered.

He stood beside her, enjoying her joy as she gazed through the clear window wall overlooking the blinding white mountains and the dot-size skiers skillfully taking the slopes, swerving and dipping like birds to avoid the treacherous moguls.

"I adore it," she said softly. "And I adore you."

That night in his darkened bedroom they had drunk champagne and then lain nude on a fur rug, hypnotized by the licking flames in the fireplace. Almost languidly he rolled above her and her long white legs enfolded him.

Later, still a bit drunk, they sleepily counted the stars visible through the undraped windows and promised each other eternal fealty.

By the time her babies were born Marianna was thoroughly captivated by the chalet in St. Moritz. It became a home, more meaningful than the palace in Ryal, the seaside villa in Kish, or the town house in Paris. In St. Moritz they were a family, living a life that was almost normal.

Holiday fever possessed them as soon as they boarded Ramir's jet in Ryal and the pilot pointed the plane toward the Swiss airport at Samaden. Every year, after considerable weeping and pleading, each of the children was permitted to bring a favorite dog. With their yipping pets they tore

through the plane's lounge, bedrooms, and galley—unrepri-
manded savages, lapping up approval from their worshipful
mother and usually stern father.

At the chalet, the routine was fixed. In the morning,
Marianna and Ramir rose early to breakfast with the children. Breakfast over, the youngsters—dumplings in garish ski
pants and parkas—were hugged, kissed, and sent off with ski
instructors. If the previous night had been a frenetic whirl of
disco dancing and drinking at the King's Club or the ancient
Chesa Veglia, Marianna and Ramir would stumble to their
separate bedrooms and fall into deep sleep. Other mornings,
rested after dining with friends in a nearby villa, they would
squeeze in an exhilarating hour of skiing before joining
friends for lunch at the super-exclusive mountaintop Corviglia Club.

Marianna's memories of one special morning were bitter-
sweet.

The air had been nippy, the snow blinding when she and
Ramir closed the door on the children. Well-slept after a rare
evening alone, they were zipped into skintight jumpsuits,
ready to join their own instructors on the slopes.

Ramir leaned against the door. "I love you," he said. "I
love you for giving me all this."

She pressed her face to his and circled his lips with kisses.
"Tonight?"

"Now."

"But people are waiting!"

"Let them wait. Your sovereign is giving you an order." He
found the zipper on her jumpsuit and jerked it downward in a
single motion. His cold hands flew over her body. Reaching
her crotch, he grinned as he massaged the telltale moisture
dampening her thermal underpants.

"Now," she said. She led the way up the wooden staircase
and turned toward his bedroom.

"No, your room this morning." His expression was sly.
"We will pretend I am a new lover sneaking in while your
husband is away."

"That's impossible—" Then she winked and shrugged a
shoulder. "Why not? The old fool will never know. He'll be
gone for hours. We have all morning for each other."

When he entered her it was with the lustful abandon she
recalled from their earliest encounters in Paris. How odd, she

thought—she hadn't realized it had been missing from their recent lovemaking. She was briefly disquieted, but when she released herself to him, her mind and her very soul detached themselves from her body, burning out of control off on some distant planet.

Exploding within her, he mumbled another woman's name. Descending from her own peak she heard it and felt threatened.

When they moved apart, he smoothed her brow. "I know what's troubling you. You must forget it."

"I don't understand—"

"Lovers fantasize, even you. Coming up the stairs you played at make-believe. Another name? What is it? Just a collection of syllables. It means nothing. There is only one Marianna."

Did she fantasize too? She had to confess she did. Still, the incident had niggled. She told herself she was a fool to let anything mar the sweet soaring ecstasy they had shared that morning.

Later, aboard the funicular climbing to the Corviglia Club, they held hands like newly met lovers.

The Corviglia Club was not Marianna's favorite luncheon spot. A modest log structure flaunting the flags of neighboring countries, it is perched on a mountain ledge high above the town of St. Moritz. Even loftier than its location is its strictly enforced code of membership. Royalty, both incumbent and deposed, are welcome, as are international jet-set figures and heirs to old money. Occasionally a carefully screened guest, invited by a member, penetrates its doors. Although the decor is unpretentious, snobbery bounces off the walls.

Marianna preferred the noisy vitality of the unrestricted Corviglia Restaurant. Ramir had submitted to a single luncheon there, coldly returned the stares of gawking patrons, and refused to return.

"Here in St. Moritz we can relax only among our own kind," he stated. "We cannot eat comfortably while rubbernecking tourists watch us swallow every bite."

"What does it matter?" she asked. "They're curious. That's normal. But they're harmless."

"You Americans, forever pretending we live in a one-class world."

"We don't and I know it," she replied. "Still, a bit of

tolerance wouldn't hurt that smug Corviglia Club crowd."

"You're still thinking about the Texan."

"I am. I'm thinking it was disgusting of the Club to seat him one day and toss him out the next. And the members— shrinking against the walls as though death was stalking the room."

"The first time he came, the Texan was the guest of the Chilean ambassador—the second time he barged in without an invitation. You know the rules about gate-crashers. You knew them when you sent for the maître d' and defended the Texan."

"Embarrassing you."

"And everyone else."

"You shouldn't have married beneath you." She paused and studied him quizzically. "Why did you?"

"Foolish Marianna. I married you because you are the only woman in the world for me."

Her blow for democracy struck—and struck down— Marianna had fallen into the late afternoon routine Ramir had predicted would please her. While he, garbed in turtle-neck sweater and heavy corduroy leisure suit, worked at his Suvretta House retreat, she napped, read, and played with her children. Each evening before her personal maid arranged her hair, she browsed among her closets filled with gowns and furs and her traveling cabinets of jewels, delightedly assem-bling a costume that would excite Ramir in the night ahead.

Promptly at eight she and the tuxedo-clad Ramir would meet in his study and ease into the evening with double martinis. Relaxed, they would send his valet for their furs— "You have more than I," she had noted with astonishment —and brave the cutting wind for the few steps it took to reach their waiting limousine. A local chauffeur, familiar with the curving roads concealed by the deep snow, would slowly and cautiously deliver them to a dinner party at a nearby chalet.

Although the routine had continued, Marianna never for-got the day the dream died.

She had left the children drinking milk in their nursery and was descending the stairs to join Ramir when she was as-saulted by the sounds of vicious quarreling spilling from be-hind the closed door of the study.

Ramir's voice, lifted in rage, was the first she could make out. "Now you've done it, the worst thing possible! How can I rescue you this time?"

"My dear brother." It was Azar venting her anger. "You'll manage, you always do."

"It's that baby-faced Austrian leech, isn't it? He's the one who got you into this."

"Kurt? No, it wasn't his idea. It was mine."

"But why?"

"Because I needed the money. There is no other reason. If anyone is responsible, it is you."

"Me?"

"I am older than you are. You were the first male, so everything falls to you. I am tired of dropping to my knees, little brother, to beg for handouts."

"Handouts. I grant you a huge allowance, larger than my wife's."

"But not as large as your own. Anyway, Marianna doesn't have my needs."

"Your needs," he said with contempt. "Your needs for a string of young swine lovers—pretty boys who service you because you buy them cars and clothes and jewelry—and who knows what else?"

"Exactly," Azar said hotly. "Why are you surprised? Blame yourself. You left me no other choice."

"Blame myself? Because you are trafficking in heroin? Because the Swiss police caught you?"

"Remember last year? You were furious, so self-righteous because my little lovers were growing more expensive."

"It was revolting. You were making a laughingstock of yourself and of me."

"And you retaliated by reducing my income. Imbecile!" Azar's voice rose to match her brother's. "You hoped to teach me a lesson. You expected me to discard my friends. Well, you made a mistake. I will never let them go. And I cannot keep them on my measly allowance. My playmates are costly—but no more than yours."

Standing at the door, Marianna had heard Ramir utter a threat, and then she had heard a hand against a cheek, followed by Azar's drawn-out moan. Appalled, Marianna grabbed the door handle. It would not budge. Azar's next words froze her in place.

"Do you think your romances are a secret? Not here, they're not! You and your holier-than-thou attitude!"

"What are you talking about?"

"The same thing everyone is talking about—you and the parade of expensive whores you entertain at the Suvretta House. Diplomatic business, is it, that you conduct over there? I know better. I know all about General Mojeeb and his pimp assistants! 'Don't serve me the local talent,' you tell them. 'Travel around. Bring me beautiful ones, fresh ones, but not too fresh—a bit of experience never hurts.' And you're generous, they say, Your Majesty. 'Bring back one or two for yourselves,' you tell them."

"Be quiet!"

"I am not finished. What about Marthe from Hamburg, and last week her sister Helga? Only sixteen, wasn't she? And the Danish girl, younger than my Kurt. They don't come cheap, do they? Rolex watches won't buy them these days. General Mojeeb's Paris account at Cartier's—that takes care of them, doesn't it?"

"Stop!"

"Not yet. Not until I tell you their best reason for coming to you. They're celebrity-fuckers, that's what they are! Do you think it's your talent as a lover that appeals to them? What a joke! No, you're a Shah. They can't wait to tell their sister prosties they've just left the Shah of Bahrait whimpering for more. Who can blame them? Jewels? Gowns? In the high-class trade they can get them from anyone. But a real honest-to-goodness Shah? That's something to boast about. And with his wife just up the road? That adds to their jollies. And to yours, too, I suspect."

"Azar, I've heard enough!"

"Not yet, you haven't. Before your whores leave St. Moritz, before the next shipment is brought in, the news is everywhere. The hotel maid tells the waiter, the waiter tells the hairdresser, the hairdresser tells his clients. At the King's Club they keep a tally. Eleven since you arrived. A bit slowed down since last year, they're saying."

"Shut up, will you! Marianna and the children are in the house!"

"I'll shut up if you get the Swiss police off my back."

"I can promise you nothing. Here I am not the ruler. Drug trafficking is deadly serious to the Swiss. If I can persuade them to drop the charges, they will never again admit you to Switzerland."

"I'll settle for that. Call them off and I'll leave the country. And my last demand—"

"I don't want to hear it."

"Restore—no, increase—my allowance. If you don't, I may embarrass you in France and England and Germany."

Marianna heard him slap her once more. "Azar, get out of my sight! You'll have your money but don't let me see you ever again!"

"Thank you, Your Majesty. My account is at Crédit Suisse, across from Hanselmann's, only twenty minutes down the road."

Azar unbolted the door and flung it open. Face to face with Marianna, she drew in her breath. "You heard," Azar said. She shrugged. "Well, you might as well know. You're the only one who doesn't."

When Marianna did not respond, Azar stepped back. She saw Marianna's wide staring eyes, saw that her face, normally pale, was drained of all color, that her body was rigid.

"Ramir," Azar shouted over her shoulder. "Come here! Now! Bring her a whiskey—"

They had faced each other near the waning fire in his study. Marianna, still in evening dress, sat unmoving in a deep chair. Ramir, wearing a dressing gown, was stiff-backed on an ottoman at her feet.

"Marianna." He leaned forward, rubbing her cold hands. "Azar has always fought that way. Wild, dirty. Even as a child. Mean and jealous because I was the favorite."

"Was it true, what she said to you in here?"

He tightened his hands over hers, rubbing harder, trying to restore warmth. "Yes, all true." He watched her eyes, searching for any expression, even shock, that might replace the vacant stare.

She withdrew her hands from his and folded them in her lap. "All true," she repeated dully.

"There is no point in lying—not now. Naturally I did not want you to know. There was the possibility you might misunderstand, be hurt."

"*Might* misunderstand, *might* be hurt?"

"Exactly that. You think those women are important to me? They are nothing—no more than bobsled rides."

"Then why—?"

He sighed, patient with this difficult child. "So many years, yet you do not know me. What a puritan you are. You believe it must be one woman for one man at one time."

"Don't you?"

He waved off her question. "Before we met you knew I came from a different culture. Traditionally our men—and only our men—take every pleasure they can afford. Our women do not complain nor do they retaliate. Within my culture I am more than an ordinary man. I am the Shah. I am the richest, most powerful, most spoiled man in Bahrait. Did you really believe marriage would change me?"

"I believed I would change you."

"You have. You and the children have given me more happiness than I have ever known. You are my Empress, my wife. We will be together till the end of time."

"And the other—the other women?"

"You must disregard them. They will always be unimportant."

For Marianna, the remainder of their holiday was a ceaseless nightmare. Azar had departed quietly. Ramir considered the distasteful subject closed. Without further discussion he continued his daily routine, skiing in the morning, lunching at the Corviglia Club, skiing again for a few hours, all with Marianna beside him—more than ever attentive to her most casual needs.

In the latter part of each day, accompanied by aides, Ramir stepped into his black limousine to be driven off to the Suvretta House. Standing behind a window watching him leave, Marianna observed his quick steps, the sober set of his lips, the briefcase he held close to his body—every inch the concerned leader, the devoted servant of his people. Then, powerless to reject the image, she had imagined him entwined with the latest succulent call girls selected by his dutiful staff. She saw him doing the things he did to her, savoring the quirky sex she knew he demanded and had believed only she could provide.

Too stunned to deal with what had happened, she considered summoning Selma from Hollywood. She quickly discarded the idea when she remembered that Selma, too, was married to a man who was blatantly unfaithful. A year earlier Selma had joined Marianna in Paris and confided the saga and the insult of Gino's ongoing affairs.

Marianna had held the weeping woman in her arms. "Why do you put up with it? Where is your pride?" she had demanded.

"I've weighed my options, I have no place to go."

"Nonsense. You can go anywhere. You have plenty of money, no responsibilities, a brilliant career ahead."

Selma lifted her mottled face and wiped the sloshing tears with the back of her hand. "It's not no *place* that I mean. It's that I have no *one* to go to."

Sad, lost Selma.

Sad, lost Marianna. She was sure all of St. Moritz was whispering about her, smirking behind her back. She wondered why she hadn't noticed before—the covert glances, the laughter that ceased when she entered a room, the expressions of pity in the eyes of good friends.

She had reminded herself she was an actress. Those scavengers of gossip would never know from her that she was dying inside. She would hold her head high, show them she was immune to the muck on their tongues, impervious to snickering and sympathy alike.

In rare rational moments she knew she imagined the reactions of others. No one truly gave a damn about Ramir's ladies-for-hire. Most people didn't know. Those who did passed it off, considering it no more abnormal than the seasonal melting of the snow and the coming of spring wild flowers to the Swiss countryside.

Yet the terrible feeling persisted. She had recognized the symptoms. Depression. Not the kind that made you blue for a day or two but the real thing, the kind that grew from the marrow and paralyzed the mind and body. She had been there before, in recollected bouts of her childhood and once, in a lesser way, over Doug Braden. Depression. It was enveloping her and she could not control it. Going through the motions of the day, she was forgetful, indecisive, her brain muddled. Fatigue was unremitting. Her only desire was to drop into sleep and never awaken.

She despised Ramir. Surprisingly it was not because of the quickie lays he desired and thrived on. Perhaps those women were, as he said, only bobsled rides. No, she despised him for his callousness, his lack of remorse, his uncomplicated ability to continue to gratify himself while aware of her suffering.

Although she had not realized it at the time, years ago he had raped her. Not in the classical way, not in an assault on her body. He had never forced his swollen penis inside her. Indeed, she had welcomed and adored that long shaft almost as something separate from the man.

His crime was that he had raped her emotionally. Coming to him vulnerable, concerned about betrayal, she had confided her fears and he had held her and promised she would be safe with him. He was a compassionate man, a faithful man, he swore. And gradually, very gradually he won what he wanted, what she was most reluctant to give: her trust.

And now he had robbed her of it. He had turned her into an empty woman, a zombie, more bereft of faith than in those black days following her parents' deaths when she could still find comfort in the God of her Church.

For that she could never forgive him.

One bright afternoon, pleading weariness from the disco rounds of the past night, Marianna had begged off the skiing and found her way to the wooden sun deck adjoining the Corviglia Restaurant. Cushioned lounges and canvas umbrellas in gaudy tropical yellows, oranges, and greens gave the deck the appearance of a sun-belt cruise ship incongruously afloat on a snowy mountain-top.

Fortunately there were few people about. Marianna selected a lounge, leaned against the pillows and tried to concentrate on the spirited skiers as they started their descent of the slopes.

"Your Majesty!" The voice behind her was strong and cheerful. Marianna had looked around to seek its owner. Dismayed, she recognized Alida Heinrud, the dreary, submissive wife of a blustering German automaker.

"Hello, Alida." Marianna acknowledged the intruder and turned back.

"Why are you hiding yourself? I told Rudi, 'Go away. Today I do not wish to ski with you.' I came with my book but it is better we have a little visit, *nicht wahr?*" Alida Heinrud, uninvited, took the neighboring lounge, her birdlike body barely impressing the cushions.

"*Nein,*" Marianna had wanted to reply. "*Nein,* not now or ever. I never liked you, and now I find you unbearable. Because you are my sister, you are myself. You are a fool. Your husband humiliates you and you accept his humiliation. You are an ant crushed beneath his boot and you lie there waiting for the next crunch. You make me ashamed because I see myself in you. A doormat with *my* fear of abandonment, *my* humiliation, *my* loss of self-respect."

Aloud, she said, "I am not hiding, only resting."

"Is the sun in your eyes?" Alida asked. "Would you like a blanket? The wind will be coming up soon."

Alida snapped her fingers at a passing steward. "Here," she ordered. "Come here, young man. Her Majesty and I would like our umbrellas tilted. And bring us blankets, the new fluffy ones, not last year's rags."

"Yes, madam." The steward quickly adjusted the umbrellas and hurried off to fetch the blankets.

"And steward," Alida called after him. "You will find my son in the snack bar. Tell him I wish to see him at once."

Marianna observed the steward scurrying away. She heard Alida chuckle lightly. Appraising Alida, she saw that the woman was beaming.

"You find me changed, perhaps?" Alida asked. "You think maybe a ventriloquist behind a tree is throwing his voice through my mouth?"

"Well—you are different."

"Different, yes. Let me put it this way. Never before in my life have I been myself. Always I envied the rest of you, so bold, so in command. You saw how it was with me—afraid of everyone, Rudi such a boor, my children dreadful. It became painful to answer the telephone. I could not request a spoon from a waiter. It is a long, sad story how I got that way. I must not impose on you."

"You're not imposing."

"The whole story we will leave for another day. The important thing is that I have changed. And who changed me."

Marianna turned fully toward this interesting woman. "I'd like to hear about it."

"A minute—Friedrich," she shouted at a pudgy teenager struggling up a snow-packed hill. "Friedrich, you know you are to be at your French lesson in ten minutes. On your way, do you hear me? *Mach schnell!*"

"Yes, ma'am." The youngster tugged at his cap and sped down the hill.

Alida's eyes followed her child. "Ah, Dr. Lasseaux—if she could see me now she would be proud. She might say, 'Alida, you are overdoing, ease up a bit.' But she will know that at last I am free to assert myself. My husband, he is more irritable than before with me. I am hopeful one day he will understand. If he doesn't . . ." She dismissed him with a wave. "It is not my concern. You see, I have swung from one end of the pendulum to the other. Now I bark at everyone. Soon, with Dr. Lasseaux's help, I will settle somewhere in the middle. When I am finished with my therapy—two, three years, more, who knows?—people who have dominated me may be furious. It will not matter. I will be in charge of my own life."

"Therapy? Dr. Lasseaux? Who is she?"

"Dr. Rose Lasseaux. In Paris. She sees patients in her sound-proofed office on the rue Jeanne d'Arc. Near the Jardin des Plantes."

"Soundproofed? Is it so painful?"

"Not in the way you imagine. It is painful to change, naturally. The soundproofing is for the music."

"*Music?* Alida, what are you talking about?"

"What the ancients talked about—the blessed qualities of music when it is used for healing."

Marianna shook her head in bewilderment. "I don't understand you at all."

"Music therapy. In the Bible we learn of the young David playing his harp for Saul and soothing the king. Plato wrote of the therapeutic magic to be found in music and Aristotle agreed with him. Always, throughout history, music has been used to influence the emotions. Now it is merged into contemporary psychology."

"And this woman—?"

"Dr. Lasseaux? She is a graduate of the Berlin Psychoanalytic Institute. Music is the tool she uses to touch the innermost being of each patient—with music she helps the patient release repressed emotions that lie buried in the pre-memory."

"Impossible."

"Possible. Music has the power to reach a deeper level of the personality than words can. It is an overwhelming experience to revive and to understand your most primitive feelings."

"Alida—you're talking about witchcraft."

"Ha! That is what Rudi says. 'Look what militarists do with their martial music,' he tells me. 'Rhythm is like tribal drums. It makes warriors of the meekest followers.' " Alida laughed. "Rudi is right. Dr. Lasseaux has turned me into a warrior. The enemy is that part of myself which once invited and accepted punishment from others. Soon the victor will be the other side of me which says, 'Alida, you have suffered enough. Now *you* take charge of your life.' "

"But music is to be enjoyed," Marianna said. "You're describing manipulation. . . . I could never surrender to such a device."

"But you do, Your Majesty—so does everyone else—all of the time. Forgive me—in Germany I saw your films. You were a gifted actress. But always there was music in the background suggesting to your audience when to be gay or frightened or sad."

"The studio musicians—they came later when my work was done. If I thought about them at all, I thought they were there to fill dialogue gaps in the scenes."

"I must not single out the movies," Alida apologized, "nor nations which inspire their citizens with rousing songs and marches. Let us be honest—the Church, too, understands the power of music. The choir, the splendid organ, the tolling bells—each awakens a response in the listener. Mood-altering? Yes. But is it so bad to let yourself be spiritually comforted and inspired?"

Marianna frowned. "The Church . . . I can't answer that."

"Dr. Lasseaux is a healer," Alida continued. "One goes to her willingly and with hope. She is not like those who inflict music on captive audiences in office buildings and factories for personal gain. You think perhaps the music is to entertain the workers? Think again. No, the employers are concerned only with what benefits them." Alida sniffed. "My Rudi is one of them. In his factories the employees must serve long hours anyway. They welcome unobtrusive music. It makes the silences and the tedium easier to bear. During their worst periods of boredom and fatigue, special music is programmed to brighten their spirits. The workers become more energetic, therefore more efficient."

"Your Rudi is even worse than I thought."

"I agree," Alida said. "But Rudi is not alone. In America you have canned music. Experts and clients decide when and where to use it. Mr. President Nixon insisted upon it when he occupied the White House. It is piped to cows and chickens to increase their productivity, and into reptile houses, prisons, and dentists' office to provide calm. All over the world it is heard—from a thirty-nine-story high-rise cemetery in Rio de

Janeiro to office buildings in Tokyo, Brussels, and Madrid. They are tricky, these businessmen. Always they avoid lyrics which might distract the listeners and cause them to *think*."

"That's the commercial use of music," Marianna said. "It is your Dr. Lasseaux I can't comprehend."

Alida paused, embarrassed. "I have talked so long, Your Majesty. You do not mind?"

"I do not mind."

"Last winter," Alida began, "I left St. Moritz determined never to return. I could no longer tolerate Rudi's bullying, the way he made me ashamed before all of you. At home in Munich nothing changed. I took to my bed and stayed there, weeping when I could not sleep—sleeping when I was worn out from weeping.

"My family thought I was too stupid to be desperate." Alida laughed. "I showed them. I swallowed every drug in the house. Rudi committed me to a hospital. No one, nothing could help. I wanted to die. Then a nurse suggested Dr. Lasseaux. Rudi was opposed. The doctors urged him to give me a chance. From my first visit I began to feel cherished. Even in my sickness I sensed I was as important as Rudi, the children—even people like you." Alida laughed again. "Listen to me now. Not only am I confident, I am obnoxious."

"Tell me about your doctor," Marianna said.

Alida's face softened. "Rose Lasseaux. She is my doctor, but she is much more. Working together, we are also friends, with tenderness and trust between us. In music therapy I am the 'traveler,' she is my 'guide.' Her office is in the rear of her apartment in Paris. The treatment room is plain, comfortable, nothing much to see. A few pastoral paintings, green plants and fresh flowers on the tables and around the room, shelves and racks filled with classical music albums, and many, many books. We visit a while over tea. I talk of what is happening in my daily life. Then Dr. Lasseaux lowers the fabric shades, to dim the room. I lie down on the daybed against the wall where the real work is done—the work that is saving my life. It is good to kick off my shoes, close my eyes, and cover them with a soft black mask, knowing she sits beside me. In her lovely voice she leads me through simple relaxation exercises. And then the magnificent music begins. It comes through earphones—worn loose so the traveler can hear the guide, too. Always the music is classical: Renaissance . . . Baroque through Bartók. Unfamiliar works of great composers—

Bach, Vivaldi, Mozart, Schubert, Debussy. Never standard concert repertoire or chorales. It is important that no intellectual response be evoked—only emotional."

"And then . . . ?"

"And then Dr. Lasseaux starts you on your journey. She describes scenes from nature—a mountaintop, a brook, a field of poppies . . . You may allow entire compositions to envelop you, or if you prefer you may follow a single instrument. The choice is yours. The music takes you where you wish to go. You begin to talk. Of the past, of happenings—of hopes you once held. She helps you understand why you took the wrong turn at a crossroads . . . how to go forward with courage."

"I'd like to meet your marvelous doctor."

"I know that, Your Majesty. Dr. Lasseaux can help you, too."

"I didn't say—"

"Forgive me. I misunderstood."

"Don't apologize. Dr. Lasseaux would not approve."

"No, she would say I was sliding backwards."

"Alida—"

"Yes, Your Majesty?"

"We all have problems, don't we?"

"Of course, Your Majesty."

"Even small ones?"

"Oh yes, yes."

"Can you arrange for me to visit your doctor? I am frequently in Paris."

"I will do that." Alida placed a forefinger on her lips. "You need not ask it, Your Majesty. I will be discreet."

And soon it would be ended, the wonderful, difficult, revelatory adventure of the soul shared with Dr. Lasseaux. The experience that had brought her to an esteem of Mary Anna Callahan she had not believed was possible. And that had brought her to decision.

Unlike Selma, she was prepared for risk. However, she would be patient. She would not make her move until after the Jubilee, until her own future was at least reasonably assured.

As the royal jet banked over the French Alps, Marianna signaled Freddie for her last martini.

"Paris in an hour, Your Majesty. Feel like a sandwich?"

"Thanks, no. I'll lunch with Dahlia." She offered Freddie a drunken, unempressy wink. "We're going to have a talk—girl talk," she said.

In another hour her mind would be ready for Dahlia. At this moment it was on herself. Throughout the past four years Dr. Lasseaux had remained her best-kept secret. Faithful to her word, Alida had arranged the first appointment and never again referred to Dr. Lasseaux. Encountering each other the following season in St. Moritz, the two women had chatted pleasantly with no hint of their brief intimacy. Nor had Dahlia been taken into her confidence. Only Freddie knew about the visits to the rue Jeanne d'Arc in the thirteenth arrondissement.

Marianna was grateful that Ramir never demanded an accounting of her time. On the surface he appeared to be as unconcerned about her sexual activity as she pretended to be about his. He had come to her bed several times since the wretched scene in the chalet. Their few efforts at making love had resulted in fiascoes. She resented his attempt to use her as a vessel and he, confronted with her inert, ungiving body, could not come to erection. Without discussion they had mutually called off the farce.

Dr. Lasseaux was a more serious matter. The outcome of her therapy could very well have a more drastic effect upon the family—on Bahrait itself—than any extramarital affairs she and Ramir indulged in. She had arrived at the crossroad —she knew the path she would take. Barring detours, her final sessions with Dr. Lasseaux would send her on her way.

With effort she brought her thoughts around to Dahlia and Dahlia's present lover, Regis. In her last telephone call from Paris Dahlia's words had been cautious, her tone wavering between fright and defiance.

Lik her stepmother, Dahlia seemed to have leaped puberty. At sixteen, while she was a student in Paris, an artful plastic surgeon had trimmed away much of the fleshy nose inherited from her father, leaving her with a pert button that dwelt in harmony with the rest of her fine features. Transformed, literally overnight, into a ravishing beauty, the once-shy Dahlia had promptly set about being ravished.

Marianna deplored Dahlia's choice of lovers: a married jockey she met at Auteuil, a homosexual mechanic she foolishly believed she could change, a British rock musician who introduced her to cocaine, an aging count who was sexually stimulated only when his name appeared in the press linked to the Shah's teenaged daughter. And the list went on.

Somehow Dahlia emerged unscathed. She offered her body more liberally than her affection, successfully bouncing from affair to affair without psychic wounds.

This one, Regis Holden, was different from the others, Dahlia said. She loved him but there were problems—and there was danger. Not to herself, she had insisted, but to Regis. No, she did not want guards assigned to her, she said firmly. Years ago she had fought her father on that point and won. Now that she was a student at the Sorbonne living in her own flat on the rue de l'Université in the Latin Quarter, she wanted to keep a low profile, to mingle normally with other young people.

"You have that understanding with Marianna," she had argued with Ramir. "Protection on state occasions, freedom in private life. I demand the same."

"You *demand . . . ?*"

"Exactly. I'm not chattel—I'm not even your heir. Let me breathe. It's impossible with watchdogs at my heels."

"I can bring you home," he threatened.

"And cope with me every day?"

"Then stay where you are," he said. "Take your chances. You're a stubborn fool."

"Thank you, Father."

The royal jet touched down at Le Bourget and bumped to a halt. Marianna zipped up the suede boots she had kicked off on leaving Ryal and slid into the suede coat Freddie held out for her.

"She's over there, Your Majesty, behind the fence. What a looker. And those legs—mon Dieu!"

"Freddie, she's a child."

"They mature fast in this climate." He sighed with longing, then got down to business. "Your bags will be waiting for you in Neuilly. I'll deliver them myself. Will the toast of Paris be there?"

"Moira? Freddie, don't tease me about her. She's the aunt I always needed."

Moira Campbell, a middle-aged widowed Scotswoman, had been the housekeeper at Blair House in Washington, D.C., when Marianna made her initial trip to the United States as Empress. Routine arrangements had called for Marianna to reside with Ramir in the Bahraitian Embassy on Massachusetts Avenue. As Ramir's plane neared the eastern seaboard, word was relayed to the aircraft that hostile students were demonstrating before the embassy. The State Department, fearful of danger to the royal couple, suggested other housing arrangements. Infuriated, determined not to be intimidated, Ramir had insisted upon being escorted under guard to his own embassy. Yielding to the State Department, he had permitted Marianna to be delivered to Blair House, the nation's guest quarters on Pennsylvania Avenue.

Mrs. Campbell, an ample, round-cheeked woman with heavy gray hair coiled and pinned to the top of her head, had welcomed her cheerfully and ushered her to her suite. Barely settled, Marianna had heard rhythmic catcalling coming from the street. Hurrying to a window, she was stunned to see crowds wearing stocking masks marching below.

"Kill the killer! Down with the Shah! Murderer go home!" they shouted.

Marianna panicked. "What does it mean?"

"They know you're here," Mrs. Campbell said. "They're giving you the same business the others are giving your husband at the embassy."

"But why?"

"They hate his guts, ma'am. They want to get rid of him."

"Will they hurt him? I'm going to him."

"Stay put, ma'am. They're just letting off steam."

"They're insane."

"They're bitter is what they are. They've lived in Bahrait. They know what they've seen and heard."

On the street, demonstrators waving banners bearing inflammatory slogans continued to shout: "Murderer! Murderer! Murderer! Down with the murdering Shah!"

"Why aren't they chased away?"

"Free country, ma'am."

"Why can't they understand? Bahrait has a different form of government from the United States. The Shah is absolute ruler but he welcomes all legitimate criticism."

"And then—?"

"And . . . and then he does the best he can for the people."

The voices below grew louder and she shuddered. "There are immense problems in running our country. Certain unpopular actions are necessary. But my husband is no murderer!"

The din had continued. Marianna was approaching hysteria when Moira Campbell took her unresisting hand. "Come, Your Majesty. We'll go to my room for coffee. You won't be able to hear them there."

Before she left Washington, Marianna had enticed Moira into her service. Hesitant about living in a country as remote and threatening as Bahrait, Moira agreed to accept the post of housekeeper in the town house on the Boulevard Maurice Barrès. From the start she had run the sullen French staff efficiently, disregarding their resentment of a foreign overseer. Eventually she softened their hearts by mastering their language, which she now spoke with a faint Glasgow burr.

Moira's bizarre French was a source of a glee to all who heard it. To Marianna, Moira the woman was an island of safety, a provider of good sense and genuine affection liberally showered on her mistress and the children. Moira had her reservations about the Shah. Astutely, she kept them to herself.

Freddie led the way down the plane's ramp. Over his shoulder he said, "If I don't see Moira, please tell her *'Je t'adore'* for me."

"You're a hopeless flirt. Have a good time in Paris. And Freddie, don't forget—day after tomorrow."

Dahlia was still behind the fence when she sighted Freddie and Marianna. Breaking through the gate, she raced toward them.

"I thought you'd never get here." She hugged Marianna and tossed a "Hi, there" at Freddie.

"We're exactly on time. What's going on?" Marianna ruffled the girl's close-cropped black curls and saw the squint of anxiety in her dark eyes.

"Can we go somewhere to talk?" Dahlia said.

"This minute. How about the house?"

"No, Moira's there. She could hear us."

"Your apartment then?"

"No, no, that's worse. There's a bistro in the old winery district. The proprietor knows me. He'll give us a quiet table."

At the wheel of her yellow Peugeot, Dahlia was strained and uncommunicative. She swore as another car cut in front of her. "Dammit, Paris would be perfect without the French," she muttered.

When they arrived at Le Petit Navire, the proprietor greeted them almost imperceptibly and led them to a table in the rear. Without delay he presented a bottle of wine, which they approved. He filled their glasses, handed each a plastic-covered menu, and tactfully withdrew.

"All right, Dahlia, let's have it."

"Regis Holden, I told you about him. We love each other. We want to be married. Don't look shocked. He's nothing like the others. You'll like him."

"Then what's bothering you?"

"It's Father. I'm afraid of what he'll do when he finds out about Regis—if he hasn't found out already. Regis isn't the husband he'd choose for me."

"Easy, baby. Your father doesn't intend to choose your husband. Someday he'll pick a bride for Karim, but you—you're home free. Unless there's something about him . . ."

"He's American."

"So am I. My act's been a smash for years."

"He's an economics student at the Sorbonne."

"Good."

"He's Black."

Marianna replenished the wine glasses. "Your father has his faults but he's not a bigot."

"All right then, how does this hit you? Regis is a revolutionary. He wants to overthrow the government."

Marianna lifted her glass and examined it distractedly. The conversation was beginning to tire her. "So many young people do. I imagine the United States will survive."

"You don't understand. It's not the United States' government he wants to overthrow. It's Bahrait's. It's Father and his secret police and his military apparatus Regis wants to get rid of."

"You're joking!"

"You know I'm not. Everything Regis tells me makes sense. Things are rotten at home. You close your eyes to keep peace in the family."

"Never mind that. We're talking about you and the man you want to marry. Does he work alone or is he part of an organization?"

"There are hundreds of students involved, of all nationalities. They don't always agree with each other. They're united on one detail, though—Father and his crowd must go."

"You didn't answer me. Where does Regis stand?"

"He's not a terrorist, if that's what you mean. He believes in change through political pressure."

"He'll never succeed. You know that, don't you?"

Dahlia shook her head mournfully. "Regis and the others, they recognize the odds. They know about Father's army and the planes and the tanks and the nuclear devices. They know about the aid from foreign countries that keeps Father in power."

"Then why are you worried? Why do you fight in lost causes? Regis should go back to the States. You should go with him and live happily ever after. Are you concerned about your father? Don't be. He's always lived with danger. He means to keep that throne for Karim, and he will."

"Father's secret police are everywhere, even in America. They're a pack of goons. They don't have the patience or the brains to learn the difference between violent and nonviolent protesters. There's no place Regis and I can be safe."

"Bahrait has friends as well as enemies in the United States. I'll admit there have been unfriendly demonstrations, but there have been friendly ones, too. Last year we were received splendidly, not just by the White House but by plain citizens parading spontaneously in support of your father. Frankly, I was surprised."

"When will you face the truth? That parade was bought and paid for by Father's secret police. Your friendly demonstrators were brought in from Los Angeles, Detroit, Chicago, a dozen other cities. I've seen airline stubs, money orders, telephone transcripts, hotel bills, that prove the pro-Shah parade was nothing but a television spectacular dreamed up by our Minister of Propaganda." Dahlia paused for breath. "Sure, a few decent steps are taken—you visit hospitals and open schools. I've watched you on television. But try getting out of line and *your* life isn't safe, either."

"Ridiculous. You're being melodramatic, paranoid."

"And you won't open your eyes. Not that it makes much difference. Early on, if you'd known what Regis and his friends know, you might have had some influence. It's too late now. These past few years, well, I've seen how it is between you and Father."

"Doesn't that tell you something? The distance your father puts between himself and me isn't the world's best-kept secret. Yet he wouldn't dare threaten me or you or anyone you love. Think of what it would do to his image—"

"Then Regis is safe?"

"If you and he hold tight. Don't do anything reckless. Trust me. I'm planning a surprise for all of you."

"Marianna, I'm desperate. This is a helluva time to be coy."

The proprietor was approaching for their order. "I can't tell you anything more. Doctor's orders," she said lightly.

The redheaded driver of the mud-spattered Citroën pulled up to the shabby building and stretched to release the lock on the rear door. It was understood between them that Freddie was not to leave his seat to assist her from the car. Marianna wanted her present visit to this place to be as inconspicuous as her visits in the past.

She found the familiar bell on the shiny brass plate, pressed it, and waited for the buzz from above that would automatically release the heavy door.

Standing on the *rez-de-chaussée*, waiting for the lift that would carry her to the third floor, she recalled the first time she had arrived in this entry. For an instant she had regressed to Pete and Madge Callahan's flat in Boston. There had been no elevator in the old building, of course. But this white-tiled floor in Paris, so worn and cracked, and the pungent cooking odors that permeated the air were evocative and nauseating. She was immediately sympathetic to the many French doctors who were compelled to practice their profession in their homes in order to save office rent.

She had wanted to forget Boston then, but as the lift had clanked to a halt she'd reminded herself that she had come here to remember the past, to resurrect Mary Anna Callahan, and to understand the convoluted journey that had brought her from the slum of her birthplace to this near-slum in Paris.

On the third floor a sign with an arrow had pointed her to the domain of Dr. Rose Lasseaux. She knocked timidly and was admitted by a swarthy, heavyset woman dressed in black who, Marianna guessed, had been born looking matronly.

Following the doctor down the narrow interior corridor of the apartment, past walls papered with dingy overblown cabbage roses, she had glanced right and left through curtained glass doors into the rooms beyond. Observing the solid Biedermeier furniture in the dining room, the cheerless maroon velvet chairs and ugly floor lamps in the sitting room, and the bedroom with its pink chenille bedspread and more of the cabbage rose wallpaper, she could not believe this dreary place and this somber woman could accomplish the miracles Alida's story had promised.

In the treatment room she accepted a cup of steaming tea from Dr. Lasseaux. Sipping the tea, she peeked at her wristwatch and wondered how quickly she could get away. Yet within minutes, under gentle questioning from this total stranger, she found herself releasing long-choked memories and feelings, not only of the woman she was but of the child she had been. Two hours later, tearful and exhausted, she halted abruptly. "I've taken too much of your time," she said. "You've been kind. If I may, I'd like to come back."

Dr. Lasseaux left her chair and drew Marianna to her vast bosom. "You will always be welcome," she said.

"Thank you. Tomorrow?"

"Tomorrow. And then we will begin with the music."

Four years had gone by since then—four years of stolen visits in which her fears and guilts had diminished and, by some subtle alchemy, been replaced with new strength and a healthier appreciation of self.

Fragments of past encounters drifted across her mind . . .

A rainy afternoon, lying on the daybed with eye mask in place, she had listened to Bach and Handel and sobbingly re-experienced the traumas of her parents' deaths . . .

"Let the music take you where it will," Dr. Lasseaux encouraged, and Marianna had cried out to her mother, "Why did you go? I wanted you to live! How can you be dead? I didn't even know you . . . !"

And Dr. Lasseaux gently answering her: "You did everything you could. You were just a little girl."

"I should have saved her somehow! I took care of her and she died!"

"Mary Anna, she wanted to be released from her struggle. Try to feel as she did. She thought it was time for her to go. She was ready."

"And my father . . ."

"Can any of us keep another from dying? Do you think you are responsible for the way your father lived or died?"

"No, he was on his own path."

"We all need to be kinder to ourselves, more forgiving." Dr. Lasseaux's reassuring voice could be heard through the music. "Be that little girl again. Feel your fear and sadness one last time, then open your hands and let the pain flow out. It doesn't belong to you anymore."

"Mom, Pop—I want to cling to them!"

"They wouldn't want you to suffer. Let them go."

And another day: While listening to the music she had said nothing. When the music was ended she turned on her side and faced the wall, sobbing. "I was in boarding school, picking apples . . . the sun was on my back . . . the sky was the kind of blue that it is only in September . . . really blue, blue, blue. Everything perfect. I didn't deserve that beauty. I wanted to be in Charlestown in the old flat . . . my mother so withdrawn . . . the boys moved away . . . the family dissolved, disappearing. I felt I'd deserted them. Pop, he made his own world after Mom died. I thought no matter what happened we'd always be together, a family . . ."

Good memories had surfaced too. "They're real. Just as important as the darker times," Dr. Lasseaux said. "Mary Anna, are you in another time?"

"Yes."

"How do you feel?"

"Dreamy. Contented. A quiet kind of joy. I'm an adolescent, off in Vermont, in the woods. Full of expectations. And longing."

"Longing?"

"To be accepted. To be part of something. To belong. I'm privileged to be alive. It's not enough. I want to belong."

Another day, riding the crests and dips of Villa-Lobos, "I see wild black-eyed Susans, summer field flowers, rays of sunshine through the trees, the sort of light where you see little particles floating in the air. And a bird swooping, very happy, looking at the trees and forest below. The bird has real freedom. I soar with him and I see all of the earth, yet I feel grounded. The ideal state. Grounded but free."

And a recent session, the music wild and bouncy, unlike her reverie.

"I see Rembrandt . . . I feel a kinship with him. He seems alone. Nobody understands what he is doing, what drives him. In his creative world he is alive but he is separated from the reality around him. He has a bridge to cross. He is telling me I do, too."

"Take off your earphones. How do you feel?"

"Like I've been asleep. I'm waking up."

Over the years, whenever Marianna was in Paris she and Dr. Lasseaux had met like a pair of old friends, coming together with easy familiarity however long the separation. Marianna learned after a while that Dr. Lasseaux, who lived alone, dressed in black at all times, occasionally brightening her neckline with an artificial white camellia which she shyly refused to explain.

Once Dr. Lasseaux spoke of her daughter's troubled marriage, the anguish of an impending divorce.

"Can't you help her?" Marianna had asked. "There must be a way to spare her the pain."

"Marianna, you know better than that." Dr. Lasseaux had reproached her. "I have no panacea, no utopia to offer to my child or to you. Suffering is part of being alive and human. Remember, from the start our goal was to free you from neurotic suffering. My daughter, like you, must accept the fact that there are no solutions—only ways to cope with problems. When we are finished with our work, you will be more confident, more assertive. For the first time you will be strong enough to control your own life. Oh, you'll make mistakes—many of them. But they will be *your* mistakes, freely made—and yours to correct."

"I dreamed of a cure . . ."

"Cure," Dr. Lasseaux said with disdain. "The word doesn't belong in therapy. Here you discover your self-worth, how to stand independently—which does not exclude healthy dependence on others. Cure," she repeated scornfully. "You have a rectal problem, you see a proctologist. Maybe you come away with a cure."

To explain her last extended visits to Dr. Lasseaux so soon before the Jubilee, Marianna had casually mentioned to Ramir that she would linger awhile in Paris to complete her shopping and that Dahlia would accompany her. She needed sixty-odd changes of clothes for the anniversary fête alone, she added.

"After I find what I want, I'll have to stay long enough for fittings and accessorizing," she had told him at dinner.

His disinterest was almost audible, his face barely visible through the flower arrangement and gold candelabra that isolated them at opposite ends of the nine-foot-long table.

"The couture people will come to Ryal if you prefer," she said.

She was prepared for his reply. "It makes no difference. Stay as long as you wish." They had finished their meal in silence.

As they were leaving the dining room to go to their separate apartments, Ramir had stopped and spun her toward him, his look one of sorrow. "You are a beautiful woman. It is such a pity, such a waste."

"Your life or mine?"

"Both."

"You mustn't think of it that way. There have been good times. We have a wonderful family. We needed each other for that."

"We did. I will never forget the day Karim was born. I was delirious," he said. "Karim is a good boy. He will be a brilliant Shah. You will see him on your way back from Paris?"

"It's all arranged. Luke will come from Ryal and meet me in Geneva. We'll go to Le Rosey together to consult with Karim's instructors."

Ramir's face became unreadable.

"Don't forget, you hired Luke to supervise Karim's education until he was ready for college," she said.

"Ah, Luke. A fine choice we made there. Give Karim my love. Have a pleasant holiday."

She had fully intended to have a good holiday. Although the scheduled sessions with Dr. Lasseaux dominated her thoughts, she nevertheless anticipated many frivolous hours of couturier-hopping. From that first lunatic shopping binge —when Ramir had selected her trousseau—to the present day, she had responded to the excitement that charged through an haute couture showing like an overloaded circuit reaching its point of explosion. Declining designers' bids to dispatch their best clothes models (including slim graceful males passing as women), and their one-of-a-kind gowns to the town house in Neuilly, Marianna chose to sit among the keyed-up audience on the traditional wobbly gold-leafed chairs in the salons. With order card in hand, she knew she was among the dinosaurs—it was said that fewer than a thousand women in the world could replenish their wardrobes with haute couture clothes. It never ceased to astonish her that as Empress of Bahrait she could possess all of the magnificence paraded before her.

Dr. Lasseaux had not let her forget that. "Here we have worked so long on the dark side of the moon. Yet there are aspects of your present life that give you enormous gratification. Your private plane, the palace, the seaside villa, the yacht, the chalet in St. Moritz, the *hôtel particulier* in Paris, servants who do everything but your breathing. Have I left anything out?"

"The children, though they'll always be mine. We've gone over that," she said. "There are other pluses. The attention, the flattery wherever I go. With the exception of my husband, everywhere I turn I'm surrounded by people who wish to please me.

"Time and the children have softened my mother-in-law. There's Azar. She precipitated all this but she's out of my life. And there's all that caviar." She had swung off the couch and burst into tears. "I guess you could say I live like a queen."

On the plane to Geneva she accepted her first martini of the day from Freddie. The steward, she noted, was pleasantly spaced out. Freddie had a whale of a time on their trips to Paris. Except for her visits to Dr. Lasseaux, he was on his own in the city. Unfailingly, he returned to duty satisfied and depleted.

Occupied with Dr. Lasseaux, with Dahlia, with the bumblebee flightiness of shopping, she had slept poorly in her bedroom on the Boulevard Maurice Barrès. She was a woman who needed a man in her bed, not just for a romp but to bestow his love and to receive her love. Dr. Lasseaux had been explicit about that.

She had glowed then, a little girl winning approval from mother. "Migod, I'm normal!"

"Not abnormal," Dr. Lasseaux had replied carefully. "The

picture is out of balance. You want to give too much, always to men who want to take tòo much."

"Luke isn't one of those."

"Perhaps not. I am no oracle. When you change, we will see what he is made of."

Now, just hours away from Geneva and Luke, she squirmed, feeling disloyal. Soon Luke would be tested. No question, he gave more than he took. The question before the court was a simple one: Would Luke remain at her side when he realized that her old patterns, so slowly and agonizingly altered, had led her to a decision that would disrupt the neat little niche he had carved for himself in her life?

What *did* she want him to do? Dahlia's reminders of Ramir's secret police had once more aroused her fears for Luke's safety. Soon after the disastrous confrontation in St. Moritz, Ramir had obliquely suggested that the royal privilege of taking lovers did not extend to his Empress. Yet, if he had knowledge of her affair with Luke—and she was positive he did—he had taken no steps to bring it to an end. When he learned of her plans would he turn vengeful, use his loyal killers to dispose of Luke?

She shivered, pulling her golden sable coat about her for security rather than warmth. If Dahlia was right, the time had come to warn Luke, to tell him he was in greater danger than he knew. She would urge him to leave Bahrait. She would promise him that somewhere, somehow, they would be together again. She would see to that.

Unless he chose to go over to Ramir's side.

Luke was standing there beyond the customs barrier. The driver who had brought him to the airport signaled a friendly customs official, then carried her unopened luggage past a grumbling line of ordinary travelers.

Luke and Marianna acknowledged each other with a polite handshake. While the driver stored her bags, Luke assisted her into the car and moved in beside her.

He found a cashmere lap robe and arranged it about her. When she was certain the driver was giving his attention to the road, her hand slipped out, took Luke's, and drew it under the robe. It was a game they had played before. Staring straight ahead, Luke said nothing as she loosened her coat and trailed his fingers beneath her skirt to her inner thighs.

"Your Majesty," he said, pulling away. "There's something we must discuss. Now, before we get to the school."

Puzzled, she watched him shut the sliding glass panel that separated them from the driver.

"It concerns Karim . . ."

"Karim! Is he all right?"

"He's the healthiest kid in Le Rosey. You can relax about that. And his schoolwork is up there with the best of them."

"Then what . . . ?"

"Something's bothering him. He won't discuss it with his advisers. He won't discuss it with me. He's morose, clams up if anyone tries to get close to him. I can tell he's bursting to confide in someone. Whatever it is, he can't carry it alone."

Marianna inspected a lacquered fingernail. Her eyes became slitted and thoughtful. "Karim is fourteen. Could it be a girl, a pregnant girl?"

"I hadn't thought of that."

"Why should you?" Her mouth twisted bitterly. "Karim and his father have done a lot of talking about what he can expect of life when he becomes the Shah. His father may very well have hinted at the dynastic privileges he can look forward to. Maybe he decided not to wait."

"I think you're wrong. He's too upset. A pregnant girl? Unsettling, to say the least. But Karim and I have had talks, too. He'd confide that to me. He knows there are ways to deal with such a situation. No, this seems to go deeper."

"Will he talk to me?"

"I can't say. Lunch with him, just the two of you. I'll be in the visitors' room if you need me."

In theschool anteroom she shed her sable coat and waited on a bench. When Karim appeared he was bundled into a fleece-lined jacket and rough pants. On his head he wore an ear-muffed leather cap that clasped under his chin. Sighting her, his face crumpled as he fought back tears.

She jumped to her feet. "Karim, where are you going?"

"Out, with you. I have something to tell you." He looked about nervously. "It's a secret—I guess." In an instant he was through the door. She grabbed her coat and followed him.

The freezing air stung her cheeks and a gust of wind blew the loosely knotted scarf from her head. Her teeth chattered and she shivered inside the sable coat.

"Karim, can't we go back?"

The boy shook his head. "Not yet, not till you hear what I have to say."

"Then please begin. I can't bear this."

"It's better than what's coming."

And he had told her. Of his father and another woman.

"Look at me," she commanded, stopping on the road. She grasped his shoulders, forcing him to face her. "Who told you such a thing?"

"Jasper. You know him, the American kid whose parents travel for the government. He came back last week. His folks are in Sweden. He heard about it from them."

"Heard what?"

"That Father—well—that Father has this woman."

She hugged him to her, relieved. "Darling Karim, is that it? How cruel of your friend to gossip. How humiliating for you to hear such a thing."

He looked at her oddly. "Humiliating for me? What about you?"

"Your father and I have been married fifteen years. Some men need another woman from time to time. What you're saying is meaningless to me."

"But—"

"Let me finish. If the story is true, then this woman, whoever she is, is unimportant. We've talked about it, your father and I. I'll admit I was hurt at first. Now I understand him better. It's not serious. They come and go. I close my eyes and ears. You must, too."

"Mother." His eyes clouded with tears. "That's not the whole story. The woman, Pia Larson, she's here, in Switzerland. In Lausanne, in a house Father bought for her. Jasper didn't mean to be cruel, and it's not just the house. He thought I ought to know the whole story before the others find out."

"Find out what?"

"That there's a baby there. Father's and that woman's. Father was with them last week."

"Impossible. He was in Brussels. Don't you read the newspapers? Didn't you see his picture?"

"I read the newspapers. I know he was in Brussels. And last month in London and Bonn. And before that Rome. But each time he insists on rest stops. And each time he comes to Switzerland to be with them, with his baby and its mother. She's like a—wife."

She sat apart from Luke in the rear of the limousine, the cashmere lap robe at her feet. Hurt and rage tore at her, making her head throb. Luke reached out to her but she shook him off.

"You're making a mistake," he said. "Karim, Jasper, those babbling parents, they've got to be wrong."

"Then I'll invent some excuse for intruding. I must know and Karim must know."

"What does it matter now? You know about Ramir's women. You told Karim you did."

"Can't you see? The others, they're unimportant. I'm convinced of that. But a home, a baby ... that's an emotional commitment."

"It can't be."

"It *can* be. I've got to find out. If he can love anyone, it should be me. If he wanted another child, it should have been mine."

"But you don't love him."

"He wanted me to stop loving him. Why?"

The car eased to a stop before a gray stuccoed house set back from the street by a winter lawn. It was surrounded by a tall, spike-tipped iron fence.

"I'm coming with you."

"No. If it's some terrible joke, I'll be right out. If there's something to it, I want to see it through myself."

She waited alone in the simply furnished parlor. The white-capped maid who admitted her had been gone for several minutes. "Who shall I say is calling?" she'd asked.

"Mary Anna Callahan."

"May I take your coat, Mrs. Callahan?"

"Thank you, no. I'm not staying."

"I'll find Mrs. Larson."

After the maid had disappeared up a flight of stairs, Marianna circled the room with mounting horror. At first glance the room had appeared so middle-class, so *ordinary*, totally unlike any environment she could imagine Ramir in. Lace curtains covered the windows. Heavy overstuffed velour chairs and a matching sofa, their arms protected by linen antimacassars, were set stiffly in a symmetrical arrangement. The only handsome piece of furniture, a baby grand piano, rested on a flower-patterned carpet.

I've made a ridiculous error, she told herself. I'll wait for Mrs. Larson, apologize, and run like hell.

Then she saw the photographs. They assaulted her from every corner. On the piano, a formal portrait of Ramir in military uniform. Beside it, another of Ramir with an infant in his arms. A series of out-of-focus snapshots—were her eyes fogging?—of Ramir in this very room, on this very carpet, with the child grown older. And yet another—now she could see that the child was a boy—of Ramir and the youngster, laughing together, sinking their fingers into the frosting of a birthday cake that read "Happy Two."

Spinning about, she faced a round oak table and another bank of pictures. She fell into a chair, her eyes riveted to a framed portrait of Ramir and a pleasant-looking brown-haired woman holding a little boy between them. The child, clad in lederhosen, smiled into the camera. Behind him Ramir and the woman faced each other, their eyes locked in affection and pride.

"Mrs. Callahan?" The voice was husky and revealed the merest trace of an accent.

Marianna, gripping the chair arm, came to her feet, unable to respond.

"Your Majesty!" The woman who spoke stopped in the doorway. She was tall and large-boned. Her thickly-lashed green eyes were glazed with dismay. "Oh my God! Please sit down. I must too. My maid didn't say . . ."

Marianna stared at Pia Larson. This was unreal. No, a trick, that's what it was. A trick set up by Karim's schoolmates. She fell back into the chair. The woman, whoever she was, started to speak. Marianna forced herself to listen.

". . . understand the shock. You were to be shielded. We never wanted you to know."

"But I *do* know—about the others."

"So do I. They never bother me. They count for nothing. A man like Ramir must have his release."

Marianna shook her head, comprehending nothing. "You, who are you?"

"No one very special. You can see for yourself. That is why you are so shocked. I am not beautiful, not too young. Nothing like the girls in St. Moritz. Yes, he told me about them, too, and about the dreadful incident that occurred there."

"Why you?"

"Who can explain these things? For me, why him? Look around. None of the trappings of wealth here. It is a quiet, lonely life for Eric and me when his father is not here."

"Eric," she repeated tonelessly.

"Our son. The child you have seen in the pictures. Fortunately, he is napping now. For all of us it is best that you do not see him. Myself? I am—I was an economist with a fine future. Ramir came to Stockholm for a conference. I was assigned to him as liaison. You were in South America on a goodwill mission. He spoke proudly of you."

"Are you trying to comfort me?"

"No, no, please forgive me. I did not intend to sound patronizing. I meant only that neither of us was looking for what happened. I had my career. It was to be my life, the dream of my parents to see me working in our government. They know of this. They are not happy for me. They see only misery ahead. I suppose they are right. Ramir promises nothing more than what we have now—our love for each other and the joy of our child."

"I'd like a drink." Marianna dug her nails into her palms. "The others, I tried to understand—" Her voice trailed off.

Pia brought a bottle of brandy and two snifters. "Maybe this will help. Tell me, who told you of us?"

"My son. It's beginning to be gossip in his school." Marianna emptied her glass in a gulp. "My head is splitting. Ever since St. Moritz, I've asked myself a thousand times—how did Ramir and I get off the track?"

Pia drew up a needlepoint stool and sat before Marianna, cupping her own snifter. "A man in Ramir's position, we both know too well, he must make many compromises to survive. We all make compromises, but a Shah, he must make more. You must not blame yourself or me. You must have realized that sooner or later he would choose his own mate."

Marianna slapped the snifter out of Pia's hands and came to her feet. She watched the brandy make its way through the slithers of glass on the flowered carpet. "What did you say?" she demanded.

Pia's large hand flew to her open mouth. Appalled, she stared at her visitor. "You don't know! No one ever told you! Ramir never warned me . . ."

"He probably didn't plan for us to meet. You can be the

one to explain everything to me." Marianna stood threateningly over the Swedish woman.

Pia shook her head vigorously. "I can't. I mustn't. He will be very angry, very cold if I talk more. I couldn't bear that. He and Eric, they are all I have."

"Then I'll get it out of him myself. Damn him—whatever happens, he's always the winner! Listen to me, Pia. Don't tell Ramir I've been here. I won't say anything either. Nothing would be gained. I'll reassure my son. I'll say I've called on Mrs. Larson, that the story is ridiculous. When I finish he'll believe he's been the victim of a filthy lie."

She picked up her coat and took a last look around. "Nice cozy place you've got here," she said and hastened from the house to rejoin Luke in the waiting car.

Aboard the plane for Ryal she pushed away the food that was growing cold on the table separating her from Luke.

"At least Karim's flying high. I gave an Academy Award performance. Convinced him he was being had, listening to gossip, the kind of crud he'll come up against all his life. He wanted to find Jasper's parents and beat the hell out of them."

"Great. You get the door prize for conning your son," Luke said. "What about yourself? Overflowing with compassion for the star-crossed lovers?"

"I'm in an emotional stew. Sure, I'm sorry for Pia. It can't be fun having a married lover who's an absentee father and who screws around besides. She's a nice lady. Too bad you couldn't meet."

"A tragedy. She'd have told me her story—I'd have told her mine. We could have wept on each other's shoulders."

"It's hardly the same. Pia and His Majesty aren't flying over Europe in public. They're prisoners. They don't dare go into their backyard together. It's incredible. I thought I'd faint when Pia told me where I fit into the picture." She laughed. "What picture? I'm outside the frame. Actually, I'm in shock. I've been used for some purpose. I'm still being used, and I don't know why or how. I can't begin to deal with it."

"Do you have to? You hinted you had some plan for us before you ever heard of Pia Larson."

"I do have and I'll tell you about it later. But Pia does

make a difference. Now I want to go further, to hurt Ramir, to humiliate him ..."

"Shh, Freddie's behind you," he whispered. "We'll talk tonight when we're alone."

After dinner he came to her suite, opening the door with the key she had given him. He wore an old T-shirt and jeans and carried his briefcase filled with school papers. He was not interested in what the children had accomplished in his absence, nor did he expect that she would be.

They had been apart so long. There had been her stay in Paris—difficult but bearable because she was not near him physically. However, from the moment he sighted her in the Geneva airport, he had been absurdly occupied with crossing his knees or fastening his topcoat to conceal the tormenting bulge in his crotch. Walking to her quarters, he had held the briefcase, an improvised leather shield, before him.

She was waiting for him in her sitting room. Her champagne chiffon peignoir, newly purchased in Paris and brazenly designed for seduction rather than concealment, exposed her breasts with their freshly rouged nipples, and the downy triangular puff he had often nuzzled with pleasure.

"Jeezus. Cover up," he begged. "I can't hold back." He closed the door carefully and tossed aside the briefcase.

"Neither can I," she murmured.

In her bedroom she dropped to one knee to loosen his jeans. He stood above her clumsily peeling off his T-shirt. Still kneeling, she brought his shaft to her lips. Again he pleaded with her to stop. On the bed he pierced her like a schoolboy who hadn't refined his skills. In seconds it was over.

Mortified, he rolled away. "Bitch. I feel like an idiot."

"Don't," she said, concealing her own disappointment.

"You were gone so damn long. Three weeks. I'm sorry..."

She consoled him, holding his face between her breasts. Suddenly she felt his fingers in her, over her, squirreling everywhere, bringing her to the edge of orgasm. She felt his hardening return, then burrow into her. Legs high, she tightened her muscles, sucking him deeper and deeper until, at last, she came.

Almost instantly, she fell asleep.

In the morning, he was gone. They never did talk about her plan and she wondered if she had the courage to go ahead with it.

Scrutinizing herself in the Hotel Danieli bathroom mirror, Selma Shapiro shuddered and concluded that her face was an insult to the human race. At best she was no beauty. But this morning in the honest early light she was a disaster. Her skin was blotchy, her hair chose its own direction, and her lashless eyes, bloodshot and swollen, reminded her of the hapless fish who swam in the window tanks of the seafood trattorias off the Merceria waiting for someone to select them for dinner.

In the next room Gino was still asleep in the bed they had shared for the past three nights. His body had been turned away from her when she awoke. Removing her weight, she had caused the mattress to tilt. Gino, restless even in sleep, had groaned and drawn himself closer to the wall.

It was her own fault that she would breakfast alone and leave Venice's Marco Polo Airport with no one to see her off. Last night at dinner she had told Gino he need not bother to get up and he, relieved, had agreed to sleep through her departure. She had resented his ready acquiescence as she had resented so much of what had transpired since her arrival in Venice.

The stopover in Venice on her way to Ryal had been unplanned. Although she and Gino had been apart for more than two months, she had intended to hold to their agreement that she would not stick her nose into his business when he was on location. Never mind that he owed this directorial job on *Pantheon,* as well as his earlier assignments, to Selma's clout at Hanover Studios.

"You distract me from my work when you're around," he'd said charmingly, running his hands over her ample hips. From the start she knew it was bullshit. In his fashion he was telling her she interfered with his personal freedom. Nonetheless, she had played it his way, coyly slipping out of his reach, smiling sweetly, pretending to believe he found her irresistible.

Other Hanover pictures under Gino's helm had proven financial catastrophes for the studio. The board in New York, aware of Selma's value to them, had closed its collective eyes, understanding the marital blackmail that made Gino's assignments essential to Selma's peace of mind.

They had both expected it to go on and on that way, with Selma providing the jobs in return for an occasional tumble in the hay and the privilege of being Gino's wife, and Gino accepting each assignment as his artistic due, invariably insisting upon faraway locations.

The afternoon Hanover's budget director, Charlie Knight, reached Selma through the studio switchboard, his first words had thrown her into panic.

"Something funny's going on over in Venice, Selma. I think you'd better drop in and check it out."

Her memory flashed to party gossip she'd overheard. Gino and young Italian women. Gino and very young Italian boys. The women came with the package that was Gino. But little boys! She knew she could never bail him out of that one. Her stomach roiled as she recalled the famous American novelist, assigned to write a screenplay in Rome, who had seduced the angelic ten-year-old son of a local leather merchant. To forget the affair the boy's father had demanded a cash settlement of a quarter of a million dollars. Fearful of an even greater loss in revenue which a scandal might engender, the studio had paid up, charging off the sum to miscellaneous overhead. They would not do it a second time, not for Gino, not for her.

"Hey, Selma, you there?" Charlie Knight's bark had brought her to attention.

"Sorry, Charlie, someone opened the door. They're gone now. What's this all about?"

"*Pantheon*, baby. It was supposed to be a cheapie. Well, the costs are running up faster than a monkey in a tree. And the footage that's coming back—between you and me, the boys in the cutting room say it stinks."

She had hurried to a screening room to view Gino's work. When the lights came back on she felt sick. She offered a choked "thank you" to the projectionist and somehow made it to her office. Four days later, after phone calls had failed to locate Gino, she cabled him she was coming to Venice.

Selma had seen Venice for the first time when she was twenty-six years old. Some girls in the steno pool had arranged a European tour and Selma, by then a script supervisor, had asked in. After three frenetic days in London and three more in Paris, the group had arrived in Venice. Selma was instantly beguiled by the city. When the steno group moved on to Florence and Rome and Naples, she chose to remain behind. Enchanted, she wandered the back streets and alleys, encountering ancient bridges arched over narrow canals, obscure piazzas, and friendly faces everywhere. Guiltily, she sat in tiny churches praying that her God and her parents would forgive her for the serenity she found there. She fed pigeons and stray cats and shamelessly reveled in the harmless leers and ass-pinching dispensed by Venetian men who would have considered it insulting to allow her to pass unnoticed. It didn't matter that there was no follow-through. Their lasciviousness did what the men intended it to do. It transformed her, however briefly, into the desirable woman she had always dreamed of being.

In the years that followed, as she gradually rose in status at Hanover and traveled abroad to supervise European productions, she never failed to visit Venice. She knew it in all its seasons the way one knows a sharing lover. The way she did not know Gino.

On her arrival at the Marco Polo Airport just three days ago, Selma had been unable to locate a porter. Tugging her arms had reached out from behind her. Miraculously the heavy bags from the Alitalia luggage wheel, she stumbled toward the customs counter, feeling tired and apprehensive about the confrontation ahead. To her surprise two strong arms had reached out from behind her. Miraculously the chafing bags were removed from her hands. Even more miraculously, the arms had belonged to her husband.

"Selma, my darling. You have come at last." Gino dropped the bags and held her close, attempting to kiss the astonishment from her face. "You knew I'd be here," he said. "I could hardly wait."

In the rear of the rented motor launch that bore them over the marshes into the Venetian lagoon, he stroked her bare arms and fondled her abundant breasts. Parting his capped teeth (she had paid for them), he tongued her lips until her mouth opened to receive his promising thrusts, and she was happy again. In his suite overlooking the lagoon he drew the drapes, and hurriedly made her happier still.

That evening, dining at Harry's Bar, grown tipsy over Bellinis, the Venetian concoction of champagne laced with fresh peach juice, she forgot about Charlie Knight and the reason she was here. She did notice that Gino was an overly familiar figure to other diners and to the raucous barflies they passed en route to their table, but she had quickly rejected any train of thought that would mar the evening. In her Bellini-heightened pleasure at being in the city she loved with the man she loved, she banished all doubts about Gino.

In bed that first night he was the quintessential Italian lover—passionate, flattering, artful, insatiable. Carried along by his endearments, she felt herself transformed into an eighteenth-century contessa, high-breasted, velvet-skinned, fragile.

"Rest, my beauty," he had crooned as she drifted into sleep. "Tomorrow I must shoot in San Marco. Enjoy your day. We will meet here for cocktails."

She had nodded, hardly hearing. Yet in the back of her head something niggled. Then she remembered. She'd intended to visit her sinus specialist in Beverly Hills for one more nose-vacuuming treatment before coming to Venice. In her haste to depart she had not gotten around to it. Early in their marriage, at home in Bel-Air, Gino had accused her of snoring. He had demanded his own bedroom. Heartbroken, she had moved across the hall.

The morning after her arrival—overcome by Bellinis, sex, and jet lag—she had slept till noon. A cold cutting shower and espresso thick as molasses had reminded her of where she was and why.

The night before had been something to write home about. In daylight it was all too clear. Gino, the slimy bastard, had duped her again.

In a rush she had pulled on the first outfit that came to hand and slapped on some of the makeup the studio experts had created for her. Tearing through the hotel lobby, she had glimpsed herself in a gaudy Venetian mirror and conceded that she looked lousy. She was a fat frump in a terrible temper but, dammit, she was also Selma Shapiro, production head of Hanover Studios, and she was going out there to do her duty.

Elbowing her way over the crowded Ponte della Paglia to the right of the hotel, she had rudely stepped in front of tourists focusing Nikons and Rolleis and Instamatics on their loved ones and on the Bridge of Sighs and the canal below. She ruined a dozen snapshots in her passage but she never looked back. She whipped past souvenir stands, *gelati* vendors, and bookstalls, a determined Joan of Arc ready to do battle for the kingdom called Hanover Studios.

When she reached the Piazzetta her heart was pounding and her feet hurt. Spitting mad, she flopped onto an outdoor chair of the Gran' Caffè Chioggia to recover her wind. She hadn't decided what she would say or do when she caught up with Gino and the *Pantheon* company. As studio boss she knew it was her responsibility to observe, as dispassionately as possible, an incompetent director at work and at day's end to call him aside and fire him. It was with that resolve that she had left the hotel.

From the chair in the caffè where she sat slurping chocolate ice cream, she could see the Basilica of St. Mark and before it, roped off from sightseers, the production company of *Pantheon*. Gino was nowhere about. Like a leaderless army the costumed cast and the crew occupied themselves reading *Il Gazzettino,* dozing in the sun, playing cards, laughing, flirting, or lounging against the facade of the church, just plain bored.

Jeezus, what am I going to say to Charlie Knight, Selma had asked herself. Before Gino was set for the job, Charlie had drawn her aside to remind her that costume pictures usually were budgeted at astronomical cost, that she was begging for trouble if she allowed Gino to direct *Pantheon.* She had promised to trim the budget if Gino could have one more chance. Gino, sensing that the job was slipping away from him, had glided beneath her bedcovers for one of their increasingly rare nights together. By morning the assignment was his.

As she scraped the bottom of her ice-cream dish, Selma had heard good-natured hoots and a smattering of applause rising from the Basilica set. Dropping hr spoon, she stood up to see what had inspired the burst of liveliness. She was not surprised when she saw all heads turned toward Gino.

Nor was she surprised to see that he was accompanied by a woman. With hands clasped high overhead, bowing left and right, Gino was a returning gladiator acknowledging the plaudits of the populace. Beside him Monica Farinelli, the leading lady Gino had personally cast in *Pantheon,* fluttered false eyelashes and fumbled with the lacing on her deeply cut camisole.

Selma never took her eyes off the pair crossing the Piazza San Marco, Gino swaggering and Monica languid, satisfied,

leaning against him. They were coming from the direction
of Quadri's, a centuries-old caffè on the far side of the
square.

On an earlier trip to Venice Selma had lunched at Quadri's.
Returning to her table from the ladies' room upstairs, she had
asked the waiter what went on behind the closed doors that
lined the corridor on the floor above. The waiter, a cheerful
old-timer, had winked, then shrugged his shoulders and
grinned. "Signora, you know how men are."

She didn't know—then. Studio life had done little to
sophisticate her. Despite her shock the day she had invaded
Marianna Curtis's dressing room, Selma still believed in
courtship, love, and marriage, still regarded the scene with
Doug Braden as aberrational.

Life with Gino had given her a quick case of the smarts.
She asked only one favor of him, that he conduct his
fornication with discretion and that he never—repeat, never
—allow her to learn about his affairs.

And here he was, the fucking bastard, flaunting his horny
prick, practically before a cast of thousands, and with his
own wife just around the corner. She was hurt and furious.
Still, she tried looking at the brighter side.

At least it wasn't a little boy.

She had ordered another dish of ice cream and sat back to
think over the situation. The first conclusion she came to was
that she would make a fool of herself if she confronted Gino
in her present mood—and his. The second was that a show-
down was in order. She would have to tell him that the hour
of reckoning was near. Unless he brought the picture in at
budget and upgraded the quality of his work, he was risking
his job and hers. She would be blunt. Other studios would grab
her if they were certain she would dump her husband. He,
Gino, would wind up where she had found him, modeling
men's fashions on the Via Condotti in Rome.

Satisfied with her decision, she had attacked the ice cream
and turned her mind to the repercussions a hard line would
have on her marriage. Now she was in murkier waters. Gino
would defend himself, justify added costs by complaining
about bad weather and his lazy Italian crew. She would
remind him that costs were only part of the problem, that the
film reels he was returning to the studio were clumsy and
amateurish. They would bicker over that. Then, as he had in
the past, he would take her to bed and perform like the stud

he was. When it was over she would wriggle voluptuously and another round would go to Gino.

Her mother, the *nebbish*, had been the first to see that her daughter was being exploited.

"Selma, why do you need him? So many nice Jewish men around."

"Ma, you know you don't care about that. Cousin Shirley married Catholic. Nobody cared."

"Her James is a big lawyer, a settled man."

"You wouldn't mind Burt Reynolds."

"Also a settled man, sort of. He has a profession."

"Look, Ma. You're skipping the point. We both know it. I'm thirty-four years old. I'm dying on the vine. Plenty of men look at me every day. What do they see? A not-so-young girl with character. Character? They have uncles with character. Why do they need me?"

"Selma, you're a fine-looking—"

"A fine-looking what? A dog, maybe. You told me yourself, I got a strong family resemblance to your brother Sam. A big lawyer would fall for somebody who looks like Sam?"

"But Gino, he's using you."

Selma smiled wryly. "And you think I'm not using him?"

Selma had signaled the waiter and paid for her ice cream. She'd permitted herself one more bitter glance at the sloppy *Pantheon* company. Then, sunk in misery, she'd wandered back to the Hotel Danieli. This time she wove her way carefully among the people jamming the bridge. She didn't shove, she didn't interfere with tourists' snapshots. She paused only once, to acknowledge mutely her kinship with those other condemned wretches who centuries ago had dragged themselves across the Bridge of Sighs to enter the dank dungeons in which they were doomed to die.

Back at Harry's Bar that evening, it had occurred to her that although the same group of barflies and diners, male and female, cheered Gino's entrance, he introduced her to no one but the waiters.

She had speared her green noodles viciously. "Lots of chums you have here."

He surveyed his friends tolerantly. "Italians. Frivolous. You wouldn't like them."

"Probably not. By the way, I was in San Marco's this afternoon. I passed the set."

"My darling, you should have stopped. Why didn't you? What did you think?"

Moment of truth. "You know why I'm here."

"Naturally. You're on your way to Ryal. You missed me and thought we should have a few days together." He raised her hands to his lips and nibbled her fingertips. "You have made me extremely happy by coming." Then he looked at her questioningly. "Any other reason?"

She plunged her fork back into the noodles. "Where will you be shooting tomorrow?"

"In front of Santa Maria del Giglio, near the Gritti. Will you come? We will lunch alone on the Gritti terrace." He sighed happily. "A little more time with you. I am a lucky man."

"Gino?"

"Yes?"

"There *is* something. Never mind. We'll talk about it before I leave."

That night he had exhausted himself pleasing her. Later, while he slept, she stared at the ceiling and weighed her options.

The next morning, after he'd gone, she had dressed carefully and stopped at the hotel beauty salon to have her hair and nails done. Thus reinforced, she arrived at the Church of Santa Maria del Giglio. She was not yet ready for Gino. She wanted to watch him at work, to see if there was the faintest possibility he could bring off *Pantheon*.

This day was even more disheartening. Because Gino was trying. Somehow he'd pulled together his troops. The cast and crew were attentive, following each direction faithfully. Yet the results were sluggish, uninspired. Gino was giving it his best and his best wasn't good enough. He had no talent.

Over lunch on the Hotel Gritti terrace she had let him have it, calmly, sympathetically. Staring into her plate, she told him the studio was disappointed. There was talk of replacing him. Someone had gone over her head to the boys in New York. When she returned to Hollywood from Ryal she would make a strong pitch to retain him. Meanwhile he was to try harder. If he couldn't get more out of his cast, then he would be wise to tighten the budget. Yes, she had seen the film reels he'd sent back to the studio. *Pantheon* was not going to be a blockbuster. The studio would take a kindlier attitude toward his future if he cut costs drastically, thus leaving Hanover with the possibility of recouping its investment through later television bookings.

He did not interrupt her. When she finished speaking she saw that he was gazing over the terrace rail, following the progress of a slow-moving gondola. Instinctively she knew he was doing what she had done the night before: He was weighing the options.

Filled with her own fear, she had waited for him to respond.

He touched the palm of his hand to his forehead. "I'm so tired," he said. "To work so hard. To hear this from your wife."

"Gino. It's not *me* speaking. I don't *own* the studio."

"You could fight for me, explain to those money brokers that I am an artist. I work with flesh and blood, my own and my actors. This is not the stock market or the shoe business."

"Of course I'll fight for you. I have and I will again. You have my word. I'm not without power."

He brightened, struck by a new idea. "I need to rest, to get away from here, to refresh myself."

"You mean you'll step aside for another director? New York suggested—"

"I mean nothing of the sort," he struck back. "*Pantheon* is my picture. I intend to see it through."

"Then—?"

He chucked her under the chin with a breadstick, his demeanor softening, his voice seductive. "I mean, my darling, that we must shut down the production for a week. I will go with you to Ryal. The change will do us good. It will be another honeymoon." He ran the scratchy breadstick up and down her cheeks. "I will return to Venice a tiger. And you, sweet Selma, will go back to the studio and convince your bankers that I am not a man so easily replaced."

Disbelief had rendered her speechless. The rotten cheating stud. Even with his pants zipped he was playing his trump card.

"Maybe you didn't hear what I said," she finally croaked. "We were discussing cutting costs, saving *Pantheon*. We were not talking about goofing off at summer camp. Either you get cracking or I, good ol' Selma Shapiro, will see to it that you're replaced. One great roll in the hay isn't worth six million bucks, not to Hanover *or* to me. As for that breadstick—shove it!"

She had run from the terrace through the bar and the lobby to the Campo del Traghetto. To steady herself, she pressed her head against the show window of a chic boutique. Passersby, seeing her break into a spasm of laughter, thought she was crazy when all she was doing was asking herself if he had enough money to pay for lunch.

That evening, trailing the maître d' past the antipasto table and dessert cart in the Ristorante do Forni, Selma had offered up thanks for small favors. The picturesque room, a favorite dining place of native Venetians, mercifully was dimly lit. Candles glimmered in glass-shaded wall brackets and in a central chandelier, spreading a softening glow over the tables. Opposite her on a rustic bench in the corner, Gino, looking unbearably handsome, lifted his aperitif in a toast. Selma clicked her glass against his and heard him say, "We will forget this afternoon. To us, forever." She saluted him with her drink and said, "Forever."

Forever? She was sick to death of his remote politeness since her flare-up at the Gritti. She wanted to deal from a straight deck before leaving Venice in the morning, but she didn't have the guts. She sensed he was as trapped as she was, calculating the deal they'd made, poking at corners for escape, yet not prepared to give up what could still be extracted from their pact.

It was Selma who took the plunge. Bolstered by strong wine and the scent of sex Gino threw off like the skunk he was, she had felt secure enough to bring up the subject of *Pantheon*.

"In Hollywood, I must tell them *something*." She hesitated, measuring his mood. Would he storm at her and threaten divorce? Would he play it safe a while longer, promise to strain his talent for the picture, or better still, walk away from *Pantheon* but not from her?

"My love," he said, "I will do whatever is best for you and the studio. After Ryal you will screen my latest rushes. You will be happy with what you see."

On the short walk back to the hotel he had caressed her in deserted alleys, and sprinkled feathery arousing kisses along her chubby arm. For good measure he rubbed her generous, ungirdled behind. As always, her knees went weak.

In their bedroom he had undressed her slowly, erotically.

The night maid had laid her gown across the bed. He picked it up with disdain and tossed it onto a chair. He played with her breasts, her stomach, her clitoris. He whispered something in Italian and left for the bathroom.

On the bed she wiggled with greedy anticipation. Then she parted her legs and waited for him to return. When he did appear he was naked. Soon he was stretched beside her, but he did not move.

"Gino?"

"Yes?"

"I—I'm waiting."

"I know."

"Well—?"

"I am waiting, too."

"For what?"

"For you to decide whose side you're on."

"On your side of course. I'm your wife."

"Then you'll tell them you saw me doing a good job? You'll tell them *Pantheon* will be a success?"

"I—I don't know what I'll tell them. Must we talk about it tonight?" She reached to touch his hairless chest.

Spitefully he turned his back.

"You have given me your answer."

"Gino!" she cried out. "Gino, what am I supposed to do?"

"Fuck yourself," he replied.

She had crept from the bed and found her robe. In the bathroom she knew she was about to succumb to a record-breaking crying spell. She closed the door and switched on the water in the tub. Then she sat on the toilet, head in hands, and wept until she was exhausted.

When she crawled back into bed he was asleep.

On awakening she had left him a note. "You snore too."

Now, standing on the swaying plank dock in the Venetian lagoon, she watched the private motor launch weave its way into the narrow berth in front of the Danieli. Two porters clad in gray and white uniforms stood guarding her baggage. They were indecently cheerful for this time of day. She looked at her watch again. Six-thirty A.M. Ghastly hour.

When the boat was safely moored the porters transferred her bags to the launch and lightly supported her elbows as she stepped aboard the rocking craft. She found her way to the open area in the rear, and while the launch revved up she took a last look at Venice, at the spire of the Campanile visible above the incomparable Piazza San Marco, at the Church of San Giorgio Maggiore, an illusionary two-dimensional marvel built by Palladio shimmering on its own island, at the friezes on the Doges' Palace, at the shuttered bedroom window of the Hotel Danieli where Gino, her husband, slept.

Perversely, she adored Venice more at this moment than she ever had before. It was still the only lover she'd known who gave and gave and gave, and asked nothing in return.

Boarding the commuter plane to Rome where she would pick up her flight to Bahrait, she felt a refreshing burst of confidence.

She was, after all, Selma Shapiro, production head of Hanover Studios, and she was on her way to see her best friend, Marianna, the Empress of Bahrait.

12

Agnes Curtis scowled at the black-uniformed driver of the hired limousine. The jackass, with total disregard for her spanking new tapestry travel bags, was hefting them into the trunk of the car, placing them on the very floor where moments ago spare cans of gasoline and a clutter of oily rags had reposed.

"Hey you, go easy on that stuff," she yelled. "They're not paid for yet."

"Doing my best, madam."

"Yeh? Well, treat them like babies, will you? They're going on a long trip. You'll have them beat to shreds before we get to the airport."

The driver shot her a sour look. He knew the type. Classy as an alley cat, no matter how fancy she got herself decked out. The beige suit with a narrow white stripe running through it was kind of smart and so were the shiny brown pumps and matching purse. The neighborhood wasn't bad either. Still, he could spot her kind a mile away. One of those dames who scratched part way up the social ladder, then got stuck far from the top. He could say the same for her husband. The heavyset man with the boozy shakes was descending the stairs slowly. His full face was freshly shaved and unhealthily red. His conservative clothes looked as though they had just come out of a department store box and were on their way to a funeral.

"Come on, Joe—get a move on," Agnes snapped. "We got twenty minutes to pick up Father Flynn. This guy knows the way to the parish house. Hey, driver, give him a hand with his bags, will you? We can't miss that London plane. We got a connection to make. Joe, for crissakes, careful! You're scraping your goddam bags!"

In the rear of the limousine Agnes and Joe had little to say to each other. The glass panel dividing them from the chauffeur was shut tight. But you never could tell. Some of these guys could eavesdrop through concrete.

It had been Marianna's wish that the Curtises and Father Flynn travel as a threesome. Marianna was concerned about the unworldly priest, she'd written in a recent letter. The flights to London and Rome and then on to Bahrait could be bewildering for him. Flatteringly, she'd reminded Joe and Agnes they'd been around. They'd flown to Bahrait, with stopovers in Paris, after the birth of each of her children, and they'd made all those trips to Arizona, California, and Hawaii. On the other hand, Father Flynn was a timid sheep in need of shepherding.

To Agnes, Father Flynn was a pest and a drag. She and Joe didn't see much of him anymore, not since Marianna had gone off to marry her Shah.

In better times, when they could afford it, Joe and Agnes had responded with checks to the priest's fund-raising appeals. "So soppy you can wring the tears from the page," Agnes had complained. Written in Father Flynn's neat hand, the appeals had invariably evoked memories of the poverty Joe and Agnes had put behind them. Lately they'd disregarded his letters. They had troubles enough of their own, God knows, what with Joe's liver problem and the recession in the building trade that was gradually sending his business down the drain.

This trip should have been a ball, a vacation from their worries. Instead, they were stuck nursemaiding an aging priest. Because Marianna had requested it. Ordered it, would be more to the point.

Father Flynn threw the last of his toilet articles into a battered suitcase borrowed from Alfred Connors, a widowed policeman who used it once a year when he visited his married daughter in Minneapolis.

"It's been a lucky bag for me, Father. Never had a bad trip. Makes me feel good every time I pack it, knowing Nancy or Phil or one of the kids will grab it soon as I'm off the plane. I wish the same for you." Alfred flushed. "Excuse me, Father. I didn't mean that about Nancy and the kids. Of course it's different for you."

"You meant no harm, Alfred. I accept your good wishes in the spirit intended."

"When you see Mary Anna, the Empress—whatever she calls herself—will you tell her 'hello' for me? That scrawny, scared kid—who'd have guessed she'd rise so high?"

"Depends on what you mean by rising high. Sometimes we

stay in one place and our hearts soar. Other times we move up in the eyes of the world and our hearts never leave the old places. I think Mary Anna is like that. She hasn't moved away from us."

"Then tell me, Father, how come you never got invited before?"

"I have been, Alfred, many times. I just wasn't ready. This time I am. Ready and needy."

In New York, embarking on the Concorde for London, Agnes Curtis led the way, her high heels clicking on the metal platform atop the ramp leading to the aircraft. After flashing her boarding pass she followed the stewardess to her seat in the middle of the plane. Lumbering behind her, Joe Curtis stopped in the entry and waited for Father Flynn to catch up.

The old boy was slowing down, Joe decided. How old was he? Joe calculated rapidly. Sixty, sixty-five maybe? That wasn't *so* old, yet he was having a hard time negotiating the steps. He had appeared pale and distracted in the limousine that sped them to Logan Airfield, and had summoned a porter to carry the single bag he carried. Sick maybe? Over the Atlantic, eyeing the priest poking apathetically at the elaborate hors d'oeuvres on his plate, Joe was tempted to say something. On second thought, he told himself, why get into it? It could be fear of traveling or even the peculiar food. The lousy airlines must raid garbage dumps for the junk they set before passengers these days. If the elegant Concorde let him down he would tell them so on the comment card the stewardess had handed him. Satisfied with this solution, Joe took a long pull on his straight scotch and fell asleep.

In Beverly Hills, the Bistro on North Camden Drive hummed with the voices of the rich and famous. Dressed in expensive-casual, they were assembled for luncheon—all voyeurs, all exhibits.

With a bravado he did not feel, Watson Wagg entered through the etched half-glass doors and prayed the maître d' would honor his reservation. It hurt him to think of how much time had passed since he'd last visited his favorite haunt. Today he had invited Douglas Braden to be his guest. His relief was enormous when he spotted Doug already seated at a corner table. Watson Wagg waved at former studio associates and stopped to chat with other acquaintances before taking his place alongside Doug.

"Great to see you, old man," Wagg said after they had ordered drinks.

Doug's scowl was only partly facetious. "Old man? You've got years on me."

"Touchy, touchy. You look marvelous and you know it. Everyone knows it, even the little Empress."

Doug checked his midriff. "Thoughtful of her to have given us two months' notice. Another inch and I'll be in fighting form."

Wagg raised his eyebrows. "For what?"

"Let's not bullshit each other. We're seekers in the same marketplace. You want something from Marianna and so do I. The question is: What does she want from us?"

"What makes you think she wants anything?"

"Do you believe we're invited for Old Home Week? Just like that, after fifteen years? Do you think she sent us those first-class tickets, with the Concorde thrown in, because the airlines need the business? No way. I hear there's a bit of a strain between Their Imperial Majesties. A gap to be filled perhaps?"

"You have a dirty mind. How do you account for my invitation?"

"That's a puzzlement. What can you offer her? You don't have a kingdom anymore. She does." A thought struck him. "Maybe she likes you."

"Thanks," Wagg said dourly.

Doug patted his midriff. "Yup, whatever she needs I'm prepared to give it to her. All she has to do is name it."

"You're dreaming."

"I don't think so."

The waiter served their drinks and brought them the menu easel. Watson Wagg ordered eggs Benedict with plenty of hollandaise sauce. Doug requested a green salad—"easy on the oil and vinegar"—and a pot of hot coffee. He saluted with his wine glass. "To Ryal. You can take the window seat. I'll be first out the door."

The United States Secretary of State, garbed in threatening black, his long arms and legs churning like a windmill in a

gale, crossed the lobby of The Madison hotel in Washington,
D.C., and slid between the slowly closing doors of the
elevator. Apologizing to other passengers, he reached past
them to push the button that would discharge him on the
eighth floor.

Damn Calvin Gropper. Despite his departure from office
with the termination of the last administration, Gropper
seemed not to have got the message that he was no longer
head of the department. The fact that another political party
was now in power affected Gropper not at all. Shortly before
the inauguration he had obtained the ear of the new President, subtly superseding the newly appointed Secretary, Owen
Belmont.

Even this meeting in Gropper's suite was an insult. True,
Gropper's cooperation was needed in handling the delicate
situation in Bahrait, but properly the meeting should have
been taking place at this very moment in the State Department Building, in Owen Belmont's office, with Belmont himself behind the desk and Gropper, his subordinate in this
mission, facing him from an ego-diminishing pull-up chair.

"Sorry, Owen," Gropper had said when Belmont telephoned to suggest they confer. "My schedule is tight. I have
other business in Washington and some packing to do before
I meet Hilary at the airport. Why don't you get one of your
department hearses to bring you over? We can talk while I
roll my socks."

"Perhaps one of the hotel maids could do that for you,"
Belmont had replied tightly.

"I'm waiting for phone calls, also." Gropper was firm.
"Shall we say three o'clock in my suite?"

Belmont glanced at his watch. Three on the dot. He hated
himself for being there. Still, what else could he have done,
faithful public servant that he was? The President had insisted upon the meeting.

Suppressing his anger, he rapped on the door with as much
authority as he could muster and waited for Gropper to
appear. He could hear the shuffle of slippers behind the
door.

"Owen, my dear fellow, step in," Gropper said jovially. "A
man in your position doesn't linger in doorways. May I order
up something for you to eat, to drink?"

"Don't bother, Calvin. This shouldn't take too long." Belmont seated himself in a deep chair and leaned forward, his stork knees almost touching his chin. He waited while Gropper disappeared into the adjoining bedroom.

"Calvin," he called. "I'm sure the President of the United States, his Cabinet, and the entire Congress would be grateful if you neglected your underpants for just a few minutes and joined me here. This is a matter of importance."

"Certainly, Owen. Don't be testy. I must separate a few items for the stopover in Rome or Hilary will be upset with me."

"How is your wife?"

Gropper strolled back to the sitting room and sat down opposite Belmont. "You know Hilary. There's a dog show in New York. She'd rather be going there."

"Why isn't she?"

"Owen, unless your operatives are asleep at their posts, you know very well that Hilary and I have been invited to Bahrait for a preparty visit with the Shah and the Empress."

"We know that."

"If Hilary were to choose the dog show over the invitation from the Empress, relations between the United States and Bahrait could suffer some disruption. Marianna is assembling a group of her friends for this private party. Hilary and I have no illusions. Ramir himself insisted that we be included. He wanted someone to talk to besides those Hollywood oddballs and Marianna's past-life relics."

"Calvin, I follow your social life breathlessly in the *Star*. It enthralls everyone," Belmont said acidly. "However, if I may, I'd prefer to get down to the reason for my visit."

"I think I can guess."

"Very well. You know the Shah is asking for new military hardware. Claims he must have it to defend his country's position against threatened Saudi incursions. Poppycock. We know he has more enemies inside his borders than outside. He also has one of the largest war machines in the world. It's his conceit and the mounting unrest at home that's making him greedy."

Gropper nodded but did not interrupt.

"In other years our government has acceded to his demands without too many complaints from our easygoing citizens. Those days are over. Lately we've been running into flak. We have younger voters asking questions about the political mess in Bahrait. Older voters want to know why we support a regime so corrupt the Shah himself has admitted to the press that his palace clique needs cleaning up. Congressmen are worried about offending their constituencies. They're only human."

"If you say so."

Belmont ignored the remark. "Taking an American wife was the shrewdest move the Shah ever made. A real coup, Calvin. You can be proud of that one. The public didn't blink when we gave Ramir all the armament he asked for—it was a dowry the taxpayers were happy to bestow on Marianna Curtis. Same thing each time she had a baby. Instead of rattles and teddy bears, we shipped tanks and planes. No one questioned our actions. Today it's a different ball game. The public wants to know what they're getting back for playing footsies with a dictator."

"What would they like?"

"Listen carefully. I've discussed it with thoughtful congressmen and all the powers that be, right up to the President himself. The consensus is that a foothold in Bahrait, a modest American military base on the Caspian Sea, would make sense. Something like Guantánamo. We're not exactly embracing Castro but it's a comfort having a toehold on Cuban soil."

"You're suggesting our flag on Bahrait?"

"Hell, no. I'm talking about American soldiers, American military equipment under American control nestled in Bahrait, not too distant from Russia or the Gulf States, just keeping an eye on things. *That* our good people would understand. Not those let's-keep-our-noses-out-of-everything Americans, but decent, conscientious citizens who spend their dollars thoughtfully and want to know their government is doing the same."

"Owen, I hear you. Does the President believe I can persuade Ramir and his advisers to transfer a piece of their country to us?"

Belmont suppressed his annoyance. "Don't be playful, Calvin. Not *transfer*. Merely lease us some land. Did you think I had another motive for being here? If you fail, then we've all failed."

Belmont unwound himself from the chair and stood over Gropper. "It's not just the country's reputation for diplomacy that's at stake. It's yours as well."

At the door, the Secretary of State got in the last word.

"Sometimes, Calvin, I wonder which you consider more important."

The two plainclothes officers assigned to guard the Empress within Bahrait lurked at a discreet distance from their royal charge. The officers' names were Ahmed and Munni. Ahmed was clean-shaven, Munni bearded. Both were jittery.

From their positions in the observatory of the Ryal Airport, their glances darted in all directions and back to the Empress. They were distressed, as always, to see her standing alone, pressing her nose against the window of the observatory overlooking the landing field.

Compelled to approve the Empress's token disguise—thick-framed tinted glasses and a silk scarf to conceal her blond hair (a compromise when she refused to wear a wig)—the guards personally considered her attempts to avoid recognition inadequate. Equally unsettling was her practice of running down the moving steps of the escalator and onto the tarmac when she sighted an expected guest.

It was known to Ahmed and Munni that the Shah shared their disapproval of the Empress's indifference to security. A bitter quarrel between husband and wife had been overheard and repeated by servants. The Shah had imperiously directed that the Empress await visitors in the curtained rear seat of her steel-plated car. The Empress had refused to be so confined. From her present behavior, it was evident the stubborn American had won.

This was a particularly strenuous day for Ahmed and Munni. In the morning they had accompanied the Empress to the airport to meet a plane coming in from Rome. When the loudspeaker announced the arrival of the Alitalia flight, the Empress had vanished from sight. Fearful of losing her, the guards had rushed to the tarmac and found her embracing an untidy overweight woman she called Selma. Later, in the palace courtyard, the Empress had informed Ahmed and Munni that her guest, Miss Shapiro, was feeling unwell and would go directly to bed to recover from her journey. "I remind you," she said, "in two hours we leave again to meet the flight from London."

Attentive to the loudspeaker for the second time that day, Marianna heard it call out the arrival of BA's flight #203

from London. Tugging the silk scarf closer to her face, she
sped to the escalator, determined to escape the security men
struggling to match her pace.

It appeared to Marianna that the plane was disgorging an
unending stream of sleekly tailored businessmen bearing
briefcases. She watched impatiently as each man hesitated at
the head of the stairs and looked about until he located his
counterpart, another sleekly tailored businessman carrying a
briefcase, waving behind the arrival gate.

Then she saw them. Joe first, heavier than she remembered.
Wobblier, too. She knew the airline had a cutoff time for
serving drinks. She also knew the Curtises never left home
without a private stash of the hard stuff to see them through
to journey's end. Behind Joe loomed Agnes, her suit rumpled,
her orange-red hair soldered beneath its cap of hair spray.

Behind Joe and Agnes, Marianna saw Father Flynn and
her eyes dimmed with teary disbelief. The once robust priest,
now gaunt as an El Greco cardinal, descended the steps
gingerly, his bony frame adrift in an oversized suit. Clutching
the rail for support, he stopped once or twice to catch his
breath.

"Marianna!" Agnes grabbed her arm. The shouted name,
intended to be a whisper, caused nearby heads to turn and
Marianna knew the distraught security men would be closing
in.

"My darling, let me look at you!" Agnes hugged, then
released her. "Joe, isn't she the most gorgeous creature ever?
How are the kids? Who else is coming? I don't know when
we've been so thrilled." Agnes dabbed at moist eyes. "Joe,
didn't I always say she was our little queen?"

"You look marvelous yourself, Agnes. You too, Joe."

"Father—" She ducked away from the Curtises and took
the priest's hands in hers. "Dear friend, how good to have
you here. I knew you'd come when I needed you." She
scanded his face. "We have so much to talk about," she
said.

She was perplexed when he avoided her eyes.

Time was a bitch.

Marianna sat at the dressing table scanning her mirror
image for the ways in which the bitch had betrayed her. The
beauty was still there. She supposed it would be if she lived to
be eighty. But reproachful signs of the passage of years were

beginning to stand up to be counted. Lightly etched lines crossed her brow when she grimaced, the twin curves bordering her nose and mouth were deeper, and those other devils, euphemistically called laugh lines, were clearly emphasized when she was animated.

"You must not be so hard on yourself," Dr. Lasseaux had insisted. "To look twenty-three when you are thirty-eight would be grotesque. Maturity is what you have achieved."

One thing was certain: With all her wisdom, Dr. Lasseaux knew nothing about show business.

These past months, anticipating her reunion with Doug Braden and Watson Wagg, she had seen herself frozen in time, barely out of girlhood, forever distanced from maturity. This morning, with the moment of reunion approaching, she had appraised herself objectively and acknowledged that the days of her glowing youth were gone.

She was less critical of her body. Standing nude, she turned and twisted before a mirrored wall, examining herself with detachment. Yes, the body was still superb. With no unsightly "maturity," thank God.

She owed its perfection first to inherited genes, then to Martha Lyons, her shrewd onetime dramatic coach. Back in the New York theater days Martha had latched on to the teenaged Marianna Curtis and lectured her on the value of daily exercise.

"It's ridiculous," Marianna had argued. "I'm firm and flat and round in all the right places. I refuse to punish myself."

"It's not for today, dummy," Martha said. "Later on, in fifteen or twenty years when you're not so young, it'll be harder to hang on to your career if you lose your figure. You'll be grateful for disciplines begun now. Think of the future."

"That's tomorrow."

"The hell it is. Look at me. Forty-seven. Face lift, ass lift, silicone sacs in my boobs. Plenty of exercise, too. And how old do I look? Forty-two, maybe. Because there was no Martha Lyons around when I was a kid, telling me it's never too soon to start tightening. Don't laugh. It's a fight hanging in there. New gals are coming up behind you all the time. Play now, pay later—is that what you want? Those that can, do—those that can't, teach. You're a doer. Head high, shoulders back, *stretch*. You're going to the top. I'll watch from the sidelines."

The last she'd heard, Martha had thrown in the towel. She'd married a gentleman farmer from Virginia and gone to live with him in a state of contentment and obesity.

Now, flexing on the exercise bar that ran the length of the mirrored wall, she gave thanks to Martha Lyons. It was all still there—the long taut legs, the tight buttocks, the flat stomach emphasizing the high bust that an enamored theater critic, viewing her in Elizabethan costume, had lauded as "magnificent globes of such radiance as to light the universe."

She was beginning to cheer up. The coming encounter with Doug and Watson seemed less formidable. She'd evaluated her face and figure and on the whole she'd checked out fine. Hadn't a poll in a current London magazine placed her second among the most beautiful women in the world? The loyal British had awarded first place to their queen, a position Elizabeth herself had privately acknowledged she did not deserve.

Time had not left the men untouched either, she reminded herself. Over the years, magazines and newspapers had run photographs of Doug and of Watson. Less frequently than in former days, but often enough for Marianna to see that the years had changed them, too. She had observed Watson's hair graying gradually and been saddened. She had seen it abruptly turn a rich mahogany and had applauded his fighting spirit. Nor had Doug remained the classic movie idol at whom she had thrown herself so rashly. A recent photograph taken on the beach during the Cannes Film Festival displayed his sinewy torso. Barely covered by the briefest trunks, his body was embarrassingly familiar. His face, however, was altered, not by character but, she surmised, by a surgeon's knife. The loosening neck skin and the soft puffs beneath the eyes she had once kissed so lovingly were gone. Not unexpectedly, the girl to whom he was tossing a beach ball was a nymphet.

She congratulated herself on sending an aide to the airport to welcome Watson and Doug. It was theatrical, clever, to postpone her meeting with them. She had issued instructions that she was not to be interrupted by their arrival. "Say that I will see them tomorrow," she'd told the aide.

With Selma and the Boston contingent confined to their suites by fatigue, she planned to use the evening to be with her children and to relax. By morning, when she returned from her ride in the forest with Luke, she hoped Doug and

Watson would be suitably ill at ease, cowed by this new environment in which no hostess had stepped forward to greet them. She would make her entrance according to her own script. She would be rested, in control, a star.

"How do you figure it, her not being here?" Doug Braden grumbled. "Makes me feel like a dayworker picked up at a bus stop."

"Shove it, Doug. Think of that first-class round-trip ticket in your pocket, bought and paid for by Marianna Curtis. And there's a Rolls-Royce waiting over there with a chauffeur and that palace fellow who found us at the plane. We're lucky to be here, even if we'd had to thumb our way from Los Angeles."

"She did this deliberately, to humiliate us."

"You're behaving like a child. She's an Empress and we're a pair of has-beens. You damn well better pull out your plastic smile, and keep it in place till we get back to Los Angeles. If Marianna has any alms to dole out to old friends, I don't want them lost because you think you're still a heartthrob."

In the Rolls, Doug sat in pouty silence. The suave aide, Colonel Badar Noori, addressed himself to Watson Wagg, who was absorbed in watching the passing landscape.

"Only fifty years ago all of this was sand and scrub," the colonel said. "Our Shah and his father before him have made the desert flower."

"Flower?" Doug Braden said sarcastically. To the right and left he could see only low-lying brick factories, a scattering of roadside shops displaying food and clothing, some garages and gas stations, jerry-built shacks, and shabbily dressed children at play. "Flower?" he repeated.

Watson Wagg nudged him. "A figure of speech, Doug. Bahrait's made tremendous progress."

"Indeed we have, Mr. Wagg," the colonel said, bypassing Doug Braden. "We are not so dishonest as Americans. We do not conceal our less privileged citizens behind Potemkin walls as you do."

Wagg nodded understandingly.

"Potemkin?" Doug asked. "Who the hell is he?"

"*Was* he, Mr. Braden. He's been dead over two centuries. Catherine the Great of Russia enjoyed him as a lover. To reward his services she gave him the post of overseer of much of her land, and large sums of money to be spent on improving the lives of the peasants. Potemkin squandered the money, never dreaming Catherine would wish to see the improvements he had supposedly made. When he learned she planned to visit the impoverished villages he ordered facades of pretty cottages to be constructed along her road of passage. The facades concealed the wretched homes the peasants dwelt in. Catherine rode past and was immensely pleased with the results. We can assume Potemkin breathed a sigh of relief. Ever since, similar deceptions have been known as Potemkin walls."

Doug sat forward. "What's that got to do with Americans?"

Colonel Noori welcomed the question. "It has been my privilege to accompany a mission to Washington, D.C. My colleagues and I were met at Dulles Airport and were sped through the magnificent Virginia countryside to your nation's capital where we were put up at The Madison hotel. I am an ardent sightseer. In one week I visited every lovely museum and monument mentioned in the guide books. I saw well-dressed workers in the streets. I was enchanted by the gaiety and historic charm of Georgetown. When my visit was ended, a friend accompanied me for a leisurely return to Dulles Airport. I congratulated him on his good fortune in residing in such a magnificent and prosperous city. Immediately he ordered our driver to reverse our route. In the capital he showed me back-street Washington, the city behind the walls. I saw the unemployed loitering against abandoned buildings, as miserable as the peasants concealed from Catherine. I saw the tumbledown schools, the filthy streets, the rows of houses with broken windows, uninhabitable but inhabited anyway. I was stunned. I had not dreamed such poverty existed there. Were it not for my friend, I could have come and gone with my illusions intact. That, Mr. Braden, is what we call a Potemkin wall. Our Shah does not believe in deception. We may be seen for what we are, the good and the bad."

Braden mumbled in apology.

Mollified, Colonel Noori continued. "Empress Marianna has taken our needy to her heart. Since she came here as a bride, she has sought to effect valuable changes and improvements in Bahrait. We are lucky to have her. You know the Empress well?"

"We were good friends before she met the Shah. We

haven't seen her since her marriage. She was very beautiful then," Watson said.

"You will find her more so now."

"When we reach the palace, will she know we've arrived?"

"Indeed yes, Mr. Braden, although she will not see you today. The Shah is in Europe. The Empress has pressing matters she must attend to in his absence. I have been asked to extend her apologies and tell you she will join you tomorrow."

Once again Doug turned sulky. "When do we get to the palace? I need a shower."

"Look ahead, Mr. Braden. We have almost reached the park. It will not be long after that."

"Where are we now?" Wagg asked as the Rolls, immediately recognizable to the uniformed soldiers in the guardhouse, drove through gold-tipped iron gates onto a leaf-shaded road.

"On the palace grounds."

"But there is no palace."

"You will see it soon. This is—what do you call it in America? I remember—this is the front yard."

Watson Wagg shifted his body until the dashboard speedometer came into view. "My God, you've clocked three kilometers since we passed the gate."

"Be patient, Mr. Wagg. Just around the curve. Ah, there it is, the palace of the royal family, the center of the Paradise Throne."

Rising beyond an artificial lagoon, the pink marble of the palace spread across the horizon like a gleaming sunrise. Visible behind it, outlined against the cloudless sky, the onion-shaped gold dome of the royal mosque shone brilliantly.

Doug Braden whistled. "A bloody Taj Mahal. I've never seen photographs . . ."

"The Shah has discouraged picture-taking of the palace, although he recently permitted a television tour by the Empress in honor of the Jubilee. Unlike your White House, the palace does not belong to the people. It was built by His Majesty's father, Shah Gahlil, and is the personal possession of the present Shah."

In the marble entry hall Colonel Noori clicked his heels and bowed from the waist. "I will leave you now, gentlemen.

You will each have your own suite. Your bags will be taken there by the valets. Please follow them. When you are refreshed you may dine in your rooms or join the other guests in the family dining room."

"What other guests?" Doug asked.

"The parents of the Empress, Mr. and Mrs. Curtis, and Father Flynn, a priest from Boston. Miss Shapiro will not be down tonight."

"Miss Shapiro . . ."

"Miss Selma Shapiro of Hollywood."

Doug sighed. "I guess it was inevitable." He looked at Watson Wagg. "Mr. Wagg and I will dine in my suite. We have business to discuss."

It was midafternoon, a wicked time to be in bed. Outside on the Avenue Montaigne the Paris traffic, muted behind clasped metal shutters and velvet draperies, hummed agreeably like summer insects, distant, unthreatening.

Calvin Gropper lay on his side in a state of untroubled drowsiness induced by the champagne he and Hilary had downed in the salon of their suite in the Hotel Plaza-Athénée.

Minutes before, Hilary had joined him, fitting her body spoon-fashion behind his. She had thrown back the covers and her bony fingers had found his flaccid penis. With boyish pride he observed its immediate tumescence. Half drunkenly he recalled his bachelor days when his jack-in-the-box response had inspired wonder in boudoirs around the world. Since his marriage he had offered himself to no one but Hilary, yet he could not relinquish the memories of past conquests and glories.

Soon, he knew, Hilary would shift her position until her head dropped between his chunky thighs and only her heavy chestnut hair and her sharp raised white rump would be visible.

Calvin reveled in Hilary's aggressiveness. Murmuring encouragement, he rolled onto his back and drifted into his favorite fantasy. In his mind's eye he saw Hilary's Puritan forebears begin their familiar arabesque around the bed of the sinful couple. Round and round they went, black-clad men and women in funny hats and stiffly starched white collars, clucking in shock as they observed the issue of their issue perform with lewd abandon. They were often party to his marital sex life, those long-dead Puritans, and they excited him as much as Hilary's rapacious mouth and hungering cunt.

Lost in delicious reverie, Calvin did not hear the sudden blast of the telephone. When it persisted he rubbed his eyes and shook his head until it cleared. Gently he removed the enraptured Hilary from between his thighs.

"The phone," he said, his voice thick.

She looked at him blankly.

"My darling, I must answer the telephone."

Her eyes filled with reproach.

"I don't understand," he said. "I left orders—only the most important—"

"What can be so important?" She was seated on her haunches, petulant, her sex-hardened nipples a pair of accusing headlights. He leaned forward to kiss them. Then, brusquely, he turned away and lifted the phone.

"Gropper here," he rasped.

"I have disturbed your rest. Forgive me." The voice at the other end revealed no regret. "My dear Calvin, you are still asleep. This is Dr. Narid. I am with His Majesty. He wishes to speak with you."

Gropper was fully alert. "Is anything wrong?"

At the end of the phone Gropper could make out whispered dialogue tinged, he thought, with prurient laughter.

"Calvin." The familiar voice of Ramir came on the line. "Rotten of me to intrude at a tender moment. I do so for your benefit, however."

"Where are you?"

"Still in Brussels."

"I will see you tomorrow in Ryal. Why—?"

"That is what I wish to explain. I shall be detained in Brussels several days longer."

"I see."

"I knew you would. A tiny brunette with overwhelming breasts. Toothsome as a breakfast croissant. And she has a friend."

"Please, you know I can't come to Brussels. Hilary—"

"Calvin, I apologize for a tasteless notion. Actually, it is Hilary I'm thinking of as well as you. Since I will not be in Ryal for several days I see no reason to subject you and Hilary to Marianna's house party. Without me you will expire of boredom."

"What do you want me to do?"

"Cable, telephone, send a homing pigeon. Let Marianna know you will not arrive before—shall we say—Thursday? Pressing business—whatever. Let her enjoy her Americans without us. She will be just as satisfied. Meanwhile," Ramir chuckled, "continue your holiday with your wife. I will not interrupt again."

"Ramir . . . ?"

"Yes?"

"You're on holiday too. Why not Switzerland?"

There were sounds of people being sent from the room. "Don't you think I would rather be with Pia?" Ramir responded in a lowered tone. "I am barred from going to her and the baby. You heard me—barred. Pia's parents have come from Sweden for a visit. They refuse to meet me. They have no forgiveness for what I have done to their daughter. Can you believe it? Two gross peasants from Göteborg have laid down the law to the Shah of Bahrait. 'So long as we are here, he must not come,' they said. The father, a butcher, threatens to kill me. My beloved Pia. She has sacrificed so much already, I cannot ask her to give up her parents, too. And Calvin, one thing more. Visit with Dahlia. Let me know what you see and hear."

"Of course."

"My best to Hilary. Good-bye."

Calvin replaced the gold-plated receiver in its cradle and sank back into his pillow. From her crouched position between his legs, Hilary moved over him expectantly.

"Go down, baby," he grunted. He closed his eyes. "Down, baby, down."

They were in the room again, those momentarily banished Puritans, circling the bed, a phantom audience, aghast at what they were witnessing. "Watch the Jewish boy," he said for their ears alone. "See what your daughter is doing to him. Listen . . ." He stiffened, then emitted a fearsome prolonged groan. When he opened his eyes Hilary was above him. The Puritans were gone and they were alone.

In his professional life Calvin Gropper was a tidy man. He visualized his brain as a complex warren of cells furnished with folders, slots, cabinets, and boxes, holding everything from hard facts to false rumors. He took pride in knowing that each item was meticulously filed and available for easy reference whenever he chose to tap the secret vault in his head.

It irritated Calvin Gropper that Dahlia Zahedi was not yet satisfactorily categorized. As the firstborn of his friend Shah Ramir, she belonged somewhere, yet he couldn't be certain whether she was friend or foe. In childhood she had been too insignificant to warrant more than a reference card. Later, under the tutelage of Marianna. Dahlia had emerged as a lively teenaged entity, but still unworthy of serious recognition by Calvin Gropper.

Only recently had Gropper perceived Dahlia—a second-year student at the Sorbonne—as a distinct flesh-and-blood figure who, unfortunately, also possessed a mind. That this mind held political opinions as strong as his own. and often opposed to his, was disconcerting and possibly dangerous.

Calvin Gropper did not relish his assignment from Ramir to seek out Dahlia and bring her father a report of her activities. He was on holiday with Hilary. He had promised his days and nights to her.

Now, seated in the rear of a taxi, observing the outrageous Beaubourg museum, he heard Hilary's high-pitched voice. "Another Paris monstrosity. The French have gone mad."

Calvin squeezed his wife's hand and agreed. Actually, he rather liked the rainbow tubing and gleeful circus colors that were the exterior of the museum conceived by the late president of France, Georges Pompidou. At this time, however, his mind was on neither Hilary nor the museum. He was still trying to figure out what to do about Dahlia.

Dinner with both Hilary and Dahlia present was unthinkable. Once before, Gropper had received a call from Ramir. "Ring her up. You and Hilary take her to dinner. Bring me more information about her American friend. I don't like what I hear."

Dahlia had suggested meeting at the Restaurant Hiep-Long on the Left Bank. "It's Vietnamese. Authentic cuisine. You and Hilary will adore it."

Excited by the promise of someplace new and exotic, Hilary had come along willingly. One step into the restaurant and her bright hopes had faded. Tiled flooring, crudely finished oblong tables laid with vinyl cloths and paper napkins assaulted her eyes. In a corner, Dahlia and a handsome black man introduced as Regis had already appropriated the padded bench along the wall, leaving two unfinished wooden chairs for the Groppers. Adjusting her long torso to her seat, Hilary encountered a splinter on the leg of her chair and swore openly as a wide ladder crept up her nylon stocking.

There were no menus. Dahlia and a distinctly hostile Regis, without consulting them, took over the ordering of dinner in fluent French and what Gropper accepted to be fair Vietnamese, since there was considerable banter in both languages between the young couple and the waiter.

Hilary had tried to be a good sport that evening, Calvin recalled. She conceded the food was passable and she consumed strong gin to lighten her mood. Unhappily, the gin and the alarming revolutionary propaganda spouted by Dahlia's lover had brought on a headache. Excusing herself, Hilary had asked for the bathroom. The owner had led her to the rear of the restaurant, past red and blue beaded curtains to a door marked *toilette*. Finding herself in a cubbyhole available to patrons and employees, both male and female, Hilary had retched over the sink. After rinsing her mouth and hands with tepid water and patting them dry with coarse paper towels, Hilary had returned to the table looking green. "We're leaving," she announced, snatching her jacket from the back of her chair. "Calvin, I must get back to the hotel at once."

In the taxi, her head resting on Calvin's shoulder, she had recovered sufficiently to deliver an ultimatum. "Choose between us," she said. "You are not one of Ramir's henchmen. You were Secretary of State in the Cabinet of the President of the United States . . ." She paused for emphasis, then continued, "of *America*. You are an illustrious man. I will not be subjected to another insulting evening with those radicals. And you, Calvin, will lose my respect if you ever again toady to that asshole Shah."

The miserable scene had taken place months ago. Hilary, too, had a file-cabinet memory. Whenever she thought Calvin's behavior in distinguished company bordered on the obsequious, she never failed to remind him of the evening in Hiep-Long's.

Dinner, lunch, breakfast, even a street encounter with Dahlia was impossible.

His only alternative was a telephone call to the apartment Dahlia shared with Regis on the rue de l'Université. He prayed to high heaven for a few minutes free of Hilary so that he could place his call. And then he prayed that neither Dahlia nor Regis would be there to answer. Gropper had his

informants also. He knew that Dahlia and her lover frequently passed their time at one of the radical-infested brasseries
that flourished on the Left Bank, or at fiery meetings held in
cobwebbed attics.

The question was: Who was endangered? The rumor repository file in Gropper's head told him Dahlia was capable
of action against her own father, yet he could not believe it
was possible. Political wisdom made him certain her lover's
activities were under constant surveillance by Ramir's secret
police operating in Paris.

Did Ramir believe he, Calvin Gropper, could hold a
reasonable conversation with Dahlia and change the mind of
the firebrand she had become? Unlikely. But he had his
marching orders. He would try.

Bouncing along in the taxi, he agreed with Hilary that
bombs did indeed have a purpose in the world and one of
them was to blow up M. Pompidou's museum. When she was
sufficiently appeased—a light pubic pat took care of that—he
suggested she ask the taxi driver to drop her off on the
Faubourg Saint-Honoré to have her hair fixed by Alexandre.
He, meanwhile, would dispose of a few unavoidable business
calls.

"I have no appointment," she fretted.

"Tell them you are Mrs. Calvin Gropper. There will be no
problem." He repeated the pubic pat. "And tell Alexandre
your husband wishes your hair arranged in a loose, careless
style. I intend to disarrange it later." He paused. "Several
times."

With Hilary disposed of, Calvin proceeded to the Plaza-
Athénée, walking part way to postpone his unwelcome assignment. In his suite he settled on the edge of the bed and
dialed Dahlia's number.

Luck was against him. Dahlia was at home.

"Darling, it's Gropper here. Hilary and I are in Paris."

"You're calling about dinner."

"Not exactly. Your father talked to me from Brussels. He
asked me to inquire if there was anything I could do for you
before you leave for Bahrait." His marmalade charm oozed
through the receiver. "I won't suggest a meeting. Clearly you
and Hilary are not meant for each other."

"A diplomatic understatement."

"I'll be frank. Hilary is at Alexandre's. I stole this moment
to talk to you."

"Calvin, if that's all you steal today, the world is a safer place."

"Funny child," he said cheerfully. "All going well?"

"Perfectly. Why do you bother to ask? Father and his secret police know all there is to know about Regis and me."

"Come now, Dahlia. You hear foolish lies about us and you believe . . ."

"*Us?* Calvin, you're getting sloppy. When did you join Father's fraternity?"

"My sweet Dahlia, I can tell you are inflamed by those youthful fanatics. It's a phase. I went through it myself. Let us talk about it in Ryal, shall we?"

"I'll be there."

"Alone?"

"Say it—you want to know if I'm bringing Regis. The answer is no. I won't feed him to Father's local piranhas."

Gropper's annoyance increased. Didn't Ramir know his daughter was defiant, willful, stubborn? And somewhat stupid, too? Why was he talking to this unpleasant child? Why, after years of friendship with Ramir, after becoming a figure of international awe in his own right, was he still fawning over royalty? He could suppress his irritation with Dahlia, but he could not deal with the image of himself as a lackey.

He heard a key turn in the lock of the adjoining sitting room. "I must go. There's someone at the door," he said nervously.

"Hilary, back from Alexandre's?"

"Probably."

"And you're afraid to be caught talking to me?"

"It wouldn't be wise."

"Calvin, you're pathetic."

"We'll talk about that too," he mumbled and hung up.

He hurried to the sitting room. Hilary was there, coiffed and shellacked, waiting to be disarranged—and he had promises to keep.

13

The tapping on the door was timid but insistent. Whoever stood behind it knew the way to her suite and was known to the security guards stationed along the corridor.

Groggily, Marianna pulled on a robe and walked barefoot from her bedroom to the entry door of the salon. She was certain it wasn't Luke, who had his own key and who never came to her in the middle of the night without telephoning first. Nor would it be one of the children. Ramir had decreed almost from their infancy that they remain in their own wing of the palace throughout the night. No matter that one of them might call out for mother or father. They had nurse-maids to see to their needs. They were to be raised as he had been, to be tough and independent, with none of the unneces-sary coddling that ruined American children. She had put up a ferocious fight for their privilege to come to her, and she had lost. No, definitely, it was not one of the children.

More curious than concerned, Marianna swung the door wide. Selma stood there shivering. With her eyes hidden behind dark glasses, her body wrapped in a terry-cloth robe, she might have been a forsaken punch-drunk boxer. "Lemme in," she said.

Marianna stepped aside. "What's wrong? It's three in the morning."

"Wrong?" Selma dropped into a chair. "What could be wrong? I just got out of that black onyx clamshell you call a bathtub. Look, I'm a Botticelli virgin risen from the sea."

"Sorry to spoil the illusion. You look terrible."

"You're not mad because I dropped in—?"

"Don't be foolish. It's time we talked. You weren't ready on the drive from the airport."

"Now I'm ready."

"Hold it. I'm pouring you a drink and then you can start." She led Selma to a sofa, poured a shot of whiskey, and handed it to Selma as she sat down beside her. "What happened in Venice?"

"Instant replay or the edited version?"

"Up to you. What's Gino pulling this time?"

"Usual tricks. Insisted on his directorial prerogative to cast *Pantheon*. Naturally he chose his leading lady from a distinguished clan of Venetian pimps and sluts. To eliminate competition he picked a leading man who comes from a long line of Venetian fags. Remarkable family. Every generation one male jumps the fence long enough to keep the ancestral name from dying out. The picture stinks but Gino's having a ball."

"Selma, my poor darling. Why do you stand for it?"

"Why do I stand for it? Because every time I make a noise he throws me another of his best samples, that's why. He reminds me what a lucky klutz I am even to know him."

"There are other men for you. You told me so yourself. Dr. Sternbaum, that nice dentist . . ."

"Periodontist."

"Okay, periodontist. You still see him. He could give you a good marriage, kids. What's the matter with him?"

"Wrong drill."

"Not funny." Marianna watched Selma pour another drink. "Gino's exploiting you. It'll get worse."

Selma's eyes grew narrower. "You're antagonizing me, Queenie. That's no great prize you pulled from the Crackerjack box. A Shah? Big deal. Call him a husband? You're as stuck as I am."

"Selma, put down that glass," Marianna said sharply.

Selma stared at this new Marianna. "Yes, *ma'am.*"

"You and I are friends," Marianna said furiously. "That doesn't mean we're alike. You're stuck because it pleases you to be stuck. Well, it doesn't please me. Not one single goddam bit! I'm getting out, do you understand? Out!"

Selma blinked. "Out of what? Where you going?"

"I'm leaving Bahrait. Not forever. But for a good long while. I'm going back to Hollywood. I intend to make another movie—maybe more than one." Her voice rose. "I'm going to do what *I* want—I'm going to be in charge of my life again."

"Oh no! Is that why those creeps are here? I saw them, Wagg and Braden, in the courtyard. You're not going to fool around with *them.*"

"They don't know it yet but, yes, that's what I'm planning to do."

"But why them? If you wanted to make a picture, why didn't you come to me? I never guessed . . ."

"I couldn't. I wouldn't. I see how you sweat to keep Gino working. You don't need another hanger-on begging you for favors."

"Favors! What's with favors? It would be a coup if I could bring you back to Hanover."

"Are you so sure? Marianna Curtis disappeared from the screen a long time ago. She's big on the late, late show. The movie buffs adore her. But this is *me*, fifteen years later, with no identity except as Mrs. Shah—a consort, a satellite. Am I still a star or have I been stashed away with memorabilia?"

"You're known all over the world!"

"So is Grace Kelly. Can you guarantee the kids would line up to see her comeback? I wouldn't bet on it. How about Empress Soraya? She was married to a Shah, too. What happened to her picture career? Or Rita Hayworth's. Did it help anything when she became Aly Khan's princess? Naturally, my first thought was to turn to you. You'd have come through, but I couldn't let you take the risk."

"Then what do you expect that pair of nobodies to do for you?"

"They're smooth, especially Watson. Behind that Stanford exterior is the soul of a con man. I'll tease them along, let them think they're tempting me. When I give in, Watson will find someone to put up the financing, someone outside the industry who admires me and who doesn't understand box office the way you and I do. Watson can't do it alone, but my name reunited with Doug's—who can tell? we might have a hit."

"Like MacDonald and Eddy?"

Marianna smiled. "Not exactly, but you're catching on."

"What does Ramir think?"

"He doesn't know. Luckily he's been detained in Belgium. Before he returns to Ryal I'll have Watson and Doug in a fever. It'll be a *fait accompli*, a huge surprise to Ramir. He's dealt me a few lately. Now it's my turn."

It was dawn before Selma lifted her bulk and shuffled down the hall to her own rooms.

Marianna lay abed, praying for sleep to overtake her. Without a sedative, there was no way it would. She was too keyed up, yet a pill at this hour was out of the question. It would leave her bleary and she wanted her head clear for the day ahead.

Bypassing the palace switchboard, she used her private line to reach Luke in his cottage adjoining the schoolhouse.

"Professor," she said. "I'm wide-awake, overstimulated. I need something to burn up my energy."

"Be right over," he promised. "Don't move."

"No, dopey, not *that*. Meet me at the stables. Half hour? Perfect." And she rang off.

Their early morning canters into the pine forest were a ritual that kept them close even when Ramir was in residence at the palace. Once, when mist still shrouded the trees, they had gone deep into the woods and Luke had made love to her. Terrified of discovery, alert to the chatter of curious squirrels and the crackling of each pine needle, she had been unable to respond. They had agreed that lovemaking outdoors was not for them. Not here, not yet.

On the bridle path she told him what she'd been loath to bring up before—that despite her love for him she needed to get away, to Hollywood, to make one more picture.

"Luke, you're not angry?"

"I'm not angry."

"When Ramir comes home I want to present him with the whole package tied tight with a bright pink bow. If it's not settled he'll go after my insecurities, bully me, scare me out of the whole idea. Luke, they'll want me, won't they?"

"You have nothing to worry about. *I* do, though. How long do you think you'll be gone?"

"Six months, seven at the most."

"I'll be climbing the wall."

She laughed. "Don't you think I'd be, too? I have everything figured out. Once the deal is set, you can arrange your trip to the States. You visit Stevie every year. This time bring him to Hollywood. Let me meet him. I'd love that. Promise him Disneyland, the beach, the mountains, a tour of the studio. He'll be mad about California. You and I, we'll be together, not always, but often enough to keep us sane. Always—that's for another time."

The mist was gone, the sun bright when they returned their horses to the stableboys. Arm in arm they strolled toward the palace, breaking apart as they approached the clearing.

General Sahid Mojeeb, commander-in-chief of Bahrait's armed forces, stood in the forecourt, waiting. As Marianna and Luke stepped into the clearing he hurried toward them.

"Your Majesty, you are more radiant than ever. Mr. Tremayne, you are a fortunate man to share our forest and our Empress on such a magnificent morning."

"I am indeed, sir," Luke said. "After Switzerland, it's good to be here."

"Welcome home, General," Marianna said. "You're radiating confidence this morning. Your meeting with King Fouad must have been rewarding."

"It went well enough. The King has agreed to a private visit after the Jubilee."

"Good. May I say, General, you're also looking more dapper than usual."

General Mojeeb smiled self-consciously. His uniforms were made in London by the haberdasher to Prince Philip. Although he disliked his reputation as a dandy, he was not sufficiently offended to give up his tailor.

"Are you here to greet us?" Marianna asked.

"That and something more. I have a message for Her Majesty. Mr. Tremayne, if you will excuse us . . ."

Luke stepped away. "As the Empress wishes."

"Please, Luke . . . tell the children to expect me later."

She turned her back to Luke and addressed the general. "What can be so important? Why can't it wait until I've had my breakfast?"

"My apologies, Your Majesty. I thought you would want to know at once."

"Know what?"

"That a message has been received from His Majesty. He wished to speak to you. Unfortunately you had already left with Mr. Tremayne. I was requested to deliver it personally."

"Yes?"

"Just this. His Majesty finds it impossible to return from Belgium as scheduled. He will be detained for several days."

"But our guests—doesn't he know they've begun to arrive?"

"He does. His Majesty appreciates the importance of this week to both of you. Only a most urgent affair of state could keep him away. Mr. Gropper will be involved in certain meetings with His Majesty. The Groppers will be delayed as well. His Majesty begs you to be understanding."

"That was the entire message?"

"That, and his expression of love for you and the children.

He will advise us when we may expect him. If there is anything . . ."

"Thank you. It's all right." Her smile surprised him. "It's really *quite* all right. It makes everything easier."

There was no escape from those eyes. They were chilling and arrogant and they glowered relentlessly from the portraits lining the brocaded walls. Glaring out of burnished gold frames, they openly disliked the two men hastening down the corridor.

"Those beggers are making me perspire," Doug complained.

"Don't let the Shah hear you. They're his ancestors—generals, tribal chiefs, other Shahs. One day Ramir will be up there with them."

"Jeezus, look at that ferocious bastard with the twirly moustache. And the next one with the ruby in his turban. Wonder who he murdered before he stole it."

"How about the guy alongside him, the one with the scimitar in his hand? Must have bloodied a hundred heads with that chunk of steel."

"Why do they keep *staring?*" Doug asked.

"An ancient artist's trick. Subjects focused their eyes on the eyes of the painter. The painter caught the look and transferred it to canvas. Gives the illusion the eyes are following wherever you go."

"Creepy s.o.b.'s. What's with Marianna, making us walk the plank before we can get a cup of coffee?"

"She isn't making us do anything. You wanted to see the palace. The valet told you to go to the end of the hall for breakfast and here we are. Problem is you're afraid to face Marianna again. You don't know if she's wooing you or preparing to have you castrated. My advice is, stay cool. If she has anything in mind for either of us, let it come from her."

"Open the goddam door. I can't deal with this conversation on an empty stomach." Doug looked over his shoulder and grimaced at the portraits. "And you, punks, stay where you are."

"I beg your pardon, sir?" A uniformed officer stood in the open doorway, eyebrows lifted. "I am Major Lahari, chief of the Palace Household Staff. I have been expecting you. Gentlemen, please follow me."

Doug and Watson did as they were told.

"Hey, what's this?" Doug stood openmouthed, taking in the room ahead.

"Obviously a perfect reproduction of a room in an English hunting lodge," Watson replied.

"Why are you surprised, gentlemen?" Major Lahari asked. "It was the whim of a former Shah, the great Rasim. He traveled widely in England at the invitation of Queen Victoria. Due to her kindness he was an honored guest at numerous country houses belonging to members of the peerage. He delighted in early morning fox hunting and savored the splendid breakfasts that followed the hunt. Upon his return from abroad he imported the finest English architects and commissioned them to re-create his favorite room."

"Wasn't that—eccentric?"

"Not at all, Mr. Wagg. Everything you see—the oak paneling, the oak furniture, the hand-carved fireplace, the portrait of the late Shah in his hunting pinks, the carpets, the leaded windows—everything is authentic. American designers come to Bahrait in the service of your millionaires to study our architecture and decor. Then they rush home and attempt to duplicate it overnight in places like *Texas*. That, gentlemen, is eccentric."

Rebuked, the men from Hollywood followed Major Lahari to a curved buffet table. "An *original* hunt table, Mr. Wagg and Mr. Braden. And a typical hunt breakfast. In the covered serving dishes you will find kippers, potatoes, kidneys, scrambled eggs, sausages, cheeses. Over here we have native fruits —papayas, mangoes, figs. Whatever you do not find, you may request of the waiters. They are here to serve you. If you will excuse me, I will leave you to each other."

"Touchy bastard," Doug grouched when they were settled at one of the round oak tables. He surveyed the room and with his coffee cup addressed the portrait of the late Shah hanging above the mantel. "Here's looking at you, buddy," he said.

His eyes roved the room in wonder. "Marianna Curtis— who'd have believed it? I've tracked her progress from the day the Shah came on the scene." He grimaced, pretending pain. "It sure hurts a fella, being forgotten so fast. But I console myself. Her happiness was my dearest wish. Happiness? Who wouldn't have it in a setup as plush as this? Her

Majesty, Miss Callahan, must be knocked out every day of her life."

"No, Doug, I'm not."

They had not heard her open the door, nor seen her move toward a far window. Shafts of sunshine pierced her deceptively demure dress. Shrewdly chosen in Paris for this very moment, it was made of lemony cotton, so gauzy it concealed her with the thoroughness of a cobweb.

The effect was perfect. With her face shadowed and her figure silhouetted, she was damn near flawless. Later they might discover an imperfection or two, but they would never forget their first reaction to Marianna Curtis since her flight from Hollywood fifteen years ago.

Caught unaware, the two men fell silent. Slowly they placed their knives and forks on their plates and pushed back their chairs.

"Marianna." Doug tightened his stomach as he approached her. "You're magnificent." He spoke with honest awe. "And a witch. You've made time stand still."

"Thank you." She touched his extended hands, then turned toward a hesitant Watson Wagg. "And thank you, dear friend, for coming." She kissed his cheek. "Such a long time . . . Remember our first meeting at the Los Angeles airport? I can tell you now, I was terrified."

"I knew that."

"And you were kind, always kind."

"No kinder than you to extend this invitation—to allow me to be here, a cat looking at a queen."

Twitchy at being excluded, Doug broke in. "A sentimental reunion for me, too. So many years."

Recalling their parting, she offered him her best Mona Lisa smile. "Yes, so many years."

Now, sizing him up in the Hunt Room of the Paradise Palace, she asked herself how she could have been so stupid. He was still handsome and he still had his hair. She was pleased about that. It made her plans for him feasible. She was certain he had remained shallow and that, too, pleased her. She could manipulate him easily. The challenge would be to convince him—and Watson—that they were the ones who were manipulating her.

"Do go back to your breakfast, please," she said. "I couldn't resist stopping by. I wish I could stay but it's time for me to visit the schoolhouse. My children are expecting me."

"When will we see you again?" Wagg asked.

"Shall we say in one hour? There's a terrace beyond the Reception Hall. I'll be there."

"At the end of the corridor?"

"Yes, Doug. It means passing those ferocious portraits again. Don't look surprised. Major Lahari reported they disturbed you. Listening devices are prohibited in the palace. However, we do maintain our own old-fashioned methods of keeping in touch."

Marianna, unqueenly in white jeans and a plaid shirt, dashed outdoors. Ahead she could make out Joe and Agnes Curtis proceeding unsteadily on the path to the palace schoolhouse. Increasing her own speed, she looked beyond them to the low-lying cream-colored structure. Once again she experienced a flush of pride, recalling that because of her persistence, the schoolhouse had become a reality.

Even now she could smile, recalling how she had resisted Calvin Gropper's role in choosing the headmaster and how tongue-tied she had been the first time she set eyes on the American professor with the mocking eyes and defiant moustache who was to become her lover.

She remembered how, working together, she and Luke had selected each student, stocking the school like a stable of thoroughbreds, with the finest specimens available. When it had been readied Ramir himself had opened it in a formal ceremony.

She wondered sometimes if Ramir knew that by the time the first class graduated she and Luke had begun their affair.

Shaking thoughts of Luke from her head, Marianna overtook Joe and Agnes and slipped between them. A whiff of whiskey assaulted her nostrils and she glanced from one to the other.

"It's her," Joe whispered. "Hitting the spirits. Started about a year ago." His shoulders sagged and he kept his voice low. "Always did like the stuff, she did."

Agnes winked. "You two have secrets? Why don't I just toddle along. Keep talking, Joe."

They fell back and watched Agnes, wearing stiletto-heeled pumps, wiggle her way down the path.

"I like a bit myself," Joe confessed. "But we made a pact after your mother died. Better go easy, we said, or we'd wind up the same way Madge did." He caught Marianna's cold glare. "Marianna, I'm sorry. Shouldn't be bringing skeletons out of the closet at a time like this."

"It doesn't matter. What kicked her off?"

"Forget I said anything. We're here for a good time. It's not fair, me dragging out our troubles and spoiling your party."

"You're stalling, Joe. You know you're going to tell me. Get it out fast."

"It's the business, honey. The construction trade isn't what it used to be. We got carried away. Expanded more than the times called for. Just to show Them."

"Them?"

"You remember Them, Marianna. You were our little girl when we began running around with Them. We bought the house in Concord, the summer place on the Cape, and we joined the country club. Wherever They went, we went too. Still do. Agnes eats it up. It's what she dreamed of all her life, exactly like your mother. Get off Pleasant Street, out of Charlestown, as far as possible from the old neighborhood."

"You both got what you wanted."

"Yeah, and now it's sliding away. Scares Agnes half to death. Thinks one little step down, she'll catch her goddam heels and fall all the way back to Charlestown."

"That's nonsense."

"Sure is. At worst we could make do somewhere in between. Only Aggie can't see it that way. You and I, we got another loony to deal with—sorry about that, Marianna— unless we do something in a hurry."

"Let's hear it, Joe. What do you want from me?"

"Money."

"Money. Just like that? A handout so you can keep up with Them?"

"It wouldn't look good, your own folks cracking up financially, Agnes going over the edge with the bottle, and you traipsing around in your diamond tiara."

"Joe, you're trying to blackmail me."

"Wouldn't be the first case of blackmail in our family. Father Flynn sure did a job on us. Of course it worked out fine. You brought us nothing but pleasure." He grinned, showing irregular teeth.

"Dammit, I was only twelve years old. I wasn't making my own decisions then. I cut out as soon as I could."

"Water under the bridge, darling. Once we had you, we realized the Lord had bestowed a treasure."

"Crap, Joe. We never liked each other. You're not stuck with me anymore. And I'm not sure I'm stuck with you. What did you have in mind?"

"Your hubby's looking into American investments in case things get shaky over here. Near Salem there's land for a shipbuilding development. It'll mean housing, a shopping center, practically a new town. He's interested in it. If he could just throw the job my way . . ."

"Why hasn't he?"

"Some big shots are fighting over it. You know Massachusetts politicians. If His Majesty could lean on them a little. An extra bonus here and there in my name . . ."

"That's bribery."

"This country of yours hasn't got such clean hands. Not from what I hear. Another smudge won't hurt it any."

Ahead they saw Agnes tottering toward the schoolhouse door.

"Hey, Aggie, hold up," Joe called. "Let's go in together." He faced Marianna. "See what I mean? I better hang on to her. How many students you got in there?"

"Twenty-three, twenty-four. Why?"

"Bahraitian kids?"

"No, they're from everywhere. About a third are Americans."

"The American kids are okay. They've seen their folks get loaded at home. They'll think Aggie is funny. But the other kids, chances are they'll be scared shitless."

"Joe, she can't go in like that!"

"You're seeing the light. I'll head her off and have her sobered up by teatime. You won't be ashamed when Ramir gets home, either. I'll read her the riot act, and I'll ditch the bottles she brought in. That's the way we play the game, isn't it, my girl? I scratch your back and you scratch mine."

The shaded terrace obviously was failing its purpose. Conceived as an area of repose with comfortable padded chairs and flowering plants, it overlooked a glossy lawn that sloped into an unrippled pond. For Watson Wagg and Douglas Braden the terrace could just as well have been a windowless cell. They paced it side by side, intently engaged in dialogue.

"Do you think she'll do it?" Doug lit a cigarette, drew on it once, and ground it into the tile flooring.

"For the hundredth time I remind you, *she* sent for *us*."

"She never had anything against you."

"True. Still this is my first invitation in fifteen years."

"What about me? She's so high and mighty, could be she brought me here to rub my nose in it."

"Not a bad idea," Watson agreed. "That's what you deserve."

"Up yours. I've already got the shakes. Stop hitting me."

"Sorry. Sometimes I forget you're sensitive and not too bright. Didn't you read anything into that stagy appearance in the Hunt Room? She's after something herself."

"What? She's got the whole damned world putting out for her."

"On the surface, yes," Wagg mused. "That's why it doesn't add up. She was so *actressy*, in an obvious way. Could be the Shah's talked her into some stunt—like get Marianna Curtis back on the screen. Soften the great American unwashed. Americans are sore as hell at this country. They watch television and sputter into their newspapers and want to know why the U.S.A. is supporting a dictator. So what does the dictator do? He trots out his idolized movie-star wife. He says: 'Sweetheart, put the crown in the vault for a while. Step in front of the Hollywood cameras again. Grant interviews. Tell the world what a wonderful guy your husband is.' They'll figure if Marianna Curtis goes on loving him he can't be that bad." Watson beamed, entranced by the beauty of his logic.

Doug was still worried. "How do I fit in?"

"Perfectly, that's how. You handed her a raw deal. You owe her a shot at getting even."

"Meaning what?" Doug's brows came together in a frown.

"Meaning, I have a gambler's hunch she wants to return to Hollywood and when she does it'll be a Marianna Curtis picture the whole way. Former Screen Lovers Reunited! That'll be the ballyhoo. But when it comes to the nitty-gritty, Doug, you won't be the star anymore. You'll be there, but you won't reach her shoulders. Think you could handle that?"

"I'd hate it."

"Where are you now? In the pits."

Doug was thoughtful. "So she takes me on and at least I'm alive professionally. Is that what you're saying? She hands me a part where I climb on my hind legs and beg and she gets her revenge."

"See, it's flawless." Wagg said.

Doug scowled. "I love it already, you son-of-a-bitch. What about a property?"

"That's the best part. For years I've had my eye on a certain novel. I don't own it but once Marianna agrees. I can swing an option. It's a woman's story. They're going to be hot again. The male lead is definitely second banana. Your agent won't get rich, but it's a start. You may be a very lucky guy."

"You too, chum."

"I'm not being condescending. My view of my place in the industry is painfully clear. No one questions my talent—they just won't let me touch their money. 'Light-fingered Watson Wagg.' That's what some smart-ass called me in *Daily Variety*. They won't believe I've changed."

"Have you?"

Wagg shook his head. "Who knows? A little penny-ante stuff now and then—I don't count that. The big stakes? Since the scandal I haven't been tested. No one ever again has placed financing in my hands and said 'Go, man.' With Marianna in my pocket—and you, Doug—it's a lead-pipe cinch."

Arriving at the terrace. Marianna saw them moving restlessly, their hands cutting the air as they talked. From the range of their expressions she suspected they were conspiring and she was satisfied.

After inviting them to be seated she settled between them and joined in a rapid exchange of compliments and platitudes. They had run through the latest Hollywood gossip when Watson Wagg released a deep sigh.

"What an enchanting corner of the world," he said. "How do you tear yourself away . . . ?"

"Not easily."

"You have everything here," Doug put in. "Unearthly beauty, love, peace." He was pensive as a pair of courting swans emerged from a cove. "Look at those two—right on cue, like a couple of actors who know their lines."

"They're real. It's all real."

Doug nodded. "Perfect marriage, adoring husband, children. No threatening harem . . ."

"Ramir's grandfather banned harems when he was the Shah. He thought one woman at a time was enough for any man."

"Smart old bugger. You must be very happy."

"I'm content."

Watson pulled his chair alongside hers. "Are you?"

"Of course. What more could I want?"

"Excitement, Marianna. Excitement, the emotion that surpasses contentment." He bounded from his seat and stood above her. "This is heavenly but are you ready for heaven? Don't you miss it? Tell the truth."

"Miss what? You're confusing me."

"Hollywood. The thrill of moviemaking, the company of fellow artists. What can match the joy of a piece of work well done? Remember the tensions, Marianna—the bickering on the set, the anxiety of viewing daily rushes, the sneak previews where you sat biting your nails? Not always fun but you knew you were *alive*. Contentment—that's for the swans out there, not for you."

"A young woman like you," Doug added.

"Young?" She turned on him angrily. "You both know how old I am. Thirty-eight. And I know how old you are, Doug—three times the age of that child you brought to Cannes."

Braden looked at her, bewildered. "What . . . ?"

"*Paris Match*," she said. "They checked you out—not in the *Motion Picture Almanac* but in your high school yearbook back in Winnetka. Your own daughter is older than what's-her-name . . ."

"Lila," he said sheepishly. "She's nothing—a face, a body that dispenses favors without discrimination. She's ambitious like the rest of them." Haughtily, he sat erect in his chair. "I'm still a name, you know. Lila thinks I can advance her career. If I don't it makes no difference. She's had a romp with Doug Braden, an experience she can brag about to her friends."

"Doug, shut up!" Wagg ordered. "Marianna, don't take him seriously."

She shook her head. "Same old Doug."

"No," Wagg said. "Time tempers us, humbles us, makes us re-evaluate. Even Doug. It pains me to see you two argue.

You were magic once. Watching you this morning, I can imagine it happening again."

"What happening?" Her eyes widened innocently.

Wagg picked up steam. "The right story, a sensitive director—and Curtis and Braden once more burning up the screen."

"And Watson Wagg producing?"

"Exactly. It would be a major event in motion picture history, bigger than *Shadow Darkens*." He stopped, chagrined.

She stared at Braden. "I have a long memory."

Doug squirmed, bravado gone.

"Don't fret," she said. "What I remember isn't all bad."

Watson Wagg broke in. "The three of us, Marianna, think of it. . . . Your husband would be proud."

"My husband *is* proud. Do you think he needs a public exhibition of my acting skills to take pride in me?"

Wagg deflated. "It was a ridiculous notion."

"I'm afraid so. If I hadn't personally invited the two of you, I'd suspect you had contrived this entire scheme in Hollywood and flown over for the hard sell."

She rose and Doug came to his feet beside her. "Gentlemen," she said, "you're here to taste the pleasures of our palace. Would you like to swim, ride, play golf or tennis, visit my husband's zoo? Lieutenant Naggi." She snapped her fingers and a slender uniformed officer materialized in the doorway. "Watch over my friends. I want their stay with us to be memorable." She turned to her guests. "We'll meet again over cocktails. Lieutenant Naggi will direct you to the family wing."

She watched the two men trail the lieutenant. "Doug, Watson," she called after them. "Don't be discouraged. What you've proposed—it's tempting. A woman can change her mind, you know."

They looked back at her expectantly. "For this woman it's more difficult," she added. "An Empress has more than her own mind to change."

Joe Curtis peered through the slit between the double doors of his suite and checked the corridor to the right and left for signs of life. With glee he noted that the security guards were not about. Taking a leak, he surmised. Blessing the saints that Aggie was dozing off the strains of the day, he started on his prowl. Aggie gave him hell whenever he did this, blasting at him that she hadn't known she'd married a goddam Peeping Tom.

Aggie didn't understand. He wasn't after anything dirty. He had normal curiosity, like any healthy man. He liked knowing what was on the other side of doors and windows and walls. Especially doors. Aggie had come down on him like a ton of bricks that time she caught him sneaking along the third-floor corridor of the Hotel George V in Paris.

"I just want to know how the other half lives," he had whined when she finally came up for air.

"*We're* the other half, stupid," she retorted.

"The hell we are. We're *tourists*." He spat out the word. "Marianna got on to the manager and he gave us two rooms for two days. The other half, they take mile-long suites on a year-round basis. Some years they pay and don't even show up."

"That's none of our business. Get your tail back inside before we both get thrown out."

Today Joe had a particular purpose in pussyfooting from door to door. Previous prowls had familiarized him with each of the suites. He knew some were grander than others. It was easy enough to figure out that the fanciest went to the most honored guests. Others were assigned, in declining order, according to some mysterious rating system employed by Marianna and her Shah.

On their initial visit to the palace Joe and Aggie had been the only guests. They had been escorted to large airy rooms looking out on the lawn and the pond. Overwhelmed, they had expressed their appreciation to Marianna. She had promptly designated the suite as Mr. and Mrs. Curtis's. She promised they would have the same rooms each time they returned to Ryal, and she had kept her word. By the second or third visit it dawned on Joe that he had been deprived of his measuring stick. He had no way of finding out how he and Aggie ranked on the royal guest roster.

His frustration did not diminish his interest in how other guests rated.

Padding close to the wall he could make out the voices of the two Hollywood hotshots—not so hot these days according to the dope Joe picked up. They had adjoining accommodations, similar to Joe and Aggie's. Joe didn't begrudge them their equal status. It was their first visit to Ryal and probably their last. If Marianna wanted to dog it up in front of them, more power to her. What good was being an Empress if you couldn't show off to old friends now and then?

Farther down the hall he put his ear to another suite. Silence. He knew it belonged to that tub of lard, Selma Shapiro. He also knew it was a larger suite than his own and that bugged him. Yesterday he had spotted Selma as her bags were being carried in. Marianna had introduced them as they passed on the marble staircase. Selma had looked at him blankly, mumbled "Glad to meet you"—although she had met him before—and kept moving. Joe hoped someone would have the good sense to stick her under a shower, fix her hair, and get her into fresh clothes before tonight's get-together. He didn't think he could possibly eat his dinner with anything that unappetizing at the table.

Reversing his route, Joe headed toward his own quarters. He listened at the bedroom door, satisfied himself that Aggie was still asleep, and returned to the corridor. He stepped firmly. He knew where he was going. To the end of the long hall, to the suite to end all suites, to the ballroom-sized rooms usually reserved for esteemed heads of state.

The oversized double doors lording it over the corridor didn't scare him. He had learned from the servants that the expected occupants would not appear for another day or two. Besides, he'd entered those doors before—uninvited to be sure—and he was familiar with what lay on the other side. It was time for another lone visit to see what, if any, high-toned changes had been made. He tried to enter, found the doors locked, and gave them a swift ineffective kick.

Not that it mattered really. He could still picture the suite as he had seen it last. A corner sitting room stretching from here to tomorrow. Two posh bedrooms. Mirrored dressing rooms alongside marble bathrooms with tubs like Olympic swimming pools. The la-de-da suite had its own kitchen and servants' quarters for the around-the-clock staff. Billionaires from the Gulf States and Europe and beyond had occupied the Royal Guest Quarters. On those occasions the floor was swept clean of other visitors. Personal entourages took over adjacent rooms to be at the service of their leaders.

Joe had never been in Ryal during a state visit. He read about them in the Boston newspapers and he and Aggie kidded on the square about never getting the super grand treatment themselves.

This time Joe was especially pissed. The suite was reserved for Calvin Gropper and that conceited prig he had married. Joe had never met Calvin Gropper but, like so many citizens of the good old U.S.A., he detested the man. Joe had seen enough of the sarcastic, smirking, self-satisfied bastard on TV to know Gropper wasn't the type he and Aggie could cozy up to. Nor had it warmed Joe's heart to learn that the Groppers couldn't be bothered arriving until near the day His Honor, the Shah got back.

Screw the Groppers, Joe decided. What really counted was that he and Agnes were here. He was proud he had laid it on the line with Marianna. He intended to get his cut of old-fashioned patronage from their Royalnesses—or else. Marianna hadn't said yes, exactly, but she hadn't said no either. Let her hold out on him and he'd throw some surprises of his own at the world. Marianna's husband and her fans might guess at her affair with Doug Braden and a few studs before him. But how would they like to hear that her humping career dated back to age fourteen—before it was fashionable to start so young? And that she'd opened wide for every male in boarding school except the pimple-faced homos?

Satisfied he had his royal relatives nailed to the mat, Joe started down the hall to rouse Aggie and hustle her into shape for the cocktail session.

A single door he'd ignored in his many excursions along the corridor now caught his eye. In the past the door had been kept shut. Joe had never seen anyone enter or leave through it. The one time he'd given it any thought, he'd concluded it concealed either a linen closet or a pantry. In a spread like the Paradise Palace no hour was ever too early or too late to punch a button and bring waiters and maids on the double.

This afternoon, not only was the interior visible, it also gave off noises of occupancy. Someone could be heard shuffling about before dropping onto a creaking chair or bed. Joe sidled along the wall and peeked into the room. Of course, Father Flynn. Preoccupied with the suite assignments meted out to more important guests, Joe had completely forgotten the old guy. What he saw did not stir any jealousy. The plain whitewashed room furnished with a chair, a floor lamp, a small desk, and a narrow bed resembled a monk's cell.

Joe moved closer. Seated on the bed, his bent figure clothed in black, Father Flynn fingered his beads and rocked back and forth. The scrawny priest had been quiet and into himself since they left Boston. Now he was crying. Joe backed away. Whatever was going on, he wanted no part of it. Marianna had sent for the priest—he was her problem. Smart girl to have settled him in simple surroundings. A grand suite like the rooms he shared with Aggie would have freaked out the padre for sure.

Joe closed the door quietly. Everyone was entitled to problems—even men of the cloth. By the time he reached Aggie, Joe had discarded the priest from his mind.

Dressing for her dinner party—one of few at which she had entertained without Ramir—Marianna recalled an exultant day that followed the birth of Karim. Ramir and his mother were visiting the state-owned hospital where Marianna lay recuperating.

"Mama and I have been talking," Ramir began. "You've given us the greatest gift possible, an heir to follow me on the throne. How can we repay you?"

Marianna was incensed. "You and I are the parents of a baby boy. He is not a gift of your mother. Neither of you need repay me."

The Dowager Empress came closer to the bed. "Naturally you're upset, my dear. At this moment you feel your whole world consists of your husband and your son. You don't understand that your child also belongs to the royal family and to the nation."

Anger blotched Marianna's cheeks. "How do I fit in? Was I brought here to be a brood mare?"

"Mama, Marianna, this squabbling must stop," Ramir interrupted.

"It's a matter between the two of us," the Dowager Empress replied. "Leave me with Marianna."

Like a docile child Ramir returned to the hallway.

Marianna turned her attention to her mother-in-law. "I haven't forgotten how you looked me over when we first met in Paris. You didn't like me then and you've never liked me since."

The Dowager Empress smiled sadly. "I was unfair. My view of actresses was unfavorable—unlike my late husband's. But that is a story for another day."

"I didn't know—"

"Someone should have told you. Perhaps it was my duty. Others have relegated the subject to history. Unhappily, I have not. It was never you who distressed me. It was my memories."

Marianna reached for the older woman's hand. "Are we friends?"

"More than that, I hope. You've made Ramir happy and you've made me happy. Sharing your child with a country isn't easy. Who knows better than I? It's a fact of life when you're Empress. If you will accept me, I'll help in any way I can."

By the time Ramir reentered the room, the two women were in emotional embrace. And Marianna had the gift she wanted—a promise that the family wing of the Paradise Palace, austerely decorated by the Dowager Empress herself, could be transformed from its present frigid formality to a colorful area of enticing friendliness in which Marianna could feel at home. In the salon a wall of books rose to the high ceiling. A library ladder riding a brass pole made every book accessible. Other walls glowed with paintings by Miró, Calder, Warhol, and Matisse. The sofas and chairs covered in tawny suede, the muted Persian rugs—an unspoken concession to her mother-in-law—and a grand piano vivid as a ripe tangerine completed the room. In the dining room, plants and trees clustered in corners, living harmoniously with more of the lively paintings.

Her mother-in-law had lived to see and approve the changes Marianna and her California decorators had created. When the Dowager Empress died, Marianna mourned her. In recent years, with a faithless husband of her own, Marianna missed her profoundly.

It was to this transformed wing of the palace that Marianna had arranged to bring her guests tonight.

14

"Regal, make the entrance *regal*." She could still hear the peevish voice of Carter Frost, the choreographer of her only musical, *Fantasies*. "Head tall, Marianna." He had clapped his hands fretfully. "Don't tip the tiara!"

Heeding Frost, she had stepped into camera range, a stunning Marie Antoinette. Breasts pushed high and waistline pinched by a cruel boned corset beneath a camisole, she had lifted her chin and raised her petticoats slightly. Without blinking she had descended the *faux* marble staircase and moved into the arms of her costar, Roger Marat. Costumed as a general, Marat wore a tunic festooned with braid and prop-department medals that bit into her soft flesh as the two danced across the parquet floor. Impassive, still regal, she had demanded between clenched teeth that he hold her at arm's length. He had refused. Meanwhile hundreds of extras had lined the ballroom floor, drenched in the fluid splendor of the radiant couple, and in their own envy.

It had been so beautiful, so phony.

Tonight the scene flooded her mind as footmen opened the door to the sitting room.

No prop men, cameras, directors, extras disturbed the cheerful warmth of the room. For an instant she yearned for the unreality of the Hollywood set, for the transient mood that could be broken by the director's call of "Cut."

Here, she was the director. The cast that looked up as she entered could not be dispersed so easily. A day's salary would not send them home satisfied.

Doug Braden was the first to see her. His eyes swallowed her whole—the cornsilk hair swept into a chignon, the ivory face barely touched with color, the understated black crepe de chine dress unadorned except for a long string of luminous pearls.

"You've grown lovelier since morning," Doug said. He appeared overcome by his discovery. From his manner she could not guess if he intended to kiss her hand or faint. He did neither, just stood there seemingly entranced.

"Doug, that's charming," she said. She turned to Father Flynn. "Did you rest well?"

"Quite well. These are strange surroundings for a priest. I managed a catnap." He smiled fondly. "Little Mary Anna, how dear and sweet you've remained."

"Thank you, Father. If I have, I owe it to you." She urged him into his chair. "We must talk privately. I have so much to tell you and to ask you. And you, Watson, did you have a good afternoon?"

"Perfect, except for my uncontrollable jealousy. Your palace was conceived in Eden."

"Then you must visit more often."

"I hope to." He moved away, wondering why her smile reminded him of the ancestral portrait gallery.

"Agnes and I think it's the greatest here," Joe blustered. "Good to be back in the old rooms. Saw the kids. Cunning, each one of them. That little princess—" He shook his head and addressed the others. Expansive, smug, belonging. "That doll is going to be a great beauty. Except for the dark hair, she looks more and more like her mother. Aggie's side of the family," he explained.

Agnes was modest. "Skipped me," she said good-naturedly.

Marianna cast about for rescue. "Has anyone seen Selma?"

"Right behind you, baby."

"Just in time," Watson said. "Grab your drinks, everyone. I want to propose a toast."

Marianna reached out to stop him. "Not yet. After dinner, if you don't mind. And I'd like to make the toast myself."

The dinner was over. Servants stationed behind each chair had removed the last course. In the ash-paneled dining room the conversation had been impersonal and without depth. The guests had laughed a bit over pleasant memories of the past and noted the happy aspects of the present. No one had spoken of the future. On the surface the ambience, enhanced by candlelight and the liberal consumption of wine, appeared tranquil. At one point Agnes had actually elbowed Father Flynn to rouse him.

"Sleeping, Father?"

"Thinking," he replied.

The butlers hovered, their eyes on Marianna. When she

lowered her lashes they responded to her signal. The moment had come to set the fluted champagne glasses before the guests. The iridescent crystal, fashioned by Baccarat in Paris, bore the royal crest etched in gold. As the butler poured the champagne, the slender, footed glasses were transformed into rows of twinkling fireflies.

Marianna, observing her guests, sensed they were growing restive awaiting her toast. The dinner wines were making her imagination play tricks. She saw the mélange of characters at her table as dress extras summoned from Central Casting, forced into roles that did not suit them. Joe and Agnes, she knew, were thirsting for beer. Father Flynn, unaccountably perspiring, forcused on the bubbly champagne, a seer searching a crystal ball for answers. Doug and Watson were tensing, daring to hope her promised toast would include words that could salvage their future. Only Selma sat at ease, prepared for what was coming.

When the last glass has been filled by the wines stewards, Marianna lowered her lashes again. To M. Bruyere, the chief dining room steward, who bent to hear, she whispered, "Clear the room of servants. Leave with them. Forbid anyone to remain near the doors."

At last the room was emptied of everyone but the guests. Marianna, champagne glass in hand, rose from her chair at the head of the table.

"Please don't get up," she said. "When you hear what I am about to tell you, you may prefer to be seated." She lifted her glass, and her eyes roved her guests. "This is a toast to me. I have arrived at a crossroads in my life. A major decision had to be made and I have made it. I have confided in no one." She glanced at Selma. "No one," she repeated.

"In some way each of you may be affected, yet I know you will understand my position." She paused. "When my husband returns I will tell him what I am about to tell you. Listen carefully. After the festivities, I am leaving Bahrait. I am returning to Hollywood."

From the table there were sounds of bafflement and sounds of applause.

She raised her hand for quiet. "And I am never coming back."

At the far end of the table, Selma's chair fell backward as

she vaulted to her feet. "What did you say? You told me . . . !"

Marianna smiled wearily.

"Ladies and gentlemen," she said. "I am abdicating."

15

Selma kicked at a cold log in the fireplace. "Oh God, you blew it! What you needed was a writer, a director, and a producer for the smash abdication scene. What got into you—spilling your best lines to that bunch?"

Marianna grimaced. "I guess the actress side of me took over again. I wanted an audience for my big exit."

"So why didn't you send for the kitchen staff instead of those barracudas?"

"I should have. They're sweet. Dammit, I was just plain impulsive and hammy. Someone should have muzzled me. Now I have something new to worry about. Who's going to muzzle my guests until I break the news to Ramir?"

"Don't worry. They won't squeak to a soul. They don't dare. You might change your mind."

"I won't."

"You have already. That was a different tune I heard before dinner last night."

"Fair enough. When the invitations were mailed I was stifling. I wanted to work again. I needed moral support from you and Father Flynn. I hoped for practical support from Doug and Watson—decent exchange for what I could offer them. Talking with you in the middle of the night, that was all I had in mind—getting away, going back to Hollywood to make a picture. But there was something else gnawing at me, something I was too ashamed to tell you. After you left it forced itself out and made me look at it."

"Back on the track, sweetie. Let me look at it, too."

Marianna spoke quietly, without bitterness. "There's a woman in Lausanne. Her name is Pia. And a baby called Eric . . ."

Selma heard her through. "Terrific twosome, aren't we?"

"Luckiest on earth," Marianna replied.

They sat brooding.

Suddenly Selma slapped her palm to her forehead. "The kids—what'll the bastard do about the kids?"

"No problem. Ramir would love to punish me through the children. He can't. The family linen is dirty on both sides.

The children will belong to us equally. Our fadeout will be friendly. If it isn't, Ramir will make a grave mistake. The world will see him as a son-of-a-bitch in his own home, too."

"I suspect the world has a fairly good idea already."

"I'd stay if I had a meaningful role to play in Bahrait, but it's hopeless. Ramir never listens to me, never has. All he needs around him are toadies who provide for his pleasure, lick his boots, and applaud the way he runs the country."

"How about the way he runs his family? He'll expect applause for that maybe?"

"No problem. He'll put on his Paris-made military uniform with the epaulets, and all his ribbons and medals including the little number he won on the swimming team at Le Rosey, and then he'll appear on television. He'll inform his subjects that the Empress, whom he loves dearly and who loves him, is no longer happy away from her Hollywood career. She is an artist, a great artist, and he respects her creative needs as he would those of anyone Allah in his wisdom chose to bless with a rare talent. He'll say I leave with his encouragement and deepest devotion, and at his personal sacrifice. He may cry."

"They'll buy that crap?"

"Without question. Unless they'd rather be shot in the back by his secret police."

The silvery gravel crunched beneath their Gucci loafers. Ahead the path was deserted, lit only by a halfhearted moon and a few unwilling stars.

Doug inhaled deeply, appreciating his expanding chest. "Okay, we're alone." He deflated his lungs and went on. "Why did you kick me under the table? I was busting to celebrate. That gorgeous Porcelain Madonna is ours! Hallelujah, we're saved!"

Watson Wagg sighed. "Doug, you're just another pretty face."

"What in hell does that mean? And why are we floating around the garden like a pair of Halloween ghosts? We should be inside knocking off the Shah's best brandy."

"Keep your voice low," Watson warned. "This isn't an audition. As it is, we're taking a chance. These trees may be bugged, no matter what Marianna said. Our words could be piped into her bedroom this very minute."

"What of it? We're getting what we want. She said she was going back to Hollywood, didn't she? She meant with us."

Watson groaned. "Start using your brain. Too bad it hasn't had as much exercise as your prick. Exactly what do we have? Not the Empress we dreamed of, not the glamorous wife of one of the most powerful men in the world. What we have is an *ex*. Not only an ex-actress but an ex-queen. Who gives a damn about an ex-anything? Remember Soraya? The Shah of Iran screwed her day and night trying for an heir. She couldn't conceive so he divorced her. Coldly, the way Ramir dumped his first wife. There was talk of making Soraya a film star but nothing came of it. She was an *ex*— and ex equals nothing. Peter, ex-king in Yugoslavia, Constantine, ex-king of Greece. No one would pay a dime to look at them once they slid off their thrones."

"Not the same situation," Doug said confidently. "She's still Marianna Curtis, isn't she? What difference if the Empress bit is behind her?"

"Behind her. Those are the key words. Sure, everyone worships her. She never misses the list of the World's Ten Most Admired Women. But will audiences pay cash to see an ex-Empress, a used-to-be movie star? Dozens, hundreds of actresses have come up since Marianna Curtis removed herself from the screen. Why should audiences rush to see her? She never was Garbo."

"Someone's bound to come along to finance us," Doug persisted.

"Yes, but ask yourself what kind of *shlock* operator it would be. She could very well turn us down. As reigning Empress—and she still is—she's the hottest thing in show business. As an *ex*—Doug, I'm sorry to break it to you—she's not a sure thing. In the language of our trade, *she's not bankable*."

"Impossible."

"It's true. The big money won't be there. Hard-nosed theater distributors want to know an actor's recent track record. Hell, I don't have to explain that to you. In our business unless you're one of the greats you become a Golden Oldie before you're thirty."

Doug stopped on the path. "Okay, what can we salvage?"

"First we go back and talk to her as old friends," Watson replied. "We explain we're putting her interests before our own. We press her to reconsider the abdication. We remind her she's more beautiful than she was as a girl. At least we won't be lying about that. But as two who love her, we urge her to consider the liabilities of starting over in an industry that has changed radically in fifteen years. No major studios, no long-term contracts, no tough-minded tycoons left to protect her career. One shot at the brass ring—that's what she gets. She could come up roses—but if she doesn't, what's left? She already has money and position. What she's after is her own place in the sun. And the sun shines brighter on an Empress who returns to her Shah than it does on a Hollywood has-been."

"Mr. Nice Guy," Doug said. "You're more devious than I thought. She keeps the title and we squeeze everything that's exploitable out of her. Right?"

"Right," Watson nodded.

"We tell her it's cold outside," Doug went on. "We say she'd be smart to keep her options open. We tell her she can abdicate later if she wants to."

"You're getting the drift."

"If she doesn't score," Doug continued, "we drop her back in the sea."

"Exactly."

"You, my friend, have the makings of a first-rate shit."

"And you, dear Doug, have always been one."

They shook hands solemnly and returned to the palace.

Back in the Curtises' suite, Agnes kicked off her shoes and sailed them across the room. "Fuck her!" she screeched.

"Quiet, Ag, someone will hear you," Joe cautioned.

"I don't give a damn. What difference does it make now? You were there for the finale—a real tearjerker. 'My husband will be shocked.' " Aggie mimicked Marianna's voice. " 'He may try to dissuade me. If he does, I will not be moved. There are times in life when one must take risks.' "

Joe picked up the speech. " 'My time is now. That is why I called you here. You are old friends. I will need your support.' "

"She sure as hell didn't mean us. We're nothing to her but family window dressing. She forgets who took her in when she needed a home, who educated her and gave her every opportunity an orphan could ask for. Just when she can show some gratitude, she pulls the plug."

"It's not hopeless."

"You know it is. That snooty husband of hers never took us seriously. Our only crack at the contract was through Marianna. She runs off, what have we got? Zero. Zilch. Even if she's loaded in her own right, she still can't come up with the kind of cash and influence Ramir can. She's not that crazy about us anyway."

"Right, Ag. Never sent you so much as a card on Mother's Day," Joe muttered gloomily.

"It's back on the skids for us. Unless you can think of something."

"Gimme time. I'm trying." Joe poured two whiskeys and passed one to Agnes. "Hey, how's this? We appeal to her upbringing. Remind her she's inviting a divorce. The Vatican wouldn't stand for it."

"Stupid, you know she's not Catholic anymore. The Vatican forgot about her long ago. Ramir will take the next step. He says, 'Abracadabra, I divorce you,' and she's out in the alley. No, she's got to hang in there until we get a written pledge from him—signed, sealed, delivered."

They fell silent. "Aggie," Joe said finally, "suppose it doesn't work out? There were good days, too, before we hit the money."

"You're getting maudlin, Joey. You're forgetting how the old days stank. We're not going back to that. Start thinking."

"I've got it!"

"Shoot."

"Remember what a religious girl she was at heart? Well, we get her to wait till the dock deal is set. We get the dough in the bank, then we cream some of it off the top."

Agnes eyed him suspiciously. "What for?"

"We build a home for unwed mothers maybe, or a playground for one-eyed orphans—whatever she wants—and we name it after her. For a few favors I can ring in the mayor, make it look like a tribute to her from Boston. Renew her ties to the mother country. Ease her suffering about turning her back on the Church."

Agnes sipped her whiskey. "I've heard worse ideas. I can't remember when."

"Got a better one?"

"No."

"Then that's the one we go with. Who tells her?"

"You do. Tomorrow morning. I'm her blood relative. She'd spit in my eye."

Roused from sleep by the grinding noise of parting draperies, Marianna welcomed the new day by burying her face in her pillow. Reaching out with one hand, she caressed the crushed pillow beside her.

Confused, she could not recall exactly when Luke had joined her. Perhaps Selma had sent for him, perhaps she had summoned him herself. No matter. He had been there and he had held her through the night. He had reassured her when she told him about the abdication. And he had gently forgiven her for blurting her decision—one that affected his life as well—to others before confiding in him. "No one will hurt you," he had promised. "Wherever you go, if you want me, I'll be there." She had clung to him, not for sex but for security. He had understood her need. Restraining his own, he had soothed her, murmuring like a comforting nanny, and she had been grateful for the unabashed tenderness behind his confident masculinity.

Now he had gone to his own cottage, to ready himself for another day with the children, leaving a little of his strength with her.

Bathed, dressed, breakfasted, Marianna moved into her salon to wait.

She knew they would come. They weren't finished with her. Not yet.

The gaunt figure with the anguished eyes stood in the doorway and addressed the young second maid. "I wish to talk to the Empress," he said. "Is she here?"

The maid had never seen a Catholic priest before. The strange figure, garbed in black except for a starched white collar that circled his throat like a noose, frightened her. She mumbled a few words and shook her head uncertainly.

From her desk at the far side of the salon Marianna heard their voices. "Kiri," she called out, "who's there?"

"Go to her," the man said. "Tell her it's Father Flynn."

The girl retreated a few steps, still staring, then turned and scurried to her mistress. In a flash she was back. "Her Majesty asks that you enter the salon. If I may be excused, sir—she wishes to be alone with you."

Moments later, Marianna stood before him. A last-minute sprinkling of face powder emphasized the whiteness of her skin. "Father, I'm happy you're here."

"I had to see you, my child."

She clasped his hands, then sat down opposite him. "Last night, only Selma came to me," she said. "And now you."

"You shocked the others."

A cynical smile crossed her lips. "I wanted to. That's the actress part of me. But afterwards—I secretly hoped they'd show some concern, or at least curiosity."

"You were not realistic. Most people think of themselves first."

"Not you, Father."

"Even I. Your decision stunned me. You couldn't know you were giving me my last chance for happiness."

She looked at him skeptically, not comprehending. "What do you mean?" Then, assuming a more cheerful attitude, she said, "Tell me about it. You were always straightforward, an example for the rest of us. The whole neighborhood would say, 'Father Flynn—his face is easier to read than the Boston *Globe*.' "

"It's a shameful story, Mary Anna. A terrible act I committed."

"I can't believe that."

"It concerns you, Mary Anna."

"Me?"

"Soon it will be clear. I am overjoyed you are abdicating."

"Why does it matter to you?"

He let her question go by. "You'll be coming back to America? Coming home?"

"Yes."

"Then you'll be returning to the Church?"

"The Church? I haven't thought about it, not in years. In the beginning, yes. But after I converted, well, I just put the Church behind me."

"You were such a good little girl," he said irrelevantly. "The nuns were very proud of you. Always so obedient, so studious, an innocent child of Our Lord."

"Not always, Father. I tried to make your values mine. Sometimes I failed."

"But you trusted me."

"Of course."

"I sinned, Mary Anna."

"No one ever said priests were exempt from sinning."

"I sinned with your life."

"Ridiculous."

"You have your reasons for abdicating. I won't pry. Just tell me this—have you found joy in your marriage?"

She smiled. "You can't be asking me to make confession . . ."

"Informally."

"Then I'll tell you. Dammit, no, I haven't found joy. I have my children—they're my only family happiness. A few brief years with Ramir, five, maybe six, were romantic. A new role to play. That was distracting. Later there were doubts, and then disillusionment. Now it's over. Today my husband doesn't need me. He loves someone else. I am nothing more than an attendant in his court. I've been lost, Father."

He clutched her hands and held them between skeletal fingers. "Christ will help you."

She pulled away. "What's this about? Where was Christ when I needed him? What happened to the blessings he promised?"

Father Flynn dipped his head. "I beg you, hear *my* confession."

"*Your* confession—of what?"

"He came to me."

"Who came to you?"

"Calvin Gropper. He came to me first, before you met the Shah. He knew everything about you, about my influence over you. He arrived without any announcement . . ." Father Flynn hesitated.

"I'm listening."

"Kate Moynahan opened the door. Gropper was an adviser to the President then. Kate recognized him from the television. She saw the black limousine outside, and the bodyguards. He came out of the rain. He stepped into the entry before she could say a word. He told her it was a matter of utmost urgency. Kate kept her head. She asked him to wait. When she opened my study door to announce him, I was the one who was shaken. He pushed past Kate and ordered her to leave the room. He sat down without invitation. He told me what he wanted."

"Go on."

"He said the Shah of Bahrait had decided to marry you.

Gropper had assured the Shah he could deliver you to him. He asked for my cooperation."

"Before I'd met Ramir? Why did Ramir want me?"

The wan priest began to sway in his chair. "I was told he had fallen deeply in love with you. There were also political advantages to the match. The Shah desired more intimate ties to the United States. He was an unpopular figure in our country. A marriage to a famous and beloved American woman would be helpful. There was only one obstacle."

"I was Catholic."

"Exactly."

"They knew that if anything was to come of their scheme I would have to convert," Marianna said. "What did you tell Gropper?"

Father Flynn grew agitated, remembering. "I demanded to know what he expected of me. He said if everything else went according to plan, I was to persuade you to leave the Church. He knew you would listen to me."

"And you agreed."

"No, no. It wasn't like that. I was infuriated. A Roman Catholic priest does not encourage any parishioner to leave the Church. Naturally I threw the man out."

"Go on."

"A few days later Gropper was back. 'I was too subtle,' he said. 'I thought you were smarter than you are.' 'What are you talking about?' I asked. 'Money, Father, money. I am suggesting Miss Curtis will come to you for guidance. She will have difficulty coping with her dilemma. And you will help her resolve it—for money.' Gropper was very sure of himself. 'The Shah of Bahrait is an extraordinarily attractive man. He is also forceful. He seldom fails to obtain whatever —or whomever—he wants. At this time he wants Miss Curtis. We know she has recently been wounded in a love affair. She is hurt and lonely—and wary. If she turns to you for comfort, you will assure her she will meet another worthier man. In time, after she knows the Shah, you will convince her that love may sometimes be placed before faith. It will be your responsibility to help her renounce Catholicism.' "

Father Flynn buried his face in his hands. "I told Gropper he was mad, that he and his Shah were insane and insulting. He wasn't through. 'Naturally, we were prepared for your outburst. Listen carefully. We never accept a favor freely given. We prefer to pay for what we get. We wish to create a bond between buyer and seller. A sound practice, don't you agree?'

"He was making me ill. I didn't answer. 'Bahrait is a wealthy country,' he went on. 'It would astonish you to know the number of—shall we say—arrangements the Shah has made with personages in the highest reaches of our government. Often they are self-serving and questionable. But never illegal. We are prepared to deal with you the same way.' Are you following me, Mary Anna?"

"I am."

"Let me describe how he convinced me. He took me to the window and raised the curtains. He commanded me to look outside. 'What do you see?' he asked. It was an ordinary day. Up and down the street there were women with babies in arms, bending under the weight of market bags. Some had little ones pulling at their skirts. Older children were playing in the road, tossing balls, dodging cars that picked up speed as they barreled down the hill. It was right after the Sheehan boy had had his legs crushed. While they played, the children listened for cars, scared, on guard to jump to safety if necessary. Gropper said, 'The kids out there, they're thinking about what happened to Tommy Sheehan last Thursday.' Then he dropped the curtains.

"I glared at the man. I realized he had eyes everywhere. 'Don't you want a better fate for those youngsters?' he asked. 'And think about the others, the unemployed boys too old for street ball, idling on corners. You wouldn't want another gang rape in the neighborhood. That sweet O'Hara girl, coming up the hill from work last week, when will her sanity return?'

" 'What can I do?' I asked him. 'It's what *we* can do,' he answered. 'We can provide something for these young people, to keep them off the streets.'

" 'We have a playground—behind the school building.'

" 'That miserable patch of concrete?' Gropper said. 'You call that a real recreation center? It's like an exercise yard in a prison. The youngsters can't wait to escape. However, there is an empty lot on the next street, fenced with barbed wire, littered with garbage. The owner won't let you use it. But he is prepared to sell it to you. How many years of passing the collection box will it take—ten, twenty, thirty—before the nickels and dimes add up to enough to buy the lot? Then you'll need grading, paving, grass, a community building where mothers can gather and rest and keep an eye on their children. And think of the jobs, Father, jobs for the loiterers. Jobs and training and self-respect.'

" 'And for this?' I asked.

" 'For this, you must ensure Marianna Curtis's conversion to the Moslem faith.'

" 'Never!'

" 'Then let me go on. After his marriage to Miss Curtis, His Majesty will wish to show further tangible gratitude to the community in which she was reared. He has expressed his desire to construct—and provide a permanent endowment for—a school of higher education right here in Charlestown. How many of your young people go on to college when they leave the parochial school?'

" 'Very few. They need money. They look for work. If they are lucky, they find it.'

" 'Exactly. His Majesty recognizes the trap they are caught in. That is why he is prepared to be most lavish with scholarships and support for worthy students. And most of them are worthy, are they not?'

" 'I don't know what to say.'

"He looked at me as though I were a dim-witted child. 'It is so little to do in return for so much.'

" 'Not for a Catholic priest.'

" 'Others have performed worse deeds. You know that . . .'

" 'My answer is still no.'

" 'Then view it another way—and mind you, I do not withdraw my original offer. Try to see it as an act of true altruism, one that goes beyond the limits of the Catholic and Moslem faiths. Marianna Curtis and the Shah of Bahrait are revered symbols, each beloved by millions. If they unite in love, if they allow their joy in matrimony and in parenthood to be known to the world, give proof that religion and race—although the Shah is an Aryan—are no obstacles to harmony, consider the example they will set for mankind. With the simplest compromise of conscience, you can bring this about.'

" 'I must give it more thought.'

" 'Do so. And ask yourself—what is the loss of one Catholic soul weighed against the suffering of hundreds of thousands who face the misery of prejudice and senseless religious wars?' "

"You agreed with him?" Marianna said abruptly.

"Finally, yes."

"You delivered me to him?"

"In a way. To the Shah actually."

Her eyes blazed. "So it was all arranged! Did you believe the Shah loved me?"

"Oh yes. Mr. Gropper seemed most sincere on that point."

"Was anyone else involved in their scheme?"

"I don't know. I never asked."

"And you were pleased with what you did?"

"When I saw the good that followed your marriage, I was. The public acceptance of your conversion, the success of your marriage, satisfied me that I had made the right decision —for others. But every day since your conversion I have borne a heavy burden. From Boston I followed your progress, the birth of your children, your worthwhile missions abroad, your efforts for the people of Bahrait. I sought every photograph of the family at home, on holidays. Always you were smiling. I was convinced you were happy. But I knew I had sinned in the eyes of God. I could not face you."

"Why are you here now?"

"Because I heard rumors your marriage was troubled. Because I am responsible if you are unhappy. Every day of my life I pray forgiveness from the Lord, but I have received no sign that He has heard me. My heart is pained beyond endurance. I seek absolution. I beg for your forgiveness."

"And you've come to me with your confession."

"Yes."

"For your peace of mind? Without knowing what these last years of marriage have been like for me?"

"I couldn't know fully, of course. When you announced your intention to abdicate, I could only guess at the reason. The enormity of my mistake sickened me."

"And you ask my forgiveness as well as God's?" She rose and stood over him, her body trembling. "Get out of here," she said. "Get out and stay out of my sight forever, you— you ecclesiastical pimp!"

Although still haunted by her scene with Father Flynn, Marianna faced her new callers with composure. Watson Wagg leaned against the mantel, sipping tonic water. Doug reclined in a chair across from Marianna's. Both men wore tennis clothes still damp from their game.

"We're not disturbing you?" Doug asked.

"I've been expecting you," Marianna replied.

"Of course you have," Watson said smoothly. "We had a long talk last night, Doug and I. We came to tell you how thrilled we are that you're returning to Hollywood. Do we dare assume we're included in your plans?"

She nodded affirmatively.

"Ah, good." Watson placed his glass on the marble mantel and rubbed his hands nervously. *"Very* good. Doug and I are thrilled," he said. "How is your mood? Ready to talk about the glorious future?"

She nodded again.

"Obviously we aren't here to discuss your reason for abdicating. That's your affair. We wouldn't presume to pry. Still it does alter the situation somewhat." He hesitated, looked to Doug for confirmation, found none, and went on. "Abdication presents certain pluses and certain minuses. On the plus side, it would be to our advantage—Doug's and mine—to present our bankers with an agreement for more than one Marianna Curtis film. They'd snap it up."

"And the minus side?"

"It could work to your disadvantage to commit beyond one picture."

"You think that?"

"Let us suppose—unlikely as it may be—that you find your first experience a disappointment. The picture itself will be a success. Have no concern about that. But what if stardom is less fulfilling than your present life as Empress? Have you forgotten how tedious moviemaking can be, and how arduous? Think of the predawn makeup calls, the boring hours hanging around sets, the tiresome costume fittings, the personality conflicts, the anxiety of screenings."

"I have forgotten nothing."

Watson found his tonic water and took several quick glups. Marianna was not making it easy for him. Seeking rescue, Watson was met by Doug's vacuous smile and flashing capped teeth. Nothing more.

He plunged again. "What I am suggesting is that you reconsider your abdication. Hang on to your alternatives. Leave yourself free to return to Bahrait as Empress should you wish to do so. Avoid the entrapment of an extended contract, the possibility of a legal suit, ensuing bad publicity. Why take chances? Try the Hollywood waters one step at a time. Abdicate later if moviemaking is what you truly want."

Her stomach knotted with disappointment. Yesterday they had seen her as a gusher, a fountain of hope that would restore them to cinema eminence. Today, with the expectation she would become an ex-Empress, they saw her as a dry well. She knew they were right, yet she had foolishly hoped they would come to her as friends, not users. In their desperation they were lewd. She wanted to tell them so, but she didn't think they were worth the effort. Tiredly she rang for her maid. "I'll think about it," she said. "Kiri will show you out. I'm expecting other callers. Tonight we'll talk again."

Agnes, with her profligate use of Kleenex, was well on her way to disposing of the palace supply. Marianna watched with amusement as the older woman sniffled up a mound of tissues. Beside her on the sofa, Joe patted his wife's knee and told her to pull herself together. This was a solemn time, a kinfolk time, he said. They had come to talk things over. For Marianna's sake.

"Our job's no easy one," Joe said. "Think we like sitting here reminding you of the terrible consequences that could befall you if you take this step? But what are nearest and dearest for if not to stand by and offer a little advice where it's needed?"

"You have a heart of gold," Marianna said.

"None of your sarcasm, miss. Sure we've had differences. You're entitled to your doubts about Aggie and me. Only this time you're making a mistake if you don't hear us out."

"I'm listening."

"And you're laughing, too. Let's get to the point. We have eyes and ears. We know you're having trouble with your old man. Backstairs gossip has it you're not above a bit of fooling around yourself. The rumor is you're getting straight A's from that professor fellow. Pardon me for being blunt. I got to do it my way to bring you to your senses."

"Joe, your style is impeccable. No apologies necessary."

He snorted his disbelief. "What about your children? Have you given them any thought? Don't they come before other considerations?"

"First and foremost. They won't suffer. How I manage that problem doesn't concern you."

"All right then, how about you? You know what that Shah

of yours is going to say when he hears you're skipping? Divorce—that's what he's going to say."

"Divorce," Agnes wept. She reached for another clump of Kleenex. "Your own dear mother had her share of misery. Lord knows I don't wish Madge's fate on you. She, poor darling, didn't have your advantages. She suffered plenty. But divorce! There's never been one in the family. What will people say?"

"I'll be a nine days' wonder, no more."

"Why can't you do like other people?" Joe put in. "A trial separation till the domestic blues blow over. Plenty of royals do that. Remember Prince Bernhard? Gave that nice fat Dutch lady, Juliana, a rough time. She had class. She stuck with it. Princess Margaret and that Snowdon fellow—they had differences too. Waited till the kids were older before they split. What about Jackie Kennedy? She didn't go flying out the White House door just because her man played around. You know what you're asking for? A swift kick back to the U.S.A."

"With loving arms like yours to return to, I can hardly wait," Marianna said.

Joe pulled out his last card. "Listen, Marianna," he said slyly. "You don't want to come home with your tail between your legs. Why not hang around till the dock contract's set? I can fix it so you return to Boston in glory. Remember that college your husband gave to Charlestown? He grabbed all the credit. Well, how'd you like a street named after you, a park, whatever you want? We cover a few palms and I guarantee you'll be a bigger queen in Massachusetts than you are in Bahrait—among *your* kind of people."

"Joe, you're too funny to rouse my Irish temper. Take Agnes and that box of tissues and get the hell out of here. Let's forget this whole conversation. Enjoy your day. You're taking the Tent City tour this afternoon. See you at dinner."

Back in his austere cell-like room, Father Flynn dragged his shabby suitcase from an overhead shelf and packed his few belongings. He removed the crucifix he had hung on the wall facing his bed, kissed it, and placed it carefully between his shirts. Mary Anna's parting words tolled in his ears, making his heart pound. He stumbled to the window to fill his lungs with the fresh morning air. Through misted eyes, he looked down on the pleasant garden and the gold-domed mosque beyond. In the distance he could hear the spiraling wail of a muezzin high on a minaret balcony calling the faithful to prayer.

Long ago, in the seminary, Father Flynn had studied the religions of the world. Accepted into the priesthood, he had become too deeply immersed in his own faith to give further thought to others. After his capitulation to Calvin Gropper he had not dared to contemplate whatever it was that Mary Anna now believed in.

Suddenly it became urgent to know. What *had* he done to the soul of Mary Anna Callahan?

Drawn by a force he could not identify, the priest found himself walking down a path shaded by an arched trellis vividly overhung with scarlet bougainvillaea. At the end of the path he could see the entry to the mosque. A bearded man clad in white robe and green turban stood waiting for him.

"Father Flynn." The bearded man spoke softly. "I am Aljavad Raheni, the mullah of the royal mosque. I hoped you would come. Would you like to step inside with me?"

The priest hesitated. "I've never visited a mosque before."

"Then you must do so now. You will not object to following our rituals before entering?"

"No, no. But I'm afraid I don't remember . . ."

"You need only do as I do," the mullah said.

The bearded man led the way into an outer courtyard and paused. "I must ask you to bare your feet, Father. It is a mark of respect to the house of God, and to others who come here to pray."

Father Flynn loosened his laces, pulled off his shoes, and looked at the mullah uncertainly.

"Next we must perform our ablutions." The mullah indicated basins filled with water. "Here we wash our faces, our hands, and our feet. No one enters a mosque unless he is scrupulously clean."

Step by step, Father Flynn emulated the mullah's movements.

When they had completed their ablutions the mullah spoke again. "Let me prepare you for what you will find in the mosque. Islam is a religion of simple beauty. We have no icons, no pews, no music. Beneath the great dome you will find nothing but the beautiful prayer rugs which cover the floor."

Trailing the mullah, Father Flynn stepped into the mosque. Instantly he was impressed not only by the shimmering rugs but by the eerily lovely light that filtered through the stained-glass windows.

"Does the Empress come here to pray?" he whispered.

"Women who follow the true orthodoxy pray in their homes or courtyards," the mullah replied. "I do not know what the Empress does. Come, it is the time for me to pray to Allah, as I do five times each day when the muezzin calls. The muezzin's chant tells us, 'There is no God but Allah, Mohammed is his Prophet.' "

Father Flynn looked uneasy.

The mullah smiled. "I will not ask you to join me in prayer."

Leaning against a pillar, the priest watched as the mullah knelt facing the holy city of Mecca, touching his forehead to a richly designed rug. The mullah murmured a few lines and rose.

"The words you heard first mean 'In the name of God, the Beneficent, the Merciful, praise be to God, Lord of the Worlds.' The rest I need not translate, except to tell you that the basic tenets of Islam, when they are not abused by fanatics, seek peace for all men."

The priest nodded approvingly.

"Are you thinking of your own religion, Father? There are differences between our faiths, but there are many good things we share. In Islam we accept that Jesus walked on earth as a prophet, just as we believe there were many true prophets—Jacob, Noah, Moses, and others. But to us Mohammed was the *greatest* of all the prophets of God. The Holy Koran says, 'No difference do we make between any of them, and to God we are resigned.' "

Father Flynn inclined his head, listening intently.

"Mohammed could not read or write, yet Allah chose him among all men to be His messenger. Others wrote down the Holy Koran as they heard it from Mohammed's lips."

"As the Holy Bible came to be," the priest said.

"Yes, a parallel. May I remind you of a difference? Our religious men marry, as Mohammed did. By his first wife Mohammed had seven children. Not until her death did he create a harem of nine wives, as was permitted then. It is known he lived out his life in love and peace."

While the mullah continued to expound, and to respond to Father Flynn's questions, the two men strolled to the entranceway of the mosque. They replaced their footwear, stepped beneath the bougainvillaea-decked trellis, and were about to shake hands in parting when they heard a woman's voice crying out.

The mullah saw her first. "Your Majesty!" he exclaimed. "What brings you here?"

Marianna, yellow hair flying, tore down the path. "Father! Father!" she called. "I'm so happy I found you!" Brushing past the mullah, she flung herself into the priest's arms. "Will you forgive me? Please forgive me," she pleaded. "I was awful, horrible."

"*I* forgive *you*?"

"Yes, yes, say you will. I've been thinking—I know now—you did what you thought was right. You never could do anything else. The Koran tells us no man is to be condemned for mistakes he does not honestly know to be wrong."

Father Flynn embraced her. "Dear Mary Anna," he said brokenly. "None of us knows what awaits us. At least on earth we can try to make peace." He looked back at the mosque. "There is only one God. The God I taught you to love is the same God you love in Islam."

Hilary Gropper sprawled on the vast bed, loose as a carelessly dropped puppet. She touched her clitoris lightly, then stretched her lanky body until her fingertips reached the padded headboard and her toes wiggled at the edge of the mattress. Restless waiting for Calvin, she rotated her hips until the white voile peignoir, Calvin's favorite because it implied purity, fell open, exposing flattened breasts and a broad pubic mound.

It was part of her foreplay, this touching of her body, like the lip-licking porno scenes she unreeled in her head as she anticipated Calvin's arrival in their palace suite.

The flight from Paris to Ryal aboard the aircraft belonging to one of Calvin's consortium clients had been erotic. She and Calvin had gorged on caviar and grown languid on champagne. Like exploring adolescents, they had doubled up in a lounge chair, where they had sneakily stroked each other's arousal points.

While serving another administration Calvin had learned from the President himself that the leader of the free world achieved his most powerful orgasms fornicating aboard Air Force One. Something about the plane's vibrations combined with the skills of specially selected professional partners would, as he put it, "blow me straight out of my goldanged skull." Presently retired to his New Hampshire farm, the former Chief Executive was busily writing a memoir of his presidency. Calvin was certain the hanky-panky aboard Air Force One would be excluded from the record and forever lost to history. The President's explicit description of his recreational flights still tantalized Calvin. It was an experience he craved.

The plane Hilary and Calvin had boarded this morning at Le Bourget Airport was luxurious enough. Unfortunately, its interior had been stripped down and made into a single large salon without private quarters. Mindful of the crew and of the stewards who regularly appeared offering services, the Groppers had spent their flight in intermittent teasing and mutual frustration.

In his bachelor days, Calvin's reputation as a lover, hinted at by the press and humbly confirmed by Calvin himself, was that in bed he had the endurance of a long-distance runner. Hilay knew better. Calvin's penis maintained its holding position only briefly. On their first encounter Hilary had attributed his hit-and-run method to the excitement of conquest. Many encounters later she realized that she was, to put it vulgarly, getting his best shot.

Too wise to shatter his illusion of mastery over his ejaculations, she often masturbated herself to arousal and permitted Calvin to enter her and orgasm immediately. Sometimes she amused herself by viewing their lovemaking in bullfighting terms—she the taunting picador, Calvin the matador moving in for the moment of truth.

She was showered, she was scented. The maid had been sent away. But where was Calvin?

On their arrival at the palace they had been met in the reception hall by one of Hilary's court favorites, Colonel Samid Mussadi. The bearded young aide to the Shah was an outrageous flirt whose welcoming compliments unfailingly made Hilary feel like a cuddly doll. Today Colonel Mussadi had been curt. He had greeted her with the cool respect reserved for fellow officers, then he had drawn Calvin aside and whispered into his ear. Calvin's horn-rimmed glasses had steamed, a sign he was annoyed.

As two porters gripped their luggage for removal to their waiting suite, Calvin had indicated to Hilary that she was to follow the leather-aproned men. "I will join you shortly," he had promised.

Well, how long was shortly? A half hour had passed since Hilary, glancing over her shoulder from the head of the marble staircase, had observed Calvin and Colonel Mussadi disappear into a small anteroom off the main hall. Since then, Calvin had not troubled to ring the bedroom nor to send a servant to explain the delay.

Torn between the heat of her temper and the heat in her body, Hilary decided to bring herself off, once at least, then lie back until Calvin appeared. Calvin, unaware that she frequently accommodated herself while awaiting him, found it delightful and flattering that she was well along in arousal when he approached her.

Hilary squirmed like an eel, muffled a squeal of gratification, and lay still. Whenever Calvin showed up, she would be ready—again.

In the sparsely furnished anteroom Calvin Gropper seated himself on the edge of a wooden chair and waited for Colonel Mussadi to close the door behind them. He ancitipated a brief exchange of ideas over whatever it was that troubled the colonel. He would dispense some wisdom, the problem would be resolved or diffused, and he would join Hilary in the well-remembered bed.

He was surprised when the colonel, obviously distraught, moved to a chair behind the small desk and with his pencil began rat-a-tatting on its surface.

"What is it?" Gropper demanded. "I have had a long journey. I wish to rejoin my wife."

"She's leaving," the colonel croaked. "She made the announcement. Last night at dinner."

"Who is leaving? Why are you hysterical?"

"The Empress. She's abdicating!"

"Absurd!" Gropper came to the edge of his chair.

"No, it's true. The Shah himself does not know, nor have I told anyone but you. Thank God you have come to advise me."

"It's insane. My mind does not accept your words. Where

did you pick up such idiocy?" Gropper removed his steamy glasses and wiped them hastily with a clean handkerchief.

"From Monsieur Bruyere, the chief dining room steward, a most responsible man. Years ago the Shah discovered him working as sommelier at the Hôtel du Cap in Antibes. He hired him away, gave him a better position. Bruyere is extremely grateful and very loyal to His Majesty. He supervised last night's dinner party for the Empress and her foreign guests. When she instructed him to clear the room of the servants and to leave with them, Monsieur Bruyere became suspicious. He removed everyone from the area but he kept his own ear to the door. He heard her say it in that stagey voice she sometimes uses: 'I am abdicating.' "

"You're certain the Shah doesn't know of this?"

"He would return immediately if he did."

"Then we must locate him. Do you know where he is?"

"In Belgium."

"I know that much. He called me from Brussels a few days ago. Where is he staying?"

"In a private residence with his chief of staff and some aides. King Baudouin himself made the arrangements. I have the telephone number."

"Then what are you waiting for? Get him on the telephone."

"Who, who—will talk to him?" The colonel's voice shook.

"I will, you imbecile. Just locate him for me."

The two men sat across from each other, the call to Belgium concluded. Gropper stared at the floor, his back rounded, his entwined fingers between his knees. "They can't find him, they said. He's spending the day and night in the country. They did not know where. I said it was important. They asked me if the matter was political or domestic or if it involved the children. I said the children were well but yes, it was domestic. They promised they would ask him to contact me as soon as they hear from him."

"We cannot afford to lose time," Colonel Mussadi said. "Those people at the dinner table—one of them will talk. His Majesty must be informed before the news becomes public. Perhaps he can dissuade her. Coming now, before the celebration—it's terrible. We must tell him."

"We?"

"*You*, sir. There is no one else he would believe."

Gropper slammed the fist of one hand into the palm of the other. "No, I will talk to her first, to the Empress. Perhaps your former sommelier spends too much time in the Shah's wine cellar. Perhaps he contrived this madness. It was good fortune we did not reach His Majesty. I was stupid to try. Only the Empress knows her true intentions. I will insist she tell me what they are."

"Good luck sir."

Upon leaving Colonel Mussadi, Calvin had poked his head into his bedroom, mumbled something to Hilary about a crucial matter concerning their hosts, and dashed away. Aroused and abandoned, Hilary had rolled on her stomach and furiously concluded her sexual business by herself.

In the corridor Calvin located Marianna's maid and learned the Empress was in the pool area. Hastening outdoors, Calvin tiptoed to the topmost terrace step and stationed himself behind thick greenery.

From his perch Calvin spotted Marianna and envied the grace with wiich she cut the water. When she arrived at the chrome pool ladder he ducked his head. Observing Marianna —clad in a translucent ivory silk maillot—mount the ladder, Calvin reluctantly conceded that she was magnificent and Ramir was a fool. With inappropriate though momentary lust, he followed her movements, irritated to discover himself stirred by the enemy.

Below him Marianna shook her head vigorously, tossing off beads of moisture that clung to her hair. Satisfied, she stepped onto the pool deck and strode in the direction of the steps.

"Calvin, Calvin, come out, come out, wherever you are!" she called.

Shamefaced, Gropper sprang from behind the shrubbery. With false cheer he galloped down the flagstone stairs. After kissing her European style on both cheeks, he held her damp body away from his rumpled traveling suit and eyed her with genuine admiration.

"You look splendid," he said heartily. "More beautiful than ever."

"At last, dear Calvin, you've said something I can believe."

Her good spirits unsettled him. Unless he had been grossly misinformed, this was a critical time in her life. He was primed for a discussion of the utmost solemnity, yet here she was, behaving with such disconcerting cheer that he did not know how to begin.

She came to his rescue. "Come sit beside me," she said pleasantly. "How is Hilary? Resting, I hope. Is your suite comfortable? I ordered fresh flowers from the greenhouse for your rooms. We're fortunate to have you and Hilary with us before we're invaded by all those stuffed shirts and dignitaries. Was it a smooth flight? Paris as a glorious as ever?"

Gropper began to breathe easily. Listening to Marianna chatter on, he concluded she expected no response. Obviously she wanted nothing more than to get this visit off to a good start. He nodded placidly, not bothering to interrupt while she told him trivial anecdotes about the children. She gossiped about her guests from Boston and Hollywood. She boasted of the tent city and of Ramir's contribution to the miracle in the desert which would live on in legend like Camelot. She rattled off names of kings and presidents, sheikhs and emirs, premiers, chancellors, and ambassadors soon to arrive.

Calvin unbuttoned his jacket and allowed his stomach to expand. He lay back among the pillows on his chair, hands crossed behind his head, and angled his face to catch the filtered sunlight. Mussadi, the fool, had got him worked up over nothing. Obviously Marianna was enjoying her life. Whenever Ramir called back he would say there had been a misunderstanding, a matter of no importance. He might even deny having phoned. He could decide that later. He was tired. He would remain with Marianna a few minutes longer. Soon he would be with Hilary.

Suffused with relief, he permitted his eyelids to close. He thought he had fallen into a dream.

"Calvin, you son-of-a-bitch!"

His eyes snapped open. This was no dream. He bolted upright and stared at Marianna. The malevolence on her face frightened him.

"Father Flynn came to me yesterday," she said.

"The priest from Boston? I remember him."

"You *remember* him! You dropped into his life and you ruined it! That sweet unworldly man. You manipulated him and you destroyed him."

"You're upset about *that?*" Gropper said, confidence restored. "It's ancient history. Your little neighborhood—

Charlestown, is that what it's called?—benefited as I said it would. Every promise made to Father Flynn was kept. Is the good Father remorseful? That is unfortunate. His Maker will forgive him."

"You slimy bastard, who'll forgive you?"

Gropper shrugged. "I need no forgiveness. I had a job to do, I did it well. You and Ramir have enjoyed a successful marriage . . ."

"A *political* marriage."

Gropper shrugged again. "What difference does it make how it began? It was a priest who arranged the meeting between Prince Rainier and Grace Kelly. An exemplary marriage resulted. All marriages are entered into to serve selfish purposes. The most devoted couples may not understand their motives, yet each partner acts to fulfill his own needs. You had yours. Ramir had his. You were a luckier bride than most. Your groom was head over heels in love with you."

"Briefly."

"Everything changes."

"Only you are consistent. Did you expect me to believe you sprinted down here because you couldn't wait to say hello?"

"But, of course."

"Without Hilary? With nothing in particular to talk about? Just a friendly chat between the two of us?"

"Why should that surprise you?"

"Because we aren't friends. Because as an actress I recognize a lousy performance. Because there's something explosive about to happen and somehow you've found out about it. What more do you want to know?"

"Is it true?"

"It's true."

"Have you told Ramir?"

"I telephoned Brussels. Major Bijan wouldn't put me through. 'Orders,' he said. 'His Majesty is resting. I am not permitted to disturb him unless it is an emergency.' Bijan said that to *me,* to Ramir's wife."

"The man is a fool."

"I was fighting mad. That's when I decided not to wait another day. That's why I disclosed my plans to my guests first. I still haven't heard from Ramir." She looked at Gropper questioningly. "Have you tried to reach him?"

"I have, with no more success than you. Bijan was barely cordial. I didn't press. There was the possibility the whole story was a lie."

"Now you know it's not a lie."

"When are you leaving?"

"I'll stay through the Jubilee. When the captains and kings depart, I'll be right behind them."

"But why at this time? Other women? You've known about them for years. Ramir's flings are without depth. They have nothing to do with his devotion to you."

" 'Mere diversions'—that's what he calls them. I've hinted I want more than diversions. I want my own identity. After fifteen years of playing the same role it's getting harder and harder to breathe. Ramir listens to my complaints but he pretends not to hear me."

"He's clever. He hears you," Gropper said. "He guessed you wished to return to Hollywood. I made him promise me that when the time was right he would encourage you to do so."

"Ramir promised *you*."

"As usual, he consulted me. I pointed out it would be as useful to Bahrait as to you. Good public relations with the United States is just what he needs."

"Public relations!"

"And of course your happiness means much to him," Gropper went on smoothly. "We understood why you invited your Hollywood friends here. To ease the way. To protect your comeback. To bring you home to Bahrait refreshed by success. That is what I cannot understand. Our plans were moving along perfectly on parallel tracks. Why an abdication? It's senseless."

"Is it, Calvin? I took a side trip the other day."

His eyes narrowed. "Where did you go?"

"To Lausanne. I've talked to Pia. I know about the baby."

The shiny new bus waited in the gravel forecourt for the appearance of the Empress's guests. Manned by two Americans clad in khaki and hip holsters, it baked in the afternoon sun.

The American drivers, ostensibly lured to Bahrait by the hefty salaries the Shah offered skilled foreign technicians, were known to the palace staff as "those CIA bastards." Unperturbed, they quietly performed their menial tasks by

day. In the evening they returned to their apartments in Ryal
and wrote secret reports on all they had gleaned during their
hours on duty. Occasionally the two men swapped shifts with
the night team. The change in routine was thought by their
supervisors in Washington to keep everyone on his toes.

The Americans relished their job and suffered no twinges
of guilt. Today's assignment to drive the Empress's guests to
Celebration City promised to be fruitful. The drivers had
checked out their passengers and knew them to be gabby and
imprudent. A thorough account of the excursion, kicked up
through channels, was certain to be useful to their superiors.

The men were agreed they could handle today's assignment
without the presence of Colonel Badar Noori. To the CIA
men Noori, the handpicked aide of General Sahid Mojeeb,
Commander of the Armed Forces, was small-time, an amateur snitch probably assigned to spy on them. Despite their
doubts about the colonel, the Americans put forth no complaint. General Mojeeb, who also kept the Shah's secret
police under his thumb, was no man to fool around with.

"Her Majesty is sending a watchdog, too," one driver
said.

"Who's that?"

"The schoolteacher fellow, Luke Tremayne. He reports
back to her."

"Our business is getting crowded. We need a union.
Where's the Shah?"

"Still traveling."

"His doctor with him?"

"What do you think? The Doc's busy taking the boss's
blood pressure and working along with the palace pimps.
Gotta be sure the Shah hires the healthiest stock. I hear
they're bringing in a regiment of new talent for the party.
Those big shots aren't coming to this garden of heavenly
delights just for caviar and lute strings. The Doc must have
both hands full, examining so many candidates. His Majesty
wouldn't want to pass out the clap for souvenirs."

The other driver snickered. "Word's out they're hiring male
prosties for the ladies. Duchesses and princesses get horny,
too."

"Quiet, stupid. Here come the tourists."

Once in a moment of sexual fervor Luke Tremayne had
sworn to Marianna he would lay down his life for her. At the

time, neither took his pledge seriously. Surely this afternoon's
excursion was further than Luke had expected to go in the
realm of sacrifice. Accompanying Marianna's group of weir-
dos into the desert was a miserable way to pass an afternoon
created for tennis and swimming.

"Why me?" he'd asked Marianna. "Noori can give the tour
pitch without help."

"I need you to keep them under control. They're shocked
by what they heard last night. They'll want to talk about it.
They're not interested in the tent city. It would be disastrous
if Colonel Noori learned about the abdication before I have it
out with Ramir. If one of them opens up, you'll be there to
change the subject."

"I hope . . ."

"Do your best, Luke."

She hadn't wheedled, she hadn't commanded. Yet here he
was, doing her bidding because she made sense and because
he loved her. Luke dug a packet of matches from his jeans.
Pretending to be absorbed in lighting the cigarette stuck to
his lower lip, he stood apart from the bus and winced as
Agnes Curtis, trailed by Joe, came through the wrought-iron
gates.

"Christ, it's hot," Agnes complained. "We got better weather than this in Boston."

"Stop bitching. I told you to leave off the girdle, didn't
I?"

Agnes looked around peevishly. "Where are the Hollywood
jokers and Father Flynn? Aren't they coming?" She rubbed a
limp Kleenex across her dampening chest. Distractedly, Joe
handed her another.

"Hey, schoolteacher," Agnes yelled. "When do we get the
show on the road?"

"Mr. Wagg and Mr. Braden will be along in a moment.
Miss Shapiro is in the bus."

"Bus!" Agnes shrilled. "Where are the limos?"

"His Majesty commissioned a fleet of buses to be custom
made in Detroit especially for the Jubilee. The buses are
comfortably upholstered and fully air-conditioned. Next week
they will be the principal mode of transport for our guests. A
representative of the Pope will be among them, Mrs. Curtis."

"I recognize a put-down when I hear it, Mr. Smart Guy,"
Agnes said.

"We will be crossing desert for an hour each way, Mrs. Curtis," Colonel Noori volunteered. "You will appreciate the spaciousness of the bus. Take any seat you wish. From time to time I will address you through the loudspeaker—tell you about Celebration City. Not too much—it would lessen the impact of what lies ahead. All I ask is that you try to picture it in your mind's eye as it will be next week when it is filled with the greatest assemblage of world leaders since the funeral of Charles de Gaulle."

"Bravo, Colonel." Luke applauded.

The colonel reddened. "This will be a happier occasion."

Joe Curtis peered at the colonel. A new worry had entered his mind. "Where do we stay when the biggies get here?"

"In your present quarters, Mr. Curtis," Luke responded. "Your accommodations, I assure you, will be grander than the King of Saudi Arabia's. Celebration City is a marvel but it contains nothing as splendid as the palace."

Placated, the Curtises descended to the forecourt. "Let's get the show on the road," Joe said. Sighting Wagg and Braden in the doorway, he shouted, "Get your asses down here, boys. We're ready to go."

Joe followed Agnes toward the bus. Suddenly he stopped and looked about, puzzled. "Hey, schoolteacher," he called out, "where's Father Flynn?"

"Forgive me. Father Flynn asked me to express his regrets to the rest of you. He was summoned home unexpectedly. At this moment he's airborne on his way to Boston."

"You got to be kidding." Agnes reversed her steps. "Fifteen years to get him here and he flies the coop just like that? What's going on?"

"I am not in his confidence. Father Flynn gave me no further information."

"I'll be damned," said Joe.

As the bus rolled south on the newly paved road between the palace and Celebration City, Luke struggled to capture the attention of his five charges. Except for Wagg they exhibited little curiosity about the history of ancient Bahrait or in the passing scenery. The actor contributed a few toothy smiles and then, like the Curtises and Selma, withdrew into silence.

Colonel Noori tried rousing them. "Bahrait is the oldest nation in the Islamic world," he began. "Over the centuries many dynamic Shahs have emerged. Through agreements and compromises with its neighbors the territory of our country has been substantially enlarged."

"Agreements, compromises?" Wagg asked.

Colonel Noori remained unruffled. "Like land expansion everywhere, the drawing of new borders was accomplished through moderate use of force. In the end Bahrait proved more persuasive than its opponents. The father of Shah Ramir was a man of exceptional strength and patriotism. He forged a powerful nation, freeing the present Shah and Empress for more peaceful pursuits of benefit to the people."

Selma stirred in her seat. "Colonel, that's a crock. In the past half hour we've passed fleets of motorized tanks and enough Quonset huts to house Hitler's army. What's that about?"

"Defense," the colonel replied evenly. "Every nation, however peaceful its intent, must stand prepared to protect itself against predatory neighbors. Shah Ramir entertains no expansionist dreams. As a responsible head of state he is obliged to maintain a sizeable military force and constantly update its capabilities. But for defensive purposes only."

"Who's threatening you?" Selma demanded.

"To my knowledge, no one, I am relieved to say."

"Then it must be the natives who are restless."

"I doubt that."

"So what's everyone hollering about? You have riots and arson going on in the streets. We read about your demonstrations back home."

"And we, Miss Shapiro, read the same about your country."

"A minor difference, sir. In the U.S. an uprising is an event. Here it's a way of life."

Luke pushed his way between them. "You two are getting off the rails. Selma, the rest of you, please pay attention to Colonel Noori. You'll find his capsule history of Bahrait a remarkable story."

"Bug off," Selma requested and returned her gaze to the window.

Luke glanced about. The others were slumped in their seats, some with eyes closed. They were boorish but they were quiet. It could be worse.

The colonel acknowledged defeat. "Ladies and gentlemen,

you are wise to rest. I, too, must save my energy for Celebration City."

The driver of the bus clipped along the road seemingly oblivious to the goings-on behind him. His companion shot him a wink and the two men exchanged grins. So far no one had observed that the vehicle they commanded was equipped with extra rearview mirrors, a pair for each of them. With luck, their evening report would be juicy.

Celebration City rose like a mirage. It spread before them—glistening lawns and trees, a storybook village of Arabian Nights tents draped in lustrous multicolored silks. Cooling fountains splashed everywhere.

In the heavy air the blues and yellows and oranges and purples of the silk rippled sensuously as an occasional small animal or bird found its way between the plywood frames of the tents and the concealing folds of the draperies.

Workers bustling about stole furtive peeks at the party of strangers, then returned to their jobs, moving furniture into tents, testing locks and fastenings, dropping trees and shrubs and full-blooming flowers into earth newly prepared to receive them.

A wispy man in a stylish jump suit stepped away from the gardeners.

"Jules!" Colonel Noori's voice rose above the clatter. "Come meet our guests from America. Here is Monsieur Jules Le Brun, on leave from the Tuileries Gardens in Paris," he announced. "We owe his presence to the generosity of the premier of France, a great friend of our Shah. *Ça va bien,* Jules?"

The little man, an agitated exclamation point, brought his fingers to his lips and smacked them loudly. "See for yourself. Exquisite already. Tomorrow the peacocks will arrive. In a few more days—ah—Louis the Sun King would have wished such beauty for Versailles!"

"Who's responsible for that thing of beauty?" Selma pointed to the barbed-wire fence encircling the compound. "How about the guardhouses at the gate and the boys with rifles who blocked our bus? Some Versailles."

"Security, Miss Shapiro," Colonel Noori said blandly. "They had it at Versailles, too. I admit the uniforms were prettier then. Do not be disturbed. Our friends are safe."

Luke tugged at Selma's sleeve. "I suggest you remain a

friend. I'm responsible for keeping this sewing bee under control."

"And if I won't play?"

"In the words of Her Imperial Majesty, the Empress Marianna—'Luke, the others are apolitical. They won't see anything but the glitter. It's Selma I'm worried about. If she gets difficult, bat her in the mouth.' "

"That's the royal pronouncement?"

"From Herself."

"Your round. Censorship, repression, torture. Whatever happens, I'll be dumb as a rock."

"Good girl. Let's follow our leader."

Colonel Noori greeted them. "I was explaining to the others—the tents are hardly primitive. Each bedroom—even those for the servants—is supplied with Porthault linens sent from Paris. The bathrooms are marble with solid gold fittings. Women will find bidets. Persian carpets cover parquet floors in the salons. Baskets of scents and soaps are in place. Entertaining ranking heads of state such as the King and Queen of Spain, the King and Queen of Sweden, and the papal emissary is a delicate affair. One wishes to provide the most exquisite accommodations short of individual palaces.

"The tents do not have their own kitchens. At the touch of a bell one of our forty French chefs will respond straightaway. The chefs have been instructed to satisfy any culinary whim without delay. Dinners will be formal, hosted by the Shah and Empress in the ballroom of their tent. The Empress has granted me permission to escort you through the royal quarters. Ready?"

Colonel Noori rounded a corner and pointed to a grassy hillock. "Up ahead," he said. "You can't miss it."

"Miss it?" Agnes squealed. "It's like Fenway Park in silk pajamas."

"A compliment, Mrs. Curtis?" the colonel asked.

"You bet."

"Thank you. I will lead the way."

A covey of uniformed guards, rifles slung across their shoulders, awaited them. At a signal from the colonel they parted the scarlet drapes, exposing carved ebony doors.

Selma shoved her way to the head of the group. Brushing past the startled guards, she opened the doors. "Get a load of this ballroom," she shouted. "Doug, Watson, over here, quick!

Remember when Hanover made the life of Marie Antoinette? Budgeted at six million, a pretty penny in those days. The costs doubled before we had a ballroom half as gorgeous as this. Look at the crystal chandeliers, and the frescoes on the ceiling, and the paintings on the walls. Migawd, they must be museum pieces."

"They are, Miss Shapiro. They will be restored to the National Museum in Ryal when the parties are over. In this room. Their Majesties will hold their receptions. An adjoining room similar to this will be used for dining. In the rear we have the royal sleeping quarters. Not so lavish as those at the palace. However, the Shah believes he and his family must properly remain among their guests."

Doug Braden fell behind with Watson Wagg. "She must be crazy to walk out on this," Doug said. "What's going on with her?"

Watson shook his head. "My mind is as empty as yours. Someday we'll understand. Meanwhile, we've got to think of ourselves."

"I've done my best, Watson. I offered her a strong shoulder to lean on. I gave her a brotherly kiss and an extra hug. Hoped it would stir those old embers."

"What happened?"

"She shook loose. Gave me a 'drop dead' look and walked off."

They were back on the bus, recrossing the desert. Luke sat beside Colonel Noori. Both were exhausted, and relieved that the strain of the trip was nearly behind them.

They came to attention when Selma called out from her window seat. "That's an amazing job your team's accomplished, Colonel. When did the Shah last visit Celebration City?"

"Several weeks ago. He will be overcome when he returns."

"Yeah," Selma agreed. "I guess you could say that."

She fell back in her seat. To Luke's relief, she kept her eyes and her mouth shut until they were again in the palace forecourt.

The two CIA men dismounted from the bus.

"Slim pickings," one remarked.

"A bust," his partner agreed.

Calvin Gropper, looking like a Prussian general, turned his back to Hilary and stood stiffly at their second-story window, watching Marianna's guests straggle from the bus. His expression was stern, his jaw jutted, his feet were planted wide apart, and his hands on his hips were taut.

"*Achtung,*" Hilary called from the bed. "Calvin, darling, you forgot your riding crop."

He refused to face her. He knew she was furious. Moments before, he had wrenched his head from the shallow crevice between her breasts, indifferent to the puckered nipples she had jabbed into his cheeks.

"Don't be nasty, Hilary, not now. I must find a solution to this mess." He tipped his head contemptuously in the direction of the forecourt. "They're back, those little people with their little problems. What do they know of the magnitude of mine?"

"Yours? Why must all the problems of the world be yours? What if she does abdicate? She's common. Ramir is tired of her. There'll be a flurry in the press. What of it? She'll soon be forgotten. How old is she?"

"Thirty-eight."

"Almost forty," Hilary gloated. "Her film future is limited. She'll end up like other royal castoffs—a villa on the Mediterranean, casino nights in Monte Carlo, younger men. She doesn't have the class for Palm Beach—"

"Stop it! You don't understand. We need her."

"Who needs her? I don't."

"Our government needs her. She's the best ambassador the United States had had since Benjamin Franklin. The State Department considers my role in arranging that marriage the coup of my career. I shouldn't have let you wheedle the whole story out of me. I thought you would appreciate what I had accomplished. But you are incapable of comprehending. You're not usually this stupid, Hilary. Can't you understand? Almost singlehandedly, without firing a shot, I planted the American presence in a foreign country. Now we're about to lose that presence."

"Agreed, you've been a hero. You got to take home the door prize. Who cares anymore?"

"I care. Ramir will care. Our State Department will care. How can you be so moronic?"

"Calvin, you're making me cross."

"Listen to me." He swung about. "Try to grasp this.

Marianna is the key to our arms deals here. Her abdication would be a catastrophe, a dangerous breach between the United States and Bahrait. Our armament industry needs Bahrait. Bahrait needs our armament industry. Billions of dollars are involved. Should Marianna leave, it will raise fresh doubts among Americans who are already lukewarm toward our trade with Ramir's government.

"Marianna as Empress is a symbol, not merely a former movie star. We have no understudy for her role. If Ramir can no longer bring his military shopping list to us, he'll turn to the Soviets. Marianna stands in the eye of a hurricane. We must keep her in place. And you, my sweet, had better pull in your fangs and tone down that fancy Boston Brahmin act when you're around her."

"Calvin!"

"Obey me. This is vital. Marianna is not a political creature. She doesn't recognize the fallout of what she's contemplating. She doesn't know that right now she is the most important woman in the world."

Marianna snapped her fingers and the projectionist high in his booth caught the signal. He dimmed the theater lights gradually, but not before Marianna's eyes swept the room, confirming that none of her guests was missing.

They were there, each and every one of them, sunk into buttery leather chairs scattered in random rows across the room. Watson Wagg, grown nearsighted over the years, had rolled his chair closer to the screen. Joe and Agnes, usually undemonstrative, had sought each other's hands and held tight, a pair of frightened children abandoned in a threatening world. Doug Braden squinted at the screen, too vain to pull out the glasses in his breast pocket. At the far end of the theater the Groppers, mutually hostile during dinner, were behaving like snapping turtles.

Beside Marianna, Selma chuckled. "You had them scared to death back in the dining room, telling them you had one more surprise to announce."

"It was bitchy of me," Marianna admitted. "I only wanted to say that I'd be running an old movie tonight."

"So this is where it began, the romance of the century."

"Please, Selma, don't—"

"I'll never forget it, sitting in my cubbyhole at Hanover, writing the press release. Jerry Crane, the son-of-a-bitch, liked it so much he swiped my by-line." She began to recite. " 'Night after lonely night, as the celluloid reels revolved, the widowed Shah of Bahrait sat alone in the projection room of his palace and watched the films of America's most beloved movie star unfold before his eyes. I knew she was performing," the Shah said today, speaking lines written for her, yet her personal sweetness and beauty of soul radiated beyond the make-believe. Viewing her over and over in that darkened room, I fell in love. Yes, in love with a woman I had never met.' "

"Stop that, Selma."

"No, I want you to remember the whole bit. Besides, the best part's coming. 'When dear friends brought us together, my faith in Allah, always unquestioned, grew stronger still. There she stood, warmer, more gracious and lovely than I'd dared to dream. Since the moment she promised to become my wife I have known happiness given to few men on earth.' "

"You believed it. Selma."

"Yes."

"So did I."

The room was in total darkness. Only the whirring sound of the lead film could be heard. Then the familiar head of the Hanover lion filled the screen, tossing his mane, roaring as he had at the start of thousands of Hanover films. Melancholy violins poured from the sound track, followed by ominous oboes and drums warning of tragedy to come. Then violins again, joyous this time, covering a pastoral long shot of two faraway figures running toward the camera—a tousled youth wearing homespun breeches, pursuing a laughing barefoot girl with flying yellow hair who was racing across a field of synthetic purple heather.

"It's *Shadow Darkens!*" Doug Braden bounced in his seat. "Marianna, what a treat."

"Quiet down front," Selma called out. "We wanna hear the dialogue." She studied Marianna's unhappy profile. Dropping her voice, she said, "What a tasty dish to set before a king."

"Fifteen years ago."

"Fifteen years from now, too," Selma said loyally.

Marianna was wistful. "You do think I have a chance? They won't have to shoot me through a scrim?"

"You look better than ever. Who needs the Empress crap. Kids will find out there's life after forty. Older fans will be inspired. Can't you see that?"

"No. Inside I feel dry and wrinkled. Audiences will sense it."

"That's tonight, here. Who wouldn't feel that way? It's anti-nature, the things you put up with. In Hollywood you'll come alive. You'll be with Luke out in the open. Or meet other men if that's what you want. There are plenty of guys—smart, exciting, not like that lox, Braden."

"I'm scared."

"What else is new? After the crowd splits I'm giving you a pep talk. How much longed does this turkey run?"

"Another hour or so. Shut your eyes if you're bored. I'm sick of it myself."

"So turn it off."

"Can't. Look at the others. They're eating it up."

"The hell they are. They're just happier in the dark than looking at each other."

While Selma dozed beside her, Marianna reviewed her motives in running *The Shadow Darkens*. Number One: She wanted to remind the Groppers—particularly Calvin—that she had once had, and would again have, her own identity. Number Two: She hoped to put starch in the dissolving backbones of Watson and Doug. As a trio, they'd pulled it off before and they would again. Number Three (which should have been Number One): She needed the satisfying strokes derived from watching her own radiant image on the screen.

Her thoughts were drifting away now, away from this room, this palace, this country, this marriage. She saw herself in another place, vague, undefined—without a past, free.

She did not hear the door handle turn. Not until a slither of light entered the projection room was she aware of the tall military figure in the doorway, agitatedly seeking someone in the audience.

She started to rise but the man—with the light behind him she could not make out his face—waved her to be seated.

He closed the door carefully, throwing the room back into darkness. Marianna followed his progress as he moved crab-wise along the opposite wall. It was Calvin Gropper he wanted. In the light from the screen she finally recognized the officer as Major Jaafar Sanjabi of the palace security staff.

Major Sanjabi tapped Calvin on the shoulder and mumbled something in his ear. Calvin scrambled to his feet. Brushing off Hilary's irritation, he followed the major up the aisle. The slither of light came and went as they disappeared into the outer hall.

Marianna's eyes refocused on the screen but her thoughts remained with the brief charade she had witnessed. When the men did not return in a few minutes, she dismissed the episode from her mind. Calvin, although no longer the United States Secretary of State, had never relinquished the notion that he ran the world. He remained a one-man CIA, KGB, and SAVAK, the repository of every nation's most secret scraps of information, however obtained. Possibly a decision was needed by the Emir of Oman, or the President of Mexico, or the Prince of Monaco. There seemed to be no pie without Calvin Gropper's finger in it.

The Shadow Darkens was nearing its climax. Only a few minutes more and it would be over. For those who did not seek immediate escape there would be snacks of caviar and pâté de foie gras served with drinks. For herself, a quick visit with Selma, then bath, bed, and oblivion.

Viewing her screen image in the final reel, Marianna was cheered. She was a damned good actress. Dr. Lasseaux's words, spoken in Paris, came back to her. "You were born with precious gifts. You developed great skills. They will always be there when you need them. You did not get your Academy Award for your beauty but for your art."

Dr. Lasseaux was right, of course. She'd won the award for her role in *Timothy's Dream*, in which she'd impersonated the drab, shabby, beaten wife of a besotted, unfaithful prize-fighter. Without makeup, her hair combed through with oil to make it stringy, she'd had nothing but her talent to carry the performance.

The award had been doubly gratifying. *Timothy's Dream*, conceived as an art film, had achieved financial success, a tawdry fact that thrilled the studio but which was known to evoke resentment among certain Academy voters. Despite this handicap, a jury of her peers had discarded their prejudice and awarded Marianna Curtis its most coveted prize, the Oscar. Last night Marianna had taken the figure down from a shelf in her dressing room and held its cool gold-plated body to her cheek.

Fortified by recollections of Hollywood triumphs, confident

that with or without old friends she could make her way as an actress, Marianna allowed herself to think of Ramir.

Instantly her bravado crumbled.

He was coming home. His private plane would drop him down in Ryal in the morning. Colonel Hejazi, a member of Ramir's entourage, had telephoned with orders that everyone was to be alerted for His Majesty's return—the crew on the landing strip, the entire palace staff, His Majesty's masseur, and his family.

In the dark of the theater Marianna braced herself for the reunion.

She would go to the airfield to meet him. She hadn't done that in years, not since the terrible incident in St. Moritz. A public display of marital unity would please him. It would be a treat for the welcoming press.

She would rush forward and embrace him, take his arm, insist upon riding alone with him in the rear of the bullet-proof limousine. She would smilingly suggest that his body-guards crowd up front with the chauffeur, leaving the two of them alone, cut off by the soundproof glass partition. Ramir would ask about the children, the guests, the progress of Celebration City. He would ask about her. And she would tell him. Not everything, not at once. Just enough to prepare him before Calvin Gropper caught his ear.

She was afraid of his anger. As a pampered prince he'd had little need to control his temper. He could fling his rage in all directions—only his father had ever opposed him, and then infrequently. Later, when he became Shah, Ramir's temper, like his body, had attained full maturity. Marianna had known actors like Ramir. Made arrogant by stardom, they had been transformed from reasonable human beings into uncontrollable Mr. Hydes, hurling their power at anyone who crossed them, secure in their misbehavior because no one dared argue with a winner.

She would tread carefully. Fortunately, Calvin had let slip the fact that Ramir suspected her flirtation with Hollywood, had actually gone behind her back to discuss the subject with his friend.

But abdication? She knew there would be a terrifying scene when she mentioned the word. She would not capitulate. If everything went according to her expectations, the worst of it could be dealt with in the car. If it could not, she would employ her immediate weapon. She would tell him that unless his behavior was totally civilized she would walk out before the celebration, leaving it to him to explain to the notables and to the press that his wife had abandoned him.

This time she had him by the balls. She would squeeze and squeeze until he screamed for mercy.

The thought made her giddy. A crazy giggle escaped her lips, rousing Selma.

"Hey, what's going on?"

"Nothing. Something. An idea I have for tomorrow. I'll tell you later."

"Okay, okay, I'll wait. I mean what's going on behind us?"

Marianna looked toward the rear door through which light was once again spilling and saw Calvin Gropper hurtling in her direction.

"Please, all of you," he said to the guests staring at him, "please continue to enjoy the film. I must have a word with Her Majesty." His heavy body plunged forward, almost tripping, before he reached her.

"Of course, Calvin. If the rest of you will excuse me . . ."

Once on her feet, she permitted herself to be propelled from the screening room by Gropper, who broke into a clumsy trot as he pushed her through the door. Her eyes widened when she made out Major Sanjabi leaning against a wall, his bronzed face gone waxen. Fearfully she shifted her gaze to Gropper. His lips worked but he said nothing. When he removed his steamy glasses she could see that he was crying.

"Calvin, what is it?" She was startled by the hysteria in her voice. "Calvin!" She gripped his shoulders and shook him violently. "Calvin, what's happened?"

Gropper reached for a handkerchief, wiped his glasses, blew his nose. His efforts to compose himself failed. Sobbing, he managed a few choked words. "He's dead, Marianna. Ramir is dead. An accident—in his car. In Paris."

He fell into her arms and she tried to comfort him.

"It can't be true," she said reassuringly. "He's coming back. He'll be here tomorrow. Everything's arranged. I'm going to the airport to meet him. We're driving to the palace together. He and I, just the two of us in the rear seat. We must talk about the future."

Calvin raised his head. "No, you will never talk to him again. Try to understand. Ramir is *dead!* An accident. On the

Pont Alexandre. He was at the wheel, on his way to the house in Neuilly. A second car. Two o'clock in the morning. Fog. It was over instantly."

Realization dawned slowly. "Paris? He was in *Paris?* Who told you this?"

"The President of France, directly from the Élysée Palace. He described the accident. He promised the matter would be handled with the utmost discretion."

"Discretion? Calvin—" Her voice was dull. "Calvin, was he alone?"

"Does it matter now?"

"It matters."

"I really don't . . ."

"Calvin!"

"There was a woman, a French actress. She escaped unharmed. There will be no scandal. The President himself has been involved with her. Both have reason to be circumspect."

She didn't know why she began to cry, dry heaving sobs first, followed by moaning and tears.

She was aware that the commotion had brought the others from the screening room. They were crowding about her, blurred figures, questioning, bewildered.

Still she wept and called his name. "Ramir, don't be dead! Please, please don't be dead!"

Her personal doctor, Reza Hosseini, materialized before her, a silk robe tied over his pajamas. She felt a needle slip into her arm. "Stop," she screamed. "I have things to do. The children . . ."

"They are asleep," someone said. "The nurse has been warned to keep everyone away. In the morning we will bring them to you."

"Karim? Dahlia?"

"We will inform them."

"No, I must tell them myself!"

"In a little while. The shot will not put you to sleep," the doctor said. "It will merely calm you. I cannot permit you to lose consciousness and awaken to this nightmare. First you must try to absorb what has happened."

"Never," she insisted. "Never. I want my husband!"

Dr. Hosseini drew her to him. "My dear, my dear, how can I comfort you? There is no way now. But we have a saying, we doctors—'The tincture of time, that is the best healer.'

You must get rest. Send for me at any hour. I will come. Meanwhile, someone must be with you. Shall I call your maid?"

"No, I don't need her."

Her eyes focused on the semicircle gathered near her. "Selma?"

"Here and waiting, darling."

16

She struggled to piece it together. Images came and went, some vague, others vivid. She remembered that Selma had undressed her, led her to bed, begged her to relax against the pillows, to let the Demerol take ovar. She had fought Selma, fought the drug, protesting she had too much to do. There were calls to be made, she insisted, important calls that were her responsibility.

With Selma's help she had roused Luke, told him about the accident, asked him to fly to Switzerland at once, to return with Karim. No, she said, Karim had not been informed. She would telephone him next.

Then the call to Switzerland, to Le Rosey. Summoning her French, she had identified herself to the drowsy switchboard operator and asked to be connected with the headmaster. The headmaster, heeding her request, had awakened Karim and remained beside the boy while he spoke with his mother. To her clouded mind, Karim's cry of anguish seemed an over-reaction. She told him she loved him, she needed him, she would see him the following day.

In Paris, Dahlia's lover, Regis, had picked up the phone on the third ring. She apologized for disturbing him, stammered the reason for her call, heard his disbelieving "Oh no!" Then Dahlia was on the line. "Here, in Paris? It can't be true!" Dhalia had collapsed and Regis was back on the phone. "What can I do?"

"Contact the Élysée Palace. A plane will be made available to Dahlia. No, you may not accompany her." She held the phone from her ear to distance his sputtering words. "No," she repeated. "I forbid it. The police—you will not be safe here."

Then a call to Azar, located by Colonel Noori in Istanbul. "I will be on the first commercial flight," Azar promised.

And then, bizarrely, a call to Pia in Lausanne.

The Swedish woman had answered the telephone herself, cheerful, although it was obvious she, too, had been awakened.

"Pia, can you hear me?"

"Yes, who is this, please?"

"It's Marianna. I am in Ryal. Are you alone?"

"Your Majesty, you are asking if Ramir is here. He is not."

"I know that."

"Then why . . . ?"

"Because . . . oh, Pia, how can I tell you?"

"Whatever you have to tell me, you must tell me straight," Pia replied. "I also will be direct."

The drug was wearing off, the horror returning. "Pia," she stammered. "Pia . . . Ramir is dead."

The strong voice in Lausanne faltered. "That is the truth? When? How?"

Marianna strained to hold back her hysteria. With care she described the When, the How. She added the Where. She made no mention of With Whom.

"I had to call you. You loved him. So did I, once. I couldn't let you learn of his death from a news report. I wanted you to hear it from . . . a friend."

"None of this is real," Pia cried out. "You are making up a story because you are angry with me—spiteful!"

"It *is* real, Pia. Oh my God, it's real."

The telephone fell from her hand and she began to sob.

Someone, Selma she supposed, had sent for Dr. Hosseini. He had inserted another needle into her arm and soon she was calm. Irrational, but calm.

She could get no grip on time. She had lost all sense of it. It stood still. It raced meaninglessly. She knew awesome events had brushed past her, yet she was frozen in a terrifying, incomprehensible present.

Something else had occurred in those terrible moments outside the projection room. Something enormous. Something too important to be permitted to escape. Something she had witnessed and heard before the Demerol claimed her.

Resisting the sedative effects of the doctor's second shot, she had searched the blocked tunnels of her memory, looking for the chink, the ray of understanding that would end her confusion.

Then she had remembered and she was stunned.

How long ago had she learned of Ramir's death? An hour? Less? Whenever. . . . The buried moment had resurfaced. She had to confront it. Calvin Gropper had regained his self-possession, she recalled. Without explanation he had hurried

from the anteroom. When he returned General Mojeeb was
with him. The uniformed general had offered condolences,
and looked at her oddly. Then, with Gropper, he had stepped
outside the semicircle of her guests. She had seen the two
men withdraw to a far corner of the room, observed them
talking rapidly, urgently. Then Calvin had spun around and
stared at her, mouth agape.

"Oh no, impossible," Calvin had gasped.

And Mojeeb, anxious, audible, had replied, "It is true. Ten
years ago. I myself had forgotten. He intended to revoke it.
When Karim became sixteen."

And then Selma had taken her away to bed.

She came to her feet shakily.

"Back in the feathers for you, honey," Selma said.

"Not yet. I mustn't sleep," she said. "There's a secret being
kept from me. Gropper and Mojeeb have the answer." She
wrapped herself in the robe her maid had placed at the foot
of the bed and started for the door.

"Where do you think you're going?" Selma demanded.

"They'll be there—Gropper, the general, maybe the others.
The way they stared at me, Gropper and Mojeeb. Shocked.
Not because of Ramir. Something else. Something about me.
I must get to them."

Woozily she fumbled with the cord of her robe, unable to
tie it.

"Let me," Selma said. "Okay, you're fixed. Hang on to my
arm."

They were still there, clustered in the entry, dry-eyed, upset
yet not saddened. Low, mumbled questions and answers
erupted among them, followed by awkward silences. From
the upper landing she searched their faces, saw only dullness,
puzzlement, connivery.

Her hand gripped the cold marble rail of the balustrade.
Throwing off Selma's support, still clutching the rail, she
started down the long staircase, her footsteps muffled by the
heavy carpeting. Halfway, she stopped. Steadying herself, she
stood erect and spoke. "Dear friends," she said. "May I join
you?"

Startled, they looked toward her.

Agnes clambered up the steps. Her red hair, so carefully
coiffed for dinner, now rumpled by nervous fingers, was

shooting out in slatternly tufts. "My darling child, where are you going? You should be in bed. Let Auntie Aggie take you back."

"Agnes, let go. Everyone, stay where you are."

"Marianna." Doug started toward her.

"Don't come near me," she warned. "I want every one of you where I can see you. I demand to know what's going on. Look at yourselves. Not a damp eye in sight. The Shah is dead. Are you planning a coup, General? Are these your troops?"

"You just watch what you're saying..." Hilary's long stride brought her to the foot of the staircase.

"Sorry, Hilary, I didn't mean you. You have your own kingdom. You hardly need this one."

"Your Majesty," General Mojeeb interrupted. "It is right that you are here. There is something we must remind you of. In consideration of your present state, after the terrible blow, we had thought it best to wait until morning. However—"

Her gaze hardened. "Now," she commanded.

They cast about, searching for a spokesman.

"Your Majesty—" Gropper began.

"Your Majesty? From you, Calvin?" She giggled foolishly, made drunk by the sedation. "What's up your sleeve this time?"

"For myself, nothing. It is General Mojeeb who has given us a startling piece of information."

"General?"

"Your Majesty, I reminded Mr. Gropper of our beloved Shah's wish put before the council a decade ago."

"Go on."

"It was a time of great pressure on Bahrait. Leftist strength was growing. There was fear Bahrait would swing toward the Eastern bloc. American businessmen were reluctant to invest in our country. Do you remember?"

"Not really," she admitted.

"Our beloved Shah was determined to put down hostile elements. Evidence was needed that our ties with the country of your birth would remain strong. He proclaimed that in the event of his death, you—instead of the Crown Prince—would succeed him. Not as regent, but as sole and lifetime ruler of Bahrait. I remember his words: 'Among those who surround me in my council, none is wiser, more able, than the Empress.'"

"But he didn't mean that!"

"No, Your Majesty—I say this most respectfully—he did not mean it. Once his sincerity was established, he planned to rescind the proclamation. The right of succession was to be returned to the Crown Prince."

"Yes, that was my wish, too. We agreed, Ramir and I . . ."

"It was never done."

"Why not?"

Mojeeb smiled without humor. "The scheme backfired. Soundings revealed our own people—particularly the women —approved the Shah's action. It is true that when Karim was born everyone celebrated the arrival of the male heir—"

"I haven't forgotten. I was a heroine then."

"But later, new ideas reached Bahrait. Our women began to perceive themselves as more than chattel. They applauded Ramir for recognizing the potential of one of their own sex. Businessmen viewed Ramir's move as a long overdue step into the twentieth century. We could not risk a citizens' outcry by reversing the edict too soon."

"And your opinion, General?"

"I am a traditionalist. Like the Shah, I believe the throne belongs to the male heir. His Majesty and I planned to move slowly, to delay the reversion of the succession to Karim until the people could see the boy not as a youngster but as a responsible adult. Then you were to publicly—and proudly— announce that Karim was once again the heir. The time was near. Who could have anticipated tonight's tragedy?"

Nausea rose in her throat, the faces below merged and parted and merged again. The carrousel of her mind spun out of control. From a faraway place she heard Gropper's voice.

"Marianna," he was saying, "Bahrait is yours. Every citizen is your subject. The armed forces, the police, the inherent wealth and power of the throne—they belong to you. You are no longer a consort, an Empress by virtue of your marriage to a Shah. Tonight you are the ruler of Bahrait. Tonight you truly became the Empress."

The doctor stayed with her until morning. Before drifting off to sleep she heard him order Selma to her own room.

"You need rest, Miss Shapiro."

"Oh yeah? Who's going to watch her? I don't want any of those vultures getting in."

"I'll be at her side until she awakens."

"She'll want to see her kids right away. Their nursemaid can bring them. Does the nursemaid know?"

"I informed her myself," the doctor said.

"And you told her she's not to let anyone talk to them before their mother does?"

"I did."

"Good work, Doc."

"Thank you, madam." Dr. Hosseini's eyes bored into her. "Miss Shapiro, may I inform you the Empress is *my* patient. And not my first one. I am a graduate of Harvard Medical School. I interned at Massachusetts General. I practiced in New York City where I refined my skills and my colloquial English. Miss Shapiro, in the vernacular, will you kindly get the hell out of here."

At dawn the doctor was still there and Selma was back. Coming out of a dream, Marianna smiled up at them. In moments reality gripped her. She gazed into their pitying faces and began to moan. Selma hurried to her side but Dr. Hosseini elbowed her away.

"Sit up, Your Majesty," he said, handing her a glass of water. "Swallow these pills. They will make you feel better."

"Hold on there! What are you trying to do, make a doper out of her?" Selma said.

The doctor sighed. "Miss Shapiro, how quickly you forget. Allow me to be alone with my patient. Soon she will be mildly sedated. The children will be frightened enough. They must not see their mother in this condition."

"Sorry, Doc. Guess I can't help butting in." Meekly Selma left the suite.

The children raced into the room, tumbling, laughing, curious about this unexpected treat at an hour when they were normally in the schoolhouse.

Drawing closer, they faltered, made uneasy by the blank expression in their mother's eyes.

"Come, my babies," Marianna said. Grabbing them to her, she crushed their dark curly heads to her breast. Slipping her own yellow head between theirs, she told them what had happened, her voice inaudible to the doctor standing nearby. When they raised their faces they were tearful but controlled.

Freeing them, she said, 'Nurse will take you now. To the mosque for prayer. Remember what you learned from the Holy Koran—that our time on earth is set by God. 'No one can die except by God's purpose, according to the Book that fixeth the terms of life.' And remember, the Koran tells us of the resurrection. One day your father will be raised up and renewed. You will meet him again."

The doctor watched the children leave. "Is there anything . . . ?"

"No, Dr. Hosseini. Thank you. I see you are an actor, too. You try to hide your grief from me. Leave now. Join your wife and have your own good cry. You knew Ramir longer, perhaps better, than I did. He loved you."

"I loved him."

"Doctor, what I told the children, about the Koran, about meeting Ramir again—do you believe that?"

"I am a Moslem. Of course I believe."

"You're a man of science, too."

"That is second. What about you? Do you believe?"

"I want to believe—as a Moslem, as a former Catholic. My husband, my mother, my father—we never finished our time on earth together."

"Then you must try to believe. Gather what strength you can. The days ahead will be difficult."

"I'll stay here until the children return. I won't see anyone else today."

"Unfortunately that is not possible. There are others. Since last night I have been holding them off."

"Who?"

"General Mojeeb and Mr. Gropper. They are the most persistent."

"Can't you tell them I'm not up to seeing them?"

"I have told them, yet they remain outside the door. They are sympathetic but they insist that you talk with them."

They stood before her, disheveled, the marks of sleeplessness branded about their eyes and on their pallid skin. When she invited them to be seated they slumped into the nearest chairs.

"We're all weary," she said. "There's no need for amenities. Tell me why you came and you can go quickly."

"Your Majesty, this is painful," General Mojeeb began. "There are arrangements, matters of immediate concern."

"We regret this interference," Gropper interrupted, "but much waits on your wishes. The announcement to the public, the arrangements for the funeral, the cancellation of the Jubilee. Decisions must be made."

"Make them. You know better than I what must be done."

"An the investiture. A simple ceremony. You acknowledge your assumption of the throne, pledge yourself to the people . . ."

"I'm not ready for that."

The two men exchanged glances. "The investiture can be postponed," Gropper said.

"There is no hurry," the general added. "Later, when you are strong—"

"Then it's settled," Marianna said. "There will be no investiture until I decide the time is right. The rest I leave to you."

Ironically, Ramir's funeral attracted more notables than the canceled anniversary fête. Dignitaries flowed in and out of the small darkened reception room where the pale Empress sat quietly accepting expressions of condolence and vows of friendship to her and to Bahrait. Karim, solemn and dignified, remained beside her, hastening the callers, smoothly cutting short their speeches when the strain on his mother became too great.

Private services attended only by the family were held in the Mosque of the Faithful. A wailing mob of thousands followed the funeral cortege to the ancient cemetery where former generations of the dynasty lay buried. Soldiers using bayonets restrained the hysterical crowd when it attempted to storm the gates for a glimpse of the marble mausoleum where Ramir was entombed beside his father.

In the mosque Dahlia, shed of her Paris persona, beat her chest in grief and called out to Allah. Azar joined her, dropping to her knees, flailing her body, crying uninhibitedly.

Later, Dahlia had come to Marianna. "What will happen to you? What can I do to help?"

"Return to Paris, to your studies. Your life isn't here. One day when I need you I'll ask you to come to me."

Doug and Watson had appeared too, with offers to stay on if they could be useful through this terrible time. Without risking an answer they had embraced her and left the room.

Joe and Aggie, awash with pity and whiskey, attempted to turn her mourning period into an old-fashioned wake. Reminding her that blood was thicker than water, they pledged to come running when she whistled. She thanked them, told them to return to Boston. She promised she would send for them soon.

She saw little of the Groppers and was thankful.

She wanted them gone, everyone but Selma. She needed time to absorb the horror, to consider her alternatives.

During the weeks that followed, guilt tempered her relief in being free. Free! The idea was strange, frightening; it made her heady and ashamed all at once. She had been prepared to fight for her freedom, to face an uncertain future, to risk rage, failure, even separation from her children. And now freedom had been handed to her. Ramir had died and in doing so had given her the only gift she truly wanted. Remembrances of happier days rose to rebuke her, but they did not linger long.

She was free. Free to gather her children and leave Bahrait. Free to work if she pleased. Free to live openly with Luke, or marry him. Free. She could delay the investiture, or reject it. She could play at being ruler of Bahrait, or she could take the role seriously and act it to the hilt.

Responsibility. Luke had used the word. He had suggested that she had the responsibility, the opportunity to make amends for wrongs Ramir had visited on his country. Luke spoke of her duty to Karim.

She wanted no talk of responsibility and duty. Ramir's crimes were not hers. Let others do penance for him, she told herself.

Yes, she had alternatives, numberless possibilities for the future. She recalled a childhood street game. You rolled four lettered dice and hoped to spell out a word. She had her word. It was simply this: Free.

Selma awoke in a temper. An irritable riser at best, she sat up in bed ready to kill.

Years ago Selma had dropped out of her analysis when the going got rough. Nonetheless she continued to believe in the lingering aftereffects of her dreams. This one must have been a doozer. In seconds the details of the dream had vanished, although her crankiness persisted. So did the buzzing in her ears. She switched on her bedside lamp. Two A.M. A hellish hour. The buzzing stopped, then resumed. The goddam telephone. Drawing on her multilingual vocabulary of obscenities —Yiddish, English, Italian, and a little Bahraiti—she swore her way to the fancy French desk, lifted the receiver, and winced with pity for the delicate Louis XVI chair that creaked when she dropped her weight onto it.

"Miss Selma Shapiro?" It was the effete Oxford-educated Bahraitian who manned the palace switchboard.

"Yes, it's me," Selma answered. "What can I do for you?" She resented this obnoxious foreigner who spoke better English than she did.

"I regret disturbing you. I would not do so but the gentleman has threatened me. He is calling from New York."

New York. That would be Burton Carpenter, Hanover's chief honcho in the financial department. One thing she was certain of—he was not calling this remote outpost of civilization to offer her a raise. Something was wrong and she knew what it was without being told. It was Gino, the no-good bastard, and the picture he was shooting in Venice.

"Put the gentleman through," she said.

He seemed far away. He *was* far away. "Hi, Burt. Always a pleasure to hear your voice in the middle of the night."

"Selma, it's six in the evening here. I've just come from the screening room. The boys and I have been viewing the latest rushes from Venice."

"Let's have it. You can't wait to congratulate the director's wife."

"Fun-ny lady. The film stinks. Gino's slipping on the job."

"He's fucking on the job, Burt. I know it and you know it from the spies you've got in the company."

"I'm sorry, Selma."

"Shove the sentiment, Burt. We're both after a good picture. What do you want me to do?"

"Bounce yourself back to Venezia. Do what you can to pull the production together. Even if it means reshooting."

"The costs," she gasped.

"We're watching them here. We have to. No one's bothering over there. I've had a dupe made of the negative. It'll be waiting for you at the Gritti. Run it yourself and let me know what you think. And Selma . . ."

"Yeah."

"I hate to bring it up. If Gino doesn't shape up, he'll have to be replaced."

"I agree," she said.

She dropped the receiver into its cradle and banged her fists on the desk. Beneath her, the little chair squeaked for mercy.

"That's where it stands." Selma dug into the basket of breakfast rolls the maid had set on Marianna's balcony table. She layered butter and marmalade on a croissant and rammed the mess into her mouth. Chewing loudly, she spoke through her food. "I leave today. Gotta be in Venice tomorrow."

"Luke will make the arrangements. Does Gino know you're coming?"

"Ha! Not this time. I'm going to surprise the double-dealing rat. If he's still shoving it into that Italian cunt, ol' Gino's in for fun and games he's not expecting. Selma the Survivor, that's me. I'm through pulling his balls out of the fire. Sure I know the risk. He'll walk out on me."

"You'll miss him."

"Will I? I've got zero now. Can double zero be worse?" Her heavy jaws quivered but her rabbit eyes were hard as marbles.

"Think it over, Selma."

"I've thought . . . plenty. What am I sacrificing? An occasional *shtup*, a gorgeous escort for the Academy Awards?"

"You love him."

"You had to bring that up. So I love him. Look at me. A great beauty I decidedly am not. I didn't get where I am by putting out on the mattress. Truth is, nobody asked. Hell, I've worked my butt off all my life. I'm through taking chances with my career for what Gino calls 'our nights of madness.' "

The plump hand reached for another croissant. Marianna patted it. "It'll work out," she said without conviction.

Selma bit into the warm roll. "On top of everything, I'm a fink leaving you. How do you feel?"

"Confused. I have too many choices. Your way is clear. You've made your decision. Burt Carpenter will make the next one."

"Yeah, unless I run scared. Gino gets me skin-to-skin, I'm pudding. He doesn't give a shit if Hanover drops both of us.

He knows I've got other markers to call in. Plenty of people owe me favors. The question is, do I go to bat for him elsewhere? Do I try to find the *putz* one more job to ruin. He'shad three already. The whole industry knows Gino is a loser. You're the one with a good shot at the future."

"Think so? I go from day to day on nerves and pills. Everyone tells me I'm brave. They forget I'm an actress."

"Who are *they?*"

"Mojeeb, Gropper, Colonel Yamani, the Minister of Internal Security. They say it's time for me to take hold of the country. The people are uneasy. They need to be reassured by their Empress—a TV appearance, a press conference, anything to let them know Bahrait isn't without a leader. There are documents to be signed, meetings that can no longer be postponed. Only you and Luke know how befuddled I am. I'm the Empress. I rule thirty million people. I'm expected to know what each one wants and I don't know what I want for myself."

"When I came here, you knew what you wanted," Selma reminded. "*Out* is what you wanted. You still want that? You feel like getting off the throne? Do it. There are plenty of folks in the audience ready to grab your seat. Will that make you happy?"

"I don't know. I simply don't know. Selma, will you come back?"

"As soon as I can."

"When you get to Venice, don't weaken."

Selma blinked away tears. "Pride was never my strong point."

17

She was absolutely firm about it. She would enter the Golden Lion Room alone.

When it had been Ramir's council chamber she had seldom been permitted to join him there. From this place, surrounded by a coterie of military and domestic advisers, he had ruled Bahrait.

Now the room was hers.

She waited immobile, as courtiers on either side drew apart the massive carved oak doors, then closed them silently behind her. She did not know or care that her pearl-gray dress drained the color from her face, giving her skin a ghostly cast that alarmed the courtiers.

Her eyes, concealed by smoky-blue glasses, contemplated the chamber. The handwoven runner beneath her feet was thin, fine, very old, its once vivid turquoise and coral faded by the centuries. Ramir's desk—no, her desk—appeared to be miles away, lost in the dimness of the oblong oak-paneled room. She recalled court gossip. Upon becoming Shah, Ramir had disdained his father's smaller council chamber, had indeed demolished walls to create this vast hall. Hapless visitors passing through the doors for the first time had entered confidently. Obliged to undertake the interminable walk toward Ramir's desk, most slowed their steps like prisoners dragging chains. Ramir, as she had observed during the first meeting with Luke, sat tight-lipped and ramrod straight on his thronelike chair, his riveting eyes as unwelcoming as those of his ancestors who glowered from gilt-framed paintings on the wall.

Today the chair was empty, Ramir gone.

She had dreaded this moment, put it off as long as she could. Moving unsteadily, she focused on the desk, an ebony monster created for Ramir by cabinetmakers in France. Embellished with leaf-shaped loops of pure gold, the desk stood before the throne-chair, an ornate seat of power covered in crimson velvet, its ebony arms terminating in gold lions' heads that snarled at everyone who approached. Richly brocaded draperies, Chinese-red side chairs along the walls, and massive chests inlaid with mother-of-pearl completed the room.

Incongruous in this rigid museum setting, heaps of papers littered the desk top awaiting her attention. Gropper, General Mojeeb. Watson, and Doug had pleaded to share this traumatic moment with her. Even the Curtises, before their departure, had offered to help.

"Condolence messages have come from every corner of the world," Gropper had said. "Let Faridah take them off your hands. There is no better secretary than Faridah. Ramir trusted her with everything. She can respond to the mail quickly."

"There are pressing matters," General Mojeeb had added. "We have disposed of what we could while you were in mourning. Others merely require your signature. We can be useful . . ."

Gropper had echoed the suggestion. Still she had remained stubborn. It would be therapeutic, she insisted. She had nothing more important to do. While she remained in the palace she would deal with her correspondence, resolve problems herself.

Arriving at the desk, she gingerly seated herself on the velvet chair. It was strange how unfamiliar she was with this eerie place. Since the interview with Luke, Ramir had kept her away from the Golden Lion Room, shutting her out of the business of government whenever she asked to join a council meeting.

"You don't belong here," he had said. "We are grim men. The issues are complicated. Often there are no solutions, yet decisions must be made."

"You relegate me to tea with wives of dignitaries," she had protested. "I'm doing busy work, cutting ribbons for roads and bridges. You know I'm capable of more than that."

"Perhaps, in the future."

Now, seated behind the huge desk, she reached across the heaps of papers and toyed with the gold accessories—the telephone, the ashtray, the penholder, the box containing the royal seal, the sleek picture frames displaying photographs of herself and each of Ramir's children—except Eric, the flaxen-haired baby in Switzerland.

Determined to be businesslike, she removed her tinted

glasses and turned her attention to the stack of official-looking papers. Topping the heap was a designer's cost breakdown for a new public park in Ryal to be built around a larger-than-life bronze statue of Ramir. She studied the columns of figures, found them befuddling, and cast the proposal aside. Beneath it, a report stamped *Urgent* dealt with the construction of an automobile spare-parts factory on the outskirts of the city, and was equally confusing. A folder containing seven closely typed pages bearing the insigne of the State Department of the United States of America was hopelessly baffling.

On and on she went to the bottom of the pile, attempting to make sense of what she read. Understanding nothing, she signed everything.

Official papers disposed of, she faced the condolence notes and decided she could not cope. Faridah could deal with them with her blessings. Frustrated, fatigued, she glared back at the framed ancestors whose eyes had never left her. Pushing free of the desk, she threw down her pen and fled the room, wanting nothing more than the solace of her suite.

Before leaving his cottage on the following day, Luke Tremayne unfastened the tight collar button on his Egyptian cotton shirt, adjusted his tie to conceal the gap, and shot his cuffs to reveal his new silver cuff links. Grumbling to himself, he started for the palace. A week ago, Marianna had asked him to become her press secretary in place of the Army colonel who had served Ramir. "Please, Luke, tell me you'll take the job," she'd pleaded. "I need someone I can trust to be my spokesman. Your assistant, Will Henkin, can take over the children." Reluctantly, he had agreed. Each morning since then he had glanced wistfully at the blue jeans and sport shirts that had been his schoolmaster garb. A quick trip to a Ryal tailor plus a few hasty fittings at the palace, and his comfortable casual wardrobe had been converted into one of stifling elegance. Over his protest, Marianna had assigned him a valet. Now whenever he opened a drawer or closet he felt like a snoop inspecting the effects of a stranger. To Luke the sedate ties, the business suits, the shiny shoes, were the marks of a fop. They were also palace requisites. Because Marianna considered them important, he had succumbed.

Today he felt particularly foolish. After much debate he

had convinced Marianna that a meeting with Khali Tehrani, the chief of a remote mountain village, was long overdue. Soon the elderly gentleman would arrive, undoubtedly in native dress. And he, Luke Tremayne, looking like a department store mannequin, would be obliged to lead him to the Golden Lion council chamber.

"Tehrani *is* Hahrait," Luke had told Harianna. "His people are dirt poor and suffering. Other village chieftains turn to him for leadership. At this point, a meeting with Tehrani is more important than an invitation to Buckingham Palace."

She had acceded, none too willingly. "I'm drowning in problems. I can't deal with those I have. I don't need another one. How can I help him?"

"I'm not asking you to help him. Just meet him."

He approached her desk briskly, this scowling village chieftain, unfazed by the lengthy walk. Luke introduced them and withdrew. Tehrani stood before her, a large bearded man with a bull-like neck thrust forward from a dusty black caftan. His head was wrapped in a blue cotton turban. A beaked nose overhung his upper lip. His luminous eyes, half concealed by deep sockets below brushy brows, were unsettling. Instinctively Marianna reached toward the buzzer in the ebony desk that would bring Luke from the outer hall.

"Ah, appearances. So unfortunate," Tehrani murmured, his voice soft, very British. "In Hollywood when they cast a villain he must look like me. Have no fear. I come as a friend."

Ashamed, she rose and extended her hand across the desk to shake his. "We meet as equals," she said. "Please be seated. I apologize for the silly little chair. When next you visit . . ."

"If I visit again."

"Don't you expect to?"

"That we shall learn soon enough. You are gracious to say we meet as equals. We do not. What our future relationship will be depends upon you."

"Mr. Tremayne told me something of your purpose in coming here. I prefer to hear everything from you."

Tehrani scanned the room. "This is my first audience in the palace. For years I sought through channels to have a meeting with your late husband. Repeatedly, he put it off. He knew it would be unpleasant. That is the way of despots. Why confront hostile forces when guns can keep them at bay?"

"Despot? My husband was not a compassionate man. Many people suffered unjustly under his rule, I agree. But a despot? You must know there was widespread grief when he died. Thousands of mourners followed the funeral cortege. I myself have traveled widely in Bahrait. Everywhere I've been received warmly. That is not the response of people who are governed by a despot."

"Madame, so naïve. Ryal is a small part of Bahrait. Your side trips? They were artfully planned by others. You dwell within a cocoon. I invite you to leave it just once to visit my village. You will see people ready to explode with hatred toward the throne. Deep, burning hatred. They are not unlike millions of others who live no better than dogs scavenging in back alleys."

"Why haven't they spoken out?"

"The old are silent. To survive, even in misery, has been their only wish. It is the young who are desperate for change. Those who dared to raise their voices and were discovered are either dead or rotting in your husband's prisons. You think I have come to beg your help? You are mistaken, Madame. I am here to save your life. It is my duty to warn you of the turmoil that lies ahead unless there are immediate social and economic reforms, an end to corruption, repression, and brutality."

"My husband could not have known this. You said yourself you never spoke to him."

"He knew everything. His secret police kept him informed. They belonged to him. Now they belong to you."

"The police have not stepped forward to alert me," she said.

"You are being watched. The men who surrounded the Shah are waiting to judge you. They ask themselves if you will continue your husband's policies."

"Bahrait is wealthy. Why should anyone be deprived?"

"Ask General Mojeeb. He will tell you the Shah was determined to make Bahrait as strong militarily as the United States and the Soviet Union. That goal was long ago achieved."

"Impossible. Only today I was presented with a purchase agreement for more military hardware."

"Did you sign it?"

"I set it aside for the moment."

"Good. Then I have not come too late."

"Too late for what?"

"The criminality of further military spending."

"Further military spending? How do I know you're telling the truth?"

"Ask Calvin Gropper."

"Gropper? What has he to do with this?"

"He can tell you. I have said too much—for your safety and mine."

Watson Wagg hummed tonelessly as he strapped the last piece of his luggage. The ebullience and high hopes he had brought to Ryal were packed away with the freshly laundered shirts a valet had returned to him minutes before.

"Our future is behind us, old boy," he said to Doug Braden. "In a way, I'm relieved. It was all a pipe dream. I've said my good-byes to Marianna. Told her my door would be open whenever she decided to return to Hollywood. Tomorrow we'll be on that plane headed back to reality. This time you can take the window seat."

"I may not be leaving."

Watson yawned. "What have you got up your sleeve?"

"Marianna invited me to tea in her suite."

"What's she got up *her* sleeve?"

Doug grinned broadly. "Tell you later. Every delicious detail."

Doug had never felt better. She had asked to see him. Not in that cavern she called her office, nor in one of the public rooms. Quite the contrary. She had sent word through her elderly maid, Narit, that she wished to meet with him privately in the salon of her suite. Five o'clock. For tea.

Tea. That was a howl. He conjured up the lunch breaks in her dressing room at Hanover Studios, the cocktail rendezvous in her Beverly Hills hideaway, and he chuckled. So she remembered, too. It confirmed his belief that a woman once laid by Douglas Braden was a woman who never forgot she had experienced the best.

In his mirrored bathroom he stripped quickly. He appraised himself from every angle and approved what he saw, offering a special blessing to the plastic surgeon who had nipped a little here, tucked a little there.

He stepped into the biting shower. First hot water, then cold, then hot, then cold, and hot and cold again.

Flinching under each watery shock, he felt every pore in his body come alive. His internist back home opposed the practice calling it dangerous for his heart, but conceded that for stimulation it was safer than whips or drugs.

He toweled himself vigorously, heightening his anticipation. No woman had ever resisted Doug Braden, he reminded himself, conveniently obliterating Rita, the wife who had dared to divorce him, and who now lay buried unmourned in the dark recesses of his memory.

She opened the door herself, a good sign. She invited him to be seated. There was no maid, no tea in sight. She retreated a few steps, then positioned herself near the window. Daylight pierced her chiffon negligee, silhouetting the well-remembered ivory body. No heartbroken widow she, not *his* Marianna. She's ready, he told himself. She's thirsting for it.

Whatever else came of their meeting, of this he was certain: It would be unforgettable.

She turned slightly, and the filtering light outlined her breasts. They were rounder than he remembered, fuller, too. Maybe motherhood had done that. Her exploring eyes were on him. When they came to rest on his crotch, the tingling that had begun in the shower fanned through his body. Unendurably swollen, he attempted to hasten across the room, and failed. The pressure slowed his steps. He would not speak first. The ball, so to speak, was in her court.

"Come closer, Doug." Her voice was husky. He had forgotten it got that way. He moved toward her carefully, her unwavering blue eyes pulling him forward.

"A kiss, Doug, for old times' sake?"

He obliged without protest. His hands groped for her breasts. Drawing away from him, her fingers grazed his bulge. She parted his zipper and the flap in his shorts. His organ, grateful for release, emerged with the impulse of a triggered bullet.

"The bedroom, Doug," she whispered.

Clumsily, his aroused prick leading the way, he stumbled

after her into the adjoining room. The bed was turned down.
She had planned it all.

She dropped her negligee to the floor and began to peel
away his clothes. Off with the jacket. Off with the shirt. Off
with the pants, the shorts, the loafers. She wanted him bone
naked, she said. She backed toward the bed and he followed
her. He gulped for air as she lay spread-eagled before him,
her lips parted, her fingernails crazily scratching the satin
sheets.

Instantly he was over her, blind with craving, his body an
appendage to his appendage.

"Hurry, Doug," she begged.

"You're wonderful," he gasped. "You're wonderful!" And
then, "I'm coming in! Jeezus, I'm coming in!"

"The hell you are," she said. She rolled from under him
and sat on her haunches, convulsed with laughter. "Look at
yourself. You're ridiculous!"

His mouth went slack. His hurt eyes obeyed her pointing
finger. Like a stunned bull he stared at his abandoned
penis.

"You're on your own, Doug," she chortled. "The bathroom's over there." She indicated a triple-paneled screen in
the corner. He gripped his deflating penis and staggered
behind the screen.

Springing from the bed, she gathered up his clothes and
threw them after him.

She heard the sound of running water and his muffled
curse. Meanwhile she selected a blouse and skirt from her
sportswear closet, adjusted her hair and makeup, and saun-
tered into the salon to await him.

When he reappeared he was as dapper as when he'd
arrived. Dapper and confused and simmering.

"Would you like to talk?" She patted the sofa cushion
beside her. "Join me."

He ignored the sofa and sat down opposite her. "Why did
you bring me from California?"

'Not for what just happened. That little sidebar didn't
occur to me until I saw how eager you were to exploit me
again. I had other reasons for sending for you. I thought
you'd had enough punishment, that you deserved another
chance. I hoped together we could make a successful comeback."

"Comeback?" he snorted. "I've never been away."

"All those TV dog-food commercials? The hammy night-club act that failed? Call that a career? What about the movie jobs, Doug?"

"Commercials are no disgrace. Even Fonda and Olivier do them. So did Wayne."

"What about the movie jobs?" she asked again.

"Hollywood isn't what it used to be. The picture business has slowed down."

"Not for Fonda and Olivier."

"That's a low blow."

"Two in one day?" she said. "Not bad for an amateur."

Sighing, she leaned back on the sofa. "Fifteen years," she said. "Our affair should be a forgotten episode to me by now. It isn't. I was playing for keeps in those days. I thought you were too. I stopped loving you ages ago, but I could never forget how you tossed me out of your life so casually and never looked back. You didn't give a damn about what would happen to me."

"You did okay."

"No thanks to you, my friend. True, I met Ramir and I fell in love again. But you left your mark. After a while I needed to even the score."

"Against *me?*"

"Against you." She shook her head. "Seeing you again, I realized you were never worth the trouble. After our breakup, when I met and married Ramir I was too absorbed in my new life to think about the old days. But Selma—she's the one who couldn't forgive you. Once she had the clout, she went to work on your career. Quite effective, don't you think?"

He loomed over her. "What the hell are you talking about?"

"Blacklisting, Doug. In the beginning Selma couldn't do much about it. Too low on the totem pole. Later, as she moved up, she began her campaign. A hint here, a word there, and exchange of favors, a bad review passed around at parties. It started to get chilly in Southern California, didn't it, Doug? Eventually I joined in. It was exhilarating. I'd run into movie people and say, 'Poor Doug, he's not looking well. Another flop. So sad.' The incident in the bedroom? That was just a bonus."

He struggled to contain himself and lost. His large hand

shot out and he slapped her cheeks over and over again. She sat waiting for him to stop. When he did, she rubbed her bruised skin to ease the hurt.

"The slate's clean," she said. "Go back to Hollywood. I'll tell Selma we're calling off the game." She tried to smile but the pain was too severe. "It'll be fun watching you start over. The best years are gone, aren't they? Not that you'll starve. There's always the dog-food pitch."

Although Hilary Gropper had never suffered a faltering ego, these last weeks had elevated her self-esteem more than anything before, including her marriage to Calvin. Each morning since Ramir's death she had awakened charged with excitement, joyfully anticipating the events of the new day.

This morning was different. Her mood remained high but the day ahead was predictable. They were going home.

Stretching fully on the elaborate bed, her pedicured pink toenails curling over the edge, she could hear the agreeable clatter of silver and porcelain as waiters set the breakfast table in the next room. From the bathroom came the fussy noises of Calvin brushing his teeth, urinating, washing his hands, stepping on and off the scale—the last to the accompaniment of a high whistle unrelated to his normal guttural tones. They'd had a healthy romp upon awakening, definitely a good start for any day.

Hilary closed her eyes and smugly reviewed the past weeks. They had been glorious. Not that a funeral was glorious, ever. Still, supervising the glamorous activity that followed Ramir's demise had been a thrill, and she could not deny it. Nor admit it. After all, Calvin had lost a friend.

She hadn't sought the assignment. That would have been gross. Yet somehow it had devolved upon her—the responsibility of acting as hostess to the stream of dignitaries who came to honor Ramir in death and to pay their respects to his heartbroken widow and family.

They had poured in. The Queen of England, after declining her invitation to the Jubilee, had appeared accompanied by Prince Philip; the Premier of Italy—whoever he was that week—had flown from Rome; Princess Grace and Prince Rainier had come from Monaco; and King Juan Carlos and Queen Sophia from Spain. The United States had sent Calvin's successor, Secretary of State Owen Belmont, to represent the President. A delegation from Fidel Castro had been both a surprise and an embarrassment.

They had come from the nearby Gulf States and faraway Nigeria. Those who had not traveled great distances had spent somber minutes with Marianna and then departed Bahrait. Those who had come from afar chose to remain awhile, resting and sightseeing before reversing their journey.

And it was to Hilary Gropper they had turned. As the wife of the one man they all knew, she had taken them in tow, encouraging visitors to try the golf course, the indoor and outdoor swimming pools, the tennis courts and stables, and to wander through the late monarch's private zoo. Talking steadily, authoritatively, she had rhapsodized over the customs and history of a country she'd never understood. They had responded enthusiastically. They had invited her to be their guest and had sung her praises to Calvin.

When the last of them had gone, Hilary had been eager to leave also. To her disappointment Calvin had said they could not rush off just yet. There remained some business to be concluded. He indicated it was a routine matter, though important, something Ramir had desired. He emphasized it would have been inappropriate to plunge into certain sensitive affairs of state in the immediate wake of Marianna's bereavement.

Calvin's own relationship to Ramir and now to Marianna was highly delicate, he reminded Hilary, and required considerable finesse. He was not explicit and Hilary was too uninterested to inquire further.

Hilary could hear the buzz of Calvin's razor in his bathroom. Soon he would lumber into the shower, his absurd whistle drowned out by the rushing water. Eventually he would appear in his dressing gown and expect to find her at the breakfast table. She slipped from the bed and hastily readied herself to join him.

At the table they dismissed the waiters and toasted each other with black coffee.

"Before we leave for home," Calvin said, "we must invite Marianna to join us for a picnic, a walk, a drive, something to show our concern for her well-being. Let me be blunt. It is imperative that she believe in our friendship. Watch what you say—"

"Calvin, you're being obnoxious again. Let me be myself."

He nibbled at her fingers. "With me, my dear, always. With Marianna, until we know her plans, we must be devoted and supportive, encourage her dependency."

"But why? She doesn't want to be Empress. You know the bitch is going to walk out."

"Women are fascinating, capricious. Who knows what Marianna will do?"

An imperious rapping on the door brought Calvin to his feet. He scurried to see who dared interrupt his breakfast.

"Azar," he exclaimed. "What a lovely surprise! Come in. I'll ring for another setting."

"Don't bother." Azar slammed the door and leaned against it, breathing hard. "I swear to you I cannot bear it, not another day," she fumed. "I think about it until I am sure I will lose my mind. We must get rid of her. She has no right to remain here. This country cannot belong to her. Two thousand years it is ours, and you, Ramir's friend, sit calmly by while Bahrait passes into the hands of a Hollywood whore! Calvin, are you crazy too?"

"Shh, my darling," he said, leading Azar to his chair across from Hilary's. "I am on your side. Listen—I will speak plainly. General Mojeeb and I have had our heads together. For the present we wish Marianna to remain on the throne. We will try to persuade her to do so. She has put off her investiture, hasn't she? The details of leadership overwhelm her. As ruler she may be easier to deal with than Ramir. Azar, I know your loss. Still you won't deny Ramir could be harsh. Who can forget how he treated you?"

"I cannot forgive him even now."

"In Marianna we may have found our perfect puppet. Let her stay where she is. She is decorative. She is not political. Eventually she may be grateful to pick up her former harmless duties and let others make the hard decisions. Suppose we offer her a shadow government with the understanding that one day when Karim is older he will be the Shah? She will buy that. With you, Azar, as undisclosed adviser, General Mojeeb will be free to decide what is best for Bahrait. And I will always be available for consultation." He winked. "Available to you, and to Marianna should she seek my services. Is that clear? Any disruption at this time will throw Bahrait into turmoil and we shall be losers also. Will you have your coffee?"

Azar accepted the cup but her eyes were hot coals. "It's not that simple," she said.

Hilary checked her watch. "Excuse me. My hairdresser is waiting. I must leave you cute schemers." She waved her hand and disappeared into the bedroom.

Calvin glanced after her. "Azar," he said, dropping his voice. "Speak softly. My adorable well-bred wife will have her ear to the door as usual. What is it you are trying to tell me?"

"That our Sleeping Beauty is stirring. Obviously your informants have grown sloppy. Are you aware of what Marianna is up to?"

"As a visitor in this country and this house, I do not have your network of spies," he responded stiffly.

Azar snapped her fingers in the air. "I give this much for your plan. You are free with advice but you know nothing."

"I know you are quick with tantrums and abuse."

"Unimportant. Listen to me, Gropper. Yesterday Marianna had a visitor in the Golden Lion Room, Khali Tehrani, the chief of a mountain village in the Shiraz province in the north. The American lover—what's his name?—brought him to the palace."

"Luke Tremayne?"

"Yes, Tremayne. A bleeding heart with star-spangled principles. He'll make trouble," Azar said.

"Not for long."

"You're too sure of yourself. Do you realize Tehrani comes from a village in one of Bahrait's most volatile provinces? My brother was so afraid of the old firebrand, he never ventured into his territory. The old goat told Marianna what it's like out there. Marianna promised she would visit him. Soon her heart will bleed, too."

"What harm?"

"Calvin, need I remind you that she controls the budget. She has sole power to allocate funds."

"No matter. One sniff of those villages will send her running. Her exquisite Majesty will issue a few orders for improvements and they will be implemented. In a short time she will be bored. I predict she will spend more time in

France than in Bahrait. Furthermore, her Hollywood career will continue to be a temptation. We will encourage her to remain a figurehead ruler and the country will be in our hands."

"What is your next move?" Azar asked.

"I shall leave quickly. My mission is not helped if I involve myself in a hair-pulling match between you and Marianna. From Ryal I will go directly to Washington, where I must warm the cold feet of certain congressmen. Many will wish to withhold their approval of new arms sales to Bahrait until they know what direction the country is taking. I played a major role in pushing through this latest contract. It must not be allowed to fall apart."

"Thereby lessening your value to appreciative sponsors."

Gropper smiled. "My dear Princess, you understand perfectly. We are on the same side, you, the general, and I. My advice, for which you have so graphically expressed your scorn, is that you do nothing to rock the boat. There is no need—as yet."

At Luke's suggestion they had agreed to meet at the stables and take their horses into the forest. "It'll be simpler that way," he had told her. "If we're observed no one will be surprised. We've ridden out so many times before."

"Luke, am I Empress around these parts?"

"Of all you survey."

"Then why should I give a damn about who sees where I go?"

"I remind you, you're not the same Empress you were for the past fifteen years. You're the big wheel. You're like something freshly minted and dangerously innocent."

"A Virgin Queen?"

"Don't be frivolous. When Ramir was alive you wondered about his enemies. Would there be a coup, an assassination attempt? The threat was there, wasn't it?"

"Yes."

"Has it entered your lovely head that his enemies may have become yours?"

"You're trying to frighten me."

"Exactly. Do you think Mojeeb and his crowd will give you a standing ovation if they learn about today's expedition?"

"We're only visiting Tehrani."

"Ramir never did. He knew he could be ambushed at any

moment. The old Shah could travel anywhere. He belonged to a generation that accepted its fate as the will of Allah. Today's generation still worships Allah, but they want more for themselves and their kids than lousy mud-clay huts and empty stomachs. Did you know the villagers cheered when they heard of Ramir's death? Now that you're in charge, they're hoping for miracles."

She shuddered. "See here . . ." she started to say, but the frozen set of Luke's profile warned her not to go on. Dammit, she thought, I never applied for the top job. I never filled out an application and sat by the phone waiting to be summoned to power. We're getting out of here, she told herself—Luke, the children, and I. Whoever's fool enough to want the scepter can have it.

They had finally arrived in a small clearing at the end of the trail. She glanced about as he dismounted and helped her to the ground. "Where are we?"

"Still quite a way from Tehrani's village. Follow me."

He tied their horses to a tree and led her to a small station wagon hidden in the woods. "Get in," he ordered. "I've brought you a chador so you won't be conspicuous. Drape it around you the way the native women do. Only your eyes should be visible, remember." He bent and kissed her lips. "Damn, why do your eyes have to be so blue? Are you afraid?"

"No."

"Good. When we get to the village, look around, listen to what the people are saying. You understand the local patois. If the whole scene leaves you cold—so be it. You can turn in your badge by morning."

The village was worse than she had expected. The dirt path beneath her feet was cracked by the broiling sun. Scrawny children volunteered toothless smiles before returning to their work on dry patches of farmland. In the doorways of the mud-clay huts withered women crouched at looms, spinning rugs out of brightly dyed wools brought to them by merchants from the city. Squatting nearby, idle men glared at the visitors and a few spat in their direction. The stench of poverty and excrement was everywhere.

In Tehrani's house they sat cross-legged on mats and drank foul soup served by Tehrani's glum sister. The sister did not join them for the meal nor was she introduced. Responding to a single handclap from Tehrani, the sister twice shuffled from behind a curtain to refill their bowls with the gummy soup.

"We have no guide books for our charming community," Tehrani said in his surprising British accent. "You have seen its highlights." He smiled bitterly. "Our highways, our monuments, our recreational facilities, our museums and libraries —the village speaks for itself."

"It's horrendous," Marianna said.

"As I must seem to you. Forgive me, Madame, you do not deserve my rudeness. I am an inexperienced host."

When the lunch was ended he took her hand in parting. "The chador," he said mildly. "It is an imaginative but futile disguise. Your identity is known to everyone you passed. I will guarantee safe passage to your car but I cannot ensure courtesy. Perhaps when you return one day there will be cause to make our reception friendlier."

Later, as the station wagon jounced down the rocky mountainside, she groaned. "Luke, up there it's like the Dark Ages."

"There are hundreds of villages like Tehrani's. Someone's got to help before all hell breaks loose."

She tore off the chador and slumped in her seat. At the bottom of the road Luke relaxed his tense hold on the steering wheel and came to a dead halt. Then he cut sharply to the left, directing the car farther from the palace.

"Take me back," she demanded. "The excursion's ended."

"Sorry, that was only the curtain raiser. What I have to show you next is far worse in a different way."

"Must we go on? There are tom-toms beating in my head."

"This is vital and today's the day. Who knows when we can sneak out again?"

"You win," she said disagreeably. "What's it about?"

"See for yourself, up ahead." They were traveling through dense forest. A nearly impenetrable wall of hedge bordered the road.

Luke slowed the car, braking gradually. "Slide closer to the door. Look through these." He handed her a pair of binoculars. "Tell me what you see."

"A giant concrete block. What is it?"

"Staff headquarters, Army Air Force, Nuclear Division."

"It's not even a building!"

He smiled grimly. "Oh, it's quite a building. A bunker,

seven stories deep. Hundreds of men and women are in there right now, working to protect the nation. They're known as the Moles. They have underground parking, hidden approaches. The roof is camouflaged to blend with the landscape. A brilliant job, impossible to detect from the air. Anyway, it's outside regular flight patterns."

She lowered the binoculars and stared at him in amazement. "Bahrait has up-front military headquarters and bases. Why a mysterious hideout? It makes no sense."

"Apparently your late husband thought it did. Brace yourself, baby, there's more to come. Ramir is said to have ordered the construction of eight secret underground hangars. Must have cost billions. They're scattered around the countryside, stocked wall to wall with fighter planes."

"But why . . . ?"

Luke shook his head. "I don't know the answer. Some of the foreign engineers suspect he had a wild scheme to grab surrounding territory that belonged to Bahrait a thousand years ago."

"Surely no one would cooperate with him."

"He had cooperation all right. It's no big news that the U.S. opened the spout and Ramir opened the treasury whenever he wanted new armament. It's a cute routine they had. Under Ramir, Bahrait submitted its requests and the U.S. played coy, pretending to be hard to get. A bit of subtle lobbying, the right palms greased, and the play moved into act three. Enormous deals were okayed and American munitions makers scrambled for the contracts. See how it worked? Everyone was happy."

"Tehrani and his people didn't look too cheerful."

"Your neighbors on the borders aren't either. They're fighting mad. They'd like to know how much armament actually is stored in this country. Certain shipments arrive and disappear."

"Disappear? Where do you get your information?"

"My friend Paul Brennon. Remember, I stayed with him when you took the kids to St. Moritz? Paul's an executive stuck in that bunker doing paper work. A frustrating job. Nothing adds up, no one answers his questions. First he receives printouts of equipment that's been ordered and paid for. Then he gets reports of what's been checked in and where it's stored. But no one is allowed to see the stuff. Anytime Paul asks how come, he's told to go back to his computers and quit poking his nose into details that don't concern him."

Marianna put the binoculars on the seat and shook her head sorrowfully. "Luke, I'm the wrong person for the job. What I saw and heard today—starving villagers, missiles, bunkers, countries spitting across borders—huh-uh, not my ball game."

"You sure?"

"I'm sure. Turn around and take me back. I want to see my children. And don't forget, you have my speech to prepare for tomorrow."

"I haven't forgotten. I'd hoped this would be an illuminating day for you. What do you want to say to your subjects?"

"Keep it simple. Let's tell them I remain in shock over my husband's death. Tell them that as long as I am on the throne I will be their servant. Tell them I intend to work night and day for continued peace and their greater benefit, et cetera, et cetera, et cetera. Like it?"

"Love it," he said with sarcasm. "My heartstrings are twanging 'Dixie.' "

Angrily, he backed off the road and made a sharp U-turn. At the clearing he helped her from the station wagon and they mounted their horses. He did not speak until they reached the stables. "Your car and driver are waiting in the shade," he said tightly. "This is as far as we go together."

The speech to the nation was going well. Luke had brought it to her after dinner the night before and remained while she read it aloud. Although he had thanked her when she praised him for striking just the right tone, she'd known he hated himself for giving her what she wanted—a string of words fulsome with sincerity, a pabulum overflowing with unspecific promises. He had failed to comment on her delivery, and had disappointed her further by not suggesting they spend the night in her bed. She had accused him of behaving like a pouting child and sent him away, confident she could have him back when the empty rite of her maiden speech was done with.

Now she stood on the sunny balcony, hands folded before her, and waited for the cheers from the park below to subside. The crowd was enormous. The palace grounds had been opened and people had come from miles around to witness her first formal appearance as their ruler-Empress. With every sentence she could feel their affection lapping her skin like warm seawater. Genuinely moved, she touched the corners of her eyes with a handkerchief and composed herself to continue.

"I give you my word, I will do my utmost—"

She never heard the shot.

A cordon of security guards fell upon her and forced her to the balcony floor. A moment later they had dragged her into the adjacent room. Outside there was bedlam. She was conscious of excited voices around her and shouting coming from the crowd. She tried to sit up, to learn what had happened. And then, for the first time in her life, she fainted.

Only minutes had passed, they told her later. Yet when she returned to consciousness, it was as from a long sleep.

Dr. Hosseini was there, and Luke, General Mojeeb, Azar, and the Groppers. She could recognize other voices. The raspy, authoritative one belonged to Major Sanjabi, head of the palace security staff. The rest, she supposed, belonged to the men who had hovered near her on the balcony.

Calvin was the first to notice the flicker of her eyelids. He knelt at her side. "Thank God the shot missed you. How do you feel?" he asked. He did not wait for an answer. "The general had his own men sprinkled among the crowd. They believe they have identified the assailant and his cohorts."

"Who—who would want to shoot me?"

It was General Mojeeb who responded. "We are conducting an investigation at this very moment. I will report to Your Majesty when we have information."

"Was anyone hurt?"

"No one. It was wise that our Intelligence recommended keeping the children away."

Then she remembered. Days ago she had argued to have Nariam and Jannot with her, to present the picture of a close family, bereaved but carrying on. Colonel Larah, a brusque man unaccustomed to obeying women, had argued with her. She had remained adamant.

"Queen Elizabeth surrounds herself with her family," she'd objected. "It reassures the people."

"Ryal is not London," Colonel Larah had replied. "We cannot be responsible if Your Majesty insists."

"I insist."

On her return from Tehrani's village and the mysterious bunker she had summoned Colonel Larah. "I've changed my mind. No children."

Now her eyelids fluttered nervously. She found Luke's worried face in the group above her. "Thank you," she lip-spoke. Aloud, she said to Dr. Hosseini, "Please see me to my room. I need to rest." She did not tell them she wanted solitude and time to examine her situation.

In the morning she sat in the projection room with Luke beside her. Over and over again she studied the army's sixteen-millimeter film of the assassination attempt. She ordered it stop-framed when she thought she saw something unusual. She scanned each visible face for a clue, finding nothing. Impersonally she viewed herself on the balcony, noting that she had orchestrated her audience skillfully. The crowd—caught by the camera's panning shot, long shots, medium shots, close-ups—was with her all the way, comforted by her words, hopeful for the future she vaguely promised. Not a single face showed tension. Whoever had fired the shot must have been out of camera range. Unless . . . Abruptly she pressed the control button on her chair. The film whirred to a stop and the overhead lights came on.

"What's that about?" Luke demanded.

"I'm going to the projection booth," she said excitedly. "I want to see the negative. If it's what I'm thinking—" She dipped behind a curtain and raced up the stairway with Luke at her heels.

The projectionist was busily rewinding the film, preparing to replace it in its metal can. He lifted his eyes from his task. "Your Majesty," he stammered.

"Don't be frightened," she said. "I want you to do something for me."

"Anything, Your Majesty."

"Do you have a Movieola?"

"Yes. In the corner."

"Good. Let's get over there. We're going to rerun the negative together."

"What is that thing?" Luke asked.

"A miniature projection machine. It's used for editing film."

"Marianna, you've seen the film at least a dozen times," Luke protested.

"Have I? Have I seen all of it?"

The projectionist completed setting up the machine.

"Now, we will rerun it slowly," she ordered. "And you," she said sternly to the projectionist, "you will show me all the splices."

"Splices, Your Majesty?"

"I want to see every place the film has been joined. How many reels were shot?"

"Only two, Your Majesty."

"Good, then there should be no more than a single splice— in the middle where the reels are joined. Easy enough to find?"

"Yes, Your Majesty."

The perspiring man fixed the negative spool on the machine. Luke and Marianna stood on either side of him, watching and waiting. When the projectionist had run the film through the machine, Marianna looked up. "I counted seven splices. How about you?"

"Six," Luke replied.

"Six or seven," she said impatiently. "That's not important. What is important is that someone has edited the negative." She turned to the projectionist. "Who gave you this?"

"Colonel Larah. He brought it to me this morning."

"Who had it overnight?"

"I do not know, Your Majesty."

Luke had accompanied her to the Golden Lion Room. At the door, she asked him to leave. "I'm sending for Colonel Larah. Let him explain this."

And now he was here, approaching her ebony desk. She left the desk to meet him.

"Thank you for coming so promptly," she said.

"You indicated it was urgent, Your Majesty."

"Would you like a drink?"

He shook his head, puzzled. "No, Your Majesty."

"You may need it." She indicated a sofa recently installed amid the wall of chairs. He waited until she was settled in one corner before he took the other.

"Colonel Larah, what is your title in this court?"

"But you know. I am Head of Intelligence."

"Exactly. At what time did the assassination attempt films reach you?"

"This morning. At eight o'clock."

"Is that the usual procedure?"

He smiled thinly. "We do not often have assassination attempts."

"Of course you don't. Let me be more explicit. When the developed film was taken from the cameraman, where did it go?"

"To General Mojeeb. Everything goes to the general. My reports, the Secret Service and Police Department reports. Everything. He reviews our activities. Those are standing orders."

"And when he is finished?"

"Until His Majesty's death, he and the general had daily meetings in this room. Between them they would decide what action to take on the information provided."

"Curious. The general did not bring the film to me. I had to request it."

"Perhaps he did not wish to distress Your Majesty."

"Colonel Larah, do you like your job?"

"Very much, Your Majesty."

"Then as long as I occupy the throne you will bring everything to me first."

"I understand, Your Majesty."

"Good. Then our new relationship has begun. Did you know the film had been edited?"

Colonel Larah did not hide his discomfort. "I did," he said.

"Do you suspect the cuts were made under the supervision of General Mojeeb?"

"It is a possibility."

"And where is the missing film now? Would you venture a guess?"

"In General Mojeeb's desk. In a locked drawer."

"Bring it to me. I don't care what you have to do to get it. You have fifteen minutes. I'll be waiting in the projection booth."

"But . . ." The colonel faltered.

"Get it!"

Colonel Larah was at the projection room door, a small film can under his arm. Marianna took the can from him, removed six curling strips of film, and handed them to the projectionist. "Match and splice these as fast as you can. Run them on the screen. Colonel Larah and I will be downstairs in the theater."

While they waited, the colonel, clearly disturbed, sat at her side.

"Have you any news since yesterday?" Marianna asked.

"Very little. The assailant was at the fringe of the crowd. A car was waiting beyond the gate, a black Saab. The assailant leaped the gate and was driven away at great speed."

"Why wasn't he overtaken?"

"We have interrogated the guards. They claim there was instant commotion. The motorized unit was slow to react, also cautious about running down bystanders. They know nothing, they say, except that the car was so dusty they could not read the license-plate number."

The buzzer at her side sounded and she signaled the projectionist to begin.

She addressed the colonel. "You will double the palace guards at once."

"Yes, Your Majesty."

"And you will discharge every man who was on duty at the time the shot was fired."

"Naturally, Your Majesty."

As the projectionist reran the film, Marianna edged forward on her seat, observing it intently. Suddenly a few frames of negative riveted her. She signaled the projectionist for a slow-motion rerun and finally for a stop-frame on a young man with burning eyes and an unkempt beard.

"Do you recognize him, Colonel?"

"No, Your Majesty. In Bahrait these fanatics are a type . . . crudely clothed, usually slim and bearded, with brimmed caps pulled low over their foreheads to avoid identification. Too often we pick them up for suspicious actions. It is hopeless. We interrogate one, learn nothing, and put him in a holding room. The next one is brought in and it is impossible to distinguish him from his companion."

"I know that man, Colonel."

"Your Majesty is joking."

"I am deadly serious. Two days ago I visited the village of Paavi in the mountains. Did you know that, Colonel?"

The colonel hesitated, then decided she was too clever to deceive. "Yes, I know," he said.

"Good. I approve of people who do their job." She fixed

here gaze on the colonel's face. "They do not all look alike. This one was leaning against a hut in Paavi. He knew who I was. He never took his eyes off me when I passed. You are to go to the village today, unarmed. You may take several men with you, also unarmed. No one else is to be informed of your mission. The suspect is not to be harmed, not before I speak with him. Do you understand?"

"We will do our best, Your Majesty."

"You do *not* understand, Colonel. He is to be protected. I will expect him here by nightfall—without a scratch on his body."

18

For the first time since leaving Switzerland and Pia, Marianna felt blazingly alive. The encounter with Colonel Larah, the speed with which she had issued commands and seen them obeyed, had astonished and animated her. She *was* the Empress. She had absolute power, and the colonel knew it. Soon others would, too.

Readying for dinner with Azar and the Groppers, who were to depart in the morning, she knew the trio would consider her high spirits inappropriate to the events of the past weeks. She remembered the old show business adage about giving the customers what they want. She would do that. She would play the brave but helpless widow.

Over cocktails she informed her guests there was to be no discussion of the assassination attempt. "We've been through too much," she said. "Let's try to make our farewell dinner a cheerful one—as cheerful as possible.".

"But we must know," Azar insisted when they were at the table. "What is being done to run down those animals? Years ago, when Ramir was the target, his assailant was found immediately. He was tried and shot on the spot. Do you remember, Calvin? Overnight, Bahrait split into factions. Ramir and his wife Alyan had to be smuggled out of the country. They resided in Rome for six months until General Mojeeb restored order and made it safe for them to return."

"That won't happen again," Marianna said. "I will not permit a circus. Not that Intelligence reports much progress. The clues picked up so far have led down blind alleys. The dissidents are loyal to each other. They deny knowledge of anything."

"Why not a reward?" Gropper asked.

"No, Calvin," she said firmly. "There will be no reward, no dog packs, no bloodshed. The people do not need reminders that there are lunatics loose. My orders are that the matter is to be withdrawn from the public spotlight—and my orders are to be obeyed."

Gropper was mock severe. "My opinions are usually looked upon as gems. Presidents and kings scramble for them. Yet I must agree with you. May I say, it is best to let the Intelligence bumblers do it their way."

At the conclusion of dinner a footman pulled back Marianna's chair. She stood to address her guests.

"Hilary, I'll say good-bye to you here. I remind you, maids and valets are available at any hour to do your packing. Tomorrow I will not keep your attractive husband very long." She turned to Calvin. "A simple matter, you said?"

"Exactly. One requiring immediate attention but little energy."

"Ten A.M. in the Golden Lion Room?"

"Ten A.M.," he repeated.

"And you, Azar. Will you come to my suite with me? I have a surprise. Something Ramir would want you to have."

Azar's sharp face warmed with anticipation. "How dear you are, Marianna," she said.

Sipping liqueurs, they measured each other over the coffee table. Azar waited for Marianna to speak. When she could wait no longer, Azar thrust her body forward.

"Please, Marianna, what is it?"

Marianna did not reply. She put down her unfinished drink and went to a small French desk against the wall. There she riffled among some papers in the center drawer.

Azar, wide-eyed and eager, sat with lips quivering. "The bracelet!" she exclaimed. "Ramir promised it to me. It was a gift to our mother from a Cambodian prince. I knew Ramir would not forget."

Marianna withdrew a cardboard tube from the desk. "It's not a bracelet, Azar."

"Then what . . . ?"

"Something more valuable." She carried the tube to the table and flung it before the bewildered woman. "Open it," she said. "I insist that you open it. Here, now."

The tiny figure tensed. Azar's gaze held on Marianna as she tore at the outer wrappings.

"Inside the tube," Marianna said. "Hurry."

Azar inserted her fingers into the tube. Lowering her eyes, she withdrew several sheets of paper clipped together and covered with a primitive scrawl.

Marianna moved in closer. "Read it," she said.

Azar read rapidly. "But it's a lie," she cried out. "Someone is trying to ruin me!"

"You fool, you *are* ruined. Every word in that confession has been verified." Marianna shook her head in wonder. "Did you and Mojeeb think you could get away with it? I've talked personally with the young man who fired the shot. He was quite communicative when I promised him jail instead of death. What a stupid pair you are, you and Mojeeb. Just as stupid as the secret police. You picked rabid, misguided young men to try to assassinate me. They trusted you. You, the great humanitarian, you who promised them a better life once I was out of the way."

"I meant it!"

"Huh-uh. After their escape the young men returned to their village. The chieftain, Khali Tehrani, told them they had thrown in with the wrong side. The assailants are in a nearby prison waiting to testify against you and the general."

Azar stormed to her feet. "You don't belong here!" she screamed. "You nevar did! Mojeeb and I will have you thrown out. Our country will be restored to us, to the family."

"Perhaps it will be, one day when it pleases me. Karim will follow when I am ready to step aside. Who knows how many years from now that will be?"

"You're a madwoman. How can you hope to stay on in Bahrait? Your life will be in danger day and night. Mojeeb has the army. He'll get rid of you."

"Dear Azar, the army will be mine. A handful of elitists may stupidly remain loyal to the general, but do you think those battalions of young draftees will fight for Mojeeb and his crowd? Never. Not when they learn what I intend to do to benefit the country. Furthermore, I have my own plans for Mojeeb."

Azar's dark eyes glittered with interest.

"His life will be spared, temporarily. I don't want blood on my hands." Marianna shuddered. "Mojeeb will be informed that the two of you have been exposed. Then I will send him to England to replace our present ambassador. One day, if hotheaded Bahraitian students choose to take justice into their own hands and Mojeeb is accidentally killed, it will be no responsibility of mine. I will send a letter of protest to

London and demand immediate extradition of the culprits. Our people will forgive me if I deal gently with the assassins."

"You're that sure of yourself?"

"And sure of you. Tonight I could order your arrest. There is evidence enough—thanks to the assailant and his accomplice—to put you in jail." She smiled, warming to the idea. "There would be a trial. The outcome must be clear, even to you. You could be hanged in the main square if I so desired, or thrown into prison for the rest of your life."

"You're serious!"

"Quite."

"And you've come to a decision, I can tell."

"Isn't it more agreeable this way, to be straightforward, to show our hands? Acting comes easily to me. Still, I find it relaxing to be myself. Azar, I've detested you since the episode in St. Moritz. You knew Ramir was expecting me when you screeched about his whores. You wanted to get both of us with one shot and you did. What a triumph for a jealous sister. My life was never the same again. Now we even the score. Your life will never be the same again."

"What are you going to do?" Azar asked coolly.

"Fortunately, your Empress is a civilized woman. I will not have you destroyed. You could be eliminated overnight and soon be forgotten. No, I prefer a lingering punishment for you. You shall be sent into exile. Your stipend from the royal treasury will be cut. You will receive enough to assure your survival, but no more. It will be my continuing pleasure to watch you hang on by your fingernails. How will you manage without money? Will the young stud in Istanbul want you? Do you dare go back to drug-smuggling without Ramir's protection?"

"You bitch! You rotten lowdown whore!" Azar shrieked. "You won't get away with this!" She tightened her little fists and started for Marianna.

Marianna caught her wrists. "Careful," she said. "You're in *my* country, in *my* house. Don't threaten me or I'll think up a worse fate for you."

Azar tore free and started for the door, then turned back, eyes flashing. "Fool!" she cried out. "You think you're in control now. You're blind! Gropper's the one. Gropper will destroy you!"

Wearing a robe and soft slippers, Marianna left her suite and stepped into the corridor. The uniformed guards on duty froze to attention when she appeared. After saluting, they fell into place beside her, intending to accompany her to her destination. She rejected their presence, saying she wished to proceed alone. They did not oppose her.

Guards at the foot of the marble staircase were waved off as the others had been.

Without changing her even pace, she reached the doors of the Golden Lion Room.

It was midnight. Her meeting with Gropper was still ten hours away. "A simple matter," he had said. "Once we've reviewed it, you need only sign and initial a few pages. Hilary and I will stop over in Washington, and I personally will get the documents into the proper hands."

Let Gropper come. She would be ready for him. She would research the matter now—be prepared for his visit in the morning.

Taking a thick iron key from her pocket, she unlocked the doors. They were heavy and she had to put her shoulder against one, pressing hard until it yielded. A slit of light from the Reception Hall brightened her way. The room ahead was in darkness but she was unafraid as she stepped inside. She felt her way along the wall, located a switch and illuminated the row of crystal chandeliers that led to her objective: the ebony desk at the far end of the chamber.

Suddenly she stopped. She thought—no, she was certain—she heard a gasp for breath and retreating footsteps seeking escape. Whoever it was possessed a hand-held flashlight that flickered on and off, silhouetting an indistinguishable figure. A distant door opened and closed.

Marianna hesitated, unwilling to call out to an intruder who might be armed. Slowly she proceeded along the Persian carpet to the ebony desk. Behind the desk, cut into the paneled wall, was a door leading to an ordinary working office, the domain of Faridah, the dull faithful secretary Ramir had installed a dozen years ago. Marianna reached the office door and tried it. It was locked. She swung back. In the softening glow from the chandeliers, the Golden Lion Room appeared quite normal. On the ebony desk the papers Faridah had organized in neat stacks remained undisturbed, the document Gropper wished her to sign in clear view. Faridah—

and she was sure it was the secretary who had been in the room—had easy access to them, yet had left them behind.

Then she saw it. The familiar portrait of Shah Gahlil, Ramir's father, glaring from the wall. Only this time the smoldering eyes, always fastened on her as she sat at the desk, were slightly askew. She had never failed to grow uneasy under his stare. Tilted, he looked ludicrous.

Marianna moved to the crookedly suspended portrait and, hands on hips, studied it. Why had Faridah been there, flashlight in hand? Why had she tipped the painting? It couldn't be the weary Hollywood chestnut of the secret wall safe. The real treasures of the dynasty, diamonds the size of apricots, storied emeralds and sapphires, the multijeweled crown and tiaras, were locked in a subterranean bank vault, under constant electronic surveillance and guarded by members of the National Police Force. Even she, as Empress, did not have free access to them. "They belong to Bahrait," Ramir had apologized the first time he took her to see them. "You and I may borrow them for occasions of state but they will never be yours or mine."

Elsewhere in the palace there were room-sized concrete vaults where irreplaceable documents such as treaties and war plans were stored behind steel doors with combination locks, and watched over by rotating teams of round-the-clock armed guards.

Feeling foolish, she moved closer to the tilted picture, intending only to set it straight. But it would not straighten. Something jutting from behind the frame prevented it from sliding into position.

She tilted it further and there it was, a drab green door, partially ajar, revealing an oblong metal box, its lid held open by a protruding folder. Her mind flashed an image of the timid screenwriter who had been humiliated by Watson Wagg for introducing a wall safe into a script. "At Hanover we banned that gimmick in the forties," Watson had said cuttingly. "Go back to your typewriter and start thinking with your head, not your thumbs."

She slid her hand into the opening and withdrew an ordinary manila envelope, curving the edge to release it easily. Accordion-type, maroon, and tied about with a narrow gold ribbon, it looked almost festive. She tucked the envelope under her arm and with her free hand scratched about the interior of the vault. Satisfied it held nothing more, she leveled the heavy frame and scowled back at the old Shah. Until this moment she had not appreciated how fully she disliked him.

Nor until this moment had it occurred to her that she had the power to banish him from her sight. As soon as possible, she vowed, he would be sent off to repose forever in the dark basement of the palace he had built.

She would see to it. She was in command now.

That decision made, she returned to the ebony desk, switched on its lone lamp, and shoved aside the stacks of papers, reserving only Gropper's document, the reason for tomorrow's meeting. She upended the manila envelope and shook it vigorously until the last sheet of paper fluttered to the surface of the desk. For insurance she swept her hand through its compartments, and dug out a pocket-size diary.

Then she bent over the desk and began to read.

19

The sun was playing silly tricks this morning, making her giddy. It bounced around the bedroom, touching mirrors, dancing off porcelain lamps and mosaic tables, performing a crazily choreographed ballet on her satin bedcover. Marianna wanted to laugh out loud, a benighted child awakened from a scary dream.

Long past midnight she had left the Golden Lion Room. Passing the guards, she startled them with her exuberance and the hoydenish way she swung a folder in her hand, like an indiscreet hooker on the back streets of Ryal. In her suite she had informed her anxious maid that she did not wish to be awakened before ten. She had worked hard at her desk, she explained, and needed sufficient rest before coping with the duties of the new day. She instructed the maid to get word to Mr. Gropper that she regretfully found it necessary to postpone their meeting until eleven. As the meeting would be brief, Mr. and Mrs. Gropper's scheduled departure would not be delayed.

How long had it been since she had greeted a morning so eagerly? She would have to reverse the days of her life, going back, back, back through years of disillusionment to find another morning as unshadowed as this.

A worthless endeavor, she decided. This was a day for going forward. She was feverish to begin. She hastened through bath and breakfast, humming softly, dismaying her second maid, Kiri, who believed a widow's mourning did not end until she drew her own last breath.

She had dressed for effect. Wearing a somber navy skirt and a navy sweater set off by an innocent white collar, Marianna was at her desk when Gropper entered and commenced the long walk down the Persian runner. Approaching, he would find her with her yellow hair pulled back severely—drabbed-out, dependent, trusting.

Gropper, too, had dressed for the occasion. In his plaid jacket, open-collared shirt, rumpled slacks, and cracked loafers, he was a man with one foot already on the plane. As he came closer she could smell his spicy after-shave lotion. His eyes were bright behind his thick-rimmed glasses. He waved cheerfully.

"Calvin, darling," she said. "Sorry about putting off our appointment. Couldn't be helped. So much work, this Empress business. I'm not sure I can stay the course."

"What foolish talk. You are capable enough to do what you want to do, and clever enough to delegate the rest." He squeezed into a chair alongside her desk and pulled out his pipe.

"How is Hilary?" she asked. "Excited about going home? What an ordeal these past weeks have been. Your support has meant a great deal to me."

He dipped his head, acknowledging her gratitude. "I'll always be here when you need me."

"Thank you, Calvin, I mustn't keep you. You said this was a minor matter. We can dispose of it quickly." She gestured toward some papers. "This document—this contract—I'm to sign . . ."

"Yes." He took it from her desk, flipped through it, then smoothed the last page before her. "Right here." He pointed to a small red X on the bottom line. "Your signature, and I will be on my way." He removed a gold pen from his jacket pocket, exposed the point, and offered it to her.

"No, Calvin," she said.

"You would prefer a pen of your own? I understand. Many monarchs have shared the same superstition."

"No, Calvin," she repeated. "I'm not signing. Not with your pen or mine."

He was sure she was joking. "A quill, perhaps?"

"Calvin, I've read the document. I don't like it."

"But why?" His eyes blinked and his glasses clouded.

"Because it's a contract to acquire additional military airplanes and carriers. At a cost to Bahrait of two billion dollars. We can't afford it."

Gropper removed his glasses, wiped them on the sleeve of his jacket, and smiled ingratiatingly. It was a moment for indulgence. "Let me explain, Marianna. Acquisition of these items was Ramir's dearest wish. I devoted one year to persuading the United States Congress that American interests were as well served as Bahrait's. Congress was slow to grasp the necessity of strengthening Bahrait against its neighbors. Finally its members acceded. They were forced to do so or Ramir would have taken his business and his commitment to the Soviets."

"I didn't know Ramir considered occasional border incidents serious threats."

"*I* knew. He was overjoyed when I told him I had achieved our mutual goal." Gropper lowered his voice in sorrow. "Ramir intended to sign the papers as soon as he returned to the palace."

"It makes no sense. We are already overarmed."

"You will agree that Bahrait's strategic location requires a strong military presence?"

"Agreed."

"Then why hesitate?"

"I am not hesitating. I am flat-out refusing."

His face flushed. "Let me be frank. To return to Washington without your signature would cause me great embarrassment."

"You'll survive."

"I always do. But will you? Bahrait cannot afford enemies in the United States government."

"Persuade them you've altered your judgment. They'll forgive you."

"They would. But I have not altered my judgment. They will be told I am dealing with a willful, brainless amateur."

"Then I must be the persuader."

He glanced at his wristwatch impatiently. "Of whom?"

"Let's begin with you. At the first show of hostility toward me, I'll end your career. Are you persuaded?"

"You're speaking nonsense."

"Calvin, Faridah's gone. Skipped in the night. No messages, no good-byes."

"Unfortunate," he said cautiously. "She could have told you what this purchase meant to Ramir."

"She did, indirectly. Let's not waste time with details—you have a plane waiting. Did you know Ramir kept a journal?"

Gropper's forehead dampened and he shifted in his chair. "No. I did not."

"Faridah did. She read it. Too bad she left it behind."

Gropper found a handkerchief and patted his brow. "Show it to me."

"And waste more time? No need, you know what's in it. Ramir was a meticulous man. Every arms purchase made

through you was carefully noted. So was your cut as bro-
ker."

Gropper shrugged. "Admittedly, a suggestion of impropri-
ety, but no illegality there."

"May I quote from a random page in Ramir's journal? He
wrote: 'Eighteen planes, missile launchers, tanks, arrived at
our harbor in Persian Gulf. Never unloaded in Bahrait.
Immediately transferred to cargo boats registered to Somalia.
Payment received from Somalia in German marks and transferred to my personal account in Zurich.' "

"Ramir did that?" Gropper was incredulous. "Resold the
material I obtained for him? Impossible!"

"Oh, there's more. You know about his underground hangars?"

Gropper nodded carefully.

"You know they don't exist. Ramir announced he was
overarming Bahrait to protect it. He encouraged talk of his
megalomania. Meanwhile, according to his journal, he was
looting the country's treasury and fattening his numbered
Swiss bank accounts. I have the bank receipts he requested.
Apart from his monarchy, my husband was one of the world's
richest men. There's evidence he was worth several billion
dollars."

"Astounding! Yet who can blame him? He often confided
to me he feared a revolution or a coup d'état. He couldn't
face exile without a sizeable nest egg for himself and his
family."

"A considerate man, my husband. Obviously he felt equal
concern for you. His journal records he split his share of the
take fifty-fifty with Calvin Groppar, and that each of you
skimmed a bit off the top for General Mojeeb."

Gropper remained bland. "You've done your homework,
my dear Marianna. What now? Expose me and you expose
Ramir. An unwise move, I think. Bahrait must not be disillu-
sioned about its late Shah. It is already a wounded country.
Only trust can hold it together. You are starting with a clean
slate. Why smudge it so soon?"

"That is not my intention."

"What then?"

"First this," she said. She took the unsigned contract from
her desk, brandished it before him, tore it in half, and then in
half again.

Gropper's expression was phlegmatic as he watched the

scraps of paper drop into a wastebasket. "Very amusing. And your next move?"

"To get you and your slab-assed wife out of Bahrait and out of my life. You're right about the clean slate. I intend to take hold of this country and bring it dignity and prosperity. I'll end the graft and repression and torture for which Bahrait is so justly famous. Before the week is out, I'll empty the prisons of every political dissident. I'll ... I'll ..." She paused, breathless.

"Bravo," Gropper said sarcastically. "A rousing sermon. I applaud you." He stood up, his hands gripping the edge of her desk. "You're a child," he said. "And ignorant, yes, ignorant of the world's realities. You called me a survivor and you're right. Well, I call you a loser and you will see that I am right. Idealism? That's for morons, not monarchs."

"This country will never again be run by despots and thieves, not while I'm alive."

"And how long do you expect that to be?"

"Long enough to see you in hell."

He stepped back, placed his right forearm across his paunch and bowed grandly. "I shall be there waiting for you. Good-bye, Your Majesty—and may Allah shower his blessing on you for the rest of your days on earth."

Selma ignored the voice on the Alitalia intercom which implored her in four languages to fasten her seat belt. A ravishing Italian steward tapped her shoulder. *"Prego,* Signora," he said, indicating the belt. His grin was downright lecherous as he bent to assist her.

"You have enjoyed Venice?" he asked. "See, over there is our Campanile, and beyond, the Piazza San Marco. From here one looks down on heaven, don't you agree?"

She did not agree, although she did not say so. He was too beautiful to offend. Another Gino, but without the vicious streak. Dammit, Italian men were famous for their sweetness and gallantry. How had she managed to hitch up with the only mutation in the tribe?

The handsome steward was still there. "It always breaks my heart to leave Venice. Knowing I will be back the same evening does not ease my pain. And you?"

"It breaks my heart, too." Tears streaked down the fat face. The steward handed her a tissue and moved away.

Another son-of-a-bitch, she thought. He could have wiped my cheeks, patted my head, offered a comforting word. Anything. But no—like Gino, he turned his back.

She glanced at her Alitalia ticket. It guaranteed her transportation from Venice to Rome. Nowhere did it pledge that the steward would provide tender loving care throughout the brief flight.

Gino had said it. "You expect everything. You want to own a man. You see too many romantic movies. A husband and wife joined till eternity? I never promised that. You do not like our arrangement—go away."

She had blanched, listening to him.

"I love you, Selma. You are a wonderful woman. We have a nice understanding. Be reasonable. A man like me, so healthy, I cannot always suppress my desires when we are apart. With other women I make believe I am with you. Now are you satisfied?"

She looked around the first-class section of the plane. The steward hovered over a blue-jeaned redhead with a Vuitton bag at her feet. They were talking in rapid French and laughing.

Gino was right. She was too possessive. If she kept it up she risked losing what little she had. For his own reasons their marriage was important to him. Her reasons were just as selfish. In bed, when she could get him there, he was Mr. Magic. She would settle. Sooner or later she would trap him her way.

The plane lurched onto the Fiumicino airfield near Rome. The steward, freshly doused with toilet water, reached overhead and brought down the light coat stored above her seat. Handing it to her, he tossed her a seductive wink. She responded with a wink of her own and disembarked to await the flight to Bahrait.

Marianna crackled with energy.

"Simmer down, honey," Luke said. "You'll bust a fuse if you don't cool off."

"It was just the greatest," she said. "That meeting with Professor Emani was the biggest charge I've had in years!"

Luke smiled ruefully. "Thanks, old buddy. I've never had a nicer compliment."

"Darling, I didn't mean *that*." She threw her arms around

his neck and kissed him. "I can't help it. I'm so wound up, Emani says it's the best plan he's seen since he became Minister of Housing. Think of it. Those slums torn down, decent apartments going up. After that, the villages, the hospitals, the schools. And it'll take just a tiny bite out of the money I saved when I threw out Gropper. I could go on and on and on!"

He shook his head, amused by her excitement. "For weeks you talked about cutting out of the show. Now you want to play all the parts."

"Ramir's little diary turned me around. That, and what I saw with you. Now I can't wait to clean up the whole rotten mess."

He pulled her to him. "Still my girl, Your Majesty?"

She sobered instantly. "Nothing's changed." She searched his face. "Promise you'll never leave me."

"I promise."

Marianna paced the marble Reception Hall waiting for Selma. Bursting with ideas, she was eager to return to her desk. Her first glimpse of her friend lumbering up the stairs, followed by a servant carrying her bags and coat, gave her a jolt. She raced down the steps and hugged Selma to her.

Selma managed a weak smile. "Let me look at you. Not bad for a lady with a murder contract out on her."

"The assassination attempt? Yesterday's news."

"The Italian press played it up big. I tried calling but couldn't get through."

"That's in the past. The gunman and his accomplice are in prison. Since then I've done lots of housekeeping around the old plantation."

Selma was only half-listening.

Marianna linked arms with her. "It went badly with Gino, didn't it? Let's go to my suite. I'll tell Luke to postpone our meeting. You and I can lunch and talk."

"Suits me," Selma replied as they started up the stairs. "I'll give you the synopsis first. Another time I'll fill in the details."

"I'm listening," Marianna said.

"From Rome I telephoned my old Beverly Hills shrink. He said I sounded shell-shocked. He said I need peace and relaxation, and the love of a good friend. Now that things are quiet around here—" she squinted. "They are, aren't they?"

"Roses and buttercups."

"Good, you got yourself a boarder."

Marianna hugged her again. "Wonderful. I need you, too. What about the studio?"

"Those money-crunching bastards in New York were pissed. Luckily, Charlie Knight came through. He could hear I was cracking up. It would be bad for studio morale if the dependable Earth Mother flipped out on the premises, he said. So I came here for a quick cure. Beats Menninger's and the price is right."

"And Gino?"

"Never better. I fixed it so the slimy bastard stays on as director of *Pantheon*. I gave my word to Charlie that I'd personally indemnify the studio for a percentage of the losses. We'll publicize the picture heavily. It's bound to earn back *something*. Remember what we used to say in Hollywood? 'The town is divided into two types: those who give ulcers and those who get them.' Gino's the giver. Figure out the rest."

"How long can you take it?"

"Till I come to my senses, which is probably never. Anyway, I have a secret." They had reached the landing and Selma scanned the hall for eavesdroppers. Satisfied there were none, she dropped her voice to a whisper. "I'm going to have a baby."

"Selma, how marvelous! When?"

"After I get pregnant. When I get home, I'm giving the Pill to my cat. If Gino wants to keep working, he'll have to *shtup* me till he bleeds. When the baby's born, we'll see what happens. I hear you take an Italian lecher, give him a kid, and in front of your eyes he turns into a devoted family man."

"Great news," Marianna said flatly.

"You gotta better suggestion? What about you? Staying on or dropping out?"

"I'm staying. So is Luke."

"You're sicker than I am. Why be a moving target for another bunch of crazies?"

"I'm beginning to like the job. Luke and I have a million ideas. We're not afraid. Let's order lunch. When I tell you what's happening, you'll understand."

The evening news was ending when Selma snapped off the color television in the family room. "I don't get it." She swung around to Marianna and Luke. "Your government-controlled TV spills out everything that's shitty about the rest of the world. In Bahrait, it's flower festivals and fancy yachts. Don't the people bust a gut when they watch how the other two percent lives?"

"They don't have television sets," Luke said dryly. "They don't have shoes either."

Marianna's eyes glistened. "Don't you see? I'm going to give them necessities first. Luxuries like television come later. We'll be honest about what's shabby, but the people will know we're doing something to help."

"You're so naïve, I can't believe it." Selma shook her head. "Do you think that by not playing footsies with Calvin Gropper you can make the military melt away? You're a sitting duck, baby. And you're another, Luke. Pretty soon you'll each have a fatal accident. If not that, the army will shove its tanks through the front door and you'll end up in separate cells playing gin rummy with rats."

"They wouldn't dare," Marianna said. "Mojeeb can't risk it. The rest of the world would abandon him."

Selma sniffed. "And another thing. You don't live in such a friendly neighborhood. In Saudi Arabia they're yapping at your heels for a lousy strip of disputed territory. I read it in *Time* magazine."

"Cancel your subscription," Luke said. "*Time* is sore because we put a clamp on the assassination story. Marianna will pick up the support of the people. They can be stronger than any army."

Selma remained skeptical. "You two are adorable idealistic children. You can't go on playing patty-cake with wolves like Mojeeb. He'll chew you up and swallow you with French fries."

Luke took Marianna's hand. "Mojeeb will be dealt with at the proper time. We know what we're doing," he said.

"Marianna, what about your kids? Aren't you scared?"

"I'm scared plenty. But unless I clean up this dung heap, my kids will live in terror or exile. Once I introduce my programs, the people will be behind me. Someday I hope we'll have a hands-off monarchy like Sweden's and England's and Denmark's. Karim and I talked about it before Luke took him back to school. I gave Karim my word I'd do my best."

Selma yawned. "I hear tumbrils in the distance."

"Very funny," Luke said.

"Break it up," Marianna said. "Luke agrees with what I'm doing. Nothing, no one, forces us out of here."

20

The Swiss landscape had a poignant beauty this midafternoon. The sun, riding low on stands of majestic firs and pines, accented the hollows in the snow, creating the illusion of dwarfed craters.

Prince Karim stood apart from his rackety classmates, morose, withdrawn, as he had been since the death of his father. Switzerland evoked better days, childhood days when he had shared St. Moritz vacations with his family. He knew there was no hiding place that could erase memories of his father, yet there was a special sadness about a ski playground that made him long for the imperious, dynamic man who had first put him on skis and who now lay buried in Ryal.

Karim inhaled the biting air. It filled his lungs, made him lightheaded. There *was* something special about the mountains and the shadowed snow, something that sneaked up on him, dared to lighten his spirits and distance him from the ugliness of death.

The twinge of happiness that suffused him was quickly dissipated by a rush of guilt. It was unseemly, disrespectful, he told himself, to experience pleasure so soon after his loss. But was it too soon? He was angry because no one had helped him deal with his grief, told him how long it should appropriately consume him.

He was not homesick. Frequent telephone conversations with his family and with Luke reminded him of his lost father. He welcomed separation from familiar voices and places that revived his hurt.

It was good luck that winter had come early this year, better luck that he was in Zermatt for the first time. Annually, to break the pall of the winter semester and to offer its students every benefit of an expensive Swiss education, Le Rosey had moved its entire student body and teaching staff to a sprawling chalet in Gstaad. But this year, aware that Gstaad's glittering jet-set attractions had become too tempting to its young charges, Le Rosey's governing board had introduced an experiment. It has transferred the winter school to the more sedate village of Zermatt. There, as in

Gstaad, the boys rose at dawn, spent mornings in class, and passed the afternoons in Nordic and Alpine skiing. Like his father, Karim preferred the exhilaration and danger of downhill runs that stretched to infinity.

Surrendering his depression, he clumped back to the ski gondola now discharging a second group of schoolmates. Bolting from the gondola in gaudy down-quilted ski suits and pomponned wool caps, the new arrivals leaped in the virgin snow, squawking like huge clumsy birds. With cold-stiffened fingers they stepped into their skis, dug their hands into fur-lined leather gloves and, employing poles, brought their bodies upright before leaning into position for the run.

The first line shoved off. "Powder's great," a youngster squeaked, looking over his shoulder.

"Gentlemen, eyes forward," an instructor implored. "Careful or you'll get a snootful of snow."

"Be alert. There are moguls ahead," a second instructor called out.

"There's only one mogul on this mountain," another boy whooped. "That's Karim, and he's harmless."

Karim moved away. In his new mood he wanted to be apart from his companions, free to adjust privately to the vaulting joy he felt because *he* was alive.

"Meet you at the taverna," he shouted, pushing off.

"Karim, wait!" an instructor called after him.

But he was gone, hurtling down the mountain, swerving among the trees, skillfully avoiding the treacherous mounds of snow known as moguls.

Elated at breaking away, he knew that if he maintained his speed he would reach the Italian border and the Taverna Luciana a good half hour before the others.

Holding the tips of his ski poles behind him, he sped down the mountainside, thinking of the taverna, tasting the *vino brulé*, the strong, mulled red wine tinged with cinnamon and cloves and served piping hot in a mug. Like his schoolmates, he favored this particular run and its destination.

The noisy taverna, a ramshackle wooden structure on the Italian side of the border near Cervinia, had stood in the forest for over a century. With its raw plank floor, hewn bar and tables, and upended kegs serving as stools, the taverna remained a friendly hostel for frozen skiers, as well as a recognized checkpoint in which Italian officials sheltered their border police.

On other visits to the taverna, Karim had been enchanted by the drunken informality of the men of the patrol, their rollicking good cheer a startling contrast to the arrogant, scowling police at home. Although students were permitted to drink nothing stronger than the hot wine, the Italian guards, inventing a hundred good reasons, toasted each other rowdily with shots of strong *grappa Friulana*.

"For the freezing weather," they had explained to the delighted boys. "It is sanctioned," one of them added solemnly. "What other reason for remaining in this stinking job? The winter sports? We are not athletes. We are distinguished servants of the law." He saluted the group, then fell back onto his keg, howling at his joke. "The beautiful woods," he went on. "Never for us. A man could freeze his balls off if he ventured too far. My companions and I, we will serve our country from here, warmed by our good friends in the bottles while waiting for distinguished travelers like you."

His neighbor nudged him slyly. "And a little contraband sweetens the cake, eh? Tell the young man. Furs, cigarettes, liquor, all become invisible after certain worthy citizens do a bit of dealing with us. When we choose to look, we see only each other, right?"

"Each other, and a box stuffed with lire," a red-faced guard boasted. He uncorked a bottle of wine and poured liberally for each ot the men. "Realities, gentlemen," he said to the boys. "Those are the realities, not the foolishness they teach in your fancy school. Come back when you are older and we will tell you more about the smuggling trade."

Karim had already downed three full mugs of the steaming mulled wine when his classmates burst through the door. The boys were uproarious. The instructors, stern and relieved.

"Karim, you know we are to stay together," one said. "If anyone—especially you—gets lost, our heads will roll, understand?"

"I'm sorry, sir," Karim said. "I was carried away by the run. It won't happen again." He passed his mug for a refill, then clumsily pushed away from the table. "Leave it for me. I'll be back in a minute."

The second instructor leaped to his feet and stationed himself before the door. "Looks like you've had too much to drink. Where do you think you're going?"

Karim tugged the pomponned cap from his head and bobbed cavalierly. "Outside, sir," he said. "To pee."

They were gathered after dinner in the family sitting room of the palace. Earlier the younger children had been brought in to visit and had been taken away to bed.

Marianna paced the length of the room, pivoted for the dozenth time, and came to a halt at the grand piano where Luke was flailing away.

"Stop that noise," she begged. "Can't you tell I need quiet to think?"

Luke switched to "Hail to the Chief," and whistled a few bars before lifting his fingers from the keyboard. "What's on your mind, Madame?"

"Professor Emani brought me the report from the Agricultural Ministry. Imagine, sixty percent of the desert is arable. With proper irrigation we can feed our entire population and have enough left over for export. Tomorrow morning we start."

Selma unwound her heavy legs, hidden beneath a flower-strewn caftan. "There's nothing you can do tonight," she groaned. "Light somewhere, will you? High blood pressure isn't queenly."

Marianna collapsed into a chair. Luke swung around on the piano bench and faced her.

"Forget your ministers of this and that. Hold on—" He raised his hand when he saw her indignation. "You're ducking your biggest problem—disposing of General Mojeeb."

"You know I can't deal with him yet, not until I'm certain the army knows who's in charge here. Give me a little more time to strengthen my position." Marianna broke into a smile. "Remember when Ramir found out Mojeeb was building a summer villa on the Caspian? He rushed out to see it. When he discovered it was grander than ours, he ordered it confiscated. Ever since, it's been an archaeological museum, another of Ramir's cultural contributions to his country. Mojeeb never uttered a word. He knew who was boss then. He'll soon learn who's boss now."

Luke gave up. "At least Selma and I know who's cracking the whip." He poured liqueurs and passed them around. They sipped their drinks and lapsed into silence.

The first quick ring of the telephone did not rouse them. Not until the switchboard operator buzzed a second time did they shake loose from their thoughts.

"Luke, will you pick it up, darling?" Marianna asked.

Luke reached for the instrument on a nearby desk. Only

half-attentive, Marianna heard him say, "Yes, operator. Hold a minute, I'll inquire." He covered the mouthpiece.

"Marianna, do you know anyone in Bergamo? Are you expecting a call?" He glanced at his wristwatch. "It's around seven P.M. in Italy."

The liqueur was making her sleepy. "Don't know anyone in Bergamo," she yawned. "Who's on the line?"

"Border police. Jabbering like crazy. Either of you understand Italian?"

He did not wait for an answer. "I'm Luke Tremayne, press secretary to the Empress. You may speak freely." He covered the mouthpiece again. "It's something about Karim. English-speaking fellow on the phone now. He says the school will phone you any minute. He wanted to prepare you." Luke returned to the caller. "Hey, slow down, will you? Yes, yes, I'm sure it's not your fault."

"Fault!" Marianna flew to the phone and grabbed the receiver. "Yes, this is his mother. He's *what*? He's disappeared! Oh, no!" She listened a while longer, then her body began to waver. "He went through the door and never came back—? Kidnapped!"

Selma was beside her. "Sit down, hon. You're gonna keel over if you don't. Let Luke take it from here."

Luke recovered the telephone. "I see, I see. Yes, I'll tell her you're doing everything. Stop apologizing," he said angrily. "Get back to your job and report *anything*. We'll be waiting." He slammed down the receiver and returned to the couch where Marianna huddled. "Look, I know it sounds bad, but there's nothing definite. It was snowing. Karim stepped outside to pee. After a while, one of the ski instructors took a head count of the boys. Karim wasn't among them. So far they've found Karim's ski cap and goggles and one of his gloves. The instructor notified the Italian and Swiss police. Since then they've been out in falling snow beating the woods."

"What about footprints, ski tracks?" Selma asked.

"Practically obliterated. The fools ran around in panic. The border patrol, the instructors, the kids. What they haven't erased, the snow is covering."

Marianna whimpered and Luke took her icy hands in his. "It's not hopeless," he said. "The Italian police picked up wagon tracks in the woods. They shoved the others back and began following the tracks. So far they've found signs of a slight scuffle and Karim's second glove. No blood, thank God. We can only sit and wait."

"Wait!" Marianna cried. "Are you insane? I'll contact Rome, the premier himself, I'll call the Swiss police. We'll fly in our own police. I'll appeal for my son on television. I'll do everything but wait!"

The desk phone rang again and she caught it. "Karim!" she shouted. "Where are you? Are you hurt?" She listened intently. "No," she pleaded. "Tell them you can't hang up yet. Repeat what they said. Yes, I understand. Find out their demands. Tell them I'll do anything. I love you."

She heard him click off and dazedly replaced the receiver. "He's being held in an old church," she said in an undertone. "Someone has made it habitable. Besides the telephone, he has a bed and a supply of food. They're giving him hot milk to keep him from freezing."

"They?"

"Masked men. The call was a warning. We're not to say a word about the kidnapping. Neither is the school. In their own good time, maybe tomorrow, the kidnappers will announce their demands."

"Why didn't they tell them to you right now?" Selma asked.

"Probably waiting for someone higher up to spell them out," Luke said. "Whoever planned the operation must make sure you'll play ball before moving on to the next step."

"What can we do?" Marianna asked helplessly.

Luke knelt and kissed her lips. "We wait. If reporters get on to the story, we deny it."

Marianna shook her head. "Terrorists can't be behind this. What can they bargain for? I've released Ramir's political prisoners."

Luke poured another round of drinks. "Swallow this," he ordered. "Try to sleep. I'll wake you when the next call comes."

When the phone rang it was 4:00 A.M. and she had not slept. She sprang to answer it and signaled Luke to pick up an extension.

"Karim!" she called out.

It was not Karim. It was a new voice, a female voice speaking in precise, unaccented English. "At dawn our anonymous spokesmen in Paris will telephone members of the international press," the woman said crisply. "They will say

Karim is alive and well. That is the truth. Later, in a second story, we will make known our conditions for his release."

"You're telling the whole world? For God's sake, tell me!"

"Certainly, Your Majesty, I was coming to that. Only you can decide your son's fate."

"Anything . . ."

"Our demand is simple. You must abdicate."

"Abdicate! To whom? You're holding my heir!"

"Not exactly. With your abdication, neither Karim nor anyone in the royal family may claim the throne."

"I don't care about the throne. How do I get my son back?" she asked desperately.

"You will hear from us again."

"Promise me . . ." she started to say. But she was speaking to a dead telephone. She stared at the instrument. "Who would commit such a monstrous act? I know who my enemies are. But Italians? Why Italians?"

It was dawn before the long-awaited call came.

"Your Majesty?" It was a male voice.

"Yes."

"I appreciate how anxious you must be. I am the father of sons myself . . ."

"Where is my boy?"

"My associate told you he was safe. That is as much as you need to know for the present."

"Let me talk to him," she pleaded.

"He is somewhere in the north. I myself am in Rome, where I now look out on the Spanish Steps. A magnificent sight."

"You didn't call to tell me that."

"True."

"You know I'm prepared to abdicate."

"A splendid decision."

"How do I know I'll see Karim again?"

"Madame." The voice sounded hurt. "You have my word. You need only follow instructions."

"Whatever you want—"

"Good. I will be brief. When it is morning in Bahrait, you will appear on television. You will announce that in one week you will be leaving for America and taking your family with you. You will say the assassination attempt on yourself and

the new danger to your son have made your decision irrevo-
cable. You will say you will never again return to Bahrait."

"Who are you? Who's behind this?"

"That is unimportant. Do as I say and your son will soon
be with you, healthy as ever. Defy me and you will have him
back in pieces."

General Sahid Mojeeb inspected himself in the three-way
mirror that walled one side of his dressing room. No angle
pleased him. The military uniform was too stiff, too forbidding for the emotional occasion. He would not wear it. With
the help of his valet he stripped to his shorts, exposing a
powerful torso of which he was proud and stick-figure legs of
which he was ashamed. The latter he kept concealed in
well cut trousers except when he was alone or in bed with a
woman.

He approved the white shirt and gray Savile Row suit his
valet brought him and allowed the man to help him into
highly buffed black shoes and to knot his subdued burgundy
tie. He debated the matter of decorations before concluding
they would be inappropriate. Feeling naked, he selected a
turquoise and white rosette, a modest symbol of the Medal of
Honor awarded him by the late Shah, and slipped it into the
buttonhole of his jacket. It solved his problem. A white
handkerchief arranged in points in his breast pocket completed his costume.

The handkerchief was important. The Empress would be
justified in weeping. As a friend, he could very well be called
upon to dry her tears.

An early riser, General Mojeeb had been among the first to
hear reports of the kidnapping by way of his bedside radio.
He had lost no time dispatching a messenger to the Empress
requesting an audience. Her press secretary, Luke Tremayne,
responded on her behalf—the Empress wished to see him at
once.

In his chauffeured bulletproof limousine, General Mojeeb
considered what he would say to the shattered Empress, so
recently widowed, so cruelly struck a second blow. He would
reassure her that however outrageous the kidnappers' demands, still not publicly announced, he stood ready to support her.

Uniformed guards swung wide the iron doors as his limousine pulled to a halt before the palace. Mojeeb dashed up the

marble stairs, gratified that the unaccustomed haste did not accelerate his heartbeat unduly. Although courageous in political confrontation and in battle, the general nursed a trace of hypochondria, subjecting himself to frequent needless physical examinations. Unfailingly, he demonstrated particular concern for his genitalia, due to his predilection for Ryal's prostitutes.

Hurrying down the corridor to the family salon, he reviewed what had been revealed to him of the situation. Karim and a group of schoolboys had skied across the Italian border to a taverna. Karim had stepped outside alone. When he did not return, his instructors, classmates, and members of the Italian border patrol had searched the surrounding area, carelessly erasing valuable footprints. At a distance from the taverna, the police had discovered signs of a scuffle and wagon tracks. They had followed the tracks, but found no useful clues along the way. They had run into a dead end upon reaching a small village at the base of the mountain where the tracks merged into other tracks on a slushy, unpaved road. Karim had spoken to his mother from the kidnappers' lair.

Before leaving his own home, a call from one of his spies assigned to the palace switchboard had informed General Mojeeb of another message from Rome that demanded the abdication of the Empress and the renunciation of any claim to the throne by all members of the royal family. If the operator was to be believed—and he would not risk lying— the Empress had readily acceded to the abductors' demands.

Now she wished to confer with the commander of her armed forces.

For a few pleasant moments General Mojeeb entertained the hope that the Empress Marianna would invite him to take up the reins of government. He was experienced, authoritative, respected. However heavy the burden, he was prepared to meet the call to duty. If she told him about the abdication demand, he would be unwise to encourage her to remain. She would think him a fool. Whatever else might be said of the Empress, she was the least likely mother to sacrifice her son's life for the throne of Bahrait. These were not Roman times— this was the twentieth century.

The door to the salon opened almost on cue. He stepped inside and went directly to the Empress. "Your Majesty, this is a dreadful situation. Have you had further word from the kidnappers?"

"I have," she whispered wearily. "Luke, tell the general their terms."

"It is blackmail of the worst kind," the general exclaimed when Luke had finished. "Bahrait is accused of operating the world's most notorious espionage system. If it deserved its reputation, it would have interceded before the kidnapping."

Marianna's face, when she raised it to his, was a mask. You slimy toad, she thought, your fine hand is in this somewhere. But where do the Italians fit in? Then she wondered, could Gropper possibly be involved? Calvin was greedy, unprincipled—but would he collaborate in this—the threatened murder of Ramir's son?

Mojeeb was still talking. "Futile," she heard him say. "All is futile."

"What do you suggest, General?"

"I fear you must abdicate, Madame. I see no other choice."

"It will be the loss of a dream," Marianna said. "Mine and Karim's. His eyes shine when he speaks of what his country can be. He's young, idealistic. He would willingly sacrifice himself if he thought it would help Bahrait."

"And you, Your Majesty?"

"I want my son back," she said simply.

Luke stood between them. "Thank you for coming, General. Your opinion is valued. We'll keep each other informed."

Mojeeb backed out of the room. When he heard the door close behind him, he looked about and confirmed that except for the security guards he was alone. Walking jauntily down the corridor and staircase, he flicked a thread from the Savile Row suit and stepped into his limousine.

21

The telephone was driving her mad, yet she had refused to have it blocked. "The next call may be the one," she insisted. It seemed everyone she had ever known wished to express concern: heads of state, wives of heads of state, ambassadors, friends, and near-friends. Pia from Lausanne. The Groppers from Washington. The Boston and Hollywood contingents, volunteering to return. Unoffended by her request to stay away, they promised to phone again, and did.

And the press, the insatiable press, admitted by Luke for a single session, doggedly seeking her quotes. "How do you feel?" one reporter asked.

"You dumb bastard! How the hell do you think I feel?" she shouted.

Selma and Luke exchanged glances. It was time to end the punishment.

After dismissing the press, Luke clamped onto Marianna's wrists and pulled her to her feet. "My mistake and I'm sorry. I expected them to show more restraint. You need sleep. Why not use the sofa in the next room? I'm turning the phone bell off. If anything's important, I'll come for you."

Shivering beneath the blankets Selma had wrapped around her, she dozed restlessly, unaware of her whimpering and the nervous jerking of her body.

A firm hand on her shoulder shook her to consciousness. Groggy, sticky-eyed, she sat up and saw Luke. He held the telephone toward her. "Take it," he said. "Paris. It's Dahlia."

She gazed at him blankly.

Luke spoke into the receiver. "Dahlia, tell Marianna everything you've told me. No, better yet, put Regis on. Let him explain."

Her voice when she spoke was quavering. "Regis? Yes, this is Marianna. What—?"

Listening, she looked across at Selma and Luke, eyes coming alive. She held up two crossed fingers. "You think there's a possibility? Have you talked to him?...He said

what?" She listened again. Her shoulders sagged. "We have
no choice. When can you leave? ... Good. And Regis, be
careful."

"Marianna, honey, stop crying. Tell us what's going on,"
Selma said.

"Regis. He once had a quick flirtation with the Italian Red
Brigade. He'd just come to Paris from Detroit. In those days
he was a hotheaded radical, gung ho to change the world.
Ramir's secret police checked him out when he moved in with
Dahlia. At first, Ramir wanted him shot. Then Regis pulled
out of the Brigade and Ramir called off his killers. Regis is an
intellectual radical, not a terrorist. Leaflets, speeches, demonstrations . . ."

Selma was losing patience. "Okay, so he's a nice boy. I like
him already. Why did he call?"

"Regis had a hunch about Karim's kidnappers. The message from Rome was the trigger. He remembered an Italian
militant, an older man, who withdrew from the Brigade to
marry a contessa from Milan. Her title provides the cover for
his work."

"Which is—?"

"A crackpot's fantasy. To see a united socialism throughout Europe. He wants money for his propaganda. He'll take it
from anyone, even those he despises."

"What's his name?"

"He called himself Signore Vendicatore. Regis contacted
him through friends. The Signore admitted nothing, but he
did advise Regis to fly to Rome to discuss the kidnapping."

"Maybe he's faking," Selma said.

"Maybe he is. Anyway, Regis is going to Rome."

"How can we help?" Luke said.

"We can't. Dahlia is driving Regis to Orly to catch the next
plane to Rome. It'll be hours before we hear from him."

Later, lying back in her bathtub, Marianna sought relief
from the unremitting nightmare. Optimism had never served
her well and it did not come to her rescue tonight. Regis had
not pulled his punches. He was playing a hunch, he had said.
"Vendicatore may be faking. Or by now he may be working
some new angle."

On the wall a clock ticked away. Nearly midnight. Twelve
hours to wait. So little time before she was to go before the

people to announce her abdication. At this moment, in a basement room, cameramen were setting up their equipment under Luke's supervision. Lights and microphones were being readied, cables strung. She had insisted that this pessimistic course be pursued. Luke, sleep-starved himself, had not tried to dissuade her. Depassionately, they had discussed the television backdrop, the sparse furnishings—a desk, a chair, the national flag suspended from a flagpole.

"It'll be over quickly," Luke promised.

"Then we'll gather the children and we'll go where it's safe, my darling." She smiled. "I'll welcome the peace. It's been so long."

The clock read 12:03. The minute hand clicking around its face no longer seemed threatening. She looked forward to the deadline, to an end to the horror. Nothing mattered, nothing but her children and Luke. She snatched a terry-cloth robe from the warming rack, donned it crookedly, and padded to the desk in her salon.

Absorbed in what she was doing, she did not hear the door opening nor the footsteps approaching.

"Now what?" Selma said. "You're supposed to be resting."

"Go away, or sit down and be quiet." Marianna pointed her pen at Selma. "I'm writing, can't you see? The abdication speech."

"The speech can be written in the morning. Keep on this way and you won't have to abdicate. You'll drop dead."

"Selma, get off my back or I'll—"

"You'll what? I'm an American citizen. Short on class maybe, but long on *chutzpah*. I say go to bed. I'll wake you in time to finish the speech."

Marianna replaced the pen in its holder. "Oh, Selma, I'm so afraid for him—" she said brokenly.

Selma plumped onto the sofa. "Believe it or not, under this mound of flesh there are bones. And those bones are telling me everything's going to be fine."

Marianna slept fitfully and shallowly with Selma seated by her side. Instructions to the switchboard operators had been changed. The operators were to sift the calls carefully, put through only those which seemed vital.

When the phone buzzed, Marianna raced to answer it. "Regis! What happened? Where is Karim? Is he safe?"

"Vendicatore's men have him. He's fine. The Signore won't tell me where they're hiding him. Not until new terms are met."

"*New* terms?"

"Cash. Five million dollars. In Swiss francs. Untraceable. I'm to hand it over before noon tomorrow."

"Five million dollars," she gasped.

"He's holding firm about that. Meet his terms, Karim gets home safely, and you stay on as Empress."

"Where would I get such a sum?"

"Jewels, art, the treasury?"

"All here, but it'll take time to liquidate them. And then it's no secret."

"What do I tell him?"

"That I'm prepared to meet his original terms. I'll abdicate." She looked over to Selma, who nodded approvingly.

Suddenly Marianna brightened. She grasped the receiver tightly.

"No—wait, Regis—wait!" She cried into the phone. "I can do it, I can get the money and no one will know where it came from, not ever!" She laughed hysterically. "What a marvelous joke!"

"What's funny?" Regis asked.

"Never mind. I'll explain another day. Go back to your contact. Tell him he has a deal—five million dollars cash in exchange for Karim. Arrange a rendezvous. I'll need a couple of hours. Call me back. 'Bye."

She broke into a crazy giggle.

"No questions, Selma. Find Luke. Tell him to dress decently—suit, necktie, briefcase. He's going on a trip. I'll arrange the plane. And, Selma, tell him to bring a topcoat. It's cold in Zurich."

She had made the necessary calls. In Zurich the director of the Crédit Suisse Bank was solicitous. He had been following the case. He appreciated her torment. If Her Majesty's emissary presented the proper documents everything would go smoothly.

And it had. Luke was standing by in the Swiss director's office, the cash already in his briefcase, awaiting further instruction.

"You're going to Milan," she told Luke after Regis had called again. "Regis doesn't know what will happen next.

Only that Karim will be home by noon if you meet Regis in the air terminal and give him the money. He has a description of you. He'll be waiting."

"You hardly know him," Luke said. "Are you sure he can be trusted?"

"Sure? No, I'm not sure. It's a chance I must take."

"What if Regis absconds?"

"I still have the original ransom proposal. I'll abdicate at noon."

Drinking thick black coffee Marianna watched daybreak come, rosy and hopeful. An accidental glimpse of herself in the beveled mirror was startling. She stepped back to confirm what she had seen. She looked like a witch. The tousled hair, the blotchy skin, the robe awry. She dragged herself to the dressing room. She knew she had to be presentable. For Karim, who would be frightened after his ordeal, and for the worldwide television audience anticipating her abdication address. It was a brief, moving speech Selma had composed and left on her desk with a note: "Not that you'll need this. Just wanted to prove your ex-publicist can still rip a heart-tugger out of the old typewriter."

Suppose Regis disappeared with the money? The idea hadn't occurred to her until Luke brought it up. What did she know about Regis? He was handsome, Black, American, an avowed radical who claimed to be opposed to violence. Dahlia loved him, but how much did Dahlia know about her lover?

Applying makeup to her cheeks and lips, Marianna berated herself for again entertaining doubts. What did it matter if Regis vanished with the money? A week ago she hadn't known it was there, smuggled into secret accounts by Ramir.

She picked up the abdication speech and read it through. Unthinkingly, professionally, she read it aloud, gesturing with her hands, commanding her eyes to tear, lowering her lids, allowing her pink lips to quiver.

Selma had footnoted the speech. "You can go out with a whimper louder than a bang. The next regime will be on the skids before it's on its feet."

If Regis failed her, it would add one more disillusionment to her life, and her disillusionments were already stacked like pancakes. For Dahlia it would mean heartbreak. The passionate girl believed totally in her lover. But Dahlia was young and there would be other lovers. Regis, if necessary, could be dealt with later. She still had her option. At noon she would give the kidnappers what they wanted—what she herself had yearned for—the departure from Bahrait of herself and her children.

Savaging the brush through her hair, she began to tremble. Another possibility invaded her mind. They—whoever *they* were—could take the money, achieve her removal, and still harm Karim.

She beseeched the telephone to ring, scream, howl, to end the awful silence.

And then it rang, making her jump because she had lost hope.

"Mother!" Karim shouted. "Wait till I tell you! Wow, what a scene! Mother, are you there?"

"Yes, darling." Her voice choked. "Where are you? How do you feel? Who's with you? When are you coming home?"

"I'm great! We're in Milan. Luke and Regis are with me." He snickered. "Next to the urinals. Hey, you'll never believe this!"

"Karim, I love you."

"I love you, too. Wait. Luke wants to say something."

"Marianna?"

"Yes."

"We have the whole story. Hold on. Better be sure the men's room is clear. Okay, I can talk. But only for a minute. The plane is ready for takeoff. Italian mercenaries handled the dirty work. But it's Signore Vendicatore who runs the operation. A foreign visitor offered the Signore a pot of gold to get rid of you by snatching Karim, and the Signore made the deal. Personally, Vendicatore doesn't give a damn who rules Bahrait, you or the Pope. All he wants is more money to continue his propaganda. We topped his buyer and we won."

"Who was his visitor?"

"Figure it out."

"I have," she said.

"We'll talk about it later. Meanwhile, lay out clean clothes for Karim and fix yourself pretty. You're going on television —the two of you. And, Marianna—"

"Yes?"

"Don't go near any balconies."

In a seaside villa, an hour's drive from the palace in Ryal, General Sahid Mojeeb snapped off his television set and ordered his driver to replace his packed suitcases in the trunk of his bulletproof limousine. His instructions were delivered with his customary curtness, although his stomach was roiling and he wanted to retch.

The bitch! The dirty double-crossing bitch!

Early that morning he had requested and been granted a second audience with the Empress. Gravely he had sought permission to stand behind her in the basement pressroom when she delivered her abdication speech, insisting that his presence would reassure their countrymen. He was prepared to pledge that as caretaker of the throne he would make it his first priority to pursue those responsible for the kidnapping. He would mete out severe punishment once the criminals were in custody. He did not rule out execution.

The Empress had declined graciously. "Just myself and the younger children," she had said. "It's a family affair, isn't it? I want Karim returned. Nothing else matters. We'll go to France or America where we can be safe."

"It is a bad time, Your Majesty," he had replied. "It will pass and you will be back on the throne. I will see to that."

"Thank you, General. I'll never forget your kindness."

She had been too composed, too sure of herself. Mojeeb had picked that up at once. She knew something he did not. His attempts to reach Signore Vendicatore had failed. The Signore's henchmen had been polite but vague. The boy was still in custody, they said. They would tell him no more.

Yet he had remained suspicious. As an officer he had been trained to be wary, to exercise caution, to anticipate the worst.

From the palace he had hastened to his home and arranged for his departure from Bahrait should it be indicated. Through sympathetic contacts, he had secured passage on a freighter that would take him to Turkey and safety. Since then, he had been waiting in the seaside villa of a friend, curiosity and faint hope holding him before the television set until the last minute.

At noon she had appeared, smiling, waving, dominating the screen, with the boy beside her. The cunning whore. She had known even as she rejected his friendship that her son was coming back. Mojeeb could taste his hatred for her and for the Italian who had betrayed him. He blessed the instinct that had led him to this seaport. From his self-imposed exile in Turkey, he would get word of his whereabouts to his loyal army officers, letting them know that the battle was not yet over. In Turkey, he would plot his return to Bahrait. He rubbed his hands in anticipation. He had always relished a good fight. He was confident of the outcome of this one.

Now, standing on the pier, General Mojeeb watched an elderly bent-backed porter struggle up the gangplank and deposit his bags on the deck. General Mojeeb was sorry for the old fellow. He would tip him generously. He could afford to. His bags held a fortune in Swiss bank notes layered between his Savile Row suits.

Inconspicuous among the workers, passengers, and visitors on the pier, he turned for a parting view of the country he was leaving temporarily.

He didn't see them come, was unaware of their presence until they encircled him. They wore business suits, ordinary in cut and color. One of them flashed a brown-toothed smile and called him by name. Uncomprehending, he smiled back, thinking the ship's captain, an old friend, had sent a welcoming party to escort him aboard. The cold eyes of the others confused him.

And then he knew. Even before the brown-toothed man said, "General Mojeeb, you are under arrest."

He felt a gun at his back and stiffened. He did not deign to look at the metal cuff that closed over his wrist linking him to a stolid, pimply-faced man. "By whose orders?" he asked.

"The Empress's," the leader said.

"But why?"

"That is not our affair. We are returning you to Ryal at once."

"To see her?"

The leader was irritated. "We are not here to be interrogated by you. I have a letter for you from the Empress. Perhaps it will answer your questions." He offered another brown-toothed smile. "You appear somewhat handicapped. Shall I open it? Read it aloud perhaps?"

"No," Mojeeb growled. "Let us be on our way. I will read it in the car."

Reseated in the rear of his car, still linked to his companion on the right, he felt the constant pressure of the gun held by the man on his left. In the driver's seat, his own chauffeur stared straight ahead, ignoring the two men who had crowded in beside him.

"Now, the letter," Mojeeb demanded.

"Of course, General." The brown-toothed man ripped away the wax-sealed envelope and passed the single page to Mojeeb.

With his captor breathing sourly over his shoulder, Mojeeb read:

"My dear General,

"It is a regrettable situation you find yourself in. I too deplore it.

"How painful to find yourself betrayed by someone in whom you once placed your trust. You learned that when you discovered our mutual friend in Milan had broken his pact with you. I learned it when I was able to buy back my son for a larger sum than you could afford. An unreliable man to do business with, Signore Vendicatore, don't you agree?

"I wish I could say your pain will stop here. It will not. There is still another disillusionment we must share. When I assumed my husband's throne, I swore that Bahrait would never again tolerate the imprisonment and torture of political dissidents. That was my honest intent the day I ordered the release of those who had opposed Ramir.

"Imagine my own unhappiness at having to break my promise so soon.

"You, General Mojeeb, are my first major political prisoner, unlike the miserable young men you and Azar hired to assassinate me.

"Like Ramir's prisoners, you will have no trial. Yet I am a merciful ruler—neither will there be torture."

The letter was signed: "H.I.M., Marianna, Empress of Bahrait."

Below stairs, in the windowless room that had become his press quarters, Luke Tremayne teetered on an improvised wood platform and faced the jam of media people who had assembled in Ryal since the abduction of the Crown Prince.

"You've heard Empress Marianna's address. At this point you know as much as I do about the kidnapping and rescue of Prince Karim. What more can I tell you?"

The questions came at him fast.

"Where did the money come from?"

"From friends. Close friends who wish to remain anonymous. The Empress has given her word not to reveal their identities."

"Is the Prince going back to Switzerland?"

"Yes. Under the circumstances I cannot be precise about the date. He will be accompanied by armed officers of the Secret Service who will remain with him constantly."

"What are the Empress's immediate plans?"

"Tomorrow at dawn the Empress Marianna will enter the palace mosque with her children for the ceremony of investiture."

"What for? She's been Empress for years."

"Correct. But only as consort to the Shah. Although she inherited His Majesty's authority when he died, religious and national laws require this formality to make her absolute ruler. Something like the swearing in of an American vice-president after the death of a president."

"What about pictures? How many of us get in?"

"None of you. Sorry. The Empress wishes the ceremony held to a low key. Try to share her feelings. For a recent widow, it will be an anguishing step."

"Okay. Tomorrow she's Empress for real. Then what? Any political plans?"

"You know there are, or you'd have left town after lunch. For those among you who don't keep up with the news, there is still that worrisome border dispute with the Saudis over a strip of land in our southwest region. Discussions between a high-ranking representative of the late Shah and the King of Saudi Arabia were under way before the tragic accident in Paris. Face-to-face talks were scheduled to take place after the Jubilee. King Fouad has been most considerate. He volunteered to postpone a visit with the Empress until she felt emotionally stronger. Now, with the kidnapping scare behind her and the investiture about to be consummated, Empress Marianna has invited the King to come to Bahrait. Together they will continue the search for a peaceful solution. His Majesty arrives day after tomorrow."

"Pictures?"

"Whatever you need—of the King's arrival and departure. The meeting will be private."

"Interviews?"

"Impossible. Nor am I at liberty to promise statements."

Luke raised his hand to quiet the protesting newsmen. "Ladies and gentlemen, soon you will move on to livelier story centers. Barring new trauma, this country is back to normal." He paused. "Or so we hope."

Except for the armed guards who formed a protective arc behind her, she might have been a suburban hostess awaiting the arrival of the local bridge club.

Tinted glasses shielded her eyes from the brilliant noontime sun. A chill wind cut the air, sending strands of yellow-gold hair over her cheeks. The wind swirled against her body causing her blue cashmere dress to cling like a dancer's leotard. On the lawn below, a field of photographers jostled for favored positions. Strobe lights popped in still cameras. Movie cameras whirred as they had in the long-ago days at Hanover Studios and throughout her life with Ramir.

Calmly, her fingers laced in repose, the Empress awaited the appearance of her royal visitor.

King Fouad's willingness to confer in Bahrait rather than in a neutral, mutually agreed-upon country, had failed to disarm her, as had his insistence that she be spared the exhausting ceremonial reception at the airport. The single issue on their agenda, the disputed land that touched their countries, was too explosive to be watered down by excessive good manners. The territory, consisting of parched hills and flatland scrub, was infertile and virtually uninhabited. Its significance was purely geographical. Whoever held its peaks commanded an unobstructed view of his neighbor's border activity. Occasional sorties kept alive the threat of eventual invasion and full-blown conflict.

"Luke, our national pride and security hang on the outcome of this meeting," she had said after a briefing. "I'm determined to stand firm."

Luke had grinned. "Don't forget *his* national pride and security are on the line, too. He may overwhelm you."

"We'll see about that . . ."

The elaborate briefings from General Noori, newly elevated from the rank of colonel since the downfall of Mojeeb, had prepared her for the approaching confrontation with the King. Like a boxer readying for battle against the champ, she had spent hours in the palace theater studying films of her opponent. Reel upon reel of the leader—imposing in royal regalia, autocratic at foreign parleys, playful on holiday—had familiarized her with his style.

From Luke she had learned something of King Fouad's personal life. While moving his country into the twentieth century, he still retained what pleased him of the seventh. "He adores the ladies," Luke had said. "As you very well know, except in Bahrait every Moslem male is permitted four wives at the same time. Whenever he's ready for a new wife he sends for his least favored—but never the first one—pulls in a few witnesses and says 'I divorce thee' three times. King Fouad has never fallen below his quota. He's even been known to fill a vacancy within an hour of a divorce."

"Those poor women."

"Not all of them. Remember, a Moslem woman can get out of a marriage also, but she has only two shots—if her husband doesn't support her, or if he's impotent. No wife could conceivably bring either charge against His Majesty, King Fouad. At fifty-five, our friend acknowledges seventy-eight *legitimate* children. Three were born in a single week, courtesy of three recent brides. He's a generous husband to all of them. Periodically he takes his current batch to Paris for shopping sprees. No other man is permitted to look at them. They slip out the back door of the Hotel George V into curtained limousines wearing their ankle-length chadors. They're quite a sight, covered head to toe in black veiling, with just enough of their faces exposed to see and breathe. After riotous tours of Dior, Givenchy, St. Laurent, Cartier's, and the like, they're flown back to Saudi Arabia weighted down with opulent goodies. Know what they do when they get home?"

"Can't guess."

"It's back into the harem for them. Every day they dress up in their fabulous Paris gowns and jewels and sit in front of their television sets, drinking tea and watching Disney cartoons and *Kojak*."

"And I'm going to be alone with him . . ."

"You couldn't be safer in a convent. No offense. Fouad's tough. He's coming to talk business, and he won't be side-tracked because you're a woman. Think you can stand up to him?"

"What do you think?"

"Unlucky bastard."

The file of limousines preceding and trailing the curtained limousine which bore King Fouad rounded a curve between the guardhouses. Newsmen snapped away furiously, then fell back from the driveway to the safety of the lawn. Marianna descended the marble stairs to await the emergence of the King.

He was handsomer than she had expected and taller, too, with an aquiline nose and a muscular neck that hinted at a powerful physique concealed beneath his wind-whipped white caftan. Observing him through her glasses, she detected a glimmer of approval in his dark eyes. Without apology, he frankly scrutinized her tensing body.

Composing herself quickly, she whispered a few words in his ear. Together they faced the squadron of photographers and reporters. It was Luke who stepped forward to break up the photo session.

"Lunchtime for us," he told the press. "In my headquarters. The Empress Marianna and His Majesty, King Fouad, will dine privately. If there's an announcement to be made, you will be called back to hear it."

They were alone in the vast Golden Lion Room. She had ordered an intimate table for two set near a window overlooking the woods.

Lunching on Bahraitian food, they had flirtatiously bounced amenities between them. When the table was removed Marianna appeared regretful. Her wide blue-eyed stare fastened on the King. "Party time is over. We can no longer avoid the unpleasantness that has brought us together."

He sighed before speaking. "What a pity we meet under a cloud of misunderstanding. Your ministers and mine have found no solution. You and I will do better."

"I agree, Your Majesty." Her smile was docile.

"I know of no capitulation or compromise put forth by your side," he said.

"Oh, there won't be any. You were kind to come here. I regret your time has been wasted."

"Wasted? If nothing more, I have had the joy of dining with a beautiful woman."

"Hardly the purpose of your trip. Try to see me as you would my husband. Flattery would be absurd if he sat in my place."

"But he does not."

"Your Majesty, my position is no different from his. The disputed territory is Bahrait's and it will remain so," she said sweetly.

"You are immovable?"

"Immovable."

"Then I am sad for you. Your stubbornness leaves me no choice. In time I will order an attack with the purpose of ending this foolishness forever. It would be unfortunate to allow the situation to come to that."

"Unfortunate? For whom?" Her eyes widened farther. "Bahrait is one of the best-armed countries in the world. Surely you know that. Everyone else does."

"You mistake the facts, Madame. True, Bahrait has had the advantage of unrestricted arms purchases from the United States. My own country has not attempted to match yours. But, Madame, Bahrait is *not* among the world's best-armed countries."

His expression as he openly admired her delicate features was one of genuine chagrin. "Your late husband would have been more yielding. My Intelligence long ago brought me tales of dubious deals with his African clientele. We know the Shah acted as a conduit, that his acquisitions of military hardware frequently passed from the United States to other countries. With the aid of Mr. Gropper, Bahrait bought liberally and sold covertly to countries the United States does not openly support. I also know of his phantom underground hangars. What I did not know was whether or not Ramir's exquisite widow had been taken into his confidence. When you withdrew the ransom money from Zurich, I knew you were part of the game."

Her face flushed with anger. "I had no knowledge of such things!"

"But somehow you found out. Isn't that true?"

"You're being insulting. Do you expect me to believe you know more than I do of Bahrait's affairs?"

"I do. And I have for a long time. I have had the information, not the proof."

"Then how dare you threaten me?"

"Easily. By employing logic. Large sums of money appear in Switzerland. They give evidence of Ramir's piracy. Ramir could not sell off American-made armament without reducing the security of his own country. There are holes in your defenses. You dug another one when you rejected Calvin Cropper's contract. You are not as militarily safe as you would have me believe. My forces can attack yours and win. Wouldn't that be a tragedy for both sides?"

"You expect me to concede the land?"

"It is the only sensible move. Today you are lauded for your dedication to democracy. You have emptied your jails of your husband's enemies and disbanded his secret police. In the same spirit, you must renounce your claim to my country's territory."

"You can't be serious."

"But I am. The decision is yours. You may choose to rearm. If you do, your grand words will be empty, your image shattered. Which will it be?"

"Fuck you," she said.

He offered a rueful grin. "An Americanism. I have heard it before. I deeply regret it is not an invitation to be taken literally. If it were, who knows . . . ?"

She dismissed her impulse to slap him. She had a better idea.

Reaching for the table buzzer that would summon General Noori, she returned the King's smile. "I must confer with my ministers. In two weeks I will have an answer for you."

He came to his feet and her blue eyes swept insinuatingly over his elegant figure.

She moistened her lips. "Two weeks," she repeated. "You will hear from me personally."

He looked at her with heightened interest. "Agreed." He took a step toward her. "You have the fairest skin I have ever seen."

"Thank you."

"And wished to enjoy," he added.

"Ah, Your Majesty—who knows?"

General Noori rapped and entered.

"His Majesty is leaving," Marianna said. "I will see him to the hall. Inform Mr. Tremayne there will be no statements and no photo session."

Minutes later, she was alone in the Golden Lion Room. Pressing her back against the locked door, she closed her eyes and gave herself up to a gut surge of triumph. So this is what it's like, she thought—to sit atop the world, to manipulate an enemy, to experience a rush as exhilarating and euphoric as that found in the precious nose candy sniffed by a cocaine addict. She hadn't beaten Fouad yet, but she knew she would. Her head throbbed, her heart beat rapidly. She was very happy.

Emerging from the room, she found General Noori and Luke awaiting her.

"How did it go?" Luke asked immediately.

General Noori was offended. "Perhaps Her Majesty would prefer to consult with me first?"

"Gentlemen, I will answer both of you now," she said. "Progress was made. I am not displeased. Certain imponderables will become clearer with the passage of time. That is as much as I have to say."

It was to be the relaxed evening Marianna had decreed, with good food and wines and no talk of partings.

In the morning, accompanied by security guards, Karim would return to school. By afternoon Selma, too, would be airborne, en route to California. "I've thought it over," Selma had said. "The studio needs me. For my personality, working is healthier than resting. Besides, I can see already, an hour in Bahrait is like a week in a disco. I'm going home." Her lips twitched. "At night I can rest. I'll be alone."

Marianna had embraced the bulky body. "Gino's no dope. He sees you for the special woman you are. Don't worry, the last vote isn't in. You're strong. You'll have him the way you want him."

"I'm strong? Crap, Your Majesty. Inside is like outside. A blob of jelly." Tears welled in her eyes. She struck a comic boxer's stance. "We'll show 'em, kid, you and me. We'll keep licking the world, just like we did in the old days. Right?"

"Right."

"How do I look?" Selma had twirled clumsily. "A bit overweight for the next round?"

"I'm afraid so . . ."

"So I'll starve myself. I'll get my exercise guy out to the house again. Sixty bucks an hour, can you believe it? Gino comes home, he'll think I'm the new maid. He'll chase me into the linen closet and I'll let him catch me." She stopped and studied the hard set of Marianna's mouth. "I hate to leave you. You gonna be okay?"

"I'm going to be just fine."

They had gone down to dinner then, to the softly lit family sitting room. Luke and Karim were already there.

"We're kicking around opinions about books and art," Luke said.

"I like this guy." Karim stood before a large canvas depicting Mick Jagger, and another of an oversized anemone. "What do you think, Selma?"

"Andy Warhol? A creep."

"Sure, that's what I admire about him," Karim said. "He's an American creep. He's free to do things his way."

"That's what your mother said when she hung the picture," Selma agreed. "She said it reminded her of her other country. Your father thought it was junk. He let her keep it anyway."

"We'll have artists like that," Karim enthused. "With my mother in charge, things will change. Wait and see."

"What will change?" Marianna asked.

"Everything. Remember the way we used to talk in Switzerland? You said one day we'd be better than the United States. You said writers, artists, students, everyone would be free. Look what you've done already, letting the newspapers print whatever they want, unlocking the prisons and letting the dissidents out, and . . ."

"Hold on, Karim. Don't forget, I've already put my first political opponents into cells."

"General Mojeeb? The assassination guys? They're exceptions."

"There may be others."

"A few. That's to be expected." Karim grew excited. "The rotten secret police have been disbanded. You took away their torture toys. The army knows you're in charge—" Abruptly, he quieted. He looked about in dismay. "I loved my father. I always will," he stammered. "But he saw Bahrait another way. He became like his own father. They did what they thought they had to do. Mother and I are different. We have changes to make, don't we?"

"Let's go in to dinner," Marianna said. "Tonight we're having a party, not a political rally."

Assisted by generous pourings of champagne, the dinner was lighthearted and noisy, exactly as she wished it to be.

Karim, his mouth filled with heavily honeyed baklava, hoisted his fork in a toast. "To Bahraitian food," he said. "Some things never change."

"Cheers," Selma saluted.

Suddenly from the adjoining salon they heard the loud, prolonged peal of the telephone.

"At this hour?" Luke was surprised. "I left orders. We were not to be disturbed."

"Answer it, please," Marianna said.

Luke hastened to the next room. He spoke briefly to the caller, then laid the receiver beside the telephone. Slowly, thoughtfully, he walked back to the dining room. "It's for you, Marianna," he said. "Calvin Gropper. He's in Washington."

"I'll talk to him."

Luke glanced at her sharply. "He says he's returning your call."

"I knew he would."

Luke stepped aside to let her pass. "Would you like the door closed?"

"No, I want all of you to hear this."

Uncomprehending, they trailed her into the salon.

"Calvin," she began gaily. "Good of you to get back to me so soon." She laughed at his reply. "No, Calvin, the subject is not free elections. The people aren't ready for that." She listened, laughed again. "You must stop teasing me, Calvin, this is serious. About the arms contract—I made a mistake. I admit it. Don't gloat or I'll be angry. How soon can you be here?" She nodded. "And the delivery date, can it be moved up? Perfect. Plan to stay awhile. Bring Hilary. We have work to do, you and I. More technicians, advisers? Naturally. Splendid. I'll be waiting. Good night, Calvin."

They were staring at her as she knew they would be. She reached for Karim. When he recoiled, she shook her head. "You don't understand," she said to the boy. "It must be this way. There are threats at the border. Our people look to me for protection."

Karim continued to back away, his eyes unblinking.

"Trust me," she pleaded. "I meant everything I said in Switzerland. Reforms will come in time. If I'm weak now our enemies will stomp us out of existence."

Luke interrupted. "What the devil is this about, Marianna? I know why the King was here. Everyone does. Why do you need Gropper? Why can't you face Fouad with the weapons you have? Emplacements can be shifted from less vulnerable locations. A lousy strip of land—it can be defended easily."

"It's not just a lousy strip of land," she flared. "It's pride that's at stake, too. That man came here to nibble away at our country, to humiliate Bahrait, to bully *me*. When he left I had him wrapped around my finger. Do you know what that feels like, to manipulate an enemy? To deal from strength?"

"But your promises—the people—"

"Their time will come. They'll be helped. *I'll* never steal their money and deposit it in Switzerland. Remember, there are priorities, Luke."

"But Gropper! If you must do this terrible thing, why bleed the national treasury? What about the money in Switzerland?"

"Impossible. If I draw on it again, the whole story could spill out. The world could learn what Ramir and Gropper did. I can't risk it. Gropper would be jeopardized just when I need him."

"Marianna," Luke said, "have you gone mad? There'll be resistance. Dissidents will regroup."

"They will be dealt with."

Karim approached her, his fists raised. Selma grabbed him. "Don't!" she begged. "Your mother has her reasons."

"We've heard them, haven't we?" the boy shouted. "They're not good enough!"

"Luke, explain it to him," Mirianna implored. "Time goes so fast. In a few years he'll be the new Shah. What will he step into if I don't provide for the nation's survival? Help him understand. He's a child, he knows nothing of the world's realities. If we don't exist, we can't improve. Power, that's the name of the game. When he's older, he'll thank me."

"I never want to see you again," Karim sobbed. "I despise you!"

"Tomorrow you'll return to school. Study hard. Concentrate on history. Then you'll know how to rule."

"I'll be back," Karim said menacingly. "Like my friend, the Prince of Burundi. His father was a despot. In school he told us how he'd go home when his father died and help his people."

"What happened to him?"

Karim hesitated. "He went home. He was killed."

"I'm sorry about your friend," Marianna said gently. "I really am. He must have been a wonderful young man. Leave with Luke. I won't see you off. It would be too painful for both of us." She turned to Luke. "Take good care of him. When you come back, we'll talk about this again."

"I'm not coming back, Marianna."

"You too," she said wearily. "What will you do?"

"For one thing, I'll sleep with a clear conscience. I wish you the same. Come, Karim."

Selma released the trembling boy. "Please, Karim, kiss your mother good-bye."

Karim sagged with defeat. "I love you, Mother," he whispered, allowing her to hold him tightly. "I'm all mixed up."

"I love you, too. But I can't help you. Not now."

She watched Luke lead her son away. She thought she heard him say, "One day she'll come to her senses. We'll be together again."

When she lifted her face to Selma's, tears blurred her vision. "And you, old friend? Deserting, too?"

"No, I've got the picture. I'm not surprised."

Marianna walked to the window and gazed at the park beyond. "It's lovely out there. Full moon. Stars. How about a stroll?"

The air was sweet with jasmine and felt like solacing arms about them. They walked in silence, listening to night birds and the light splattering of gravel on the path.

Marianna spoke. "It's despicable, this thing I'm doing."

Selma did not contradict her.

"There were options . . ." Marianna continued.

"Who knows how they'd come out? You've been socked around a lot. From the beginning . . ."

"Drop it, Selma. I will not listen to a synopsis of my life."

Selma went on. "So what do you grab for? Power. Too bad. You'll be lonely."

"Lonely!" Marianna stopped on the path. Her eyes glistened. "How can you believe that? When you have power you're never alone. Power sleeps in your bed, wakes with you, wraps itself around you, caresses you. It's the greatest high in the world, the ultimate orgasm!" She paused, hugging herself. "And no one can hurt you." She was almost inaudible. "Power protects you. It won't let you feel."

Selma took her hand, squeezed it. "Poor baby," she said.

In her sitting room. Marianna drew the drapes against the distractingly beautiful moonlight. Clutching her robe around her for warmth, she sat at her desk and reread the letter she had written to Dalila in Paris.

"My darling,

"Marry your wonderful Regis. Go to America, if that's what you want. You have my permission and my blessing.

"In time you will hear news of me you will not like. Try to ignore it. Know that however ugly the practices I may revive, you and Regis will be safe.

"Be happy and one day come back and tell me what it's like.

"Love always, Marianna."

She sealed the letter and put it aside.

Impulsively she withdrew another sheet of the embossed paper from the desk drawer. Gripping her pen, she wrote:

MARY ANNA CALLAHAN

Born: Boston, Mass. 1942

Died: Ryal, Bahrait 1980

EMPRESS MARIANNA OF BAHRAIT

Born: Ryal, Bahrait 1980

Died: ?

"Dear God, what am I doing?" She lowered her folded arms onto the desk and rested her stricken face on them.

Minutes later, her period of mourning was ended. She crumpled the sheet of obituaries into a ball and tossed it into her wastepaper basket. Straightening, she pressed the button that would bring General Noori to her. When he appeared, hastily uniformed, she apologized for the lateness of the hour.

"There's work to be done," she said. "Calvin Gropper is on his way. Pull up a chair. Let us begin."